Introduction

OVERZEALOUS

ONE

In life there is chaos...in death there is peace.

Her legs were heavy. She didn't know how long she had been running, nor did she care. She just wanted to get to safety... whatever that meant. And as quickly as possible. She had many regrets, but this had to be her biggest.

Now was the time for positive thoughts...a positive attitude. Normally, this wasn't a hard task. Tonight, it was foreign to her. She was too busy trying to save her life.

No, that was only partially true. She was trying to save multiple lives.

Rain.

Her mind recalled when she loved the rain. Her father once told her that rain represented new life, the cleansing of souls. That's why it rained in some parts of the city, and not in other parts. Some parts of the city needed more cleansing. Unfortunately, in her present location, South Memphis, that was more than true.

She remembered that day. Vividly. She wanted to love her father. She tried like hell to love her father. But he was a weak man. Even as a young girl, around age seven, she recognized weakness and had a thing for strength.

She didn't miss her father. She hated that they didn't have much of a relationship. But, that was his fault, his misgiving...and now, he was gone. She did have a mother who cared, a mother who loved her. God, did she miss that lady. She still asked the Good Lord to bless her mom. She died way too soon.

If the night didn't go right, she would also meet her maker and her parents...much too soon.

She didn't like thinking in moments like this. She felt raw and vulnerable. Right now, her parents consumed her mind. Her father had died a sad, lonely man. Her mother shared the same hopeless ending. And why? Because in Jackson, Mississippi, the worst thing a daughter of a traditional, rich, white family could do was fuck a black man.

Her mother's family disowned her and the daughter she had with someone who was not her husband. Someone who was not white. Her mother's mother told her that she would die a soulless death. The family was estranged for over twenty years before her mother succumbed to death. She hoped her grandmother, the bitch matriarch that she was, would die a horrible death followed by an eternity burning in hell.

The last thing she wanted or needed to think about was death. Unfortunately, it wouldn't escape her mind.

She had created this mess. She had been told by her superiors to stay away. Hell, she had been told by everyone to keep clear of the Harvey boys. As always, she didn't listen. She never had regrets. Tonight, she did.

The boys were young and just didn't get it. In so many ways, she had a blank check, carte blanche to do her job, but they truly did not understand.

If she died, many others would die as well. He would come back. The man with the mysterious past. No. He was the man who lived death...and death lived inside of him. He would do what he does. Clean up messes with more messes. Despite this, he was good at cleaning up after her. Too good. She often recoiled at the final results. The conclusion was always the same—more deaths and more misery.

He was protective of her.

Too. Damn. Protective.

As always, he went overboard. Mass destruction. The man himself was a WMD, weapon of mass destruction. He did what he needed to do to make things right in his mind. The outcome was always hideous...someone missing body parts...or beaten badly...or worse, death.

Only she knew the real man. The one who killed an abusive father, enlisted in the Army and became one of America's top assassins. She knew far more about her former partner, her best friend than she ever wanted to know. She missed him—her protector, the man who melted her heart and convinced her that chivalry wasn't dead.

The thoughts were good. But she needed to focus.

Her legs were heavy. She didn't know how long she had been running, nor did she care. She just wanted to get to safety. Whatever that meant. And as quickly as possible. She had many regrets, but this one had to be her biggest. Now she was trying to save her life.

This was not the part of the city she wanted to be in. South Memphis. Bellevue and South Parkway. Definitely not the best area. She was sure she had run at least three or four miles, if not longer. Her black clothing and the torrential rain had helped to provide cover. She knew she was lucky. Usually this area was swarmed with people, undesirable, nocturnal dwellers of sin and destruction. From women of the night to pimps and players to criminals from all elements of life. This was their playground.

She knew that. Of course, she knew that. She was considered to be one of the best detectives in the city and had been decorated on numerous occasions. Despite her accolades, however, she was not well-liked. She was a lone wolf, with trust issues.

She had been burned before, betrayed by previous partners, fellow detectives that she entrusted, only to end up on death's door.

She used to have a savior. He was always there. He loved her. She loved him. They started off as reluctant partners, then eventually became best friends. Inside, she smiled. She was actually the reluctant partner. He was the supportive one. She was angry at herself. He offered a better life, but she just couldn't walk away. They had crossed the line, her line.

He was love. Her heart was full. He was the point guard, the quarterback, her protector. Any and everything she needed him to be—he was.

Then...he was gone.

But she knew he would be back. She was signing her own death certificate. He would definitely be back.

She was standing in the middle of the intersection, surrounded by four cars. She had a Glock, nine bullets and two spare clips. She wasn't surprised to see the driver and passenger doors of every car open. Eight against one. When she was younger she would call that a fair fight. Younger was five years ago when he was still here.

The rain had deserted the area. The hamburger stand was empty. The gas station on the west side of the street, and the park that sat on the opposite side of the street, the usual nightspots for the seedy children of the night, were both deserted.

She was alone. Now Sondra would be alone. She had failed big-time as a mother. Her work had prevented her from being a great mom, or maybe, it was her obsession with her work. Either way, that same call of duty was now taking her away from her daughter—once again. She would be alone.

Momentarily.

She had a plan. Sondra knew the plan. She would go to him... the same him that aged her. His departure was the catalyst that aged her. She loved him. She hated that she never gave in to her desires and became one with him.

He changed her life...for the best. And that, she would take— to the grave.

She smiled. One recurring thought had been with her the whole night. She was lying in her bed, completely nude on top of silk sheets and he walked in. As his eyes locked with hers, it made her flesh warm and she said the words that had been on her lips for five years, "Welcome back, Zachary Brick."

She smiled more and in one motion raised her gun and swiftly squatted as the firefight began.

He will be back...

Then...she was gone.

TWO

THE POWERFUL SHALL DISREGARD THEIR WEAKNESSES.

His day started early. He was never a morning creature. No. The night was his calling. When he was younger that calling included cleaning up the streets of Memphis in some of the worst parts of the city. He was a true night owl. The darkness was definitely the optimal time for knocking heads, which was his favorite pastime as a young cop. The best ass kicking always occurred in the dead of night.

Sometimes he still missed those days...those nights. He was the best at what he did. He could be the brute, as well as the intellectual. This versatility helped him survive the streets and the bullshit politics. Office politics among police departments were notoriously the worst. But like he did in the streets, he manipulated and captivated the office. Yes, he was always the best, regardless of his surroundings.

He didn't lack for confidence. It was the true jewel that kept him afloat. He treated every encounter as a battle of wills and wits. Even in his daily dealings with his wife and three sons, he maintained this mindset. It was his confidence that kept him above the fray.

The volume was turned down on his computer as he continued to look at the 27-inch monitor. He lost count of how many times he had looked at the video. It was grainy...shot from a cell phone at the intersection of South Parkway and Bellevue. The driving rain distorted the recording, but the woman was recognizable. Not only by him. She was probably the best and most well-known detective in the city. She was relentless and ruthless in her duties, which, ironically, made her a popular figure by both the good people and the lowlifes of the city.

If he were a man who easily displayed feelings, he probably would have shed a tear or two for Detective Alaina Rivers. After all, the numerous cases that she successfully closed, shone a positive light on him during his tenure as Deputy Chief of Detectives. He wasn't too proud to admit that he used her as a stepping-stone to reach the position he now held—Director of the Memphis Police Department.

He now hated that he had made a deal with the devil. An alliance that he made only out of necessity, a pact he thought was best for the city. What once was a good cause, ultimately became a weakness and the worst albatross that he could have ever imagined.

He didn't say anything when he heard the two knocks at his office door or when the plainclothes detective walked in without a vocal invitation. The detective was six feet tall, with a slender build. He had a thick, dirty blonde mustache, immaculately trimmed. His eyebrows were just as thick. His overt baldness made his facial hair stand out. His brown eyes were set deep in their sockets. In many ways, he was the direct opposite of his ultimate boss.

Outwardly, Director Sam Wanamaker appeared to be in good shape. Inwardly, he knew better. Yes, he exercised every other day, including hitting the exercise bike and pedaling for a good thirty minutes non-stop. However, he refused to run. Running was a demon to him...an evil to be avoided and God, he hoped that he would never have to run again

"Lieutenant Fontaine, what's my title?" barked Director Wanamaker. His six feet, three-inch frame was intimidating, in or out of uniform. He was a workout junkie when he was younger. These days, he worked out just enough to look presentable. His appearance meant a lot to him. It was a part of his identity, and the most critical part of his persona.

"Director, of course," stated the subordinate officer.

"The last time that I checked Lieutenant, when I gave an order I expected it to be obeyed." He stood up out of habit, but didn't take his eyes off his computer. He never thought he would classify himself as a computer geek, but that is exactly what he was now—a victim of modern technology, from incessant use of his cell phone to surfing the net to being a looky-loo on social networks.

"Director, it was out of my control," replied Jody Fontaine. "I don't control these fucks. Detective Rivers was a persistent bitch. You know that. She pushed too much. Didn't know when to give up. I tried telling her to watch her back and even told her to back the hell off."

The subordinate officer sat down in a chair in front of the director's desk. The director, in turn, finally gave him his complete attention.

"Did I tell you to sit down?" stated the director, as he walked around his desk to face his subordinate.

The lieutenant rose immediately once again. "I'm sorry, sir," said Fontaine in a weak voice. "I didn't mean any disrespect."

"Yeah, Fontaine, you never mean any disrespect," stated the Director, as he pointed a calloused finger in the face of the detective. "In a perfect world, in my younger days, I would have either beat the shit out of you or just shot your stupid ass."

The lieutenant knew his top boss was telling the truth. The man was truly a legend from his days as a beat cop, then to detective and eventually, to his days as police brass. The director was right...he was stupid. He realized that the best move now was to shut the hell up.

He knew of the stories of Sam Wanamaker walking up to criminals and fellow law enforcement officials and just beating the shit out of them. Regardless of all the despicable acts that he had engaged in, it didn't stop him from moving up the ranks of the Memphis Police Department.

"Who is being assigned to the case?"

Fontaine replied, "Jenifer Cassidy and Laura Richison. Both were friends of Rivers and she was a mentor to both. Plus, we can spin this on several angles—friends and close colleagues, females, one black, one white. I think we can cover a lot of bases with them being assigned."

Wanamaker often wondered about his police force. The rumors were rampant throughout the local government and the city that his force was racist, sexist, crooked and probably every other negative adjective that described law enforcement agencies in America today. He never wanted his police department to be any of those things. But Fontaine was a flaming example of everything that was wrong with the MPD. He knew it. The day he took the job, he promised himself and his wife, Donna, that he would change things. Thus far, he was a liar.

Wanamaker searched for the right words to say to his subordinate. Yes, Fontaine was part of the problem. However, Wanamaker realized that he was the biggest problem. Rivers' death was on him more than anyone else. If there was vengeance to be had, he knew his name would be at the top of the list. A list that would make the streets of Memphis flow red.

"I remember asking Detective Rivers if Brick had anything to say before he left the city," stated Director Wanamaker, choosing to change the subject rather than go down a path that he really didn't want to travel. A path that would have caused loathing every time he looked in the mirror. His face only a couple of inches away from Fontaine. "She told me that he said, 'don't give me a reason to return'."

The two men exchanged hard, long glares. Director Wanamaker knew the man's God-given name was not Zachary Brick. Hell, he didn't have a clue of what his real name was. He wasn't sure if Brick even knew his own real name. Additionally, he could not finger the alphabetic agency Brick called home. He had reached out to numerous federal government officials that he knew to get information, but all attempts failed. From having the phone slammed down on him to being told to never call this number again, it was clear that the answer was "No" in so many different ways, without anyone actually saying the word "No."

"The one person we had to keep alive," stated Wanamaker, "the only person we needed to keep alive and you couldn't control your fucking best friends. Your. Fucking. Best. Friends."

The lieutenant took a step back as he addressed his boss. "Director, I know it's bad whenever one of ours is killed, but I honestly don't think we have anything to worry about. The rumor is that Brick is dead."

The director laughed. A hearty, condescending laugh. "You really are a dumbass. Stupid as fuck. I'm a bigger dumbass for promoting your stupid ass. Brick disappeared, but not because of death, and not because he met a gruesome demise or a bullet to the head or a stake to the heart. But because he wanted to disappear. He wanted to get lost."

"But it's been five years, sir. If everything they say is true, he has moved on, never to be heard from again or he just may be dead."

The Director said, "Have you seen a body?"

"No, sir," replied Fontaine.

"For your sake, I hope that's the truth Lieutenant. The one person that kept Brick away from Memphis was killed by your friends in the most public way possible. It hasn't been a good eight hours and there are already a million hits on YouTube, with every damned news station in America and overseas showing the damned video.

"Heaven help us all if he sees that video."

"I'm not worried, Director, I'm sure we are good." Lieutenant Jody Fontaine proclaimed confidently, but internally, he felt that last night was a grave mistake. Why invite Hell to a party already full of demons and turmoil?

"We need to make this look good," stated Wanamaker dryly. "Knock some heads, ruffle some feathers and just run rampant over the city for the next week or two. I will be holding an official press conference within the hour. By the way, how are the troops taking it?"

"Half and half. You know the bitch was very popular...but on the flip side, many thought she was too damned righteous. But she was one of us and you have my word that we will kick up enough dust to make sure no stink sticks to *us*."

"I don't like that Fontaine—*us*. You were supposed to keep your so-called friends in check. You were supposed to make sure we stayed Teflon. We are the cops, the city's authority. And now... now you have put us right smack in the middle of the fray.

"If you ever call her a bitch again, I'm telling you now, I will kick your ass until you can't sit down. That's a promise."

Lieutenant Jody Fontaine didn't speak. His only focus now was to push down his fear of retribution. The older officer wished he could reverse every action and reaction that got them to this disdainful point.

In his head, Director Sam Wanamaker could hear Zachary Brick's voice, *Don't give me a reason to return.*

And the powerful shall disregard their weakness.

THREE

THE LAND OF OPPORTUNITY...A PLACE OF FREEDOM.

Paz. That was his God-given name. A name that was rich in tradition in his native Mexico. A name he was proud of. It was a name that even meant something when he moved to southern California.

The Spanish translation meant *peace*. Which, at one point in his life, he was a strong advocate for. Now, however, in this business, he walked a thin line between peace and pandemonium. In fact, in the eyes of law enforcement, he was always on the right side of *peace*. After all, he was a Paz.

He was born Nigel Paz and he was the oldest of three sons. His family name was a legacy throughout Mexico and South America. His father and five uncles were all attorneys for the biggest cartel crime families in these regions. And the Paz sons loyally followed in the footsteps of their fathers. However, the difference between them was stark. While his father and uncles were men of the law that usually stood in the background, Nigel, his brothers and cousins wanted to be at the forefront of all the action. Yes, the Paz men made a name for themselves.

It was a name he loved...but reluctantly, he had to give up when he and his family were run out of California.

Hector Harvey Senior never truly loved or embraced his new name, but he loved his wife. Their departure from California

16

was all about survival. He was a father of five children, and was desperately trying to ensure his wife, offspring and grandchildren lived to see another day.

Theoretically, it was a simple thought that should have had a simple plan to follow. But nothing is ever simple for a true crime family. The children he had introduced to a life of crime had ultimately made the one mistake that could result in the death of the entire family. A mistake not sanctioned by the head of the snake.

"You know what?" dragged Hector Sr.'s scraggly voice. The man was seventy-two with a full head of white and silver hair, and a mustache and goatee to match. He was the tallest member of his family, but his six-foot five inch frame was distorted by the wheelchair he currently needed. Though his body was physically failing him, his mind remained as sharp as it had ever been.

"This is a first. I have never made a trip to one of my sons' girlfriend's house to have a conversation," continued the old man. "But I thought it was prudent to come and talk to my sons to see what the fuck you assholes were thinking."

He was being pushed by his driver and second oldest son, Hector Junior, or preferably just Junior. He didn't have his father's towering height and was only five-nine. But he had a thick, hard body. Junior worked out regularly and was now the personal bodyguard for his dad. At one time, he and his older brother, Arturo, ran the family business. Then they had crossed paths with a female detective with a dangerous partner. That unfortunate encounter resulted in the honor of running the family business being passed to his younger brothers, Ronaldo and Damian.

"Pop, this isn't as serious as you think," Damian Harvey stated in his husky voice. "The lady detective was becoming a pain in the ass. She was like a dog with a bone, looking for bigger bones behind every fucking tree she crossed. She got what she deserved. She found the big bone and it didn't serve her well."

No further words were spoken. Damian was the youngest son and child of the Harvey children. Although he was the shortest of the Harvey offspring, he was the recognized muscle of the crime family. The man was well-chiseled. His chest was wide and thick, with larger than average hands for his short frame. He held two associate degrees, which rubbed his father the wrong way. Of his five children, Damian was also the least educated.

The Senior Hector had to practice patience when it came to his youngest child. Truth be known, he could take or leave his children. He built his business for he and his wife. She wanted brats, so he gave her brats and that's exactly how he viewed his children. His two oldest sons failed at running the business and he was eventually forced to take the reins back from them. After their chief nemesis, Memphis detective Zachary Brick left town, he turned the business over to his youngest sons, Ronaldo and Damian.

"Ronaldo, I blame you!" said Hector Sr. to his son. "You are the fucking brains! You were the one who was supposed to keep this fuck out of trouble."

Ronaldo Harvey was considered to be a pillar of the community. He held a B.S. degree from UCLA and a master's degree from the University of Memphis. He represented the power of the Harvey family, but more importantly, he represented business savvy, success and youth. He was the chief executive officer of the family's legitimate management consulting business as well as the current lord of the family's criminal enterprise. He looked the part. His jet-black hair was chopped short. He stood six feet one inch tall, with a well-defined build. Even in his casual cream white shirt and holey blue jeans, he still looked as if he could grace the cover of *Business Weekly*.

"Pop, this is on me," said Ronaldo. He sat in a lone chair that faced his dad.

"I ordered the death of Detective Rivers," said Ronaldo in a smooth, calm voice. His full head of black hair was slicked back. He wore no socks or shoes. Sitting on the back of his chair was his muse, Lacey, who occasionally ran her hand through his hair.

Hector Sr. knew the future of his criminal organization was Ronaldo. However, his son had two major weaknesses—pussy and Damian. The elder Harvey didn't mind his son's thirst for sex. But he had major trepidations about Ronaldo's closeness and desire to always defend the stupidity of his younger brother.

"I told you to leave the Rivers woman alone!" exclaimed an exacerbated Hector Sr. "Do you know what you have done? What your arrogant, over-confident, know-it-all ass has done to this family?"

"Yes, I know what I have done," said Ronaldo, as he leaned forward in his chair. "I let everyone know that we don't kowtow to anyone, that the Harvey family runs this fucking city, and whatever we touch, turns to gold."

"No shit, 'Naldo, tell him!" stated Damian excitedly.

"Shut up Damian," said Ronaldo in a quiet tone. "Pop, you have to trust me. Look at how far we have come as a family, as a business since Damian and I have been running things. As a family, we are more successful than we have ever been. And, in the eyes of the law, we are clean. It's what you've always wanted. We are a legitimate business. The only person who even had an interest in investigating us has finally met her maker."

"If it was only that easy, 'Naldo, if it was only that easy," said Hector Sr. as he signaled Junior to leave.

The family leader wasn't used to being afraid. There was only time that fear riddled throughout every fiber of his body. It was when the Cartel allowed he and his family to leave California with just enough money to start over in another state. That state became Tennessee. Now, that fear once again permeated his soul.

His fear was of one man only, a man way more sinister than the Cartel.

And his youngest sons had just rose the dead...and his name was Zachary Brick.

Part One
THE LAMB AND
THE INSTRUMENT

CHAPTER 1

THE MIND IS A TERRIBLE INSTRUMENT.

I killed my first man at age twelve. The victim was my father, the same father who killed my mother and my twin four-year-old sisters. My life was spared, as was my eight-year-old sister, Marguerite—but only because we spent the night at my mom's sister's home.

I didn't shed a tear when I heard. Honestly, it was only a matter of time. Weak men raise their hands and strike fear and pain in the souls of women who don't know the true meaning of love. Sadly, my mother was one of those women.

She was also the one who taught me about weak men. Even though I was a kid and really didn't understand much, I was a momma's boy and took in what I could from her. I also learned a lot of life's lessons by hanging out with my father and my father's father. They talked shit, which was Black talk for young boys to listen and learn from. Half of the crap out of their mouths was just that—crap, but the other half was about living and surviving in White America. Boys who truly listened, learned a lot. The others, rolled the dice on the possibility of having a tough, clueless existence.

So, no...my eyes didn't fill with tears that next morning. Instead, I just felt anger and a sense of purpose. I knew had two missions. First, I had to comfort Marguerite, whose tears flowed like rivers. She was my responsibility now.

My second mission was more sinister, more selfish. I was a kid who wanted revenge, who needed vengeance. Even in the mid-eighties, a black life in Sacramento, California was just as worthless as a black life in any other part of the nation. My father was a wanted man, but not a hunted man. He took refuge in the homes of friends and relatives.

Two weeks after the death of my mother and sisters, I found the man called Herbert Hargreaves. He smiled when he saw me. Maybe it was the fact that his only son knew how to find him. Maybe I was his favorite. After all, I was the one who stood up to him. Maybe he saw me as the son who took after his father. Hell, I don't know why he smiled at me. He was sitting at the kitchen table in his father's house, my rotten to the core grandfather. Like father, like son.

Even with a gun in my hand, he continued drinking his coffee. And he kept smiling. In his eyes, I could see that I posed no threat. After all, he taught me how to shoot, how to drink...hell, how to do everything. As I think back on those days, I was sure my father now thought that I owed him something.

The first bullet hit my father in the chest. Shock. Years later, I would learn the various effects of shock and bullet wounds. But at twelve, I didn't know or care about Herbert Hargreaves surprise factor. He struggled to get to his feet. His right hand covered the wound over his heart. His six feet three frame stood tall and provided a perfect bull's eye. I held the .22 caliber handgun with two hands—the way he taught me. Vengeance was my guide. My heart. My. True. Weapon.

My next two shots were to his gut and the middle of his neck.

When my grandfather finally entered the room with his sawed-off shotgun, the sight of his oldest son stopped him in his

from, who we came from and who we used to be. My mother used to say, "It's the simple things that count, that make a difference."

Maggie took a sip of her coffee. Her hands were shaking. I got up and sat next to her. We were at a café on the outskirts of South Omaha, the farthest we could be from the base. The café was actually pretty big, with booths along the walls, and at least two rows of tables that sat in the center, from one end to the other. The café had a red, white and blue theme. Each table alternately displaying red, white and blue tablecloths. That pattern repeated itself throughout the café. It was cheesy at best. But the place was clean and the café personnel were polite and professional.

The décor also included pictures throughout the restaurant of cowboys, settlers and Native Americans in war garb. The pictures especially reminded me of our father and his dad. Both were fanatics of cowboy and Western movies. I grew up on John Wayne movies, James Garner's *Maverick* and so many other Western movies and shows. Over the years, I had seen Sidney Poitier and Harry Belafonte's *Buck and the Preacher* over a hundred times. So, this place was like home to both of us.

I held my sister in my arm. Her head was resting on my shoulder. Over the years, we tried our best not to remember or talk about our past, our family. Just like so many years ago, I held my sister as she cried her eyes out and kissed her on the top of her head. As much as we didn't talk about the past, it was always a part of me. In fact, the bastard in me was from my early past. I couldn't escape him.

And I was a bastard.

Never deny or hide from yourself who you really are. My mother was the first who taught me that. This same notion continued to reverberate during my time in uniform and with the Company.

"I told you before, don't be afraid to tell them the truth. You can even tell them that you have a brother that you see once in a blue moon."

"I don't know, Lawrence," responded Maggie through her tears. "You know how one thing leads to another. You are family. They will want to meet you, know all about you. You know I can't tell them that you were with the CIA, and I definitely can't tell them that you are in hiding, and now own an auto repair shop somewhere in Texas."

"Well, I will leave it up to you on what you tell them, but tell them something, and let there be some truth in what you tell them."

She moved closer and I held her tighter. I hated memories. Yes, I knew how many people I had killed in my lifetime, and though I tried my best to forget them all, I just couldn't. The two that stayed at the top of my mind were the deaths of my father and grandfather. I could still see the whites of my father's eyes, his five o'clock shadow, nappy Afro and the kinked hair of his mustache. I even remembered his yellow-toothed smile and his foul body odor. Yes, these memories seared a hole in my brain.

I killed evil and the asshole that spawned that evil. Those deaths stayed with me. I wasn't there when my mother and twin sisters were murdered. But I killed in their names. I understood how and why those deaths would stay with me forever.

Thoughts of holding Marguerite that night, so long ago, also resonated through my head. We had caught a Greyhound that night and went as far as we could with what little money I had. That was Phoenix, Arizona. I placed Marguerite in the foster care system, and at the tender age of twelve, I found work.

That was the day Anton and Marguerite Hargreaves died. The day Lawrence and Maggie Travis were born.

Within a month, my sister was placed in a good home. And like now, we met up to have an occasional meal together. It would be the only time that we referred to each other using our birth names.

"I wanna meet your family," I just blurted out.

It seemed as if the whole place got instantly quiet. In my mind, the few people in the café immediately stopped eating and conversing to direct their attention on us. Of course, that wasn't the case. But those words shocked me...and equally, I knew Maggie as well.

She slowly moved her head, and I took a napkin and dabbed at the wet tears on her cheeks. Her makeup was already smeared and I was doing a fine job of messing it up even more. Maggie hugged me and excused herself to go to the ladies' room to get herself together.

During the time that she was gone, my mind cycled through a thousand and one different thoughts. I wished I had my own family, and thoughts of my sister's kids and my kids playing and growing up together made me smile.

"You have to see this," Maggie's voice surprised me, bringing me back to the here and now.

I looked up and saw a certain distress in her face. She gave me her cell phone to look at a video. As I watched it, I realized that I knew the woman in the video surrounded by eight shooters.

She was the one that I wished I had met years ago...had multiple kids with, and lived happily ever after.

Dreams weren't reality.

"Memphis needs Zachary Brick," said Maggie.

CHAPTER 2

THE DESTRUCTION OF IRRATIONALITY.

"That's your desk over there," said the detective with the short red hair to me. It was over ten years ago, but I still remember the day like it was yesterday. Alaina Rivers' back was to me as she typed on her computer. I noticed that *over there* was the next set of desks that sat about fifteen feet away from her desk and that the desk facing hers was empty. I realized that her goal was to ensure I was fully aware of who the *Alpha* was.

I didn't object. I took it all in. In my previous employment, I wasn't a profiler, but profiling was a huge part of how I did my job. The second I was told that we would be partners, I began my profiling.

In the world that I came from, profiling wasn't a word that was used. The Company had analysts, and we analyzed. I used to kill for a living. It wasn't a glorious job, but a necessary one and analyzing was an essential part of it.

Although Detective Rivers was sitting, I could tell that she was probably around five six or five seven. She was slim, yet, not too slim. She wore a pixie hairstyle...short, stylish. She wore a lightweight, dark blue jacket and faded blue jeans. On her feet were mini-combat black boots that fit like high top sneakers. Sitting at a desk was not her style. I knew immediately that she was a woman of action and she dressed the part.

The first thing I noticed about her desk was what was missing. She had no family pictures, or anything else that could be deemed personal. She was practical, protective of her space, a pragmatist. That, in itself, informed me that she didn't trust her co-workers. The least that they knew about her personal life, the better.

I knew the longest partnership that she had over the past three years was four months. Trust...or lack of. She was a lone ranger. A righteous soul. Those who came before me served others, which meant misplaced loyalty...loyalty that didn't include her.

Her sparse desk did have a compact disc player with a self-made CD. Her music was a variety. From Simply Red's *Holding Back the Tears* and Boz Scraggs' *Lowdown* to the Fifth Dimension's *Stoned Soul Picnic* and Clarence Carter's *Patches* to Elton John's *Goodbye Yellow Brick Road*...the CD was on random play. Just those few songs told me that she was missing a man in her life, be it an old boyfriend or her father. Maybe both. Regardless, it screamed of a bad relationship. That was just a thought. As time passed, I would learn that it was her dad, and indeed, they did not have a close relationship.

For the first three months, our relationship was strictly confined to work. During that time, we did something that she, nor the department's brass, was used to—we solved cases at an alarming rate. We received cases. We investigated. We made arrests. We solved crimes. We worked methodically to accomplish what we needed to do, with little to no conversations regarding our personal lives. We didn't discuss family or friends or boyfriends or girlfriends. It was *strictly business.*

When it came to me, she was inquisitive. My answers were short, but as appropriate, I would give her little tidbits of information. Half-truths at best. I wanted her to be comfortable. I thought it was important for her to be at ease, to gain and maintain trust in her partner—in me. As a CIA officer, even in the world of elimination, you worked with others. Whether it was a handler or a mediator on the other end of a headset, you had to have confidence that the person you were working with had your back.

We had confidence in one another and trust. I was sure of that. Then one day, she informed me that we had to drop by a grammar school to pick up her daughter. The school was in Cordova, a suburb of Memphis. I was told to stay in the car. Of course, I tried to do as I was told. All Alphas think that they are the lead in any partnership. Detective Alaina Rivers couldn't help herself, whether she was a team of one or of one hundred, she assumed the lead.

After ten or fifteen minutes, I got out of the car and leaned on the passenger door. Within minutes, a white woman was departing the school with a medium-sized, slightly fat ten or eleven-year-old boy. She didn't look happy. Nor did the young boy. He had gauze and white tape heavily wrapped around his nose.

The next two kids to exit the building, one black and another white, accompanied by adults who could have been their parents, were equally injured. The black kid's face was swollen. His right jaw looked like it could be broken. The third kid had a brace on his neck, along with a black, swollen eye.

I had no idea what had happened at the school. I actually assumed Alaina had been called because she was a detective and familiar to the school officials. After seeing those boys, I knew something pretty bad had occurred at the school. Judging by the surroundings, there was no way this was acceptable behavior in this affluent area of the city.

Minutes later, a little girl with nice, long sandy brown curly hair came be-bopping out the building with Detective Rivers. The little girl walked with a skip and didn't seem to have a worry in the world. The same couldn't be said for my partner. She still had that stoic, no nonsense-look on her face. The closer that they got to the car, the more I noticed the little girl looked identical to her mom. The biggest difference was the young girl's creamy brown complexion, which was in contrast to her mom's tanned, but fair or white complexion. In black neighborhoods, the girl would be referred to as a redbone. In the world of Prince Roger Nelson, he referenced girls of her complexion as little red corvettes. Even at a young age, I knew she would grow up to be a looker.

Something also told me that Detective Alaina Rivers probably had an arsenal to ensure that young boys always stayed away.

I looked at my partner and she returned the glance. We didn't speak. She wasn't the same woman. Her eyes were softer. Her demeanor was lighter. No words were necessary.

'What's your name?" asked the little girl. She sat behind her mom.

I turned around in my passenger seat and looked at her with a smile on my face. She matched my expression with a friendly smile on her face. "My name is Zachary Brick. What's your name?"

"Sondra Rivers. I'm Detective Rivers' daughter."

"And the reason we had to come to school to get you, Miss Sondra?"

"I beat up three boys in the girls' restroom," said Sondra, matter-of-factly.

I looked little Sondra up and down. She was nine, maybe average height for her age, but definitely skinny. Her right knuckles were bruised. If she felt pain, you couldn't tell. She was a happy girl, and whatever happened, didn't seem to faze her. In less than two minutes time, I surmised that she wasn't a fighter, which wasn't to say she couldn't fight. She just didn't seem like the instigating type. I had a strong suspicion that the three boys, who were definitely bigger then she, deserved what they got.

"You are so small," I said. "How did you beat up three big boys?"

"My mom taught me how to fight, plus I take Tae Kwon Do and karate."

I looked at my partner. She didn't turn her head, but she eyed me with her peripheral vision. She had a satisfying smirk on her face. I got it. The apple didn't fall far from the tree. Verbally, Alaina Rivers would never tell her daughter that she was happy with her actions, but her face clearly said otherwise.

Ironically, it took a nine-year-old to break the ice between us.

CHAPTER 3

WHO KNOWS WHY THE LAMB SEEKS JUSTICE?

It had been two weeks since her mother had died, but the pain had not erased. Still just as fresh and harrowing. She didn't know when her heart would cease hurting, but knew she had to get away. She was so tired of being watched, being followed.

This thought consumed her for a week. She was disappointed—in him. Every fiber in her body told her that he would return and do what he was infamous for...wreak havoc on a level unknown to punks and thugs. His reputation was legendary. Stories of his five-year run were rampant in the city. Maybe the stories were true...maybe not. She didn't know, but now prayed to God that they were.

He was a pseudo uncle to her, or better yet, the father she wished she could have had. Her father was alive and well...and absent. The man who loved both she and her mom was now the same man letting her down. She was beyond disappointed.

He loved her...cared for her...supported her. She hated him... *for leaving.*

Hated him for not being there...for her mother...when she died.

And hated herself...for wishing he was here now.

The dark gray sedan with the black tinted windows was very conspicuous. It didn't even attempt to hide its presence. It didn't matter where she went, or for how long, the car was always there. Even when she tried to be stealthy and sneak out the back door to go over a friend's house, they were still there. On several occasions, she called the police, but conveniently, they were nowhere to be found. Then as soon as the cops would leave, they were there once again.

She wanted to live a normal life.

Unfortunately, she didn't know what normal meant now. She knew that they weren't going to hurt her. They didn't want her. They didn't need her. She wasn't the target.

She was the bait.

But enough was enough.

"My precious girl, hopefully I will live a long, prosperous life and eventually die of natural causes. If this is the case, have no worries," her mother, Alaina Rivers, told her. "You will live a good life. I will make sure of it."

She didn't immediately question her mom. However, she knew something was weighing heavily on her mind...or worse, on her heart.

"But if I die suddenly, and if it's a violent death...remember my instructions. He will find you. No one will mess with you." She wished the long pause was just for effect. But Alaina Rivers didn't do effect. Sondra knew this best. "They want *him*, Precious. Trust me, they will get him...probably as raw as anyone has ever seen him."

That thought. It was something she wanted to forget. However, she knew if she did, she would be truly gone. Her mom would be dead. She would want her vengeance and then some. She needed to stick to the plan.

If they wanted him, then she would take them to him. She gassed up her car and jumped on Interstate 40 headed west. Her followers appeared to be caught off guard and exited the interstate.

Maybe they needed gas. The unexpected can be a bitch...and a shock.

She was still on I-40 West, on the other side of Little Rock, when the dark gray sedan took a detour. She suspected that they needed gas, but really didn't care why they had stopped. She was just relieved to be free. If they had driven another five miles, she would have pulled on the shoulder of the interstate, behind the two law enforcement vehicles parked there. One was clearly a state trooper vehicle. The other vehicle appeared to be an unmarked black sedan with dark tinted windows.

She didn't allow her thoughts to distract her from her goal. It was just like her mother to make sure every *t* was crossed and every *i* was dotted. Truth be told, she had no idea where she was going. She threw her phone away and turned on the phone that her mother had left for her. His address was programmed in the phone, on the map app.

Alaina's instructions directed her to stop at a hotel in Midwest City, a city on the eastern outskirts of Oklahoma City. She then used the phony ID her mother had left for her to check in. She was surprised when the hotel clerk told her that she had a standing reservation. She was shocked to find her room had fresh cookies and a note that two chocolate flavored drinks were in the small refrigerator.

That night she did what she had done every night for the past two weeks—cried until sleep called her name.

The next morning, she would make the final trek to her destination. She had never been to Texas. She had never even had a desire to go to Texas. But her GPS was programmed for Shelbytown, a town on the outskirts of Amarillo, south of the city.

She only hoped that this was a new beginning.

Some lambs needed a new start.

CHAPTER 4

A SMART MAN NEVER SUMMONS THE DEVIL.

I had been in the city for ten days. The city I never thought I would ever return to—Memphis, Tennessee, the Bluff City. The city famous for Elvis, the Blues, the killing of Reverend Dr. Martin Luther King, Jr. and home of the best damn barbeque in the world. I couldn't wait to get a sandwich with coleslaw, a half slab of ribs, baked beans and oddly enough, a hamburger. I think it was a Memphis thing, as the barbeque restaurants in the city made the best damn burgers as well.

Truth be told, I had been to Memphis on numerous occasions...too many to count. Partners aren't supposed to fall in love. Unfortunately, just like in a movie or TV show, sometimes *supposed to* has no real meaning at all. I probably stayed in Memphis five years too long, but had my reasons. I had originally come to the city to kill a man. However, while surveilling the man named Hector Harvey Sr., I couldn't help but notice a certain detective on the case. I was never a man who believed in love at first sight. At best, it was lust at first sight. But this feeling was different. I couldn't quite put my finger on it...maybe intrigue. Hence, I took the appropriate actions to become a detective in Memphis, and hoped to partner up with the redheaded detective.

It was the day that Zachary Brick became my newest legend.

Back in the day, I would've laughed at my sentimental thoughts or reminiscing. I now opined that I missed the woman. Hell, who was I trying to fool? It wasn't an opinion. I did miss her...terribly. I also wanted to burn the fucking city to the ground. However, that notion was the old me. The me before Zachary Brick was born. I wanted my share of vengeance. But the woman loved her city. She served her city. No, I wouldn't be the man to burn it to the ground. I couldn't say the same about the people who killed her.

Ironically, I was in a warehouse on the outskirts of Little Rock, Arkansas, about to kill two thugs. For some, even diehard killers, it would have involved some contemplation. But not me. In fact, there was no ambiguity in anything that I was about to do. My plan was to first follow Sondra to ensure her safety. I guessed that I was on the right track, as I ended up trailing the gray sedan that was following her.

Life can be crazy. In many ways, Memphis ended up being what I thought it would be. I was wrong when I thought it would be a temporary stop. However, my planned two-year stay ended up being five years. I thought that my lie about transferring from the police department in Vancouver, Washington, would be debunked in a couple of years at the most. In the CIA, it would have been my legend, my cover.

But the plan really didn't include love.

Both Alaina and Sondra had touched my heart. Now the woman was gone. The little girl that had captured my heart needed me. I didn't want her to know that I was in the city and had hoped she had left much earlier. I couldn't put my plan into action until Sondra was out of the city and safe. When she crossed the bridge that connected Memphis to West Memphis, Arkansas, my plan was officially initiated.

I think she surprised her followers when she decided to leave the city. It worked out nicely for me, as I made a couple of phone calls to law enforcement types in Little Rock, who had decided that the time was right to pull over a certain dark gray sedan. Instead, the sedan unexpectedly exited the interstate. A gas stop. A perfect stop. A perfect location.

Life is full of opportunities. Some we consider golden, others, not so much. Not involving anyone from the Little Rock Police Department was a good thing. As an employee for the CIA, using people was a huge part of the job. But all too often, it made good men bad and bad men worse. I had a couple of Little Rock detectives and a couple of police officers willing to assist me in a dirty deed. The one thing cops, agents, CIA officers and investigators had in common was the proverbial collection of favors. Many people owed me. Some of those favors I had collected. Others I had hoped I would never have to collect. But that was the biggest lie in my business—golden opportunities included calling in favors.

I was just pleased that I didn't need to collect on this one.

The gray sedan stopped at a rickety gas station with a small island of four gas pumps. I followed them off the exit ramp into the same station. The place was run down, its best days behind it. I pulled around to the side of the building. Maybe it was a stroke of luck that I parked in front of the restrooms on the right side of the building. In the prevailing climate of political correctness, the gas station would have been considered old-fashioned, or vintage. Across the street was a more modern gas station/convenience store combo, with restrooms inside the store. Even that one was outdated. Gas stations with outside restrooms probably went out of style somewhere in the eighties or nineties. But the few that still existed continued to make money. As long as they carried gas, someone would always be willing to patron the station.

Like a couple of dudes, both dressed in black, trying to keep a low profile—incognito.

It was perfect for the deed that was required of me.

The overemphasized part of a CIA officer's job is being inconspicuous. In fact, the job was covert operations. However, taking action at a moment's notice was also an essential function.

For this task, I needed to take action. Inconspicuous could come later.

The guy was white, at least six feet four, with a well-built physique and a thick neck. That was my focus, his neck. My vehicle was a dark burgundy Chevy Suburban with dark tinted windows. The seats were down in the back, turning the cab space of the SUV into exactly that—a covered cab. I lifted the back hatch up and waited.

The big dude really had to use the restroom. No telling how long he had been holding his water. He went into the station and presumably asked the clerk where the restroom was and then for the key after he was told it was on the side of the building. He didn't appear to notice me or my parked vehicle nearby. Sometimes dumb can't be quantified. Or maybe his lack of observations skills just fell to the wayside, as he made a mad dash to the men's room.

I instinctively sized him up.

I stood six feet tall and weighed around two hundred pounds to his two sixty or two seventy weight. This disparity in size was pretty insignificant for the action I was about to take.

He fumbled to put the key in the lock. As he pushed open the rustic door to the restroom, I pushed the sharp needle into his back with my left hand, and when he turned, my right hand quickly lurched forward and plunged the other needle into his neck. Within a split second the big man began to fall. I then caught and dragged him to the back of my SUV.

Then I had a choice, wait on his partner to come and look for him, or drive around to the gas pumps and accost him in public. I chose the latter. I whipped my car around and came in from the opposite direction. I pulled up next to him as he finished pumping his gas and opened the driver's door to get in. He looked stunned. Even more so when I jumped out the car and hit him over the head with a blackjack. The blackjack was made of wood with a lead weight inside. The man fell heavily into my arms. I then took him around to the back of the SUV and placed him next to his partner.

I didn't bother to look around to see if anyone was watching me. I had on a baseball cap, pulled down as far as it could go, with dark shades on. Although it was midday in December with sunny skies outside, it was still cold and people cared more about keeping warm than being observant. I had on a dark jacket with dark jeans, hopefully making it tough for anyone to give the cops an accurate description of me. Lastly, as I drove off, I didn't worry about my license plates being seen. They were covered by a dull yellow tinted license plate cover, which would make it hard as hell to read from a distance.

Assassins are thinkers. Some hate it. Others embrace it. But none of us want to have to think too hard. We can think for hours and then, when it comes time for judgment, time to do the work, we can be the most focused human beings on planet. Assassins that are married or in serious relationships, have ready-made thoughts—family and relationship-related. They deal with children, marriage, in-laws and friend issues.

Assassins that are single with no children, deal with everything else—thoughts of their single life, a life with no ties, no serious relationships and very few true friends, if any. I had my sister. As much as I wanted to say that I had her family, I didn't. If I had anything, I had a woman that I loved named Alaina Rivers, and her daughter, Sondra. Now Alaina was gone. Murdered. Cold-blooded. Killed in the streets like a dog.

They wanted Zachary Brick.

That was my main thought pattern. They wanted me. They got me. They didn't get a new me or an old me, just a more refined, wiser version of myself that came with age. The biggest change in me over the past ten years was my internal rage...or better yet, my repressed rage. For years I had suppressed a fury in me that remained dormant and refused to rear its ugly head. That was a good thing. I was fortunate that Alaina worked on me for the better of five years to calm my internal demons.

She was quite successful, as my internal rage had dissipated. However, I was still a trained killer. An assassin absent of feelings and remorse when it came to doing my job. Vengeance was on my mind. But it was a different form of revenge. I wanted the head of the snake, and the head was no longer Hector Harvey Senior. His sons, Ronaldo and Damian, ran the business now.

They wanted Zachary Brick. The problem for them is that they had never seen me in my rawest form. I had news for them. I was coming at them savagely, with blood in my eyes, ice in my veins and a shitload of weapons in tow.

In front of me were two so-called thugs. Harvey's men. Tied up. In separate chairs. Hands behind their backs. Feet shackled to the legs of the chairs.

One – white. One – black. One was my height, my skin color, bigger than me, but with more fat than muscle. The other one was taller than me, white, burly, the muscle.

Alpha Dog and Beta.

My Alpha was on my mind. I decided that she couldn't be a thought right now. Not the kind of thoughts that I wanted to have.

When I was taught to kill, I was told that the greatest friends an assassin could have were *composure* and *an empty heart.* Composure was easy.

There are some assassins who can only kill. No personal contact, no working a room, no investigating, or getting to know subjects or acquaintances or associates., as part of the job Then there are the assassins who can do the obvious, but also associate closely with others and become one with their environment.

I was the latter.

I slapped the big guy, and backhanded Alpha Dog. I, too, was sitting in a chair facing my two new associates.

"You wanna hear some crazy shit?" I said to the so-called thugs. "In the CIA, they have these duty titles: training instructor, training specialist, advanced training specialist and my favorite, master training/drill professional."

I laughed out loud. It just really hit me as funny. Only the Company could create something so stupid, yet so believable. "Excuse me for laughing," I apologized to my two guests, who were completely alert from their stupor now. "I laughed because the one word CIA officials tried their damnedest not to say was *assassin*. Can you believe that shit?

"All of these elaborate, damn duty titles, just to avoid saying assassin. Ain't that some shit. Trying to be all politically correct, when there is nothing politically correct about that damned agency. But they care about the titles of the damn trainers that trained their killers. That shit is too funny, don't you think?"

Neither man said a word. I really didn't expect an answer. In fact, I had a smirk on my face and an expression of complete disregard for their opinion. "Those titles just describe levels of expertise and professionalism possessed by an assassin. Hell, I was a master training/drill professional, and you know what that means?"

Both men just stared at me. I think Beta guy was still kind of out of it, but appeared to have a genuine interest in what I was selling. Alpha Dog, on the other hand, just looked pissed off... beyond pissed off.

I continued unfazed. "It meant that I could kill someone in at least two hundred different ways, and in a hundred of those ways the best medical examiners and investigators in the world would think was a suicide." I laughed again. "That's some crazy shit, don't you think?"

They didn't think. As much as they tried to play it off, both were scared shitless. I knew the true meaning of being scared shitless. It meant that you were so afraid, that you emptied your bowels until there was nothing left. Maybe they didn't do that, but it sure as hell smelled like they did. It was a raw funk. The kind of smell dogs or flies refused to be around. A smell that resonated, even in the wide opened space of an abandoned warehouse.

I understood. How could I not understand? I had a table with five various models of handguns, three different deadly knives, a machete, a hatchet and various small instruments that could inflict more pain than any other weapon I had on the table.

It was a show of deadly force. Looking at each man's face, I realized that it was a show that I probably didn't need. The look of anger and spite on Alpha Dog's face indicated that he knew he was going to die, but refused to show any fear. If I had to analyze the man, I would say that he was single, with no kids, and probably not much family to speak of. No one would be sharing tears at his demise, nor would anyone really consider his death as a loss. Certainly, not the Harveys. In contrast, the fear on Beta's face told me one thing—he didn't want to die.

"Ok, I will make this easy," I said. "First, by introduction, my name is Brick. Zachary. Brick."

There is always a weak link. You can have two of the strongest individuals in the world and you will still have a weak link. In this case, the weak link was the biggest of the two so-called thugs. His eyes grew to the size of half-dollar coins. He knew the name. My name.

"I don't have time for games," I explained. "The first one to tell me what I want to know...lives. And yes, it's really that easy. That fucking simple."

"Go fuck yourself maggot!" Alpha Dog exclaimed with venom. "Brick is dead and all of these parlor games to scare us ain't worth shit. So, go fuck yourself, you lil bitch! If—"

Before he could say another word, I grabbed the hatchet and brought it down with force on his left knee and left it in. His scream could probably be heard two counties over, as blood gushed from his kneecap. I didn't give a damn. We were at least five to ten miles from the nearest anything, on the outskirts of Little Rock. I pulled the hatchet out, and disregarded the gushing blood, then brought the hatchet down on his right foot, chopping his toes off through his expensive Cole Hahn shoes. He continued to scream, an octave or two louder.

His partner, Beta, had tears flowing down his face. He knew I meant business. More importantly, he wanted to live. Composure also means driving the point home. I wanted Beta to know that I meant business. I picked up the machete off the table, backward swung it to the neck of Alpha Dog, separating his head from his body.

If you ever want to send a message to a bad guy, cut the head off the so-called leader. It has a charming way of turning hardnosed bad guys into spineless bitches.

I was pleasantly surprised. I thought the severed toes, followed by the head would make Beta pass out. It didn't. His eyes were red, as tears poured down his face and snot backed up his sinuses. His face displayed the horrible fear of dying. He didn't know it, but his death was inevitable.

Regardless, I couldn't lose focus, Alaina was still on my mind. She was the reason I was here. The reason I had no mercy...no filter.

I needed what information he could tell me before I took his life. Our question and answer session lasted approximately thirty minutes. Beta was very cooperative. He told me everything

I wanted to know and more. I told him to calm down. I pulled a small bottle from my pocket. The bottle read extra strength aspirin. They looked like aspirin. I gave him three pills. I told him to open his mouth and I put the pills in, followed by a swallow or two of bottled water. My pledge was that it would calm him down and make his headache go away.

"I'm going to leave you tied up. You will be tied up for another couple of hours. When I reach Memphis, I will call the local authority here. I'm sure they will send someone to rescue you, and possibly arrest you. Which is much better than dying."

Beta just shook his head in the affirmative. The man was happy to be alive. I knew that. I was equally sure he had someone waiting on him in Memphis. Someone he would never see again.

I packed up my stuff and changed out of my blood-soaked clothing. Then, I piled up the bloody clothing on the warehouse floor, and set them afire. Within ten minutes, I was driving away.

Beta died a peaceful death. If he had family, they could have an open casket funeral. That was the best I could do.

During my two-hour drive, I would think about the woman I loved. The only woman who ever, truly got me.

And an assassin who killed for a living would drop a tear...or two...or three for the woman he couldn't tell how much he did truly love her.

They wanted Zachary Brick.
Be careful what you ask for . . .

CHAPTER 5

W̲HAT DOESN'T KILL YOU...COULD KILL YOU.

Sometimes, killing, or the methodology of death, can be the death of all of us. His name was Evan Pacheco and like me, was an officer with the CIA. His primary task was delivering death. Several years prior to me going rogue, Pacheco did the same. He went on a six-month spree of damaging operations for the Company. That damage included the compromise of over twenty missions and the killing of other Company officers and allies.

The Company did what the Company does.

Several officers were sent on training missions, with the specified intent of eliminating the threat—the rogue officer who fell out of favor with his employer. Those officers failed in their mission.

By design, officers on different missions usually have no idea what's going on with another officer's mission. Additionally, there is no daily briefing or monthly newsletter that provides information on all the current missions, or the details of past successful or failed missions. Divisions, or assassins, didn't share information. Occasionally, one would hear something in a pre-brief of a mission...and once in a blue moon, during a hot wash, which was a debriefing of a current mission. The best any field officer could hope for was a handler who shared whatever information they received. Information that may keep us alive.

I heard about the workings of Evan Pacheco during my pre-brief of my next mission—the CIA's operation to kill an asset, Evan Pacheco.

The man was smart. Manipulative. He had a team of six mercenaries working for him. At one time, they were all held up in an office building in Karlsruhe, in southwest Germany, not far from the border that separated France and Germany. The city was located in the province of Württemberg, about sixty miles from Patch Barracks, an American Army Base in the city of Stuttgart. Karlsruhe was famous for being one of the cities that our nation's capital was fashioned after. Rumor had it that Thomas Jefferson had traveled to Karlsruhe and was so enthralled with the city, that he made a sketch of it and provided that sketch to Pierre Charles L'Enfant, the French architect who was designing the layout of Washington, D.C.

The office building was a small, three-story, red brick building that was situated near the market square. This location was ironically within a couple of miles of the Federal Court of Justice and Federal Constitutional Court, the two highest courts in Germany.

I spent six days surveying the office building. I closely observed the day-to-day interactions and activities of Pacheco's six mercenaries. I had a layout, or architectural drawings of the entire building. It took me two days to hack into Pacheco's computer server, alarm system and two backup alarm systems. Field officers were superstitious and overly suspicious. Thus, they often insisted on having triple protection, hence, an alarm and double backup systems. Regardless, I was able to sneak in and plant cameras throughout the building. When I hacked into Pacheco's computer server, the things that I saw shocked me.

Pacheco was a traitor. For money. He was also the smartest officer that I had ever met. He was disgruntled. Vengeful. His mind had betrayed him. Why? Because he allowed his mind to overthink things. Then, he wanted to correct wrongs. Just too many wrongs for one man to correct by his lonesome. Hence, a team was established.

His team of six...was actually a team of nine, which included three sets of identical twins. This carefully configured conglomeration was brilliant. Super Assassin Evan Pacheco was an evil genius. I had seen the daily comings and goings of every team member and never realized that three of the people I was seeing had twins. Thus, I had to do several double takes when viewing my iPad or laptop.

Of course, it was easier to damage over twenty missions with a team of nine versus a team of six, especially if some of your people looked identical and could be in two different places at the same time. This advantage would be especially useful if one of them got caught and needed the perfect alibi. Pacheco was the tenth member, a man of great intellect that understood the inner workings of Langley, as well as the intimacies of killing and breaking the spirit of others. I was sure he had used the identical twins to his advantage. But how? I didn't know...and honestly, I didn't care.

I just admired the man's genius. Who in the hell could find three sets of identical twins that were also ruthless criminals. I understood then why the Company wanted him eliminated—he was much too cunning to keep alive.

I realized that I was able to get into the building when Pacheco and his crew departed for a couple of days to accomplish two missions. CIA operations in Sigonella, Italy, on the island of Sicily, and in Paris were disturbed by Pacheco and his crew. Disturbed was just another way of saying operations were grossly interrupted with several officers killed.

Prior to my quasi home invasion, I set up a dummy system that allowed me to walk throughout the building without the alarms going off. If Pacheco or any member of his crew viewed the office building via a phone or iPad app, the system would look normal, as if no one was in the building. If I could have accessed the building a couple of days earlier, I probably could have stopped the missions in Sigonella and Paris. That was the only viable information I had found.

I took my time placing small, directive explosives in each of the six rooms on the third floor. I then rigged the sprinkler system on the second floor with a concentrated poison that would be triggered once I initiated the explosives on the upper floor. My plan was based on my previous viewing of the crew. I noticed that the majority of the crew hung out on the top two floors. The main floor, however, belonged to Evan Pacheco and the only female in his crew.

I was waiting in the building upon their arrival. It was a Saturday morning. They had wreaked havoc in Sicily and Paris on a Friday night, sending Europe in a tailspin that would dominate the news cycle the entire weekend and continue to even be the lead story on Monday morning.

Within an hour of their arrival, I initiated my plan. The explosion on the third floor quickly killed five of the mercenaries, while the simultaneous dispersing of a concentrated poison from the sprinkler system on the second floor, instantly killed three more. Evan and his female team member were fucking like rabbits in the bedroom of his three-room flat on the north side of the building.

Being on top, the blonde woman with the red and blue streaks in her hair, was the first to jump up when they heard the explosions. The first thing I saw was the Glock 30. How could I miss it? It was a dull chrome red with a dark burgundy wood handle. It looked sleek. Hell, it even looked sexy.

But so was she. The. Woman. Was. Deadly.

So. Was. I.

One shot from my Sig Sauer 1911 got her in the middle of her forehead. My second shot was at the pillow, an inch from the head of Evan Pacheco.

The bedroom was huge. Hell, it was actually the size of two oversized master bedrooms. I had hid in one of three closets, in the one closest to the bed. I was less than ten feet from the infamous Evan Pacheco, the most prolific killer in CIA history.

"Who do I have the honor of killing?" asked Pacheco in perfect German. His smile was deceiving. The man was afraid. When I made my entrance and detonated the directed bombs on the third floor, which automatically set off the sprinklers on the second, I glimpsed the killer's hands resting on the nicely sized breasts of his mercenary.

"Elijah McCrane," I returned in perfect Spanish.

The man had a hearty laugh. "First of all, Mr. McCrane was white, and to be perfectly honest, was a little shit." His Russian wasn't as good as his German, but was still not too bad. "Plus, he really wasn't as good as you and I. Hell, he was lucky if he knew twenty ways to kill someone."

"I only have one question," I stated.

The man didn't pay any attention to me. I knew why. He was stalling, while waiting on reinforcement from the Karlsruhe police force.

"No, you are the one and only Hunt Collins," said Evan Pacheco, in English. "I have heard stories. I thought I was the best? But I always hear the same thing from my handler and probably every assassin who heard or know the stories of Hunt Collins."

"One question, Evan," I responded also in English.

"One question? Only one?"

"Why?" was my one-word question.

"Everything is not what it seems Hunt." The man's eyes were looking at me, but his mind was elsewhere. Actually, he was looking through me. I could see the pain in those eyes...as well as the fear. The confusion. The sadness. The disappointment.

"I killed Elijah McCrane," the killer said to me. Elijah was the top assassin in the Company before Evan Pacheco took the honor. That's how it was for assassins in the CIA. Second best always wanting to out-duel the best.

"He told me to watch my back and that the Company isn't what I thought it was. He was right. I came for Elijah. You came for me. Someone will come for you...I hope you survive."

We continued to stare at each other. *He was the best*. I had the gun...second best. About to become the best.

"You centralized, single pointed the bombs," stated Pacheco. "No noise outside the building, all contained within. Pretty good. Smart.

"The authorities are not coming, right?"

My shot hit him between the eyes.

I didn't have to say anything. He had allowed his left hand to shyly slide to the side of his bed. I knew the trick. He had a holster attached to the side of his bed with a Glock 37, also dull chrome red, with a burgundy wood handle.

He was right. In less than three years, the Company sent killers to take me out. Some, like me, were within Company walls. Others, were guns for hire.

Hunt Collins was the name I was given when I joined the CIA. It was my official name . . .

. . . now, my legend was Zachary Brick.

I had hidden in plain sight for five years. Then walked away to save a woman. Now I was back. Something internally told me, Memphis would never be the same.

It was a good memory as I drove back to Memphis.

With murder and mayhem on my mind.

CHAPTER 6

IF ONLY COMPUTERS COULD DO WHAT MEN CAN DO.

"How are we looking?" I said in my mouthpiece to the person on the other end. Her name was Maxwell Griffith. Max for short. She was once an assassin for hire. Then she took a job to kill me. It didn't work out too well for her.

Then it did.

"Looking good," said Max. "I can see everything, every building." She was in the big town of Shelbytown, Texas and was now my *right-hand man*. But she was no man.

And she didn't play nice with most.

Needless to say, she didn't kill me and more importantly, we became friends. Very good friends.

But whenever I thought about how Max and I met, my mind always wandered back to Evan Pacheco. He killed Elijah McCrane. I killed Pacheco. Max was sent to kill me. She was the fourth person sent to kill me.

The other three...I didn't allow to live.

I wasn't happy Sondra decided to stay in the city as long as she had. However, it had allowed me to conduct reconnaissance and surveillance on the Harveys' operations. I wanted immediate vengeance, but had to do it my way—the smart way. I couldn't just go buck wild, like a bull in a china shop. That was an amateur move, and a stupid amateur at best.

Damn, how I wanted to be that stupid amateur. I wanted to make every Harvey man suffer as I now suffered. I wanted to kill the wife and daughter of Hector Senior in front of Hector and his four sons. Mentally, I had a list of every person that I wanted to put to death before I took out the father and each son. I had killed women before in my capacity as a CIA officer, but only those that I was ordered to kill or who posed a threat to the United States. It was a part of the job and nothing I lost sleep over. I was also sure that there had been some not-so-innocent bystanders who had lost their lives as well. But I was able to justify all of these killings at the time. Now, however, even the torment in my heart couldn't bring me to kill the Harvey women if they were, indeed, innocent.

It was a million daggers that attacked my soul at night...a blackness that permeated my heart. This anger and anguish felt like a black hole, an abyss that kept me confined and unable to escape from to find some kind of solace. I knew what was going with me mentally. I missed my favorite detective. The woman I had fallen in love with. The one person who actually made me realize I had a soul and a reason for living. Prior to her, I didn't believe any of that love shit. Now, it wasn't shit to me. It was love. She was love. Alaina and Sondra did something that I never thought was possible. They made me human. Taught me love.

Now I would digress, and be what I was used to being, to be what I was.

Death.

I had placed surveillance equipment at over twenty locations in the city. Ronaldo and Damian were the youngest two sons of the Harvey family. They ran the family now. In my absence, Ronaldo and Damian had taken over the family business and from all indications, were a hundred times worse than their older siblings.

It was a long and detailed family history. One I knew well.

Now I was only concerned with these two punks. They were indeed the worst of the bunch. Although I had once put the clamps down on their oldest brothers, Hector Junior and Arturo, it was a necessity, once again, to clean up Memphis and return it to decency.

My man, Beta, told me the names of the eight guys involved in the shooting of Alaina. More importantly, he told me where I would most likely find all eight. Impending death makes the toughest son-of-a-bitch into a snitching, whiny little baby. I gave Beta the best thing that I could—a civil death. Now I was executing the first step in my plan of attack. A plan I knew would change based on the hand that I was dealt.

The Harveys were the kingpins in the Bluff City area, the nickname for Memphis. Their criminality covered all of western Tennessee, and parts of Arkansas and Mississippi. Although it didn't seem like much, one local reporter estimated that their criminal enterprise brought in over a half billion dollars per year. This money came from multiple sources, which included drugs, prostitution, illegal gambling and protection to local businesses. It was easy for them to make a considerable profit, considering how many cops and local government officials that they had in their back pocket. I was also convinced that their generosity had lined the pockets of some federal officials as well.

I was in the parking lot of Melrose High School in the Orange Mound community, one of the oldest neighborhoods in the city and one rich in tradition. This area that once boasted of having the most well-to-do black folks in the city, was now just a shadow of itself. Like most communities throughout America, it had its share of night crawlers and predators that predominantly surfaced when the sun went down.

This was my sixth and final stop of the night since driving back from Little Rock. My busy day turned into a busy night.

This was my evening to break laws and to be a menace to society. My mission was to send a clear message to the Harveys and to the city of Memphis. The message would have to be severe, and not easily forgotten. Killing the eight killers who took Alaina's life would send that message and so much more.

I had placed two small digital cameras in the trees directly across from an apartment building that sat on Park Avenue, a major thoroughfare that ran through the Orange Mound community. That apartment complex was a couple of blocks from the high school. It was a red brick, two-story building with sixteen total units, with eight apartments upstairs and eight downstairs. All of the residents worked for the Harvey boys. I knew the brothers didn't own the building, or pay rent and had a strong suspicion that the owner's payment was that he and his family would live to see another day.

It was after two on a Thursday morning...the witching hour, a time when the demons and goblins came out to play. My target was the two bad asses who occupied the first apartment on the bottom floor, on the east side of the building. There was no movement outside of the building, which was a good thing for me. But in carefully viewing my targets' apartment with binoculars, I could see their apartment was dark, no light emitting from windows or the front door. I had scouted the apartment several times, around the same time. At times, there was heavy traffic in and out of the apartment. It wasn't hard to tell if someone was there, light emitted from the slightly opened blinds and at the bottom of the front door. Additionally, the apartment next door to them, where they also did business looked equally vacant. It was clear that my targets were not home, but out in the streets somewhere. That was not a good thing for me.

As luck would have it, they returned fifteen minutes later. I quickly lost my enthusiasm. They had company.

"You see this shit?" I said to Max. We had made small talk while I was conducting my surveillance, primarily to keep her alert and astute. I did this out of habit, but found that it wasn't necessary with her. She was the female version of me. We were both professionals and this was our business. We had both been on missions where time and patience were elements you just didn't focus on or pay much attention to. If you did, it could mean your life.

"Yeah, how do you plan on handling this?" her voice was just as strong as it had been the entire day.

"What I told you earlier," I said as I drove to the apartment. "I'm going through the apartment next door and through the bedroom trap door. The only difference now is that I don't know what I'm going to do with the little girl that they have with them."

CHAPTER 7

H E WHO OPENS HIS EYES IN THE MORNING,
SHOULD FEEL BLESSED.

Regardless of how long he had been on the job, he still hated waking up early. His day officially started at five o'clock every morning, Monday through Friday, and sometimes on Saturday and Sunday. Regardless of what time sleep called his name, he was awake at three-thirty every morning and was out the door by four-thirty.

Today was one of his unusual days. That's what he called it. His unusual days consisted of reminiscing of days past. Another life. Another career. Those days used to be once a quarter. Now, his unusual days occurred once every couple of weeks.

However, he didn't allow those days to interfere with his present day. Being the chief of detectives of the Memphis Police Department required him to review the prior night's events before the city was fully functional, which was seven-thirty or eight a.m. during the weekdays. He grabbed his Pittsburgh Steelers coffee mug with hot, steaming brew that Deb, his wife and best friend, made for him every morning. Although the Tennessee Titans played in Nashville, the city of Memphis had always been Steelers and Cowboys country.

He loved Deb. She was the best. He didn't need this life. Deb was worth millions. He was fortunate that way. He felt even more fortunate that every day consisted of a smile and a blessing. A loving wife, two beautiful sons...but a profession that any sensible man would walk away from.

He had been in various forms of law enforcement for over three decades now. When he took over the chief of detectives position five years ago, he was the first Caucasian to hold the position in ten years. Nothing to write home about, and Memphis was nowhere near home, but for him, it was a major accomplishment in his life and career.

The ring tone of his cell phone caught him off guard. He scrambled to cut it off. Deb was sleeping soundly in bed right next to him.

Four-fifteen. Immediately, one word occupied his mind. *Trouble.* Phone calls before five meant that the world was falling apart. Definitely death, and usually the death of someone significant, someone famous or political, someone way too young to die, or worse, a person of Caucasian persuasion in the wrong neighborhood. He picked up on the fourth ring, prior to the call going to voicemail.

"Major Hillsmeier." He had been Hillsmeier for fifteen years now, but it still felt odd whenever he heard the name.

"Sir, it's Sergeant Harrell. Lieutenant Jeffries directed me to call. He told me to tell you to haul ass and meet him at Mayor Archibald's house."

Calston Hillsmeier hesitated. Words escaped him. A lump developed in his throat. *Haul ass to the mayor's house* meant possible death of someone important, and the fallout would be ugly.

"Is the mayor and his family okay?" Cal Hillsmeier asked his sergeant.

"Yes, they are," was the response. "But those on his front lawn are not."

Cal Hillsmeier didn't kiss his wife on this morning. It was his morning ritual, except when the world was falling apart in his adopted city of Memphis. As he pulled out of his two-car garage, he was still optimistic that he could turn an obvious bad day into something more decent. If only he could define decent at that moment.

He would soon find out just how wrong he would be.

Ensuring that the garage door closed behind him, he failed to notice the body sprawled out on his lawn. The man was laid out on his back, dressed in black and with his legs spread eagle. The victim's hands were resting on his chest, tightly clasping the eight-inch serrated knife in the middle of his heart. His face was bloody from the hole in the middle of his forehead.

As Cal pulled out into the street and looked back at his house, another morning ritual, the body stopped him dead in his tracks.

"Fuck!" was the only word Major Cal Hillsmeier could muster.

CHAPTER 8

In case you are just joining us, eight bodies were found in the front yard of five Memphis city officials this morning, including Mayor Archibald, his Chief of Staff Ryan Robison, Police Chief Wanamaker, Chief of Internal Affairs Major Robert Turner and Chief of Detectives Major Calston Hillsmeier. MPD officials are not saying at this time if the dead bodies are connected to the death of Detective Rivers. The office of Chief Wanamaker stated that he will hold a press conference late morning to address these events.

He rubbed his black, wavy hair from front to back in exasperation as he turned the television off. This was depressing on so many levels. He had just won re-election as the Mayor of his native Memphis, and discovering two bodies in the front of his house, the mayor's house, was never a good thing.

"Fuck, fuck, fuck!" yelled Mayor Kenneth Archibald to his chief of staff and four law enforcement officials. Just like in his situation, four of the five officials in attendance had also awakened to a murdered body or two on their front lawn. The only difference was the method of death.

The sixth member of this meeting was Assistant Chief of Ds, Lieutenant Jody Fontaine.

"How in the hell did something like this happen?" asked the mayor. "I'm the fucking mayor of a major city, with a security detail, and still, two bodies are found on my front lawn, and worse, the damn press know before I know. And it's my fucking house!"

No one immediately spoke. In situations like this, only two officials were authorized to speak: the director of police, and the chief of staff, and the CoS had nothing to say. In this meeting of six, Ryan Robison was probably the most innocent one in the room. He had no law enforcement experience. He was a master at public relations and staff management, the perfect combination for keeping any public politician or figure out of trouble.

"We are on it, Mr. Mayor," volunteered Director Wanamaker. "We have the surveillance tapes and my men are going through them as we speak. Additionally, Lieutenant Fontaine will head up the task force to capture these criminals."

"Cut the shit Sam!" retorted Mayor Archibald. "You, me and every fucking body, who is somebody in this damn city, knows who is responsible for this damn carnage. You assholes let the Harvey Boys run rampage over this damn city and kill probably the most honest and honorable cop on your whole fucking force, and you didn't expect Detective Brick to come home. Really, Sam? Are you assholes that fucking clueless and stupid?"

"Mayor Archibald, I respect you sir, but don't talk to me...or my men, like we are your fucking children!" Sam Wanamaker barked back.

The table was long, thirty feet in length, oak, beautifully shellacked with a maroon finish. The mayor sat at the head of the table, with his CoS in the first seat on the right of the mayor, and Director Wanamaker on the left. Major Hillsmeier sat next to the CoS, while Major Turner and Lieutenant Fontaine sat next to the Director.

Mayor Archibald leaned forward, surveying the room. He knew the mess he had on his hands. He was once one of the boys in blue. He was more than familiar with the thin blue line. He was even more familiar with the corruption that permeated police departments, especially the department that was under his purview.

"Sam, I would say that cooler heads should prevail, but you are welcome to turn your badge in if I have hurt your fucking sensibilities."

The Director didn't reply. He was a proud man, but he knew the mayor. He was easily the smartest, most meticulous man he knew. Not only did he make sure to cross the *t*'s and dot the *i*'s, but he also knew the history of each *t* and each *i*. He knew his city. He wasn't a part of the corruption, but he knew where the bodies were buried and who was responsible for burying every last one of them.

"Sir, we should probably go over our plan of attack as well as what Director Wanamaker will say at his press conference," added CoS Ryan Robison.

"No, we are going to settle this shit now," responded Mayor Archibald tersely. "If Director Wanamaker wants to turn in his badge, I prefer it happen now and not later."

Sam Wanamaker was trying to play it cool. He prayed that there would be no fallout from the death of Detective Rivers. Not in his wildest imagination, did he see any of this playing out this way, with the mayor asking for his resignation.

"Director Wanamaker, please turn in your badge, and leave my office."

"No, sir!" exclaimed the Director. "I want my job, Mr. Mayor. I apologize for my outburst." It was hard for the man to say the words. He had worked hard to be the top dog. He couldn't believe he was that close to losing it all.

The mayor was silent. He and Sam Wanamaker continued to look at each other. The silence for the director was nerve racking. Sam Wanamaker knew what was going on. Mayor Archibald was playing hardball and the director knew the wheels in his head were spinning.

The two men had a long history. Some of that history included friendship, mutual respect, professionalism and once upon a time, a partnership as young detectives. Both were hungry for leadership positions. Kenneth Archibald was higher on the corporate ladder and still climbing, while Sam Wanamaker had reached his pinnacle position, his dream job.

"Sir, would you like the room?" asked Ryan Robison.

"No, regardless of the obvious tension in the room, let's press on," stated Mayor Archibald. "It will be interesting to see and hear Director Wanamaker's press conference. Tell me Sam, how will you explain eight dead bodies in the yards of five city officials? What plausible explanation do you plan on pulling out of your ass, Director?"

"Unfortunately, there are more bodies than that, sir," volunteered Ryan Robison. "Evidently, there was a shootout in Orange Mound that resulted in six dead. However, there was a witness that said there were eight bodies, but the killer took two bodies with him, which may be the bodies that ended up on your front lawn, sir."

"How in the hell do you know that?" Cal Hillsmeier weighed in.

"I've got my sources," answered Robison.

The two men looked at each other. An environment already filled with tension, grew even heavier. Cal Hillsmeier didn't like city or office politics. Ryan Robison was a career politician, and the last thing the Chief of Ds wanted was the mayor's righthand man in his front yard.

"What did the witness have to say, Cal?" asked Mayor Archibald.

"I haven't talked to her yet, sir. I will as soon as I get to the office."

"No report from your detectives?" questioned Robison.

"The young lady will only talk to Major Hillsmeier," interjected Lieutenant Fontaine. "She witnessed the scene. She was with the men who were killed. The killer spoke to her and told her to only speak to Major Hillsmeier. They even threatened to put her in jail. But she is far more afraid of the killer than any of us."

Mayor Archibald burst out in a sarcastic laugh. He had the attention of the room. He was shaking his head as he continued laughing. "Tell me, what fucking else do I need to know? Please, get it all out, instead of fucking up my day later as well."

"Well, since we want all of the possible bad news now, sir, there are two bodies possibly related to this fiasco," Cal Hillsmeier added. All eyes were on him now, waiting on an explanation. And he obliged. "I received a phone call ten minutes before this meeting from the chief of detectives in Little Rock. Two bodies were found on the outskirts of Little Rock in a warehouse. One victim's head was cut off, along with some other injuries.

"The second victim was dead as well, but he appeared to have been poisoned. Evidently, both men are from Memphis, possibly tied to the Harvey family. It seems that they were both accosted and removed from a gas station, about ten miles from where their bodies were found. The cops arrived at the gas station approximately thirty minutes after the men were taken."

"For the press conference, concentrate only on the eight bodies," volunteered Ryan Robison. "Arkansas is not our jurisdiction, the Orange Mound killings are an ongoing matter, and there's no sense in giving the press any more ammunition. Director, if they ask about Orange Mound, just mention that it's an ongoing case, which requires further investigation and that we will provide more information when we know more."

"I'm sorry, Sam, I can't let this go," intervened Mayor Archibald. "Why in the fuck would you guys poke the bear? We all witnessed how Detective Brick ran roughshod over the city before, and guess what, we didn't say anything. We loved the crime rate dropping. We loved the fact the bad guys had second thoughts before committing a crime and the ones that didn't take a second to think, paid for it in the worse way at the hands of Zachary Brick.

"We said nothing. And no one tried to prove he was the guilty of anything. We all turned a blind eye...the mayor before me, the city council and everyone in the MPD, and then we wished he had never left when he finally did leave the city. The crime rate now is worse, probably as bad as it has ever been.

"You dumb motherfuckers had to kill the only person who kept him attached to this city."

"Mr. Mayor, we're not sure if it actually is former Detective Zachary Brick," commented Lieutenant Jody Fontaine. "There are tons of rumors that the man is dead. One thing is for sure, he is long gone from Memphis."

Mayor Archibald shot a glare towards the lieutenant. Then he arose from his chair to leave. "Sam, I know Zachary Brick, probably better than anyone in this room. I also knew Alaina Rivers better than anyone in this room. Rivers should have been your assistant chief of detectives. Obviously, we failed Detective Rivers miserably. You and I have been awarded for the work of both of these detectives. Now...as a city...we may have to pay the piper a huge bounty."

The mayor slightly opened the door to leave, before stating, "Lieutenant Fontaine, I don't wish death on anyone, but if Zachary Brick kills any cops, something tells me that your stupid ass may be the first to die."

CHAPTER 9

THE GOOD LORD DOES ANSWERS UNSPOKEN PRAYERS.

"What's your name?" Cal asked the young lady sitting across from him in his office. He didn't smile, but more importantly, he wasn't frowning either. His voice was even, polite. He didn't want to come off as an asshole to the young girl. The right optics could sometimes could result in a huge bounty. He was definitely hoping for this outcome with her.

"Camille," answered the girl. "Camille Singler."

"Well, Camille, it's nice meeting you, and I'm glad you came in," stated Cal. "I'm sorry my detectives kept you in an interrogation room without any thing to eat or drink."

"It's no biggie," replied Camille Singler. "I had something before I came here."

"How did you get here?"

"Uber."

"I wanted to ask if you have a credit card...but what I really want to ask you Ms. Singler is, how old are you?"

"I'm sixteen, sir," said Camille, with a smile on her face. "And yes, I have a credit card." She paused. Cal could tell she had something on her mind. That she had something to add. "The man who told me to only talk to you gave me a credit card with a thousand dollars on it and a thousand in cash. I guess he really wanted me to talk to you only."

"You like the man?" She didn't immediately respond. For Cal, her smile said it all. He was used to that smile. He had known women of all ages who was smitten with the man. Hell, his own wife was one of those women.

"So, Ms. Singler, can you please tell me what happened?"

Before she could say a word, there was a single knock on the door, followed by Lieutenant Jody Fontaine immediately opening the door and walking in the room. He looked at the young woman sitting across from his boss. She returned the look.

"Major, can I see you out here for a few minutes?" asked Fontaine. "Something we need to discuss."

"No, it can wait. When I'm done, I will find you."

Fontaine insisted, "It can't wait Major. We need to talk now."

Cal looked at his deputy chief of detectives. He knew what Fontaine had up his sleeve. However, today wasn't the day for games.

"Lieutenant, get the fuck out of my office," said Cal sternly. "Now!"

Fontaine left without incident. Cal took a breath. Then another deeper breath. He was perturbed. He never trusted Fontaine. He knew his deputy had an allegiance to the director, but also realized that he had allegiances with others as well. Some days he wanted to know who the others were, other days he did not.

"Are you okay, sir?" asked Camille with concern on her face.

Cal appreciated the young woman. She was brave. Now, she was protective.

"I'm good, Camille, thank you for asking and I'm sorry about that." He smiled, then took another breath. That was his ritual when it came to Fontaine, to take a deep breath, or two, or three. He refocused his attention back to Camille. She was tall. Basketball tall. He knew why she was out so late that night, and with possibly eight boys or young men. She had her reasons, but he didn't want to get into that, not unless she brought it up. "I hope you don't mind me calling you Camille. I happen to like the name a lot."

She smiled again. "No, I don't mind, sir."

"So, Camille, please tell me what happened."

This time, Camille took a deep breath. "It was late, definitely past midnight. I was picked up by two guys I knew, Patch and Red Man."

"Do you know their real names?" intervened Cal.

"No, those are the only names I know them by." Cal nodded his head and she proceeded with her story. "On our way to their place, they picked up two more of their boys. When we got to their place, the five of us were walking to their apartment from the parking lot, and that's when the two guys we picked up just fell to the ground. Then two guys that were up on the balcony of the second floor fell over the balcony. When Patch and Red Man swung around, they were both shot in the head.

"Blood shot all over my face. I was turned around too." She paused and looked down at her hands. Cal noticed that she was trembling and wringing her hands. "I saw him walking towards us, with a gun in his hand. I think it had a silencer because you couldn't hear anything and somebody was blasting music in the apartment, so I didn't hear a thing. I thought he was going to shoot me, but then two dudes came out of the downstairs apartment and just that fast he put them down."

Cal was impressed with Camille. She was composed, poised. For sixteen, she had a moxie he didn't even see in thirty or forty-year-old witnesses. "What else?"

"He walked up to me and whispered in my ear. He told me not to worry, that he didn't kill innocents. He asked me my name. I told him. Then he said he would give me a credit card and a thousand dollars in cash if I helped him. After that I was to go home, get a few hours of sleep and then come here and meet you and give you a message."

"What did you help him with?"

"I actually helped him...drag the bodies to his car. A dark Chevy SUV that your guys probably found in a park near Melrose stadium. He told me to tell you that."

"What else did he tell you to tell me?"

"He said that if I wanted to move my family out of town, to tell you and you would make it happen."

Cal tried not to smile, but he couldn't help himself. He knew he had an office full of detectives looking at him. He didn't care. Fontaine had his men, but Cal had his men as well. But Camille was in his care.

"Okay, what else?"

"He told me to do whatever you needed, whether it was helping to make a sketch of him or anything else. And he also told me to tell you two words. Hotel. Charlie."

Hunt Collins.

Cal didn't say a word. Hunt Collins aka Zachary Brick was always one step ahead of everyone else. He would have Camille do the sketch of Brick, but he knew what he would get.

In his mind, he smiled again...and hoped the city had enough body bags.

CHAPTER 10

T<small>RUST CAN BE THE POISON OF FOOLS.</small>

"Why in the hell are you late, Major?" asked Director Wanamaker, as his chief of detectives walked in the door of the director's office.

Cal replied, "Director, I had to take care of our witness. I decided to take a more personal interest. If anything happened to her, I wanted it to be on me and not my detectives."

"That's why you have men," said Fontaine.

"Shut the fuck up, Lieutenant," said Cal, with a grimace. "I'm the chief of detectives, not you. Mind your damn business."

"Major—"

Sam Wanamaker shut Fontaine down before he could respond. "Lieutenant, either shut the fuck up or enjoy your demotion to beat cop."

Fontaine turned beat red. He wasn't sure how to take the director's reprimand. Yes, he was the director's guy, but he also owed an allegiance to the Harvey boys. He couldn't get kicked out of the room, or more appropriately, the detective's bullpen. He couldn't fight a demotion, with the information the director had on him.

"Alright, Cal, what do you have?" Wanamaker wanted to know.

"Well, the young lady did a sketch of a black man with a big, curly afro, thick mustache and thick beard. He had dark red sunglasses on at night, so she couldn't see his eyes. The dark SUV he was driving was found in a park near the football stadium close to Park Avenue. Evidently, whoever the killer is, picked up every weapon and put them in his vehicle, burning all of the evidence.

"Additionally, the medical examiner verified what the young lady told me. It appears that two of the guys were killed with three or four-inch daggers in the back of their neck. They were probably the first two kills. The other four at the scene were killed with a .40 Cal, probably with a silencer. The witness stated that there was loud music coming from the apartment complex, so she couldn't hear the gun being fired. But even with loud music, she should have heard something.

"So, we think it's Brick?" asked Wanamaker, with a furrowed brow.

"Sorry, Director, we're still not sure if this is the work of Brick," stated Cal, as he rested his eyes on Fontaine.

"Personally, I think Brick is dead and this is the work of the Harvey boys or their enemies trying to set them up," added Fontaine.

"Lieutenant, are you willing to take that chance?" asked Cal. The man was six foot two, slim, bald and with a neatly trimmed silver mustache. He missed his red locks from years ago, but his baldness and mustache made him look more distinguished, which he loved. He was well-respected as the chief of detectives, but only he and his wife knew that his life before Memphis was a lie. With the exception of the one other person.

That man's name was Zachary Brick.

"No, he is not willing to take that chance, Cal," stated Wanamaker, matter-of-factly. "Hell, I'm not willing to take that chance. Nor should you be."

The two subordinates sat at a small mahogany table with a high gloss finish in the director's office. The director sat several feet away in a nice, burgundy leather office chair that was much more suited for an elaborately decorated living room than in a city government office.

"Brick is the first man I have ever made it a point to closely observe," continued Director Wanamaker subtly. "I noticed him at various events and remember him interacting with kids, and the kids just absolutely loved him. It was the only time I've ever seen him have a truly genuine, natural smile. He obviously loved kids and they clearly loved him back.

"He was dynamic, a real communicator and motivator. He was just different with those kids. It was hard for me to comprehend that side of Zachary Brick.

"Equally, at other events, I noticed a more reserved side, but the confidence was always there. And women would flock to him. He was cordial and easily engaged in conversations. Some of the women did everything except drop to their knees and give him a blowjob. Everyone was just enamored with him. Even though he didn't always reciprocate with the flirting, the women still wanted him.

"You wanted to kill him, but you also wanted him on your team."

Cal said, "Some people just have that personality, sir. As far as Brick goes, you either hate him or love him, and truth be told, most of the officers in uniform and other detectives loved him. If they needed him, he was there."

"Cal, you and I both know that we would be stupid men to really believe Zachary Brick was dead. I honestly don't think the man is capable of dying." His voice was deep, authoritative. He spoke with a tone that made weaker men cower to his power, and made stronger men think twice about crossing him.

"I really don't like this, Cal," continued Wanamaker. "Brick was the best detective I have ever known. Yes, he was a pain in the ass, but at the end of the day, he was a team player. He was also an enigma. I tried to find out about his history, because so many things just didn't add up for me. I called contacts high and low, and I could never get a straight answer. Hell, I even had contacts in high places hang up in my face.

"Define crazy. Define secretive. Define cunning. Define murderous. Define killer. You know, all of those definitions add up to *only* one person. Zachary. Brick."

"Which means what, sir?" asked Cal honestly. "Brick was mysterious, but he had a heart. He loved what he did, regardless of how crazy it was. No offense sir, you weren't the director of police then, but everyone loved what he did for the city."

"All of that is true," stated Wanamaker. "One man cleaned up the streets of Memphis. No one cared how he did it. And we all know it wasn't pretty. He literally took the law in his own hands and made the city a better place."

"If it is Brick, I think we need to flush him out," volunteered Fontaine.

Both men looked at the lieutenant. Some ideas sounded great in your head, before the words were actually spoken. "Director, I think we are skirting the obvious," continued Fontaine. "There were rumors that Detectives Rivers and Brick had a thing for each other. You can look at the eight bodies and knock just by the death of the men that this was very personal. Hell, four of the men's faces were beaten to a pulp. One even had his head half-way cut off."

"Before you press on," interrupted Wanamaker. "Do we have the reporters under control? My press conference was a success, but the vultures are hungry. They should be. Last night was not our best as a city. Tons of questions. No answers."

"Yes, we do," replied Cal.

"Lieutenant, the best thing for us to do is something we really can't do," stated Wanamaker, as he came within an inch of the man's face. "Which is to allow Brick to wreak havoc on the city. To get his revenge. Then we do the cleanup. But we are the protectors of the city. We are the law. This is our city to straighten out, not Brick's or anyone else's."

Chief Wanamaker looked at his two top detectives. He wasn't sure what he was seeing. His chief detective was as nonchalant as ever. Cal Hillsmeier was the one who got the job done, with no stress and usually, no questions involved. See crime, solve crime and bring on the next case. The chief of detectives was probably the smartest cop in the department. He handled his business. No fuss. Sam Wanamaker was sure of one thing when it came to chief of detectives—he would always come through...it was in his DNA.

Jody Fontaine, on the other hand, was full of uncertainty, possibly even fear. He knew Brick was a dangerous man. A man who would make everyone pay dearly for the death of the woman he loved. That included those who wore the uniform as well. Fontaine was an ex-Marine, with more ambition than brains. Wanamaker considered him a man who took stupid risks, but called it bravery.

Sometimes you don't know what you don't know. In this case, it could and probably would get him killed.

Zachary Brick was a killer.

Just that thought alone caused a chill to run through the director's body. The man had done unspeakable things to many bad guys. He did those things without remorse. In any other city, or any other place, Brick would be in jail for life.

Memphis wasn't any other city . . .

. . . And Zachary Brick certainly wasn't...any other man.

CHAPTER 11

THE YOUNG DO DIE YOUNG.

I knew the Harvey boys and they knew me. Did that mean anything? Probably not, but who is to say. Arturo was the oldest of the four sons, and he and his brother, Hector Junior, ran the family business during my time in Memphis. Better yet, they ran the day-to-day operations. But Hector Senior made all of the big decisions.

Arturo was a good leader. He carried a big stick. He was a big man. He was the epitome of spontaneity...and normally that would be a bad thing in this business. However, Arturo had an ace in the hole—his brother Hector Junior. Junior was the epitome of the word enforcer and crazy as hell. Much shorter than his older brother and he had a screw or two loose. He was unrefined, which in a way was the direct opposite to my crazy. His crazy was based on his family name and fear that accompanied it. Thus, he already had a ready-made audience that inherently feared the Harvey name, and which he capitalized on. My crazy was strictly based on action and in most cases, a calculated crazy to send a clear message. I realized that if I didn't have formal training, my perceived sophistication would actually be Junior's unrefined.

But for almost five years, I allowed Arturo and Hector Junior to do their business without a single word from me. They only knew of me, just as I had known of them.

Actually, I knew quite a bit about them. Not only did I know their operation in and out, I also knew which politicians and law enforcement officials they had on their payroll. That included federal officials as well. I knew the location of every warehouse, dope house, whorehouse and stash house. I could have qualified as the yellow pages on everything Harvey. I made it a point to be knowledgeable and informed of the Harvey operation. Just in case.

As much as I wanted to say that the sons were merely an extension of their father, I knew that this notion was the farthest thing from the truth. Hector Senior pushed the buttons, made the major decisions and manipulated the major players. Arturo just provided the right face for the crime family. He stood six foot five, with a chiseled thin body. His long wavy black hair and facial hair made his deep-set eyes stand out eerily. Or as some of his allies and nemeses described him—*just death*. He was a black belt in at least four martial arts styles. His hot temper was kept in check by his handling of Junior. They worked well together. The brains who could be the muscle, and the muscle who was only that—muscle.

From doing my homework, I was able to comfortably introduce myself to their so-called managers and runners. As crazy as it sounded, the Harvey operation was very organized. In fact, if I hadn't been in law enforcement, I would have been quite impressed. But I knew the right brothels and stash houses to hit to get their attention.

A month before I departed the city, I made it a point to finally introduce myself to both Arturo and Hector Junior. I met them at an inside storage facility in South Memphis. The brothers had five other workers, aka thugs, with them. It was all about work. It was the Harvey crime family. They didn't need protection or bodyguards. The Harvey crime family ran the city of criminals. They provided drugs to all the pushers in the city, ran whores and gave their blessings to the other pimps and hustlers in the city for a nice weekly fee.

Their enterprise was huge throughout Memphis, the entire state of Tennessee, and even the neighboring states. They were the rainbow coalition of crime. Their crew included every nationality and even before it was popular, and even had gays and lesbians working for them as well. Very diverse, very organized and very impressive.

During my time as a Memphis detective, I had learned patience. It was one of many reasons that I wanted to do police work. In the CIA, I had plenty of patience...until I didn't. I needed to reestablish my mojo, my moment of Zen.

Storage Number 115.

"Good afternoon," I said. It was seven against one. Of course, I thought it was a fair fight. However, I wasn't there to fight. Having a gun in each hand probably wasn't a good peace offering. I also wasn't there to make new friends.

"Detective," responded Arturo Harvey in an even tone. He was the only one who didn't appear panicked that I was there.

Three of the other six thugs, including Hector Junior, nervously reached for weapons. I politely lifted both guns, Sig Sauer 1911s and stated, "Not a good idea. I just want to talk."

Everyone who is properly trained on how to use a gun is taught the same thing—*don't point it if you don't plan on using it*. The huge difference at police academies from the rest of the world was identifying yourself as police, and actually giving the assailant a chance to comply. Often times, cops didn't recall that training...especially when it came to killing young black men. But identifying yourself as a cop was about one thing—money. As the city of Memphis, or any city for that matter, didn't want to get sued for a wrong or bad shooting.

I wasn't police academy trained. I was military and CIA-trained. You point, you shoot. Now I was a detective. I needed to comply with the Memphis Police Department rules.

I tried to comply...I didn't try hard, but I tried.

The two thugs not named Harvey continued to reach for weapons and I fired two shots, one from each gun. The thug closest to me was hit in his right shoulder and went down. The other thug who was standing within a couple of feet from Arturo took one in his left shoulder, and also went down.

"Stand down!" shouted Arturo, as Hector Junior and the other three thugs reached for their weapons. "Cool it, dammit!"

"Thank you, Mr. Harvey," I said facetiously. "Honestly, I just wanna talk. I was really hoping I didn't have to get ugly."

"Detective Brick, I was hoping we would never have to meet," replied Arturo. "We have stayed in our lane and I was hoping that you would have stayed in yours."

"I wish that was the case, Mr. Harvey, but unfortunately it's not. I heard Hector Junior and some of your boys threatened my partner, Detective Rivers. I don't like that. I definitely don't appreciate it either. I thought I would come and formally introduce myself, and let you know that I will kill your whole family if your boys don't stand down."

Arturo and I looked at each other. I still had my guns, but both were down by my side. It was June. The weather was nice, with low humidity, and a decent temperature. Out of Hector Senior's children, Arturo was the only one who actually had his dad's height and looks. Both father and son looked menacing. The big difference was that Hector Senior was older, with white hair, and no hair on his face. I could see him in Arturo's facial features, and I imagined that Senior was hell on wheels when he was younger.

Arturo had a very small writing pad in his left hand, and a pen in his right. I assumed he was recording what amount of money and drugs they were removing from the storage unit. The unit was fifteen feet wide by eighteen feet deep. Very spacious, which was hard to tell with money wrapped in clear wrap taking up half the unit, and boxes of cocaine and heroin, taking up the other half. The boxes and wrapped money were stacked around the storage unit five feet high.

"Maybe you should tell your bitch of a partner the same thing, Detective," Arturo finally said to me. "I don't allow anyone in my business and your partner just can't get that through her thick skull."

"You know what, Mr. Harvey," I began. "You don't know me very well. Better yet, you don't know me at all. One, you called my partner a *bitch* and I don't really like that. Actually, I don't tolerate that. Two, you know of my reputation, and trust me on this, my reputation is the real thing.

"I will kill your whole fucking family if you even have a dream of hurting or even going near Detective Rivers."

"Go fuck yourself!" yelled Hector Junior, as that was obviously a command for the other three thugs to shoot me.

Before even one of the three could shoot, I shot two of the three in their hearts. Simultaneously, I shot the third assailant between his eyes. Hector Junior was the last gunman, and I raised both my guns and shot at him. Each bullet zinged pass Hector's ears and it clearly freaked the man out. His arms came inward, his hands joining each other near his chin, with a Glock in one hand. I think he realized how close both bullets had come to pulverizing him.

And the whole time, my eyes stayed on Arturo.

"I don't play, Arturo," I said. "I wanted to play nice and let you know that I only had one wish—for you to stay the fuck away from Detective Rivers. The good news, I'm leaving town, Arturo, but if I have to come back to the city because something happened to the detective, believe me, nothing will keep me from killing your kids and your nieces and nephews. Understand?"

"Yeah, I get it," stated Arturo Harvey weakly.

In my line of work, one thing you learn very fast is how powerful men fear death just as much as any average citizen. Fellow assassins didn't think about death, but knew that it was a part of the game. A foregone conclusion. Criminals, both low level and major players, played the tough guy role and pretended that they didn't care if they lived or died. In reality, it was the biggest lie in the criminal world. Occasionally, you really did run into a Billy Badass, who didn't fear death. But that was only seen in about one in every one hundred criminals.

The Harvey boys were not Billy Badasses. Just two more wannabees.

Before midnight, I would blow up two warehouses and three storage units, with money and drugs going up in flames. Additionally, I blew up two brothels, sent the streetwalkers home for the night and gave them an ultimatum to stay off the streets for the next two weeks.

No one was hurt during my moment of Zen. My version of Zen.

Then I did the ultimate insult—I blew up Hector Senior's Mercedes that sat in his driveway at three o'clock that next morning. And to add even more insult to injury, Alaina Rivers and I were the first detectives on the scene.

That was over five years ago.

It was one of two messages I needed to send. The second message would not be as friendly, not be as nice. I was sure my message was received.

That was then . . .

CHAPTER 12

THIS WAS NOW...

Sleep was calling my name...in the worst kind of way.

Sondra was still at the hotel in Midwest City, Oklahoma. I was sure she was tired from her drive and stressed from the madness she endured in Memphis after her mother's death. She was a good kid. She had a lot of her mom in her. I laughed at how badly she fought her innate tendency to be like Alaina.

I only had one goal after this assignment—to allow Sondra to live a normal and peaceful life.

My thoughts were still on the Harvey family. Specifically, on my second encounter with Arturo and Hector Junior. I wanted it to be a memorable occasion for them. I baited my adversaries. I wanted a fight. However, I was sure Hector Senior told his sons to stay at bay. But the more I interrupted their money, the less they could endure.

On our last encounter, I beat the brothers within an inch of their lives. I left their beaten bodies in the middle of the street, right in front of their parents' house. I wanted Hector Senior to see the failure of his sons. I wanted their men to see their failure as well.

Two days later, I was no longer a detective with the Memphis Police Department or a resident of the city. Accomplishing that task was my last assignment. I had left a powerful message for Hector Senior...*hands off of Detective Alaina Rivers.*

Now I was back in the city to do what I should have done five years ago—to eliminate a family empire.

It was a hard lesson to learn. But I was the reason for Alaina's death. I had my opportunity to kill the head of the snake and his baby snakes. But for the sake of Memphis, I stood fast. I didn't want to make the waves that I had in the past. Like so many people I had killed in the past, the Harvey family was a threat to America and its citizens. The exception—I was at ease with killing on foreign land. Something just didn't seem right about killing on American soil.

That was then. This was now.

During my five years in Memphis, I had used my gold badge to strike fear in the hearts and minds of criminals and bad players. The city knew me. I was the Batman and Punisher of the Bluff City, rolled into one. I stepped on toes and busted my share of heads.

Unfortunately, I spared the snake and his enterprise. I paid a steep price for my failure. I was beyond disappointed. I tried to do the safe thing. I knew Alaina wouldn't change. The Harvey family dabbled in the drug trade, and the Narcotics Division had the point on their case. What little case they had. Although we were homicide detectives, this didn't stop Alaina from having her own file on the Harveys.

Now I had to live with my mistake. *Live with not killing the snake.*

Arturo and Hector Junior no longer ran the family business. That honor now belonged to Hector Senior's two youngest sons, Ronaldo and Damian. Arturo now lived in Mississippi, across the Tennessee – Mississippi border, in a small city called Southaven. But he was still deep in the business. He ran the operations outside of Memphis...Mississippi, Arkansas, Alabama, Georgia and Louisiana.

His life now was about being inconspicuous. He played the role of a family man, the doting husband and father to a beautiful wife and three children. However, he was still a very cautious man. For the past week, his wife and children were living it up at a resort on the beaches of the Gulf Coast, down in Biloxi, Mississippi.

The great thing about being a rogue assassin over the years was that I played by the CIA rules and...by my own rules. For the past ten years, in some capacity or another, I was still an assassin. I had money and had tried my best to do good with that money.

I had access to four floating, adjustable satellites. Satellites I had paid several millions of dollars to use at my will. I knew the comings and goings of the entire Arturo Harvey household. With his family out of town, his young and homely housekeeper with the nice body under her oversized clothes had worked every day since the lady of the house was vacationing. She usually only worked three days per week.

I got it. Arturo was in his early fifties now. His wife wasn't the attractive, size six model he fell in love with at a younger age. Their three children had weighed on her body. She wasn't a big woman, probably medium sized at the most. Regardless, he now desired his housekeeper...the young twenty-one or twenty-two-year-old worker, who probably had no idea what she was getting herself into.

I knew there were six bodyguards on duty, providing protection for the oldest Harvey child. I had no reason to fear anything, as I was in a house in Olive Branch, Mississippi, which also sat outside Memphis. I was on my laptop, watching the outside of Arturo's house. Patience was on my side.

The past thirty-six hours or so had been very eventful. What I desperately needed now was sleep. For the past week and a half,

I had lived off cat naps, no more than three hours of sleep at a time. That was just for the preliminary. Now everything was about to rev up and truthfully, all I could think about was the fact that I needed sleep. My body was speaking to me. I had one final act to do, before I could lay down and shut my brain down for eight to ten hours.

I grew up on technology in the CIA. I wasn't the first assassin to use technology, but it was a huge part of my repertoire. I was used to satellite coverage, a communication liaison constantly in my ear during a mission and a handler who had my back.

I still had those things. Her name was Maxwell Phoenix.

"When was the last time you slept?" asked Max. My earbud was in my right ear. Good old Bluetooth technology.

"Yesterday," I stated. "It was an eventful night. An eventful twenty-four hours. After this, I will get some sleep."

She didn't immediately respond. She was back in Shelbytown, holding down the fort. As odd as it sounded to me, she really was my best friend. We had a confusing, complicated history. A history that should have ended in my death or hers. But somehow the end result was two mixed-up souls that depended on each other, needed each other.

"Twenty-four hours? You are such a liar. Get some sleep. I will let you know when he leaves the house."

Max could see the same thing I saw. She was the one who actually controlled the satellite. She was an expert at everything. From technology to killing to knowing how to make a man feel like a man. Like I said, a complicated history.

I said, "I will be okay. If he doesn't leave within the next hour, I will take you up on that offer."

"I'm here if you need me," she signed off.

I was in a great location. I knew that the Harveys, Director Wanamaker and all of their cronies had put the word out. They wanted me and any information of my location would make someone at least a hundred thousand dollars richer. That fact wasn't lost on me.

This was Memphis. A hundred thousand dollars went a long way. The Harveys were good for it. That's how they did business. This type of money was chump change for them and just a part of doing the job.

Max was right. I needed sleep. My eyes were heavy. Thoughts were beating me up. I didn't want to think of Alaina, so my mind went elsewhere. It went to my safe place. As strange as it seemed, that place was my chosen profession.

Killing is an art and every true assassin wants to be Picasso. The art of causing death involves a certain appreciation, nothing to take lightly. Killers are not assassins. Killers just kill and usually no game plan. As ludicrous as it may sound, the operative word between appreciation and just killing is the *smoothness*.

Assassins are the ultimate professional killers. Even shooting someone in the back of the head represented a certain *smoothness*, especially if the victim wasn't expecting it.

The key is in the methodology. Hell, I didn't know how many different ways I had killed people, and really can't even say if all of them were *smooth*. But as an assassin, I knew they were at least smooth-ish. I was also aware that bombs represented the strongest and most hideous message—the one that scared the hell out of a crime family. The one that kept other professional killers honest.

My Plan A wasn't working, so I went to Plan B. I dialed my phone.

"Who the fuck is this?" His voice was heavy, breathless and weak. I assumed that this apparent exhaustion came from his young housekeeper.

"Meet me at your spot. Thirty minutes," I said.

The phone went quiet. I knew I was the voice he wasn't expecting to hear. The voice he didn't want to hear.

"I can't get there in thirty minutes," Arturo replied. I could hear the nervousness with every word. "Detective Brick, you don't need me. I'm no longer in the game. I'm just an old married man now, living in Southaven, away from all the action."

"Your family is in southern California," I stated. "Either meet me in thirty minutes or your family is dead. And I will make this easy for you. On your other phone, try calling your wife and kids."

He didn't say anything. I knew he was calling each cell phone. I knew the result of each call. A busy signal.

"I can't get through, you asshole!" he screamed into the phone. "Don't fuck with my family, muthafucker!"

"That's funny Arturo. I told you the same thing about Detective Rivers. You didn't believe me. Thirty minutes. If not, I promise you, their deaths will be far worse than your boys from last night."

"Okay. But I live more than thirty minutes away from Beale Street. One hour. I promise I will be there."

"Forty minutes." I hung up the phone. His spot was a Mexican restaurant on Beale Street. It didn't matter. That was the smokescreen.

As I looked at the satellite feed from my laptop, I saw Arturo and his bodyguards running toward two SUVs that sat in the oversized circular driveway. I knew the game plan. He was already on his phone, probably calling his dad or his brother, Ronaldo, to set up a surprise party for me. I was sure that he thought I was already in place or close to the restaurant.

It didn't make a difference. Both vehicles blew up simultaneously as soon as they started moving.

Bombs delivered the strongest message . . .

. . . And sleep called my name.

CHAPTER 13

Do Fries Go With That Shake?

She woke up. She wished she could say that she felt refreshed, but she wasn't. Her mother's death still lingered heavily on her mind. She didn't know her future. The only thing she knew was her destination.

For now.

She did get some sleep, and that was a good start. It was actually her best sleep since her mother had died. Ironically, the place was almost five hundred miles from her home. She didn't undress when she came in last night. Once her body had hit the king-sized bed, she went numb. Now over ten hours later, she had a renewed life. At least that's the lie she told herself.

She had gassed up the night before. Her hotel receipt was folded up and had been slid under the door. When she opened it to see the cost of the room, she saw a written note instead, which directed her to drop by the front desk. The hotel clerk was an older Caucasian woman with bleached white hair. She was slightly overweight and greeted Sondra with a warm smile.

"I hope your stay was a good one," the clerk said.

"Yes, it was," responded Sondra. It was still hard for her to smile and respond to niceness.

"Well, you be careful on the road, and hopefully we'll see you again," the lady clerk said as she slid a small brown box towards

Sondra. The lady's smile said it all. Take the package and get on the road. Sondra did as suggested.

Inside the small box was a note, *I love you and don't worry, I got this.*

There was no signature or name on the note. But she didn't need a name. She knew exactly who it was. Inside the box was a .380 automatic, a nine-inch serrated knife and the name of an auto repair shop.

She programmed the address into her GPS. It told her that she was approximately 350 miles from her destination. She then plugged her phone into the auxiliary slot on her radio and switched to the Memphis news station. As she drove to her destination, she had a constant smile, which was a change...a very good change.

He did have this. Fourteen men were dead in Memphis, with eight bodies found at the homes of five city officials, including the homes of the mayor and chief of police. Two car bombs had killed seven in Southaven, Mississippi, a city on the outskirts of Memphis. She knew the area well. Of the seven killed, Arturo Harvey was one of the victims. Plus, the fourteen killed in Memphis were connected to the Harvey family. She liked how the news said family and not crime family.

Then she heard another bit of news. On the outskirts of Little Rock, Arkansas, two men were found dead in a warehouse. One was tortured. The other death appeared to have been a quiet death, maybe the result of poison or a drug overdose. She was sure that those were the two men who were following her. She wondered if anyone would tie those two bodies to the twenty-one in the Memphis area.

She couldn't help herself. Yes, indeed. She did feel refreshed after all. *Sleep. Vengeance.* Yes. It did her body good. On her phone, she selected a 60 song playlist she had received from her mom.

She felt warm inside. She felt alive. Everything was going to be okay. She knew that. She could feel her heart beating, the goosebumps on her arms and more importantly, she could feel her smile.

She laughed as she parked in the lot of the auto repair shop. The name of the street was Memphis Avenue. How ironic. She knew people had been looking for Zachary Brick for the five years since he left Memphis. She knew they would never think to look for him at a place called Bluff City Auto Repair on Memphis Avenue in a town in Texas called Shelbytown.

CHAPTER 14

Love is the roadmap to salvation.

Sondra was surprised at the size of the shop. The parking lot was the largest one she had ever seen at an auto repair shop. There were spaces for at least four rows of cars, possibly enough room to accommodate a hundred vehicles. The building was big, with four maintenance bays on the front side of the building and another four bays on the back side of the building.

She didn't get it. This didn't seem like the Zachary Brick she knew...but what did she really know about Zach? The only thing she truly knew about him was that he loved her mom and he loved her, probably more than her own father did. But obviously, he was a ruthless killer. Anyone who killed twenty-one men in a day had to be ruthless.

She memorized what she needed to say as she approached the desk. The guy behind the desk was solid and at least seven or eight inches taller than her. She wasn't sure, but his chiseled body had to be in the upper 200s, probably about 270 or 280 pounds. He was white, with long dirty blonde hair tied in a ponytail. She noticed the tattoos on his neck and although he had a long-sleeved shirt on, she was sure both of his arms were full of tattoos as well.

"May I help you?" asked the clerk.

Sondra noticed the northeastern accent, which was unusual in a small southern town. Immediately, she disliked the observant gene she had received from her mom. Or better yet, what her mom had drilled into her.

"Yes, you can," replied Sondra. "May I please see Maxwell Phoenix? I need a new priority one motor put in my car."

The big man leaned forward and brought his voice to a whisper. "In this room behind me is a staircase underneath the desk. Go down the staircase and Max will meet you at the bottom."

Sondra looked at the man. She didn't know what to think. She felt as if she was in a 007 spy movie. He raised his eyebrows and she decided to do what he stated.

To her surprise, there actually was a staircase underneath the desk. The staircase was steep and long. She was sure that it bypassed another floor that could not be accessed from this staircase. When she reached the bottom, she was met by a tall woman wearing three or four-inch boots, which added to her five-seven or five-eight height. She was white with a dark tan. Her hair was cut short and appeared to be three different colors—jet black, purple and dark blue. Sondra thought it looked great on her. To top it off, the lady was model thin.

Sondra wasn't jealous, but did feel some kind of way. Intrigued, perhaps. Maybe it was the way the lady was dressed. She had on black knee-high boots, with faded blue jeans and a long black tee-shirt with a picture of Marilyn Monroe on the front.

"Welcome to Shelbytown, Texas," said the woman.

Sondra liked her voice. The woman was foreign. She knew it was a French accent. She smiled. First it was a bulky receptionist with a northeastern accent and now a woman with a French one. She wondered if they even realized the irony of having these accents in Texas.

"Maxwell Phoenix?"

"Yes, that be me," said Max, as she slightly smiled. "You are Sondra Rivers, the pseudo daughter of Mr. Zachary Brick."

"Yes, that be me," responded Sondra. "And I'm sorry, but your name sounds made up."

"Maybe, maybe not. I may share my story with you one day, if you share yours." Sondra nodded her head. "Come on, let me show you around the place, then we will get you something to eat and get you settled at Zach's place."

Sandra didn't know what to expect. The auto repair shop surprised her. She was impressed. The shop consisted of three floors. From the outside, it was deceiving to the public. The top or main floor was on the ground level. The other two floors were below ground, basement floor one and two. Both levels were only accessible by the main floor. Separate staircases. There were people in almost every office that she saw. But regardless of the appearance, she knew this place was more than just an auto repair shop. Sondra didn't ask any questions though, and Max didn't volunteer any information.

Max gave Sondra a ride around the town, before taking her to the house. She knew the girl would not be going anywhere by herself, but wanted to play it safe. Although Sondra was a nineteen-year-old young lady, according to Zachary she was a homebody. Regardless, Max didn't want to take a chance. While driving around the big town, Sondra realized it was a lot bigger than she had previously thought. Max told her that the population was around 20,000, give or take a thousand or two. She volunteered the fact that twelve years ago she came to Shelbytown to hide out. Fortunately, she liked the place and the people. When she initially came to the area, the city had about eight or nine thousand people. But the town had grown since then. She liked to think that she had something to do with that.

The house was in a large subdivision. Sondra wasn't sure how far the subdivision actually was from the auto repair shop. While driving through the area, she didn't know what to think. Every home in the subdivision was nice and unique. Being in Texas, she thought she would see homes with just a southwestern style, but there were all types of houses in the subdivision—Art Deco, Southwestern, Dutch Colonial and Victorian, to just name a few. It seemed as if the area went on forever. She was sure that whenever they reached Max's home, she would need to use her GPS just to get back to the main gate of the subdivision.

Sondra took a double take when they arrived at the house. She didn't know what to expect from Zach. In Memphis, his house was a bedroom. Nothing special on the outside or inside. This was definitely different. The style was Victorian, two stories. It was beautiful. And big. There were double garage doors and a separate garage door. The outside looked homey, with perfect green grass and equally perfect trimmed bushes. When Max opened the single garage door and parked Sondra's car inside, Sondra shook her head in disbelief. The total area of the garage was big enough for six vehicles. There were three vehicles in the garage with easily enough room for another three.

"Wow," said Sondra. "Your house is spectacular."

Max didn't say anything initially as she took off her shades. "Not my house. Zach and I both live here. Before you ask, we are just friends. Best friends, actually. If you're wondering, our friendship is strictly platonic. I met your mother and I'm sorry for your loss. While you are here, please feel at home and treat this place as your place. Understand?"

Sondra nodded her head in the affirmative, as she entered the house through the garage entryway. She then stopped dead in her tracks.

She thought, *Damn, they were right. Everything in Texas is bigger.*

CHAPTER 15

Wʜᴀᴛ's ᴀ ʟɪꜰᴇ ᴡɪᴛʜᴏᴜᴛ sᴜɴsʜɪɴᴇ?

There was silence in the room. They had been in the room for about fifteen minutes, sharing a bottle of Cognac. Each man had already consumed three drinks from their shot glasses. Years ago, when they shared a vehicle and had adjoining desks, they often talked about the future and how they would one day own the city.

Now that they did own the city, they wished they could give it back.

"We don't deserve this shit, Sam," Mayor Kenneth Archibald stated.

He and Director Sam Wanamaker were sitting at a small round table in a room that the mayor liked to call his counseling room. According to rumor, this room had been added on in the early 1990s, so that the acting mayor could hide from the press or his meddlesome staff members. It had once contained a small cot for the mayor to take an occasional nap or have an occasional rendezvous with his secretary. Now the room just had a small, round table and a little refrigerator, with an assortment of glasses on top.

"So, do you still have a doubt that it's Detective Brick?" the mayor asked facetiously.

"It's no longer *detective*. Even the worst of us wouldn't do some fucked up shit like that, and you know it," retorted the director incredulously.

"I never told you, but I saw Brick and Rivers together a couple of years ago," the mayor volunteered.

The director looked perplexed. "When and where?"

"In Mississippi, at the JSL, the Jackson Secret Lounge."

"The JSL, what's the JSL?"

"It's the most private of restaurants that sat in downtown Jackson. Very exclusive. Just to walk in the door cost $500, a cover fee per person, which does not include the meal. My wife and I were having dinner with the Governor of Mississippi and his wife, when I saw Rivers come out of a private room for two to go to the restroom. She left the door open, and boom, lo and behold, who do I see? Zachary Brick.

"I went in the room and have to say, he wasn't surprised to see me. I sat down and we exchanged pleasantries and just talked for a few. He looked good. I told him that we missed him in the city. I also told him that there were rumors that some men in suits were looking for him after he left. It was a nice, cordial conversation."

"What should we do about this situation?" the director asked, as he took another shot of his Cognac.

"What do we do? The million-dollar question." The mayor put his hand over his glass as the director tried to pour him another drink.

The director said, "Fuck. I didn't see this one coming. Arturo Harvey. Damn."

"Probably best to let it play out," added Mayor Archibald. "Clean it up later. Take our bumps in the media. Play dumb. Let Brick do his thing."

Both men were in their own thoughts. The drinking had ceased for both. Former partners. Trying to live in the present, with the past weighing them down.

"I want to ask you how deep you are in, Sam, but something tells me that I really don't want to know the answer." Kenneth Archibald's eyes were now glued to his director of police.

Sam Wanamaker kept his eyes down. His hands played with his shot glass. His mind disregarded the thoughts that were swimming through his head, and he tried his best not to answer his former partner's questions.

Unfortunately, the heart and brain don't always overrule logic.

"Mr. Mayor, I'm not in. I'm just a city employee doing his due diligence to keep his city safe."

"Nice bullshit, Sam. But like I said, I don't need to know."

"So, are you really comfortable with us letting this play out?"

"Yes I am. Fuck Hector Harvey and his kids. Let Brick do what he needs to do. One thing that I saw at that dinner was how much he loved Rivers. If you can, you need to get a message to him. Killing cops or government officials is not allowed. I'm not going to say that you or anyone else on the force is involved with the Harvey family, but regardless, I don't want them dead at the hands of Zachary Brick. Understand?"

"Understand, Mayor Archibald. I definitely understand."

CHAPTER 16

AND DEATH COMES FOR THE WICKED ...

"I want him dead, goddamnit! Dead! Dead! Dead!" Damian Harvey screamed, as he still could not believe the news of his oldest brother's death. It had been eight hours and counting, and the news was still eating him up internally.

Over the years, he and Arturo had their issues. But at the end of the day, they were still brothers. They loved each other. Arturo was the teacher, the disciplinarian for his brothers and sister. Hector Sr had business to handle, so his oldest son became his wife's enforcer for the other four children.

"We need to find his family and kill all his fucking relatives!" Damian continued. Tears of anger were flowing down his face. "Where in the fuck is that detective's bratty daughter?"

There was no immediate reply from anyone in the room. Damian, Ronaldo and Hector Jr. were in the dining room of their parents' house. Ronaldo and Junior sat at the table that sat eight. Ronaldo sat at the head of the table with Junior occupying a chair two seats down on his right. Damian walked the length of the table back and forth.

"We need to have a strategy, Damian," Ronaldo stated weakly. He was the public leader of the family, and regardless of who perished, tears were not a part of the leader's responsibilities. He had to maintain his composure and display the leadership his father bestowed on him. Like Damian, he had his bouts of hothead tendencies, but they were few and far between.

"Fuck strategy, 'Naldo. We need to strike back now dammit!"

"Strike back at who Damian?" Junior weighed in. He had dried tears on his face and reddened eyes. He and Arturo were more than just their parents' oldest children, they were the best of friends. They shared a bedroom growing up, amongst many other things. They shared so many random experiences, from girls to drugs to everything in between. The two were inseparable. And now...one was gone.

"Ronaldo is right, we need a strategy," Junior stated. "As much as I hate saying it, Brick is an ornery bastard and his rules are not our rules. He stacks the deck and that sonofabitch is always ten moves ahead of everyone else. I guarantee you that this was just the beginning of his madness."

"Fuck you Junior! You are just scared of that crazy muthafucker!"

"You should be too!" the explosive voice caught Damian by surprise. Hector Sr. rolled his wheelchair into the dining room and did something he usually only did once or twice a day. He stood upright, with one hand on the table to ensure his balance.

"Damian, you want blood son, and that's understandable," said his father in a calm voice. "We all want our share of vengeance. I had to tell the love of my life, your mother, that her oldest son was dead. Not a good feeling, son. Not a good feeling. As much as we play a dangerous game in a volatile world...this business is really a gentleman's game for crime families like ours. We left Mexico and left all that crazy kill each other shit south of the border. And I'm not ashamed to say that we were legitimately ran out of California."

Senior looked at each of his sons. The old man wasn't proud. He was smart in a way that eluded most young men, especially young men in the crime game. That included his youngest sons.

"I love my family. I love you all. The Cartel gave me two choices. Move my family and claim a stake elsewhere, or death. And that death was meant not for only me, but all of you as well. I chose my family. I chose all of you. I chose your sister. I chose your mother. A gentleman's agreement.

"Ronaldo." His son looked at him with steely eyes. "Arturo once told me that Detective Brick was a different animal. A different breed that we had never dealt with. I called bullshit. I had already dealt with the Mexican Cartel, and once worked for the Colombian and Brazilian Cartels. Hell, I should have been dead by age twenty, twenty-five. But I survived. I had dealt with the worst of the worst. No fucking American could be as bad as the gringos I had to deal with."

Once again, Senior paused for effect, carefully eyeing each of his sons. "I was wrong. Brick was a tactician, a strategist, a killer unlike any killer I had encountered before. Arturo was right. The man just wanted one thing—safety for the love of his life. He was willing to show me, Arturo and Junior how far he would go to keep her safe. He spared our lives."

Senior walked the length of the table toward his son, Ronaldo. His walk was measured, methodical. It wasn't brisk, or slow. He was a deliberate man, trying to deliver a deliberate message. His right hand stayed on the table as he placed his left hand on the shoulder of Junior.

"We broke our promise, son. Arturo paid the price. Listen to Junior. Both Junior and I didn't listen to your older brother. It's five years later, but we just paid the price. We want blood, we want revenge. We are going to get it. But we have to do this right. Listen to your brother." He looked at Junior as he said this. Then, Senior motioned for Damian to bring his wheelchair and wheel him away.

CHAPTER 17

ZOMBIES, VAMPIRES AND MUMMIES DON'T
LIVE ON MY BLOCK.

Both Junior and Ronaldo laughed as they recalled Arturo's favorite saying. It meant that he wasn't worried about anything that wasn't in his face...that wasn't real. Or at least what he didn't consider to be real. However, that notion didn't apply to Detective Zachary Brick. For Arturo, Brick was the ghost in the night. He represented the zombie, vampire and mummy all in one. The dark cloud that occupied an invisible space, lurking and waiting for his moment to shine, and that appeared out of the blue to seek and destroy his enemy.

"If the man is that bad and feared, how do we kill him?" Ronaldo asked his older brother.

Junior said, "When I was coming into my own as a kid, Pop did something I didn't understand at the time. He had me work with his support staff. I called them the maintenance guys. These guys did all of the shitty jobs. They took care of the vehicles, fetched the food and alcohol, did drug runs and guess what? They also maintained Pop's Learjet. And one thing those guys taught me was preventive maintenance.

"This maintenance applied to the aircraft to ensure that whenever he needed to fly, it would fly without any problems, but that also applied to the business. Prevent problems before they actually became real problems or became bigger problems."

"Arturo considered Brick to be a problem," added Ronaldo. "And let me guess, you and Pop had other thoughts on preventing Brick from becoming a bigger problem."

"Exactly," confirmed Junior, with a smirk on his face. "We wanted to show how big and powerful we were. In our minds, Brick had to go. We couldn't give anyone a reason to challenge our power."

Junior went quiet. His mind wandered to a time when he and Arturo ran roughshod over a city and amassed a fortune for his family. Then it all came crumbling down.

"Brick was always a step ahead of us," Junior stated. "You talk about formidable opponents. The sonofabitch rigged the game and truthfully, we never even knew what game we were playing. We never had a clue and everything happened so fast. After he embarrassed us, dogged us out, he left Pop a cassette tape and told him where every bug was located, as well as where every bomb was located.

"The man could have taken out the whole family, including you and Damian. That's why we left the detective alone. The man didn't lie to us. Everything he did, he told us about first. He wanted us to know everything he did, which was a subtle message that he could do whatever he wanted to do, whenever he wanted to do it."

"That was then, Junior. This is now."

"And Arturo is dead, Ronaldo."

The brothers looked at each other. Ronaldo wasn't used to this side of Hector Junior. The man had taken a subservient role for the past five years. Arturo was the manager for all out-of-town business. But with that, everyone inside and outside of Memphis knew who really ran the Harvey crime family—Ronaldo and

Damian. Now he was depending on a brother who was kicked to the curb of the family business.

"How would you handle this?" Ronaldo asked.

"Brick is an enigma. When Arturo told me that years ago, I didn't fully understand, but slowly got it. He is someone who is equally both a planner and spontaneous. The planning part of him planted bugs all over the place in all of our vehicles and homes. We had no idea how in the hell he did it. It was a damn shame. On top of that, just to add insult to injury, he also planted bombs all over the place.

"We were grossly outsmarted. Arturo and Pop were two of the smartest people I knew, but that damn Brick. If we took three steps to be in front of him, he was always still one step ahead. A few times we thought we had him trapped, but it ended up being a trap for us. Trying to keep up with the guy was frustrating as hell."

"Junior, what are you saying?" asked Damian, who had returned from upstairs getting his father situated. He stood in the doorway, impatiently listening to the conversation. "I didn't catch everything you said, but you make this asshole sound unbeatable, like a damn god or something. Like he can't be harmed or killed. Ronaldo, you believe this shit?"

Damian was visibly upset. His eyes lit up with anticipation, his fists balled as if he was ready for a fight. He had just left his father and mother. The sight of seeing his mother's tears as she mourned the death of her oldest son was too much for Damian to handle.

"Yeah, Damian, I do believe it," Ronaldo replied in a calm voice. He considered himself a strategist, planning right down to the most minute item, if possible. He had studied military history, as well as the history of old criminal enterprises. His ultimate goal was to one day go back to Mexico and get the respect stolen from his father. There was no way that one man, a washed-up detective at that, was going to detour his plans.

"To beat your enemy, it's best that you know all about that enemy," lamented Ronaldo. "Especially if it's an enemy that you are unfamiliar with. This Detective Brick is formidable. He killed our brother and over twenty of our men. So yeah, I want to know everything Junior can tell us about this motherfucker."

"Fuck this!" Damian exclaimed. "I'm going for a smoke!"

"Don't go anywhere, Damian," Ronaldo said.

"Just smoking, 'Naldo. Fuck, get over yourself." Damian lit up a cigarette as soon as he stepped outside. He too was frustrated. He wanted to kill this detective so badly, that he could feel it deep in his bones. As long as his family had been in the drug business, they had never lost a family member. His uncles and cousins had survived, his father had survived and up until now, his brothers had survived. Until Arturo didn't.

Along with his frustration, came restlessness. He looked at the cars in the long driveway. There were eleven cars parked in the long horseshoe type driveway that ran from one gated entrance to the other one. The driveway that led from one entrance to the house and to the other entrance represented a third of a mile. The property was big. The house sat a hundred yards from the street. The front yard was graced with beautiful green Bermuda grass. Even in December, the groundskeeper had managed to keep the grass green.

Currently, there were also nine oversized protectors guarding the house versus the usual five, and Damian liked that they were inconspicuous. These guys were handpicked by him. Security was his responsibility and he took this responsibility seriously.

As much as he wanted to abide by Ronaldo's demands, he was his own man, and restlessness was not his friend. His car was the last one on the left in the driveway, facing away from the house.

As he hit the alarm on his key fob, the tremendous bang blew up his SUV and sent the tough man crouching to his knees.

Sometimes – zombies, vampires and mummies live on everyone's block.

CHAPTER 18

LIFE AND PEOPLE HAVE
ONE COMMONALITY—CRAZINESS.

I could see the entire basement of my home in Texas on my monitors. The basement was like a studio apartment. It only consisted of two rooms, which included the huge open space and a full bathroom with a shower that sat directly opposite of my computer set-up. Near the bathroom were numerous weights, a stair stepper and an exercise bike.

The basement floor plan was over twelve hundred square feet. The east side of the room had a kitchenette area, with a regular sized stove, a full-sized refrigerator and a microwave. Four folded, portable trays stood flushed next to the refrigerator. In the middle of the room was a beige living room set, to include an oversized sofa and loveseat, a rectangular dark brown coffee table and a sixty-five inch television mounted on the wall.

I couldn't see my two computer stations, but I knew them well, and missed them. The stations sat side-by-side to each other. Each station consisted of two twenty-seven inch monitors that sat on the desk, with six other twenty inch monitors mounted on the wall. I actually worked on both monitor, but I preferred the station on the right. The left station, however, was preferred by Max. She acted as if it didn't make a difference to her—but it did.

It was a running joke between us. But with sixteen monitors, we could cover a lot of ground.

"How was your sleep?" Max asked me as she appeared at the left station. It was nice to see her smiling face on the monitor. She was a beautiful woman. Someone who always intrigued me. She was indeed a friend. Probably my best friend now. Of any assassin, she was the one who could take me out anytime she wanted. Hell, we slept in the same household...and I slept with my door wide open. That is, if I wasn't sleeping in the basement.

"Not bad," I stated.

"I'll say not bad, Max replied. "You kill one son before you fall asleep and when you wake up, the whole fucking family is scared to death and wants to kill you ten times over. What kind of sadistic dipshit, are you, Mister Brick?" Her smile widened. She had some of the whitest teeth I had ever seen. "Then you blow up a car just for the hell of it. If they ever do catch you, they may actually skin you alive."

"I want them thinking, then thinking some more, and then even more thinking," I responded.

"I heard what you heard. You are definitely in their heads. Just as you said, they are sweeping every house, picking up a whole new fleet of vehicles, spreading their personnel throughout the city, and providing everyone with bodyguards. Yeah, Mr. Brick, I think you have them doing way more than just thinking. You have them down right terrified and shitting bricks. Excuse the pun.

"The second car bomb surprised me though. What possessed you to do that?"

"Their conversation," I replied. "I wanted to give some validity to Hector Junior's comments. Plus, Davey at the car dealership, told me that he already had twenty vehicles ready for them to pick up."

"Suppose they decide to go elsewhere, to another dealership? What then?"

"They trust this dealership. I've been working with them for fifteen years or more. They give three million to the dealership at the beginning of each year and, in turn, all maintenance and anything else they need is taken care of, including new vehicles at the drop of a dime. The Harveys, or somebody from their crew, turn in the old vehicles and the dealership takes care of it, as in, they get rid of them."

Damn!" Max exclaimed. "They have it good."

"Anyway, I like how you're thinking," I stated. "It's proactive. We will deal with it if that happens to be the case. And I really hope it won't be."

"What's next? Same strategy?"

"Yeah, chill out for the next several days. Let them stir. Inaction on my part will probably result in them double and triple checking everything they are doing. I made it possible for them to retrieve over half the bugs in the family houses, warehouses, stash houses and storage locations. I want everyone to be nervous and stay that way."

"Did I ever tell you that you are one sick fuck?" joked Max.

"Yeah, too many damn times. So, how is Sondra doing?"

Max said, "That girl has a ton of you in her. I know she has none of your blood, but she is indeed your daughter. Her mannerisms, smarts, just the way she approaches things. It's like looking at you if you were a young woman. When I brought her down here, she was excited when she saw the room. She didn't say anything, but her eyes were wide and her mouth was opened. She just sat at Station A and started typing. No comment, no questions...but I could see the excitement in her eyes. They were glassy with anticipation. It was too damn spooky."

I smiled both internally and externally. For most of five years, she was my delight. From the time we met, she became like a miniature version of myself. I think at some point, she did become my child. She was more comfortable around me than her mom. Maybe because I wasn't her parent by blood, just a father figure who had her best interest at heart.

"Considering how she turned out, any man would be proud to call her his daughter," I said. "She's a good kid."

"You can try to be modest, but she is part of you."

"I don't know about all of that," I responded. "Where is she?"

"She is probably asleep...in your bed." There was something on Max's mind. I saw it in her eyes, and it was written all over her face.

"What's going on?" I asked.

She smiled. An awkward smile. "She has...questions. How do I answer her?"

"You tell her the truth," I quickly replied. "I didn't tell Alaina everything about me because I never wanted to put her in danger. But I told her enough. Way more than I thought I would ever tell her."

I paused. Thoughts flooded my mind. Too many thoughts. "You are the only one who truly knows everything about me. Our friendship means the world to me. Now, I may be the closest person to Sondra. I know she has other family members, but relationship wise, they're distant. I want her to be comfortable. And if it takes you telling her everything about me, then do that. Just take it in stages. Don't overwhelm her with too much information in one sitting."

"She loves you," Max interjected. "And I know you love her. I got your back, Mr. Brick. I got your back."

CHAPTER 19

Shock equals mental
DESTRUCTION OF THE MIND, BODY AND SOUL.

Most people don't realize the pure destruction of the human body from major weaponry, such as a bomb or high-powered rifle or even a handgun. It rocks the spirit, drains the internal workings of the brain, heart and body. That's why many regurgitate at the sight of mangled or disemboweled bodies, or the smell of death. The sight or smell of death churns the intestines and causes the best of men to lose any inner contents of the stomach.

The bomb I planted in the SUVs of Arturo and his bodyguards contained an overabundance of TNT. Enough to rip apart and burn the bodies of the seven men. It was two days later, but forensic scientists from both the Mississippi and Tennessee Bureaus of Investigation, and the Memphis Police Department's Investigative Services Branch were still trying to collect and piece together bodies and vehicles. It wasn't an easy task.

Additionally, the second bombing had brought personnel in from the Bureau of Alcohol, Tobacco, Firearms and Explosives, otherwise known as the ATF. The federal government didn't give a damn about gangbangers or cartel assholes killing each other or dying. However, that lack of concern came with a caveat—which was, as long as high explosives were not deployed. I broke that rule. I killed seven with one bomb and used another bomb as a warning. Well, actually, more of a scare tactic.

But with the ATF came other government officials. Most undesirable. Some with their own agenda. A few with one agenda—to kill me.

Even with the pending threats from others, I had to keep my focus on the mission—the Harvey family. The Army taught me how to maintain focus. From being a sniper and trained killer to just being a soldier, your focus had to stay on the mission. I spent numerous hours honing my craft. I wanted to be the best. That meant laying down in the mountains of Afghanistan for four days, waiting on my target to appear.

This trait eventually attracted me to the CIA, where I further expanded and honed my skills. I became even more versatile and rugged. From sitting uncomfortably in a four by four foot room for two and a half days, or dressing in nasty clothing, to portraying a down-on-my-luck homeless person to observe the comings and goings of cartel personnel at a rundown bank in downtown Caracas, Venezuela.

The Harvey crime family was my prize and my eyes and mind were focused. In the time that I was in the city waiting on Sondra to depart, I was able to accomplish some tasks and do some reconnaissance. I had a history with Mexico and several cartels. Each cartel knew me by a different name. However, they all knew one thing—what I was capable of. What I had done in the past.

The Harvey family was understandably distraught and devastated. Death is never an easy thing. But it's even worse when family members or loved ones meet their demise from explosives. Such a violent and gruesome way to go. Depending on the strength of the bomb, the explosion could literally rip off body parts and severely char the body beyond recognition. And that's exactly what happened to Arturo and his six men.

The family couldn't plan a funeral or memorial. I had pulled a cartel move. The cartel was good at mangling a body so badly during death that the family couldn't hold a proper funeral or burial. It always had to be a closed casket funeral. I thought the Harveys were lucky that I didn't kill Arturo and leave his ass in the Mississippi River.

Needless to say, I felt good. Everything was progressing as planned. I was excited. Sondra was safe with Max, and I was getting my revenge. Overall, they were small victories, but nonetheless, they were still, indeed, victories. In many ways, I had let Alaina down. I should have been there. Truthfully, I never should have left Memphis or better yet, even entered the life of Detective Alaina Rivers and her daughter. But I did. As badly as I felt about losing Alaina, it felt great that I got to know her. That I loved her, and...she loved me.

My rollercoaster of feelings wouldn't be my demise or my distraction. The planted listening devices had me, Max and now, Sondra, listening to multiple conversations of the Harvey family, Chief Wanamaker, Lieutenant Fontaine and Mayor Archibald. We didn't miss a beat and more importantly, we didn't miss an opportunity to obtain information.

From trivial information to that of the highest importance, I wanted to know it all. That's how I did my job. That's how I was trained. Everything had value. From someone having an allergy to certain food items to Lieutenant Fontaine having an affair with his brother's wife to Damian's bipolar mental condition and shedding tears when he was alone. It all made a difference. Everything counted. E-ve-ry-thing.

I understood the pain and hurt of the family. Hell, I caused that pain and hurt. It was intentional. I wanted to put the Harvey men in a state of rage, have them question their every decision, and make them want to kill me and everyone that looked like me.

Hector Junior had impressed me. Actually, both Hector Senior and Junior had stunned me with their emotional maturity.

It was easy for me to believe how the old man looked at this event. If it had been Sondra, I know I wouldn't have been able to control my emotions. The man was on the other side of seventy and had been in the business over fifty years. He was one hundred percent Mexican and had grown up in both Mexican and Colombian cartels. He was used to death, probably even the deaths of loved ones and friends. However, this hardened Hector Senior was a fearful man in so many ways.

Through my connections south of the border, I knew Senior had escaped death on four separate occasions. The man was good at making money, and the cartels loved anyone who could make them money. So, it was always about allowing Senior to live, in order to fatten the pockets of cartel leaders. The man had raised sons to do the thing he couldn't do—kill. Now, he was walking the tightrope where sanity met insanity, where the rubber meets the road. I knew the death of a son was tough, even heartrending. However, Senior was the backbone of the family. Arturo's death had floored him, and deeply affected his wife, daughter and Damian. The man who had kool-aid flowing through his veins, had to do something at age seventy that he couldn't do at age thirty or forty—be mentally strong and mature for his family.

Although for me, it didn't make a difference either way.

The two men who had kept their cool and handled Arturo's death like warriors were Junior and Ronaldo. None of Senior's children knew his history. They knew that they left California, and probably understood why. Now it was up to the family to carry on. Junior was back in the fold. It remained to be seen how affected he would be or how long this union could last. Thus far, Junior was on point and was holding his own. Unfortunately, for the Harvey family, I was tuned in to every word being spoken, and every move being made.

This was my game.

But Junior and Ronaldo would make this a harder fight than I wanted. Junior was correct in his assessment. He told Ronaldo that his car needed to be checked for listening devices and bombs. I hadn't planned on blowing up any more vehicles, but wanted to validate Junior's train of thought. It gave him more credence with Ronaldo and this was possibly something I could exploit later.

Then he told his younger brother that every house had to be checked for listening devices as well, and each warehouse and storage facility needed around-the-clock guards—twenty-four hours, seven days a week. Lastly, he suggested that all family members be assigned three or four bodyguards that would follow them everywhere.

I had created exactly what I wanted – paranoia, confusion and a spreading out of the troops.

At the end of the day, I wanted to own the hearts and minds of the Harvey family, assuming, there were any family members left to own their hearts and minds.

They took a life.

I planned on taking much more.

CHAPTER 20

MEMORIES ARE THE GATEWAY TO
HELLACIOUS NIGHTMARES.

"Officers sometimes lose themselves in this business, son," the psychiatrist said to me. "Even the best officers can feel the pain of death. Too many deaths have a way of turning normal people into head cases."

It was my first and only session with a CIA psychiatrist. It was a mandatory session for all training officers. *For all assassins.*

The government agency with the most psychiatrists and counselors was the FBI, followed by Homeland Security. An agency such as the CIA, which is known for certain difficult situations, didn't believe much in counselors, psychologists and psychiatrists. However, just to cover their ass, they had a few in their employ.

I was the heartless bastard the Company loved. No one to speak of to mourn my death...nor did I have the mental acumen to care much about others. The Company had no idea about my sister, and I was surprised I had been able to keep that secret for over thirty years. She was my only blood family, as far as I was concerned. The aunts, uncles and cousins we had left years ago didn't know if we were alive or dead, and I was quite sure they didn't give a damn.

I know I didn't give a damn.

I knew I needed mental help, but was pretty sure that I was just one of the hundreds of millions in the United States alone who also needed some type of mental health assistance. At the end of the day, I was too jaded by the junk I had seen or been a part of since the age of twelve to really give a shit. For over thirty years, I had been a part of the problem and not part of the solution.

Like so many others, I tried to convince myself that I was a part of the solution, but if that was truly the case, then the woman I loved would still be alive. That fact hit me like a ton of bricks. For the first time since I heard about the death of Memphis Detective Alaina Rivers, my heart deeply ached for the woman I missed. The woman I wanted to hold one more time, kiss one more time, hug and whisper, "I love you," one more time. My anguish was blaring loudly. I felt as if I was in an opening in a big, wild jungle, screaming for dear life, but with no one around to hear my screams.

"Fuck!" I said to my eight monitors, as if they would respond to me. I had the same set-up here in Olive Branch, as I did in Shelbytown. The only difference was that I only had one station here and have two in Shelbytown.

"Fuck! Fuck! Fuck!" The release felt good. I continued looking at the monitors, but it was late. Sondra and Max were doing whatever in Texas. I was monitoring what little madness was happening in Memphis. No one could hear my screams. I liked it that way. No one could see my tears, and that, I liked as well.

Alaina's body was shredded by 19 bullets out of 80 possible shots. The thought was still with me when I beat the faces of three of the eight guys who shot her. My hand wouldn't stop wielding the small sledgehammer as I literally beat the men's faces to a bloody pulp. It was rage. It was madness. It was love.

I had gotten plenty of sleep over the past three days. I was about to hit the hay for the night when I saw Hector Junior walk into the dining room of his parents' house and take a seat across from his brother, Ronaldo. Both thought they had gotten all of the bugs I had planted throughout the family various houses. The ones they had found, I had intentionally made as detectable as possible. At a minimum, each house had about ten detectable listening devices that were easily found.

However, at the home of Hector Senior, only three of four were easily found. That was the plan. I wanted the family to think they had a house of sanctuary. The fact is, I had managed to get twenty other undetectable listening devices planted throughout the house, to include hidden cameras. From cable and satellite television personnel to housekeepers to some of the Harveys own thugs, I had teamed with people I trusted and who trusted me. Looking at the two brothers as they sat and conversed, I was relieved that both the picture and sound were flawless.

Hector Junior had grown significantly over the years. Ten years ago, he was all brawn and no brains. But now he was different. It seems that spending almost every day with his father over the years had turned the man into a formidable opponent, someone who was wiser and savvier then ten years ago.

I took my headset off and turned up the volume. I wanted to clearly hear their conversation. I was hoping that just maybe I would finally learn something. Thanks to Junior, their recent conversations were basely purely on deception. They wanted to see if I would take the bait. They had come up with fake missions and meetings to see if I would bite. I didn't.

I had shaken their world. Their entire organization was in a state of flux and frenzy. Two days after Arturo's death and they were still spinning out of control, trying to get a handle on what was what. Bombing Damian's SUV resulted in several other vehicles in the driveway blowing up—a ripple effect. This sort of thing happens when multiple vehicles are armed with an explosive device. Ronaldo bought twenty new vehicles the next day.

The vehicles were already loaded with listening and remote camera devices. It helped to know people. The Harveys provided the dealership $3 million a year for vehicles and needed service, but it helped even more when I gave Davey and his two maintenance friends $50,000 each to take care of the vehicles according to my plan. I was glad that the Harvey family continued to deal with one dealership.

Davey and I had a history. Davey's cokehead brother, Robbie, had gambling debts. However, instead of the guys chasing Robbie, they kidnapped his daughter. Davey had raised his niece for the last ten of her thirteen years. He gave a damn. His brother, not so much. Davey came to me. I found his niece and the assholes who had kidnapped her. I spared Davey the humiliation his niece had endured. But I can't say the same about the three punks involved in her kidnapping. I spared them nothing. Davey was beholden to me. Regardless, he and his friends were taking a big chance helping me out. Besides the obvious danger, they still needed to get paid for their work. As much as Davey insisted payment was not required, he and his friends had families to support, and $50,000 was nothing compared to the risk they were taking.

I often laughed at my five years as a Memphis detective. The great thing about the job was establishing relationships. Most of those relationships came from just doing the job. I had assisted those who really needed a cop to be what cops were supposed to be—a servant to the people. Some tasks were easy, others required more assistance and, in some cases, required firepower. But all consisted of one thing, people who were genuinely appreciative for the assistance.

That was also what I loved about Alaina. She loved the people. The citizens of Memphis were her people. She believed in every good credo of being an effective cop. She always provided assistance whenever she could. She was all about the people. I became about the people. I liked to think that it took five years for her to change me. But that was the lie I told myself. Within the first six months, I was already thinking the way my partner thought. As our relationship advanced, our trust and belief in each other increased as well. She made me a better person. I had relationships now. People I could depend on and people that could depend on me.

"Mexico said no," I heard Junior say to Ronaldo, which captured my attention. "Remember the bombings in Bogota and Mexico over a decade ago?"

"Vastly," Ronaldo responded. "Gulardo family versus Garsay family. Garsay blew up some of Gulardo's stuff and Gulardo responded by doing the same."

"No. That's the word that got out. Nowhere close," Junior corrected. "That's the rumor that was spread with the intent to throw everyone off. No one really wanted the truth to come out. During that time, someone was spreading hell south of the border, with numerous cartel families. It was easy for them to blame one another, because there was a ghost in the night creating the havoc.

"Then three years ago, the enforcer, Vicente, the muscle and nephew of Santana Garsay, was gunned down in Tijuana. He had killed a store owner over some nickel and dime bullshit. Evidently, someone stepped in to get revenge for the store owner. Two days later, Vicente's head was delivered to the doorstep of his father, Larenz. When Larenz came to Tijuana to avenge his son's death, he and his entourage of ten walked in the store, smelled gas, rushed out of the building and jumped into their trucks. As soon as they started to drive off, the three SUVs blew up."

"Fuck!"

"Yeah, so Mexico thinks that this elusive ghost is our ghost... that Detective Zachary Brick is the ghost."

"You would think they would want him bad," stated Ronaldo matter-of-factly.

"I said the same thing to my contact." Hector Junior paused. As much as I wanted to believe that it was done just for effect. I knew it wasn't. The man was genuinely afraid. "I was told that some ghosts are left to roam the night...and hopefully, that night is many miles away."

I smiled. That smile would last me through the night, while I slept on the sofa in the makeshift computer room.

Part Two

DESTRUCTION

CHAPTER 21

LIES. LIES. AND BUTTERFLIES.

"Can you tell me about Zach?" Sondra asked Max, as they sat on the sofa watching television. Max didn't immediately respond. For her, it was a loaded and complicated question. Any and everything dealing with Zachary Brick was both good and bad, just like their relationship.

She continued watching television. It was a welcome relief from watching monitors and having earbuds in her ears for hours on end. The local news was on. She preferred finding out what was going on in Amarillo or Dallas or the state of Texas versus the rest of the nation. She needed a moment. Now thanks to Sondra, thoughts and memories flooded her mind and filled her heart.

Twelve years ago, she had a mission. She was hired by the Central Intelligence Agency to kill an officer of the Company. He was a prolific killer. A professional. No one knew how many lives the man had taken. She just knew he was ruthless...the killer above all killers. In the CIA, there was always *a killer above all killers*.

"Is that a no?" persisted Sondra.

"I was hired to kill Zachary," stated Max. She could feel the butterflies flying nervously around in her stomach. She wanted to be careful. Butterflies often led to lies. For whatever reason, she didn't want to lie to Brick's pseudo daughter.

125

"He was on assignment in Paris. He was tasked to kill an attaché to the American ambassador to France. This man was a fixer. Probably the most famous fixer in the world. The man was powerful. He killed and had others who killed for him. He did it all behind the flag of the United States of America. Behind the red, white and blue."

Max looked over at Sondra, who was sipping on a cup of hot raspberry and lemon-flavored tea. She was intrigued. She had heard the stories of her pseudo father Zachary Brick. The whole city of Memphis had heard stories of the Brick. Sondra didn't know the man that she had heard so many stories about. She only knew of the man who got her into reading, writing and computers. The one who got her.

But she wanted to hear the stories first hand—from someone who not only knew the man...but loved the man.

"There was one problem," Max continued. "He never showed himself until he actually did the killing.

"Or so I was told."

Sondra liked this. She wished she had popcorn. She was an avid reader who loved suspense thrillers. Now this was the real thing and she loved hearing Max tell a tale of someone she loved and cared about, someone she admired.

"Four days before the hit, I was in a café and before I could order a drink, the bartender brought me an apple martini. I love apple martinis. When I asked who had ordered the drink for me, he pointed to a table in a dark corner. It was so dark that I couldn't see the person's face. So, of course, I had to get a closer look."

Sondra imagined that if she really did have popcorn, she would be chomping down like it was the last bucket of hot buttered, salty popcorn she would ever have.

"When I saw his face, his eyes...I thought I was dead." Max was in another world as she slipped to another time, another place. The memories were very vivid as if she was still there, on the Seine, the famous river front of Paris.

"He didn't smile, but told me to have a seat. Then the damnedest thing happened. We talked. Then we talked some more. Then we talked even more.

"The craziest thing about that night was that we talked about everything under the sun, except killing and of course, his least favorite subject, himself. He didn't say one word about himself. But it was the most interesting conversation I have ever had.

"I told him about me...and I could tell as I was talking that most of the stuff I was telling him, he already knew. He mentally seduced me that night. I felt so aroused from having a man just listen to me and have enough interest to hear every word I said."

Max smiled. She felt the dampness in her eyes. She would always be a killer, but she loved her femininity. She loved him.

"For the next two days we spent almost every second together. Back in those days, Sondra, I was one of the coldest killers in the business. Hell, I didn't even know I had feelings...emotions like that. He touched my heart when I didn't even know I still had one."

"That last night, we had sex. I know some women would say *made love* or just talk about the passion. All I can say is that it was wild, hot and way past steamy. I wanted to have this moment before the fourth day. On that day, Zachary was going to kill the attaché, and then I was going to kill Zachary."

The two women exchanged glares. The older woman was still in Paris, and with the same confusing thoughts she had back then. Meanwhile, the younger woman still wished she had popcorn, as she latched on to every word from the mouth of Zach's best friend. Actually, she knew they were a whole lot more than friends. She just hoped that this was then...and not—now.

"I remember thinking that I woke up early, but when I looked at the clock, it was actually past two in the afternoon," Max recalled. "Zach left me a note. Said he had drugged me and that only one person was going to die that day. He signed off the letter with a smile and told me that we would meet again. He had put a Do Not Disturb sign on the door."

"Wowwww," said Sondra in a slow voice. "Were you mad? What happened next? Did the CIA come after you?"

Max smiled. "Slow down. Aren't you the curious one."

"Of course, I am," replied Sondra. "No one knows anything about Zachary Brick, except maybe you and my mom. As you know, she is dead." Sondra stopped suddenly. The words lingered in the air. The sofa was big, three cushions, with the middle cushion separating the two women.

Before Max could say something, Sondra continued. "That was the first time I actually said those words. But she is gone and plenty of thoughts, plenty of words went with her. We talked about Zach and I wasn't stupid. I knew she had seen him a lot. Going out of town on so-called business trips. But she was with him. I know he came to Memphis a lot, to help with cases, and sometimes, to just spend time with my mom. If I had brought it up, she would have told me the truth and let me know that he did it for me. He wanted to keep me out of trouble."

Tears rolled down her eyes. Max moved over and let the young woman's head find a home in her arms. "I saw him every now and then. He came to my graduation, a contest of computer geeks I participated in and other events. He always made sure I saw him. But after the event, he just disappeared."

"Yep, that was Brick," stated Max, as her hand stroked the arm of the young maiden. "Believe me, the man has the biggest heart in the world. Those who have been fortunate enough to know him or call him an associate or friend have benefited in some way from his benevolence. And you know what? We are all better off knowing him, being a part of him."

Sondra said, "I know," as she wiped tears away. "My mom wouldn't like it, but I'm glad he is about to eliminate the waste in Memphis. I hope he kills them all."

Max didn't say anything. However, she knew one thing— Sondra Rivers may not be Brick's daughter by blood...but she was the apple that didn't fall too far from the tree.

"Max," said Sondra. "Has Brick always been a killer?"

CHAPTER 22

To kill or be killed is a state of mind.

In a prior life, it was Cal Hillsmeier's job to know shit from bullshit. He was one of the best at it. He had a different name then, worked for a different organization and had different responsibilities. He remembered one ten-day stretch when he was in four different countries, selling different bullshit to four different foreign nationals, but expecting the same results. When he walked into a room, he already knew the smell of the room, like whether he was wasting his time or waiting on the other shoe to drop. Today, he already knew—the shit would keep coming until the real deal reared its ugly head.

He, Director Wanamaker and Mayor Archibald had just received a ten-minute briefing from the head of the deployed team from the Bureau of Alcohol, Tobacco, Firearms and Explosives, or ATF for short. Chief of Detectives Major Hillsmeier knew it was just a formality. The team was not a surprise, but the briefing was. The great deflection. When the team chief exited one door, and the other door opened, Cal knew the real show was just beginning.

In his prior life, he would have been the man walking through the door, about to sell his form of propaganda to the local authority. It was a false narrative that the CIA didn't operate on

American soil. Of course, they did. Hell, foreign enemies operated on American soil too, so the CIA naturally had a role. It all fell under one ambiguous and confusing umbrella.

The man was short, compared to the three of them. He was five foot seven at best, but his slender frame with the small metal-rimmed glasses and full head of red hair made him look taller. The man was a true redhead with a mustache and goatee to match. His light weight beige jacket went well with his white shirt and blue jeans.

"It always amazes me when I come to a predominantly black city and meet those high up in the local government, and only one of the senior officials is African-American and all others are White." The facetiousness of the man's comments wasn't welcomed with laughter.

"For the purpose of this meeting, my name is The One, as in I'm the one who will rid you of your problem." The man spoke with confidence. There was surety in every syllable, every word. Cal Hillsmeier knew that for every ounce of confidence the man displayed, he also possessed a pound of arrogance and two pounds of deceit.

"No one is calling you *The One*," Cal stated. The man smiled at the chief of detectives' retort. He loved pissing off the local officials. Federal trumped local government and it was always nice to show that element of power.

The meeting place was two buildings over from police headquarters. However, two buildings also equated to two streets. The building was one of the oldest in Memphis. Built in the 1940s, its fifteen floors were considered amazing back then. Although it was nondescript in its outside appearance, it was home to over twenty businesses. However, the top two floors were usually empty. When they did have occupants, it was usually government personnel from alphabet organizations from the nation's capital.

The ATF only wanted to brief the top three officials. It was unusual for the mayor to take such a meeting and equally unusual for the Director of Police to attend. But this was different. Bombs always had a way of guiding the narrative for the federal agency, with the local officieals expected to cooperate. That is, the local government didn't have a say regarding federal protocol, especially when it came to explosives.

Cal knew the ATF was the first of at least three federal agencies to occupy the top two floors. Although the FBI had a field office in Memphis, advanced explosive and counterterrorism experts from the Bureau would be arriving soon, if they had not already arrived in the city. The Drug Enforcement Administration, aka DEA, was also expected and most likely in the city now because of the Harvey family. Plus, a faction of Homeland Security and the State Department would be showing up soon.

He knew the protocol...the routine. He also knew that the CIA didn't give a damn about a drug family, a local cop being shot to death and a former cop possibly seeking vengeance. No, even those who worked for the Company had agendas.

"You guys have a Zachary Brick and Harvey crime family problem," the redheaded government official continued. "I'm hoping you men will allow me to take your garbage out for you. No questions asked."

"So, are you representing ATF, FBI, State Department or maybe...the CIA?" asked Cal, as he rose from his chair and stood against the opposite wall, sitting behind the mayor and director.

"Major Hillsmeier, one of my bosses once asked me, 'Have I ever known real fear?' Of course, I told him that I had. He told me to hold on to that belief."

Director Wanamaker and Mayor Archibald had no idea where the man with no name was going with all of this. The same could not be said of Cal. He had been asked that same question before—and by the same boss.

"My agency eradicates fear. We actually meet it head on, kick its ass and move on to the next job. We want to eradicate this situation for you. I think we can eliminate your problem within the week, and with very few deaths. So, what do you say?"

"One...agent," Cal paused. He wanted to see if the redheaded man would reveal his organization. "Why would your organization invade our area? Two, how do you figure that we have a Zachary Brick or Harvey crime family problem? And three, very few deaths, what's your definition of acceptable losses?"

"First, how do I figure that you have a Brick and Harvey problem? Because you do, Major. I know it and you know it. My definition of acceptable losses, hopefully less than twenty and no cops."

Director Wanamaker jumped in immediately, "Agent, that's unacceptable on any level, and Major Hillsmeier asked you what organization you are representing? Additionally, no one has made an official, positive identification of Zachary Brick, so how can you say for sure that we have a Brick problem?"

"Director, I'm with the ATF as well," he replied.

"I call bullshit, sir," Cal attacked the man's response. "There is no reason for two briefings or even two meetings for us from the ATF. Secondly, this sounds like more to do about Brick, than Memphis or the Harvey crime family."

Mayor Archibald turned around and looked at Cal Hillsmeier, while Director Wanamaker kept his eyes on the redheaded agent. If he was an agent.

"Though it's not important, I represent the ATF as well," the redheaded briefer stated. "What's more important is what we can do for you. Your city is under siege, with bombs going off and people dying. The person you don't want to blame is definitely responsible for all of this. And I'm the one man who can help you guys. Allow me to help."

"I'm a patient man, agent," the mayor weighed in, "however, you are trying my patience. As my men have told you, no one has even seen the man. Hell, for all we know, it could be a woman."

The no-name agent replied, "Trust me, I understand Mayor Archibald and please correct me if I'm wrong, but you guys have no photos or recordings of Zachary Brick, do you? Remember, he used to be a detective for your department and you guys have no photos to provide to your officers or staff. Now, your city may be going to shit and you guys have absolutely nothing. Just an efficient killer and destroyer of bad dreams. Someone who believes in cleaning the city's mess and taking out the garbage."

The Memphis officials all looked at each other. They didn't know what to think. Could he be right about Zachary Brick? For Director Wanamaker, the agent was right, as the biggest mystery surrounding Brick was a lack of pictures or recordings of the former detective. Even his official file had disappeared—both the paper copy and the electronic copy.

The agent added, "In a perfect world, you would think if you have garbage, this person would be the perfect type of garbage collector that you'd need to clean your city."

"We can clean our own city, Agent," Director Wanamaker said. His voice was terse, filled with tension. He had been down this road before.

Five years ago, prior to Zachary Brick disappearing from the city, Sam Wanamaker was a Major and the Chief of Ds. Brick was one of his guys. He was very respectful, the epitome of what you would want in a detective, in a cop. His investigative skills were top-notch. Sometimes, without saying a word, he would strike fear in the hearts of criminals throughout the city.

"Clearly, you are very familiar with Detective Brick," Mayor Archibald began. "Please brief us on what you know about Brick if you can."

"My boss was right about fear," the no-name agent said. "Or being afraid." He looked at every man in the room and rested his eyes on the mayor.

"My first dealing with the man you all know as Zachary Brick was in Bogota. During this time, he had wreaked havoc in two other locations and we thought we had a beam on him. I wasn't sure if Brick was a one-man team or part of a group of guys. We were pretty skeptical when we heard the reports that it was just one guy. So, we brought on a team of eight to investigate.

"Fear. Damn. I never knew true fear until one night in Bogota." The man paused. He was in another place. Not a good place. "We were in country for four days and nothing. Then one night, as I was getting my two or three hours of sleep, I woke up when someone was preparing to throw me out the window of my fourth-floor room."

His eyes narrowed. His skin grew a shade redder. He balled his fists.

"My feet were bound by duct tape. My hands were also bound behind my back. Tape was placed over my mouth and that's when I woke up. When I was thrown out the window head first, I instantly realized that this was it for me. That this is how I would die.

"But as I went down one story, my momentum crashed me into the wall. I don't think he said a thing. I don't even think he looked out the window. Three of the other seven guys met other fates, but it was a distraction. While the other four members of the team were saving us, he struck the Gulardo crime family in Bogota. Killed over thirty men, blew up five buildings, destroyed over an estimated two thousand pounds of cocaine and burned over a hundred million in cash."

The man took a seat. A sigh of relief was painted across his face. Beads of sweat collected on his forehead.

"So, you didn't see the man before he threw you out the window?" Cal asked.

"No, my room was dark and I was tired and disoriented."

"Was that your last encounter with him?" Cal quickly replied.

"No, we met again in Puerto Vallarta, Mexico. We were in the port. I thought that we had some damn good intel in place. Half of my twelve-men team were situated on the dock, in a cruiser, while the other half was dispersed throughout the dock inland.

"Long story short, a small explosion blew a hole in our cruiser forcing us to swim for our lives. Three other explosions on the dock followed. As we scrambled to save our lives, two warehouses that belonged to Santana Garsay blew up as well. Over twenty men were killed. We're not sure how much money or drugs were destroyed.

"Some time that night I went into a café to take a leak. While I'm doing my business, the lights go out, the room goes completely dark and I feel the business end of a silencer at the back of my head. The voice tells me that if he ever sees me again, I will never make it back home. Just like that. He was gone. The whole encounter was probably less than ten or fifteen seconds... but seemed a lot longer.

"Despite his threat, ever since that time, I've been hoping to meet this guy again. And no, in every situation I did not see the face of my assailant. I thought the man was lost to me forever... until I heard about a Detective Zachary Brick in Memphis five years ago. And just like that, he was gone.

"Then three years ago, in Tijuana, Mexico, a store owner was killed by Vicente Garsay, the nephew of Santana Garsay. No one paid much attention to the death of a store owner. It was just another random death in Mexico. Then, two days later, Vicente's father, Larenz, received a package at his doorstep, the severed head of his son. Santana's little brother, Larenz, had always been a hothead, so he and his boys rolled up to Tijuana, three vehicles deep.

"Three black SUVs stop in front of the store, get out fully strapped and ready to torture and kill everyone in the store. But as soon as they walked into the store, they were in for the surprise of their lives. As they walked in, they noticed Vicente's best friend hanging against the wall, opposite the door. He was beaten badly and out cold. Hanging around his head was a placard with three words in big red letters, 'Gas, Bomb, Run.' They smelled the gas and hightailed it out of there. When the vehicles were a good hundred feet from the store, they all blew up."

No one immediately spoke. The director and mayor looked at each other. Cal was still standing behind his two bosses.

"Nice stories," Director Wanamaker was the first to speak. "But how does that help us?"

"Fear, Director. That's how it helps you. That's why I'm here. You guys need me. Trust me on this."

The three officials took it all in. During the briefing, they were respectful, no words were necessary. Mayor Archibald was once a cop himself, and he knew the advantages of listening, absorbing information and making informed decisions. He had carefully taken in every word during this meeting. and listened to Sam Wanamaker's words as well. But the mayor also knew when to speak up.

"I'm impressed, agent. I would be even more impressed if I had your name, the name of your organization and a valid reason to stand down. We," he pointed to himself, the director and Cal, "are responsible for protecting and serving our community, our city. Truthfully, Mr. Whoever You Are, your stories were indeed interesting, but unfortunately, your words fell on deaf ears."

"Mr. Mayor, that would be a mistake," the agent stated.

Mayor Archibald responded, "I doubt it. You haven't given us any evidence or shown us any reason to believe it is Zachary

Brick we are dealing with. The two times that he kicked your ass, you didn't even see his face. How can we believe anything you say, especially if you are not forthcoming about your name and the agency you work for? And no, we don't believe the whole ATF story.

"Additionally, if it is Brick, we need evidence that he is your boogieman. We all know Zachary Brick, and no shit, you are right, he was the scariest individual I have ever encountered. But, you know what, Mr. Agent, he was also the most down-to-earth, be there for your fellow man law enforcement official I have ever known."

"Sir, that tells me that you don't know the real Zachary Brick," the unnamed man shot back.

"No sir, that means you have done a bad job of selling us on your theory," Director Wanamaker responded. "You want my men to stand down under the guise of your protection. Admittedly, you may be sincere in your request, and as much as I dislike the Harvey family, they are still under my jurisdiction, just like our possible suspect Brick or anyone else that it may be. The bottom line is that if the assailants are in my city, we are responsible for apprehending them."

Cal Hillsmeier added, "I'm sorry, sir, we are not the ragtag, hillbilly force you expected us to be."

The mayor was the first to rise, followed by Director Wanamaker. Cal already had the door open. As his bosses departed the room, Cal held the door a little while longer. He and the man exchanged glares, with each knowing that their history had caught up with them. They also knew this was not over and hoped they survived the man presently named Zachary Brick.

"You know what?" asked Cal. "If you were operating in Bogota and Mexico, that means you can only belong to one agency."

The unnamed man nodded his head...and with that, Chief of Detectives Cal Hillsmeier turned and walked away.

CHAPTER 23

Six degrees of separation...is a real thing.

Marlin Raymond knew the power of a phone call. After an eight-year stint with the CIA, he picked up the phone, called his father-in-law and requested a new legend, with a new life. A life away from the Company...something he could call normal. Thirty days later, he and his wife, Rosalyn, were setting up house in a place either had ever been to—Memphis, Tennessee.

With one phone call, he and Rosalyn became Calston and Deborah Hillsmeier. He was now a detective transferring from the Kalamazoo, Michigan Police Department to the Memphis Police Department. The change was good on a personal level. He and Deb could finally start a family. They always had a great relationship, but the move increased that greatness and rekindled flames that had subsided, but had never been extinguished.

However, a life consisted of both a personal life and a job or profession. For Detective Cal Hillsmeier, Memphis was different. Crime ran rampant. As a homicide detective, his days consisted of twelve to sixteen hours on the job. But he took the good with the bad, and the good included coming home every night.

Then came the Death of Angels. Officially, they were listed as a gang of murderous thugs. But they were more than that. They were organized. They were stealthy. Unfortunately, they were unknown. Murderous...that went without saying. For three consecutive months, every Friday evening, the night belonged to the Death of Angels. Killing sprees. Serial killers. A gang of ruthless killers. Whatever moniker was bestowed on the gang failed to properly describe the crimes they committed.

Their thirteen Friday killing sprees added up to over a hundred deaths. Weeks one through eleven included the deaths of minorities, mostly African-American young men, gangbangers and kids of ill repute. However, in weeks twelve and thirteen a different demographic was targeted, which included ten college-aged Caucasian adults. Dead students throughout the city. It woke a nation and put Memphis back on the map. Once again, for the wrong reason. But then time, as the Deputy Chief of Detectives, he and his boss, Chief of Detectives Sam Wanamaker, they were in the limelight.

The power of a phone call.

His name wasn't important. The man had so many legends, one more wouldn't hurt. He told the man he needed him and relayed the storied details behind the Death of Angels. He also promised that he would be teamed with the best detective in the city, with carte blanche to do whatever they needed to do to clean up the city.

The man accepted.

That was the day Zachary Brick was born. That was the day Memphis was reborn.

He heard the voices coming from the kitchen. One voice belonged to his wife, Deb. He loved the woman. She truly was his rock, the cornerstone of his sanity. In his mind, they were still girlfriend and boyfriend, trying to make this long-term marriage thing work. He made a call to save her life and begged the lady to give him a chance. She did. She was alive today. He never looked back.

It was the second voice however that grabbed his attention. He was not in the mood to deal with his shit again. He didn't like the person's voice, nor the person behind the voice...and the voice didn't like him. He didn't know how to quantify the relationship they had. He cared for the man. Even had love for the man. But you had to love family, right? Cousins were still family.

Cal made a beeline for his wife as he entered the kitchen. He kissed Deb, then turned his attention to their houseguest. "Why are you here Brice? The last fucking time you were here, Brick was very tempted to kill your stupid ass. Are you ready to die? Even if you said yes, I wouldn't believe you."

"Uncle John said hello, you dick," CIA Officer Brice Sloane said. "Told me to tell you, an occasional phone call would be nice. Even said you could pretend it was a wrong number and you guys could discuss what went wrong."

"Go fuck yourself Brice!" Cal said, as he glared at his cousin. "And tell John Raymond to fuck himself too!" The kitchen was big. A twelve-foot island with three stools on the outside sat in the middle of the kitchen. The kitchen appliances had a blackish décor, except the refrigerator, which was silver. Brice Sloane was on one end of the island, while Cal occupied the other end. Deb Hillsmeier sat at the small four chair round kitchen table.

Cal continued to look at his cousin with the same glare he had several hours ago, when Brice was an unnamed agent, pretending to be an employee of ATF, or a mystery man from an unstated alphabet government organization. "One question, Brice." He had his cousin's undivided attention. "Do you really expect Brick to spare your life a second time?"

"You mean a third time," intervened Deb, with a smirk on her face.

Brice looked at her sideways. "I didn't come here for him to spare my life," Brice said in a firm voice. "And why in the hell are the both of you still referring to him by his legend? If anything, both of you still have a responsibility to turn his sorry ass in!"

"For what?" Deb casually asked. "You can't arrest someone on a hunch, my dear cousin." She kissed her husband on the cheek as she walked past him and exited the kitchen. "Brice, Cal is right," she said at the door opening. "You need to let this go. The Company sent six people after him. He killed all, except one. You should feel blessed that she didn't die. If she wanted to be with you, she would be here now."

Deb didn't wait for a response. The two men continued to look at each other. "This does not have anything to do with that," Brice Sloane volunteered. "The man may not officially be wanted by the Company, but he is still wanted."

"Deb is right, Brice. You need to let it go. Our friendship and blood saved your life the last two times. This time, Brick won't have any mercy. He will take you out."

"He will try."

Cal motioned for Brice to have a seat at their table for six in the dining room. He grabbed a plate sitting on the island and placed a steak, baked sweet potato, half a cob of corn and dinner rolls on a large plate. "You know she doesn't cook like this for everyone," Cal stated.

"She didn't cook this for me," Brice said suspiciously, as he slid his chair back and automatically reached inside his light jacket for his gun. "She was already cooking this when I arrived."

"Hold your horses, asshole," Cal said matter-of-factly, as he grabbed a plate for himself. "I called her as soon as I left our unexpected meeting to let her know that we may have company tonight. So, sit your ass back down." He rolled his eyes at his cousin as he filled his plate. "Brick wouldn't put Deb in danger, you know that. We both know that he is the best the CIA has ever trained."

"Meaning?" Brice said, as he put a piece of steak in his mouth.

"Meaning, he knows your selfish ass is in town, on an unauthorized assignment, about to get four men and yourself dead."

"How do you know I have four men, Detective Hillsmeier?" he smiled as he mentioned Cal's fictitious name.

"Do me a favor?"

"What?"

"Grab that writing pad on the microwave and write down your last will and testament, if you haven't already done so." Neither man smiled at the comment. "Then, go see after your two men in the Suburban down the street. I'm pretty sure they were visited by Zachary Brick."

CIA Officer Brice Sloane looked at his cousin, as Cal turned up his bottle of beer to his mouth.

Cal heard the man say "Asshole" as he ran towards the front door.

CHAPTER 24

LIFE ALWAYS REPEATS ITSELF...SIMILAR TO A
DOG WITH A FAVORITE SPOT TO PEE.

Investigating is a developed skill. Especially if you were a part of the CIA. The Company wasn't about making or developing investigators. Manipulators, killers—yes. Investigators—not so much. The true job of CIA officers was to influence chaos in foreign countries. But there was not a CIA official in America who would actually admit to that. Regardless, as officers, we knew that. We lived that.

I had to work at learning how to investigate. But fortunately, trained as a killer in a military uniform afforded me access to some of the best people Uncle Sam's government had to offer: FBI, CIA and the State Department. I knew investigators from my days in the military, plus I had spent invaluable time with Bureau agents who were the best at what they did. The same tenacity I had as a G.I. and assassin, carried over as I honed my investigative skills. I watched. I learned. I practiced. I succeeded.

I wasn't sure I had the patience to be a true investigator. It was about taking what the CIA had given me—the power of observation to work a room, a scene, a scenario. I learned that all of the great investigators knew how to combine the skills of observation, with the pure element of patience. I wasn't a great investigator, but I was great at observing. Patience was now my new best friend.

Every perfect plan comes down to execution.

That's what Detective Alaina Rivers taught me.

What I knew wasn't good enough. Alaina taught me what investigating was truly about. Having a good eye was only half the battle. A good investigator had to know what they were looking for, what was important. As much as I just wanted to kill everyone in and associated with the Harvey family, it was more important to me to solve whatever case Alaina was working.

The one thing I knew for sure—it was an off the books case.

Detective Smokey Franklin was Alaina's partner when she was killed. I knew Smokey. During my five years in Memphis, Smokey was a uniformed cop. He and I had a very good relationship. In fact, he was one of the few cops that I truly could call a friend. He had assisted me on numerous occasions during my time in Memphis. I liked Smokey. Unfortunately, he had one problem— he couldn't keep his dick in his pants. Smokey was twice divorced, with two children by each ex-wife, and had another couple of children by two other women.

He was Alaina's fifth partner since I had left Memphis. The longest any of her four other partners lasted was the second one, who was around for nine months, before he was killed on the job. As much as Alaina liked working alone, she did better with a partner. Someone to watch her back and hopefully, keep her grounded...keep her alive.

Favors always had their place. Smokey was promoted to detective two years after I had left the Department and had been partnered with Alaina for almost three years. If he knew something, I knew he would tell me. Unfortunately, because of his four exes and six children, he had to find a second job. He was now a private investigator, taking pictures and recording videos of cheating spouses.

He was parked on the curb of a street in the Germantown area of Memphis. His subject lived on the third floor of a three-story townhouse apartment. The long lenses on his camera told me that he didn't need to get out of his car and his subjects were providing him with all the information he needed.

I caught myself having a little fun, by sneaking into the backseat of his black sedan. However, I was the one surprised. Upon hearing about my failed attempt at sneaking up on him, he unlocked the car doors, never once looking back to verify my identity.

"I could have shot your stupid ass," Smokey said in his powerful voice. The man was good at his job. As much as I wanted to take the credit, the best I could do was take credit for convincing him to be a detective.

"I like you, Smokey. So I won't burst your bubble." Smokey responded by giving me the side-eye, while aiming his camera and taking another picture of the lovely couple engaged in infidelity. It never ceases to amaze me how stupid people could be when it came to committing adultery—open blinds, exposed windows, fucking in cars, going on dates. It didn't matter. My favorite dumb move was fucking someone in your own house.

Smokey said, "You have been busy." He turned to look at me. "You make me nervous back there, how about bringing your ass up here with me?"

I did as requested. As much as I trusted Smokey, I could understand his lack of trust. Although he was the first person I talked to when I got to the city, it was still a tough situation to be in.

"She was a good woman," said Smokey. "I can understand if you want to kill me too."

A Glock 40 with a long slide laid on the seat between us. I surprised Smokey at a restaurant when I first arrived in the city. He was eating breakfast at his favorite café and sliding in the booth across from him almost made him choke on his food. I wanted to know what he knew about the case Alaina was working on. He couldn't tell me much though. That was the way she rolled, keeping everything close to the vest. I tried to make him feel comfortable at this time by letting him know that we were cool. But I got it—friends or not, Alaina was the love of my life. That, in itself, made me a huge risk to his safety.

"Smoke, I told you at the café, we're cool. I need you. Stop sweating the small stuff."

He laughed. "I wonder who you got that from." He was right. Alaina was notorious for saying the age-old cliché.

"You know, just about everyone on the force feels your pain, Zach. Alaina was loved. Yeah, she was a hard ass, but she made most of us better cops, made us accountable. So many of us, loved that woman, bro. And that's not an understatement."

"Yeah, she was special." Those were the only fucking words I could muster. I didn't want to think too deeply at this moment. Outside my temporary home, I didn't and couldn't give the lady too much thought. It was deadly dangerous. Plus, it was highly emotional.

"You know there are probably cops and city officials behind all of this," I added. "But I only want the head of the snake."

"That, and the whole Harvey family," said Smokey, as he looked at me with sadness.

"Don't worry, Smoke," I quickly replied. "Not the women, unless I absolutely have to. I certainly don't want to...and only will if they give me a reason."

"Talk to me, bro, what do you need?"

"I need you to do several things for me," I replied. "Take this phone, I will call you with what I need." I gave him a burner. "Thank you for looking after Sondra."

"No, thank you. I remember when I first became a detective and juvenile court was sweating me for past due child support.

Alaina gave me thirty thousand dollars and told me it came from you. As much as I am thankful for that and owe you for bailing me out, being there for Sondra and doing what you want me to do isn't about the payback, it's all about Alaina and the woman and detective she was."

I didn't say anything. Honestly, I didn't know what to say. I never gave Alaina thirty thousand dollars to give to Smokey. It was just a great gesture on her part. She must have known that Smokey was probably in a bad way. I felt reminiscent in a way, a way that made me miss Alaina even more.

I picked up Smokey's camera with the long lens, which sat on his center console. I took several quick photographs of the couple he was spying on. It was late, past midnight and the couple was more than getting their freak on. They were living dangerously, fucking on the patio where anyone around could see what they were doing. The good thing for them was that there were no apartments or townhouse buildings directly across from them. The bad thing for them was that it was a decent spring Memphis night, with low humidity.

I gave Smokey his camera back. I still didn't say anything. Smokey didn't disturb my thoughts either. With the exception of Alaina and Sondra, I had been around him more than anyone else. I reached my hand out and we shook, a soul shake. We held the shake for a few seconds. I nodded my head once, as a sign of gratitude. Even at night, I could see the glassy eyes of Detective Smokey Franklin.

As I opened the door and looked back at Smokey, I said, "Smoke, I didn't give you thirty thousand dollars. That was all Alaina." He looked at me and just nodded his head.

I closed the door and vacated my original plans of going back to my temporary home.

The Harvey family would feel my pain tonight.

CHAPTER 25

MERCY IS A FOOL FOR A FRIEND.

The Harvey brothers were big and bad to the average person, or maybe to the average Memphian, or to the average child of the night. That was something anyone could surmise. Or maybe that was just the lie that many of us in law enforcement told ourselves. Truth be told, most of Memphis was probably afraid of the Harvey brothers and their goons.

My saving grace—they were afraid of me.

"Max," I said as I turned the music down in my car. "Call the connects, have them circulate the word." I hesitated. As much as I wanted to think about this move, I couldn't. This was spontaneous. "Get information to Damian that I was seen at three different locations—near the old warehouse district in North Memphis, off Danny Thomas in Germantown, near his parents' home and in Cordova, near Alaina's house."

"What are you about to do?" Max asked. I heard the concern in her voice. She knew me too well. She knew I could do spontaneous, but planning rendered the best results. This wasn't smart and my best friend and partner knew this. "Don't, Zach, just don't."

"What is he about to do?" I heard Sondra in the background. "Max, what in the hell is he about to do?"

"Max, don't tell her anything!" I said. "Dammit, send her upstairs, to her room or something. Hell, give her something to do."

"Seriously, send me to my room," Sondra said in a calm voice. Then she cracked up laughing. That led to both Max and I laughing as well. She was a young woman now, but I still looked at her as my little butterfly, with the infectious smile and laugh.

"You sound like Mom when you said that." She laughed again. "I miss her."

Fuck! I didn't know what to say. Those three words were like a bullet in the heart. "I miss her too."

"So, what *are* you doing?" asked Sondra.

"Right now, I'm parked at a Walgreen's in Germantown," I replied. I was so happy this conversation was taken place over the phone, instead of over a monitor. Seeing Sondra's face would probably put me over the edge and make me destroy everything Harvey, including the entire family.

"Alright, you know they don't like us in Germantown. You may be in the wrong suburbs." Now it was my time to laugh. But she was right. Germantown and black people in the Memphis area had a bad, undocumented history. Only affluent people of color were welcomed in Germantown. They didn't care about political correctness. Most people of color and of average income or below didn't venture into Germantown, unless they had a valid reason. My reason was valid enough...in my mind.

"I should be good," I said. "So, how are you liking my little town?" I was at a loss for words. This was our first time talking since her mom had been gunned down. I had intentionally avoided talking to Sondra. She was more than just a loved one now, she was my weakness. I loved her the same way a father loved a daughter. She was my baby girl. The only daughter I may ever have. No, we didn't share blood and Alaina and I never got married. But in so many ways, the three of us were family.

"We haven't talked in a while and that's what you want to know?"

The question caught me off guard. But she was right...and I hated that. "Yeah, that's my question, lil' lady. I want you to be comfortable. I want you to be at home, so yes, I want to know how things are going there."

It was a bullshit answer. Borderline ranting. She deserved better. Unfortunately, right now, I couldn't give her better.

"I love the place, I love Max."

"What, Max has a fan?"

"She took her earbuds out and went upstairs. I'm sure it was to give us some time to catch up or to just talk."

"Max is a good person," I said. I was a man with a head full of thoughts, but with very few words. I didn't know what to say. I didn't want to get into condolences or how bad I felt about Alaina's death. Max seemed to be a good deflection.

"The last couple of mornings I have awakened to Pete Rock's *They Reminisce Over You,* and Annie Lennox's *Cold.* And it was wild. My mind just went back to waking up to you and mom dancing around and acting like fools to music."

I actually smiled. That was our thing, I would put on Alaina's music when I woke up. That was my way of waking her up and getting her butt started in the morning. It was a way for us to get going, by using the fringe benefits of dancing as a mode of exercise to jumpstart the heart. For Alaina, this was just the beginning of her day. She always followed this up by running two and a half miles each day. The woman was beyond dedicated. She was obsessed about staying in shape.

"I never knew she could really dance like that," Sondra continued. I could tell she had a smile on her face. "You fools used to cut a rug and man, you could actually sing and rap." She burst out in boisterous laughter. "Man, as much as I wanted to say that you old folks looked old, I couldn't. You both were the real deal."

She went on for another ten minutes or so just talking about our morning soirees. I let her talk, let her get it off her chest. Maybe this was serving a dual purpose, as I no longer wanted to kick anyone's ass or blow up stash houses or kill bad guys. The more she talked, the more I realized we both really needed this. Then she said it.

"I really miss mom," said Sondra. "I miss our life. I miss you, her and me being a family...miss us enjoying each other."

She stopped talking. The comms were silent. I knew she had so many thoughts and so much pain.

"I love you," I said.

"I love you more," she responded. That was our thing. Or I should say that used to be my thing. She would say, "I love you," and I would say, "I love you more."

"Go home Zach."

"Don't worry Sondra, I'm going directly to the house. That's a promise."

"And Zach."

"Yeah, babygirl."

"I'm giving you three or four days. Then Max and I are leaving for Memphis. No sense in telling me no, it's happening. So, do your damage. But if you don't kill them before I get there, I will kill them myself."

That was followed by dead silence on my comm system. As much as I wanted to push back, I didn't. Sondra was her mother's child. At the end of the day, she would follow her own mind... regardless of how much or how loudly I objected.

I steered my car towards my place of residence in Olive Branch, while wondering, what new hell will tomorrow bring?

CHAPTER 26

A<small>ND TIME WILL WRECK OUR VIRTUE.</small>

I was mentally drained, but my brain was active, still working overtime. I needed clarity. I remained still—just laying in my bed, looking up at the ceiling. I closed my eyes. It was my way of telling my brain to stop. To slow down. To give me peace. To wake my quaking heart.

My body had responded well. In less than a minute, both my heart and mind were in a state of calm. I could think straight again. That's exactly what I did—think. Sleep wasn't calling my name. Sondra was.

Alaina was tired that day. She was lying on her bed, sprawled out. The day had drained her. Sondra still had homework to do. My task was to help with her math. I was good with numbers. As much as I wanted to say I was good with everything...I couldn't.

People.

That was my shortfall.

"How are you doing, Mister Zach?" the little girl with the naturally curly hair asked me. Sometimes life is what it is. It seemed to me that of every four out of five people I had met in my lifetime, of interracial heritage, and with one black parent, had great hair. Little Sondra was no different.

I had learned that her father was African-American. I could only assume he was tall. Alaina and I were friends now, but neither one of us shared much about our past. It had been two years since I had first met Sondra. She was now eleven and tall for her age. She was five foot six, with skinny legs. She could look her mother in the eye. She wasn't shy—yet. Equally, she wasn't outgoing either.

"How is my lil' angel today?" I asked. "How are you doing in school?"

She smiled. She even giggled a little. She liked when I called her one of the numerous nicknames I had for her. "I'm doing well, Mister Zach. All A's except math."

"I don't know how you can be so good with computers, but struggle so much with mathematics," I replied.

Whenever I saw Sondra, she always reminded me of my self at that age. I remember thinking that at age eleven, I was a little silly and carefree boy. At age twelve, I would become a man. Not by choice, but by necessity.

I hated when I got this way. It made me feel like I was always running away from the age of twelve and that it would always catch up with me. A great man once told me that a man must put shadows behind him. *Twelve was my shadow.*

My memories of my time with Sondra were always good. I remembered helping her with her homework, watching television together and sometimes just talking about nothing. I also remembered her thing for computers, starting at an early age—it was just a natural calling. By age eleven, she could break a computer down and put it back together. She could also build one from scratch. Her skills went beyond hardware, she was just as good at programming. She was a great kid, with smarts beyond belief. More importantly, she was my little buddy. Maybe in another world, we were father and daughter.

Even before Alaina and I had become one, the three of us were already family. The sofa was my bed. I was used to various unorthodox sleeping arrangements. Alaina, Sondra and I had one thing—we had each other. I had my sister, Maggie, who had a family that didn't know I existed. And I know Maggie loved me. However, it was nice to have a family of my own to love and to be loved by. It was nice to have Alaina and Sondra.

As I strategized my next move, history was keeping my mind occupied. But even that was dangerous—remembering why I had changed from someone who didn't value life or the lives of others, to someone who cherished life and embraced love. Alaina and Sondra did that for me. They made me want to live. Want to be a better person.

I remember the day I realized that this was where I belonged. Alaina and I were ending a long, tedious day. We were looking for and had found a young punk that had killed four teenagers, not that much older than Sondra. Damn kids who should have been in school, instead of hanging out with a twenty-year-old thug who killed the kids as part of his gang initiation.

We sat around the dinner table as if we had no worries in the world. This was our moment. I wished then that the moment could go on forever. That Sondra could stay eleven forever, and that my relationship with Alaina could turn into something real, something magical. We laughed and talked, and acted as if this was just an everyday routine for us. This was a life I had never thought about, nor a life I had ever thought I would enjoy. However, this scene, this table, these people, represented a new life for me. The life I wanted. The life I suddenly desperately desired and needed.

I don't remember falling asleep watching television with Sondra, or when she actually fell asleep. But when Alaina woke me up, I was surprised to see Sondra sleeping comfortably with my left arm wrapped around her little body as her head rested on my chest, and with her feet tucked under her legs.

My lasting memory of that day was seeing the peaceful smile on the face of the woman named Alaina Rivers. It was genuine. Something I had come to like, I had come to desire. However, it wasn't the smile. It was the gleam in her eyes that made my heart pause. They say a picture is worth a thousand words...then, a look must be worth two thousand.

It was time for sleep.

With the right thoughts on my mind, I chose to call it a night. To let my mind rest and enjoy the peaceful moments of a woman and her daughter.

CHAPTER 27

THE MAN...THE MYTH...THE LEGEND.

Sondra was still stunned two hours later. It was her first interaction with Brick since her mom's death and she never thought it would go that way. It was late for her as well, but she wasn't sleepy. She was thinking about something she truly didn't want to think about—her mother.

For the first time since her death, she thought about the deaths of the Harvey crime family and all of their minions.

"Why were you so intrigued by Brick?" Sondra asked Max as she brought her wineglass to her mouth. She didn't know where the question came from. She and Max had been drinking wine. Max didn't seem to care about her age or even want to know if she had drunk wine or any other kind of alcoholic beverage before.

Her empty glass was not empty for long as she picked up the bottle and refilled her glass. Sondra was no stranger to wine. Her mother introduced her to wine when she was fifteen. Occasionally, the two of them would have a drink together while watching a movie. She missed the popcorn or nachos her mother would make. She only drank with her mom. Never with friends or boyfriends. She wished her mother was here now, with a movie playing and Alaina going on and on about how good her hot nachos were with melting cheese and jalapenos.

Max didn't immediately answer her question. They were both sitting on the sofa in the TV room. Both had their bare feet on the table with the seventy-inch television on and the volume turned down low. Three empty bottles of white wine sat on the white square coffee table and a fourth bottle was half full.

The question caught Max by surprise. She had entertained many questions from Sondra since she had arrived in Texas. Though she never quite knew what to expect from Brick's pseudo daughter, this was the one question she really didn't expect. She realized that Sondra was a young lady who insatiably wanted to know everything possible about the man her mother unconditionally loved—the man she had always considered as a father, more than just a father figure.

"In the world we lived in, some reputations were legendary," Max stated between sips. "I was flattered when I was told who it was that I was supposed to kill. But then I saw his file." She looked at her glass as thoughts lingered in her head.

"Fuck. His file was the wildest, craziest thing I had ever seen," she recalled. "Zachary Brick was not the name on the file. And no, don't ask me what the name was." She looked at Sondra and the young girl understood.

"But Zach had the reputation of being the one," Max continued. "He was a master at making people disappear. He could do the unimaginable. I have never admitted it, but just looking at the stuff in that file, scared the shit out of me.

"We lived in a silent world. You didn't talk about killing people. You never heard one operative or consultant talk about the exploits of others. You never wanted someone to get the ideal that you were weak or were in awe of someone else's accomplishments. But the truth, Miss Sondra, a few people reputations proceeded them. Zach was one of those people."

She turned up her glass, reached for the bottle, refilled her glass and took another big swallow. "There was one case in particular that blew my mind. One of the CIA's own, a handler, had raped and killed over sixty foreign nationals in ten countries. Fucking unreal. Even though the Company knew about it, they didn't pull him from the field, just shipped him from one country to the next. Four years. Four years that shit went on, before the CIA finally said enough was enough. And enough's name was Zachary Brick."

"Not really his name, but the name you are using," Sondra corrected with a halfhearted smile.

"Yeah," Max agreed. She took another gulp of her wine and looked at the glass. "The man knew something was coming, so he used his many identities and went on the run. That was the magic of Brick. He tracked the man and followed him to four countries, before he eliminated the threat."

"Why did he follow him to four countries?" Sondra asked. "Why didn't he just kill him when he initially found him?"

"That was partially Brick, partially CIA. They wanted Brick to catch their mistake in action. Of all places, the asshole was in Singapore...tried to rape a fourteen-year-old. Fortunately, Brick caught him before he did. He tortured him like I had never heard or seen anyone tortured before. Cut off all ten fingers and all ten toes, rammed rebar in both eyes, and another rebar in one ear that exited through the other ear. His body was full of razor blade cuts with salt poured in each wound. The Singaporean government didn't know what to do with something so disturbing. Once they realized it was an American, they were especially afraid to contact the U.S."

"Brick had sent a clear message. He had done what the Company wanted him to do. But it was too strong. The kill was heinous, sadistic. After this act, the Company believed that their number one eliminator, their king remover, was unhinged. So, it was time to put him down. It was time to eliminate an officer who had done as commanded. Kill the killer, if you will."

Max smiled. Now it was funny. Then, not so much. She would never admit it but viewing Brick's file did something remarkable to her. It scared the shit out of her, while simultaneously stimulating her, sending chills throughout her body. That was the day she knew she wanted the assassin. Yes, she would kill him. But that would be after she had some fun. They had some fun. With each other.

Sondra said, "I think I'm supposed to feel bad, feel afraid. But Zach is my family. He's more of a father to me than my own father. Does he intrigue me? Of course, he does. But nothing he has ever done or will do will ever disappoint me or make me feel anything but more love for him."

The ladies looked at each other. One young, the other older. They were a contrast in style and personalities, but Max saw something in Sondra. The young woman was smart. Her computer knowledge and skills were obvious. But she was wiser than her age. She had her mother in her. The other stuff she had in her was pure Brick.

"He's been like a father to me," Sondra rationalized with a tinge of seriousness in her voice. She had a newfound alertness. Her eyes were focused. Her interest in the man known as Zachary Brick was more intense.

"He's a good man," Max reiterated. "The crazy thing about what he did that it was a combination of how the CIA's rapist killer demeaned and tortured his victims. But when your kill goes viral and the victim is tied to a U.S. government agency, then all sanity goes out the window."

"And you were the solution?"

Max lifted her glass as if she was making a toast. "Yep, I was the solution."

"And I told you how that ended."

"I hope he went back to the house tonight," said Sondra. She wasn't down and out. She was drunk and the sadness of life lurked somewhere in her heart...maybe her mind. But there was no way she was going to allow it to defeat her. Not this night. Not any night.

"I'm sure he did," Max reassured her. "You have his heart. You are the one he listens to."

Sondra said, "That sounds good. But Zach is his own person."

"I think Zach's life had been untethered, unconnected for years. Ironically, that's what kind of connected us. My life was very similar to his life. The difference in our lives was that you and your mom probably saved his life. Whereas, he was the one who saved my life. It's as if our lives were gerrymandered to mimic each other's."

Neither woman spoke.

Within minutes, the young one would be sound asleep on the sofa.

While Max would look at the young girl and wonder what the future held for all of them.

CHAPTER 28

Life on the run...is a slow, laboring trot.

"I was once hired by a multimillionaire to find his father," said Max warily. "The man just up and walked away from his Navy job and family. He left a wife and three children. The son was the oldest, fifteen at the time and twenty-five years later was still mad as hell. He gave me a million dollars retainer and told me that he would give me another ten million if I found him alive."

She paused. Her eyes were focused on the computer monitor in front of her. She was on the system on the left, her regular system. She felt more comfortable on this one. She was so used to Zach being on what she considered to be the primary system, that she thought it was only right that Sondra occupied the seat now.

She had gotten up early and called Zach on the computer system to make sure he was okay—mentally. After they talked for a while, she made breakfast before Sondra woke up. She laughed as she thought about the girl. Max remembered when she was that age and how she wasn't much of a drinker as well. But Sondra both impressed and intrigued her. The young woman's future was bright, so much brighter than her future was at that age.

"Well, I traced everything I could about the man. One thing stood out—Sigonella Naval Air Station in Sicily. The man had been stationed there on three separate occasions over eight years.

I traveled to Sicily and just asked around the area. It took me over two months to finally get a lead. About thirty miles outside of Catania, the city closest to the naval station, was a very small village near the Hyblaean Mountains.

"The father lived there with his new family. The houses were probably a good quarter mile apart. I waited a couple of days until his wife and two young daughters left the house. Needless to say, I did my job, which included calling his son and asking several questions. Of course, the first question was why. I'm not even sure what he said. But I thought to myself, how many days, weeks, months or years did it take him to get fully comfortable living in a new life, without looking over his shoulder or thinking that someone would knock on his door with dangling handcuffs?"

Max paused again. Her mind was on that moment so long ago. It wasn't the death that occupied her mind. It was years later, yet she still wondered what the deserter thought about in every second and minute of each day.

"Max, you okay?" asked a worried Sondra.

"Yeah," said Max, as she let out a long breath. "After Zach tricked me, I think I became target number one on the CIA's hit list." She smiled. "The thing about doing a job as a freelancer is that you don't know who is footing the bill. You don't know if it's the Company, or a handler, or a rogue officer. You never see the person or people that you are actually doing business with. Money is wired into your account, and although I didn't complete the task, they can't get the money back. I had transferred my money into another offshore account. So, somebody wanted me dead."

Sondra wished she had popcorn. Max's story was interesting, intriguing. But more importantly to Sondra, it was a part of the man she thought of as a protector, a father figure. As cool as she was playing it, she was on pins and needles to hear the story. Max's story, Zach's story—and what made them tick, what made them kill, what made them – them.

"Guess what? I escaped to the same village," said Max sullenly. "I think I wanted to feel what the Navy deserter felt. Every second, every minute of every day, my mind was working overtime. A day was like a week, a week was like a month and a month was like a year."

Max looked at Sondra. "I found someone who had been missing for twenty-five years," she stated dryly. "However, it only took me four or five months to get comfortable. Then, it happened. Very unexpectedly. One morning, a hand over my mouth woke me up. Someone whispered in my ear, 'Stay calm, get your weapons, take the two at the back, I will take the three out front, you have thirty seconds to get your shit together."

"Who was it?" asked Sondra with a tinge of excitement in her voice.

Max answered, "It was Zach. The house had a cellar with doors that led to the outside. He quickly made his way to the cellar, and thirty seconds later, I heard a vehicle blow up, followed by three shots at my front door. As soon as the backdoor was kicked in, I took them both out.

"Zach came in, I pointed my gun at him, with every intention to shoot. He had holstered his gun. He told me to either shoot or grab my go bag and to get the fuck out of there."

Max smiled again. "The rest as they say—is history. We have been a team ever since."

"Is he going to kill the whole Harvey family?" asked Sondra. Her eyes were glassy with anticipation.

Max didn't answer immediately. The one thing that had improved for Max over the years was her ability to choose her words wisely. "No," she said curtly. "He won't kill the women, unless they are an imminent threat. But the Harvey men, yes, all will meet the same fate as Arturo."

Whether the smile was forced or natural, it appeared.

And Sondra Rivers had the whitest teeth in Texas.

CHAPTER 29

A ND DREAMS WILL GIVE US NEW LIFE.

I had slept. How long? I wasn't sure. I hadn't looked at a clock or the watch on my wrist. My body clock told me about three or four hours. A call from Max had awakened me from my stupor. She told me to jump on my computer. I eventually realized she just wanted to see me, to look at my face. I was tired, but it was nice to see her smiling face.

As much as I wanted to go back to sleep, I couldn't. I woke with a thought and that thought took me to another world.

"Make love to me like you have never done before."

Those were the words that would always stay in my heart and beat a tune in my mind. Alaina was at the kitchen sink, cutting fresh green beans. She loved cooking when she got the opportunity, which wasn't often. I was behind her, my hands smoothly rubbing up and down her waist, occasionally working their way to her breast, my groin in the small of her back and my lips teasing the back and sides of her neck.

Something told me that our minds were in two different places. For me, it was on the act of love. At that moment, I thought her mind was in the same place. I would later learn differently.

This moment would always represent a certain sense of hindsight.

I stayed on my beaten path. That included doing what the lady wanted me to do—make love to her like I had never done before. As simple as that sounded, it wasn't. We had a very active and competitive sex life. Some acts consisted of making love, others consisted of having sex, and then, there was just pure fucking. All three resonated with me.

This act began with me kissing the back of her neck, while simultaneously unbuttoning the shirt she was wearing. The only thing she had on. We often bantered about her racial makeup. With her father being half-white and half-black, I joked that she was only twenty-five percent black and that all twenty-five percent resided in her ass. As I kissed my way down to the object of my desire, I could feel the tension in her body.

That became my focus, to relieve that tension.

I slowly dropped to my knees. My lips laid tender kisses on her butt and inside thighs. I kissed down to the back of her knees and made my way back up to her butt. My hands were just as busy as my lips. I was reaching my goal, second by second, I could feel the tension releasing from her body.

When the tip of my tongue made contact with her clitoris, her knees slightly buckled. My hands went from squeezing to slightly rubbing her butt as my mouth continued to work the magic I was creating. Alaina's breathing was labored, her moaning indicating she was losing control. She needed relief, and I was trying to provide it. My tongue and fingers were busy and synchronized. From flicking her clitoris with my tongue to sticking my fingers in her pussy, I was in the zone.

I repositioned myself, getting on the balls of my feet, lifting Alaina's legs and putting them on my shoulders. She was holding onto the sink and by her moaning and occasional screams, I could tell she had come at least two or three times.

This wasn't about sexual competition. This was about a woman with something deep on her mind and needing a release. For now, she didn't need an ear to bend or a shoulder to cry on, this was about pleasure—losing control, releasing tension and sexual satisfaction.

This was about Alaina.

I let her legs down, rose up and entered her in the same position she had been in since we started, bending over the kitchen sink. I started hard and continued to pound hard. Occasionally, I would slow it down. Alaina was wet, with juice oozing down her inner thighs. My hands stayed busy as well, going from her breasts to her waist to her shoulders. I put my left arm around her neck and pulled her back towards me, still thrusting to the rhythm of our bodies.

"Island," she said quietly.

The island sat in the middle of the kitchen. I gently swung her around. We didn't change positions, just location. Alaina's body was glittering with sweat. I was equally sweating.

We moved our sexual adventure to the kitchen table. I didn't immediately enter her as she laid on the table. I admired her body. Her skin was as if she had a forever golden tan. I think it was the twenty-five percent. Her body was toned, not an ounce of fat. I knew she ran a mile and a half every morning and tried to hit the gym twice a week. Her short hair accentuated every feature of her face, from her alluding eyes to a nose and mouth that weren't too big or too small.

Her eyes told me we weren't through, that she wanted more. Whatever was on her mind was in a dormant compartment of her brain and she didn't want to deal with it now. I obliged by kissing her, a sensual kiss. Her right hand grabbed my cock and stroked it. I didn't need the help, but damn, it felt good. I slid down to her breasts and flicked my tongue over her nipples playfully, before putting one breast in my mouth, followed by the other.

I continued my mouth action, moving down to her taut stomach, her inner thighs and down to her legs and stopping at her feet. I took each foot in my hand and sucked her toes. I knew what would relieve her tension. I alternated feet and fingered Alaina at the same time. Then I licked and kissed my way back to her pussy. Saying she was wet would be an understatement.

I penetrated her again. This time I took my time. My rhythmic thrusting was mingled with sensual kisses and sucking her nipples. This was the slow release of tension. She was relaxed, floating on sexual satisfaction.

Her eyes told me to bring it home and that's what I did. My thrusts increased and were deeper, harder and more intense. When I reached that moment of gratification, it was a concerted, synchronized effort. Simultaneous combustion.

She reached her hands out. I pulled her up and picked her up into my arms. We kissed as she straddled her legs around my torso.

"I love you," she stated.

"I love you more."

We kissed again. Long kisses. "Let's go to the bedroom and let me do you."

I knew right then. Something wasn't right.

Alaina was in trouble.

CHAPTER 30

ONE DEGREE OF SEPARATION, TWO DEGREES OF PAIN.

I was still reeling from last night. I was somewhat drained, but had items on my mental checklist that I needed to accomplish today. My mind was my enemy. The saving grace was I knew my limiting factor and had to combat that. Too often we had to neutralize ourselves—stopping our hearts and minds from making the wrong decisions for us. The emotional decisions would be the fall of civilization. I couldn't remember which great American initially said that, but I decided to make the saying my own.

Lucy Bankwell was a connected person. A power player. Her name was very fitting. She was indeed a banker. But her real trade was *mover and shaker.* She was also my legitimate money person.

The woman was five feet six inches tall. Or maybe sixty-six inches short. It didn't make a difference. The woman believed in her four to six-inch heels. Her shoulder-length, dark brown hair complemented her brown complexion well. She never wore much makeup and I always thought that was a good thing. Some would say she had African-features, but for me, someone who had traveled the world, I didn't think so. Her face and nose were medium-sized, with average sized lips. Her breasts were a nice 38C. I knew that first hand.

We had history.

She was a creature of habit, reaching her office at ten every morning, Tuesday through Saturday. The first time we had ever met was on a Sunday, in this same office. I don't remember much about the office furnishings, but can easily recall that she had a black full-sized sofa that let out into a bed. In fact, that is where we closed our deal with a two-hour sexual rendezvous. It was something that just happened. Nothing planned. Not by me anyway.

That lasted for six months, until I met her ex-husband, a Memphis cop named Smokey Franklin.

"So are we talking money or something else today?" asked Lucy, in her singsong voice. I admired the woman. As she spoke, every syllable was pronounced with dignity. Every word was easily released off her sultry tongue, which oozed of sexual desire, or maybe, sexual tension. Truth be told, she was one of the most sensual women I had ever known.

"How in the hell are you, Mrs. Bankwell-Franklin?" I joked as we hugged each other. She smelled good. But hell, she always smelled good.

"Shut the fuck up, Brick," she bantered back. "So, this conversation is about that deadbeat ex-husband of mine?" She kept her eyes on me as she walked around her desk to take a seat. The woman was still a freak. I could tell by the glass desk she sat behind. It was an L-shaped completely glass desk that consisted of three pieces. I knew that with the right client, whether male or female, the woman probably sat with her legs wide opened.

"Unfortunately," I answered. "I need to know what kind of relationship Smokey and Alaina had. Also, you need to tell me what Smokey is into now."

Her eyes of steel fixated on me. She knew what I wanted to know. She not only dealt in finances, she dealt in information as well. She wasn't a gossip. She was just a woman who kept her ear to the ground, by allowing information to come to her and paying a decent price for it, in hopes that it would benefit her one day. In the case of her ex-husband, she never had to pay for information and if others didn't bring it, then she would simply get it straight from the horse's mouth.

"Every time I tried to tell your ass about Detective Franklin, you blew me off," she said incredulously. She was right. For whatever reason, I never wanted to believe the worst of Smokey Franklin. "But before I volunteer anything, you need to talk to me, Mr. Brick."

I said, "Alaina told me that you guys had become friends and I know she had changed over the years. She was more trusting of Smokey than she was with her other partners. Truthfully, I don't know if that was a good thing."

"She came to me six months ago. She wanted to ensure that Sondra was taken care of financially if—"

It was an awkward moment. We glared at each other. Lucy was suddenly uncomfortable. I didn't want that. "Don't trip, lady. She's dead. Life goes on. That's why I'm here...to do what needs to be done...to make things right."

"I'm sorry, Brick," said Lucy, as tears welled up in her eyes. I got up and walked around her desk. She stood and we embraced. "I miss her. We had...really become very...close...and...and..."

Her sobs had increased and the words were hard to get out. I let her get it out. I wondered if she had grieved at all since Alaina was killed. I wasn't in a hurry. We didn't talk. Lucy held me tight. After several minutes, her sobs decreased, until she was just sniffling. She had a box of tissue on her desk. I held the box while she grabbed tissue after tissue to blow her nose and dry her eyes.

"She didn't trust Smokey," said Lucy surprisingly. "She couldn't prove it, but she was sure Smokey was feeding information to the Harvey brothers. She was going after big fish though. She didn't want the brothers, she wanted the assholes who controlled the Harveys. She was convinced it was someone higher up in the government."

"As in the local government?" I asked.

"I don't know. I just assumed she was talking about someone in Memphis."

Lucy sat back down. I sat on the edge of her desk. She was trying to get herself together, but she excused herself to her private restroom. I was trying to think this through. Smokey Franklin. Harveys. Local government officials. Possible federal government officials. This was not the time to overthink this or to come up with a plan. I was just taking the information in, wondering how all of this would end.

Lucy looked much better when she came out of the restroom. She was carrying a thirteen-inch red laptop in her right hand. She gave me the laptop without saying a word.

"Your eyes are red," I said with a slight smile on my face.

She smiled back. "You are still an asshole," she retorted. "That's why they make dark sunglasses sir." I smiled back. "Alaina kept this laptop here with me. She came by the office, at least two or three times a week to make annotations. Many times when I wasn't here. I don't think anyone knew about it. I kept it in personal restroom here at work."

"Thank you," I said. I knew the laptop well. She had had the laptop computer for a while now. I bought it in year three of my five-year stint in Memphis. After her death, the Harvey boys had sent a three-men team to Alaina's house to find this very computer. They were careful not to disturb anything. This occurred when Sondra was making funeral arrangements.

Two of the three criminals were computer specialists, or at least, they pretended to be specialists. They bypassed the house alarm without setting off the alarm. Then they jumped on the desktop computer in the study and another laptop in Alaina's bedroom. They didn't find what they were looking for. The reason being, it was on this laptop. The laptop she added detailed information about everything she worked on, including information about her last case.

The one that got her killed.

"She told me you bought it for her," said Lucy. She was eyeing me carefully. My mind was elsewhere. I couldn't help but think of the moments she was typing something or surfing the internet or just doing whatever on this same laptop, and I would try my best to interrupt whatever she was doing. Sometimes I was successful, other times not so much.

"Plus, she wanted me to give this to you." Lucy looked inside her handbag and gave me a small burgundy box, about the size of a jewelry box for a wedding or engagement ring.

She said, "Six months ago, Alaina gave me a similar box and told me to give it to you if something happened to her. She basically made me promise. I didn't ask her what was inside. It really wasn't any of my business. We were drinking wine and having a great time, and that didn't change. We just continued our conversation.

"Then, after she came back from her last trip, she gave me this box. I returned the old box to her. But this time, she told me that the box contained two thumb drives—one for you and one for Sondra."

I then said to Lucy, "I was thinking about something Alaina once said to me, 'Never play the devil's game, because you can't win. He's too good at it.'"

That was early on in our partnership. The woman didn't know me as well as she would come to know me. Once she did, love and our deep connection covered her eyes with proverbial blinders.

If she had removed those blinders, she would have realized that I was the devil.

Unfortunately, I knew the truth . . .

. . . there were bigger devils than me in the world.

And the pain of the heart can make the best of men a gun ready to shoot.

CHAPTER 31

T HE DEAD DON'T THINK ...

"I don't usually agree with Junior...or even dad for that matter," Ronaldo Harvey declared. "But they were right, killing the detective was not a smart play, and now we are paying for it. And the debt is real."

He had dreamed of being an attorney. He had attended college, got his degree and was even accepted to law school. Unfortunately, that dream would pass him by because of the family business. His dad had other plans for him. Now he was to be the leader of the family business, to include both legal and illegal franchises. He was at the law firm of Harvey & Valens, Attorneys-at-Law, talking to the lead attorney, his sister, Kendra Harvey.

She was the middle child of their parents' five children. Her specialty was criminal law, but she was just as versed in both financial and contract law. Her business and judicial acumen had accommodated her family well by keeping her brothers and their minions out of jail and thus, ensuring the financial success of the family. Her reputation was in good standing throughout ten states in the nation. As a result, she was the chosen defense counsel for multiple cartels' top criminals. This was her claim to fame, and her burden to bear.

But that wasn't her main station in life. That was her family.

"You and Damian refused to listen to the voices of reason," Kendra said tersely. She loved her brothers, but they were also the source of her biggest headache. She had called a family meeting. She was expecting her father, and her other two brothers, Hector Junior and Damian. She had requested Ronaldo to come earlier, so they could have a talk.

"That's beside the point now," retorted Ronaldo. "We did what needed to be done."

"No, it's not beside the point," Kendra responded. "Detective Rivers wasn't a threat. So what if she made a little noise, it was manageable." Her voice was hard and authoritative, which was in direct contrast to the outward appearance of the woman. At first glance, many would probably describe her as the typical Mexican female: long, streaming raven black wavy hair, dark features, beautiful dark soft eyes and a slender body. But she was anything, but typical. Her shapely frame was compact in a five-foot three body that threw many attorneys off their game before the game even began.

"So 'Naldo, both you and Damian need to fucking curb the cavalier attitude. I asked you here early because I have a plan...and it's not popular, but it's a viable plan. We do this and we either kill Brick or he moves along."

"Plan? What plan?" Ronaldo looked confused. As much as he knew that he and Damian had messed up, he still considered himself as the leader of the family. The last thing he wanted was his older sister skirting his power.

"I will tell you everything when the family is all here together. However, I need you to support my play...no questions and no bullshit. We need to bring closure to this situation sooner than later. Simply put, I need your support."

"You need to tell me the plan now," replied Ronaldo incredulously. "You want my support, but it's like you are trying to take over as the head of this family. That shit isn't happening, sis. I still wear the big boy pants in this family."

"Figurehead wise, that's true 'Naldo." Kendra's tone was non-threatening. However, her brother knew better. Something didn't smell right to him. This was not Kendra talking. He quickly realized that his task at the moment was to let her talk. From his searching eyes to his flared nostrils, Kendra knew that was her signal to press on with her oration.

"First, I know Junior has been advising you. You need to continue to listen to him." She gave Ronaldo a few seconds to let that soak in, before proceeding on. From his facial expression, it didn't seem as if Ronaldo had an issue with that. "Ironically, you and Damian never respected Junior, but the only thing he had done over the years was listen to Senior."

"Yeah, maybe he should be running the business," lamented Ronaldo. "He has been right about everything,"

"That may be true, Ronaldo, but he is not the one to run the business. He is doing the job that is right for him now, which is to be your experienced advisor. He has learned a lot from dad and Arturo. Now he can advise you. The thing is, you need to continue to listen to him."

"I know," Ronaldo stated weakly. He was tired. He was lost. He wished he was playing a game of tic-tac-toe, or even cat and mouse. But with former Detective Zachary Brick, he didn't know which game he was playing. Worst of all, Junior was the expert on the man. He even entertained the thought that Brick was feeding Junior information and vice versa. However, he knew that this thinking was just his paranoia. In fact, he knew that Junior would prefer that Brick kill their parents before allowing Brick or anyone else to harm a hair on Arturo's head.

The two were close. Both Ronaldo and Damian had heard the stories of how Senior would beat the shit out of Junior, until

Arturo stepped in. Many times, when things went south because of Junior's actions, Arturo would take the blame. Arturo knew he was Senior's favorite and would never beat him. This dynamic resulted in the two oldest brothers becoming extremely close. Closer than close.

That's why Ronaldo had an issue with Junior. He thought Junior was taking Arturo's death too lightly—maybe that was also his paranoia.

"It's odd the way life is sometimes," said Kendra. "I have always admired Junior's power, yet he was quiet as a mouse. He would rarely say a word. Arturo was the Alpha, but Junior was his right hand and ironically, the one who just faded in the background. Now he is an encyclopedia of information. Let your big brother be there for you. He is giving you damn good counsel. Listen to him."

Ronaldo stated, "I want to ask how we got here, but we both know the answer to that. I fucked up Kendra. I really fucked up. I allowed us to be played by fucking assholes with badges and so-called official status. Arturo kept telling me to leave it alone, to step away and to step away...to make sure we didn't do the dirty deeds of the city.

"Fuck, Kendra! How could I be so damn stupid?"

"Ronaldo, your problem has always been one thing—you can't let shit go," answered Kendra incredulously. "We have a great family business. We practically own a city and a section of the United States, and you still want to be the head of a cartel. Ronaldo, it doesn't work that way. You are smart, very smart. It doesn't take anyone long to figure that out. But it also doesn't take anyone long to figure out that you want the world groveling at your feet."

Brother and sister exchanged glances. Ronaldo smiled, a halfhearted smile. Then he clapped his hands as if applauding his sister. "Well, thank you, big sis. You know I hate when you're like this with me, but I know you are right. I know that you tell me this shit to help me get refocused."

"No, my second part of this conversation will help you get refocused." Ronaldo's brow furrowed. "With the death of Arturo, Santana Garsay sent a message to you to clean this up and clean it up now. If not, we, as a family, will have a lot to pay for. He knows you and Damian are sharing the wealth with someone outside the family and outside the cartel. I, for one, didn't know that. But it's stupid on your part 'Naldo. Yes, you are the head of the family, but the question is, how long do you truly want to stay as the head of the family? An even bigger question is, are you ready to accept the responsibility for the death of your whole family?"

"Fuck." Ronaldo's eyes were suddenly glassy. He remembered meeting the cartel leader once as a child. Well, it wasn't a formal introduction or meeting, it was more of a beatdown. Santana drove a gold Mercedes, a two-door sports coupe, which he stopped in front of a cantina in Tijuana. Ronaldo and his friends were playing soccer in the street at the time. He and Damian were staying with their uncle during the summer outside, just outside of Tijuana. And that's who Santana came to see—their uncle.

With his car still running, Santana jumped out and charged into the cantina. He pulled Ronaldo's uncle into the streets of Tijuana and beat him barehanded until his face was completely swollen and bloody. When he was done, as he was walking back to his car, Santana stopped and told Ronaldo and Damian to say hello to his mom and dad for him.

From that day on, Ronaldo was afraid of the head of the Garsay Cartel. The thought of that day had put a new wave of fear in the heart of the head of the Harvey family.

He understood why Kendra had called him in to meet early. He didn't worry about Kendra sharing this news with the rest of the family. She wouldn't do that. Not because she cared about his status as leader of the family. No. That wasn't important in her big picture. She answered to a bigger power—and that power resided south of the border of the United States.

CHAPTER 32

DEATH AND ASS WHIPPINGS ARE GREAT LEARNING TOOLS.

"Tell them what happened," demanded Hector Sr. to his now oldest son, Junior.

Senior had lived a life he was proud of. The most important thing to him was waking up every day to the woman who lay next to him, his wife, Mariana. They were high school classmates, and then college sweethearts, which led to a marriage based on true love. For Senior, he had what he wanted—a beautiful woman who made him happy and someone he was proud to say was his wife.

She was, indeed, the apple of his eye, which made his children, the worms he never, truly wanted. However, the best of his worms was his daughter Kendra. She chose her father's profession and like him, was a person who had loyalties elsewhere. But she loved her family and knew that this was the time when they needed her most.

"Dad, we know what happened," intervened Kendra.

Senior was proud of his daughter. Internally, he initially wished she had been born a boy. She had the intelligence and tenacity he wished every one of his sons had. Arturo was the smartest of his sons, but he never lived up to the expectations of Hector Senior. Unfortunately, none of his sons had. But Kendra was different. She had more than exceeded his expectations. She was more than just a consigliere to Senior, she was the one he trusted to make the right decisions and the right moves, when the worms he called sons fell on their faces.

"What are we doing to find Brick?" asked Kendra, with exasperation in her voice. She didn't like the day-to-day dealings of her family. She thought her younger brothers were reckless and dangerous, and too often failed to think through their rash decisions.

Kendra looked at all of her brothers, as they remained silent. They were holding the meeting in the smaller conference room of the law office's two conference rooms. Senior sat in his wheelchair at the head of the table, while Junior and Kendra were seated to his right. Both Ronaldo and Damian sat on his left, with Ronaldo closest to his dad.

"So, I will take that as nothing is being done," she said.

"That's not completely true," Ronaldo finally spoke up. "Our connections in MPD have us covered. They are looking hard and heavy for this Brick guy. We have put out the word that for any cop who gives us viable information on Brick's whereabouts, we will give them fifty thousand dollars. No questions asked. If they capture or bring us Brick's dead body, we will pay them a hundred and fifty grand.

"Additionally, our own guys are on it as well. If they spot him, they are to call their team leader immediately, who will then, call me or Damian. So, we do have a plan."

Senior held his head down, then put his hands together as if he was praying. "No, 'Naldo. Dammit! No, you don't have a plan!" exclaimed Senior. "You have a fucking hope and a dream. More than that, you have a death wish. That wish will also apply to your sister, brothers, me...and yes, your mother."

Kendra leaned forward and put her left hand on her father's hands. He held his daughter's hand as they placed them on the table. She looked at her father. She saw and felt his pain. Of his sons, Arturo was his favorite. She knew her father would never lay claim to having a favorite, but based on all of the private conversations they had shared in the past, she realized that he clearly favored his oldest son and only daughter. Over the years, he had learned to love Junior, but had no respect for his two youngest children.

"Father is right," opined Kendra. "For one, fifty thousand is nothing. I know for a fact that you gave Detective Franklin two hundred and fifty thousand just to set up his partner. Plus, you gave him another hundred fifty thousand to steal drugs from the evidence room at MPD. Secondly, we are paying the department and city officials two million per year."

She let the words linger in the air, as she squeezed her father's hand. She was his daughter, and her playbook was his playbook. She eyed Ronaldo, who exchanged glances with his sister. Their earlier conversation was still on his mind. He knew that Kendra dropping Detective Franklin's name and mentioning the payments to city officials was her way of saying that Santana Garsay knows what Ronaldo is doing and that he better end this soon.

She continued, "This is what we are going to do. We are going to press Detective Franklin. Put eyes on him. We are going to pass the word via your gang members that we will give twenty thousand to anyone who has eyes on Brick, and have them pass out three burner numbers—one for each of you and one for Junior."

"Hold on," interrupted Damian. "I respect Junior, but he is no longer one of—"

Kendra stopped him in his tracks. "Damian, interrupt me again and I will either shoot you or have Junior kick your ass right here in this office."

She let her father's hand go and walked around the table. She stood between Ronaldo and Damian, as both men looked at their father. Kendra leaned down, with her mouth at the base of Damian's ear. "You, nor 'Naldo, know the real Hector Junior," she muttered, just loud enough for Damian and Ronaldo to hear her. "I have seen Junior beat to death three assholes at the same time and they were way tougher than you. Mother gave 'Naldo the reigns before he was ready. Now all of us are in trouble. If Junior could kick the dogshit out of the toughest guys, how much of a badass does that make Zachary Brick?"

Both brothers looked at each other. One was outwardly angry, while the other wondered how they could have fucked up so badly.

Kendra stood on the other side of her father. "You smart guys are that dumbest assholes in the family. For all practical purposes, you two are still the leaders of the family business, since that is obviously so important to you. But right now, I'm calling the shots. As I was saying before I was rudely interrupted, twenty thousand to anyone who eyes Brick and calls one of you three and you three only. The twenty thousand is payable when one of you three arrive on site and point Brick out. Understood?"

Junior voiced a "yes," but Ronaldo and Damian said nothing.

"You know what?" sneered Senior. "I begged my dear wife to abort both of you ungrateful bastards when she was pregnant." He pounded his hand on the table, catching all of his children by surprise. "Your sister asked if you understood, so answer her fucking question!" His voice raised an octave or two. His skin had turned two more darker shades of red.

"Yes, we understand," both men said simultaneously.

"Lastly, also pass the word...a hundred thousand to anyone who can tell us where Brick lays his head every night," said Kendra, her voice even more authoritative than before.

All three brothers voiced affirmatively.

"I have one question," Damian stated. "Why aren't we calling Mexico? Hell, we need the help."

"If Mexico comes up here, they will make an example of both of you for every other operation they have in the States and Mexico," Kendra answered. Many associates with the cartels in Mexico and South America were convinced Hector Senior and his family were still alive only because he had made the cartel money, including numerous prosperous investments. In some circles, the prevailing thought was that Kendra was now the person advising the cartels.

A deafening silence fell over the room. Kendra, her father and her brother, Junior, knew the truth that Kendra wouldn't voice. The easiest way to erase a problem was erasing the source of the problem.

In this instance, that included the elimination of every member of the Harvey family.

CHAPTER 33

Every swinging dick reports to a bigger dick.

"Come on in...come on in. Have a seat," Mayor Archibald said from behind his desk, as he waved his hand, signaling Director Wanamaker, Major Hillsmeier and Lieutenant Fontaine to have a seat.

The three walked in and took a seat in the three chairs that faced the front of the mayor's desk. It was obvious the mayor had been drinking. The half bottle of Jack Daniels Black and the glass in his hand were proof that the mayor had already had a drink or two. He also had three empty glasses on the desk reserved for his guests.

"I want each of you to get a glass and pour yourself a drink," said Mayor Archibald. When the men didn't immediately respond, the mayor looked at each man with a coldness in his glassy eyes. "It's not a request, it's a fucking order," he added.

Each man poured himself a drink as the mayor watched to ensure that they all took a swallow or sip. Then he volunteered, "We are celebrating the meeting I just had."

The men all looked at one another. The moment was awkward. Whatever was going on, the mayor was not in a hurry to disclose. He sat stonily in his seat. His mind was in two places: on the meeting he left an hour ago and the here and now in his office, where his people waited patiently for him to speak.

"You know what surprise meeting I was invited to today?" he asked. No one spoke. Before anyone could speak, the mayor added, "Invited. No. No, that's not the correct term for the meeting I attended. How about the surprise ass fucking or the last-minute massacre? Maybe if I wasn't drinking, I could come up with something more creative."

Director Wanamaker asked, "Are you about to tell us that the Feds took our case?"

"Sam, that would be easy, a piece of cake," the mayor retorted. "No, I had the honor of being ambushed by the governor, the governor of Mississippi and the heads of the Tennessee Bureau of Investigation and Mississippi Bureau of Investigation, and our friends from DEA and the ATF."

The room was quiet, as all three men waited on the mayor to continue with what happened in the meeting. Two of the three were surprised by the announcement. However, Cal Hillsmeier knew the meeting was coming sooner or later. He knew the optics of bombs blowing up in a mid-major city in America. Things were different now. They had been different since 11 September 2001. No governor, senator, or local or national politician wanted bombs haphazardly exploding in any American city. Cal had personally picked up the phone and called his old colleagues, assuring them that this was a local matter and not a terrorist attack.

Unfortunately, many Memphians considered this terrorism within their city borders.

Mayor Archibald continued, "The governor wanted me to allay her concerns that the city was under attack. She doesn't like the attention our city has been receiving nationally. First, a detective is killed Mafia-style, then an alleged drug dealer was killed in an explosion. Although it was in Mississippi, the national news media made sure to mention that it occurred outside the Memphis city limits, a location considered to be in a suburban area of our beautiful city. Then, once again, we have explosions within our city limits.

"So, I get where the governor is coming from. No one, and I do mean, no one, wants this kind of attention, in their city or state."

"Sir, I hate to say this, but this situation of bombs exploding in random cities is becoming commonplace," Cal added. "We live in a different world now. Even though it's seventeen years later, and despite the fact that Americans are becoming desensitized to this type of violence, they are still highly uncomfortable with explosions happening in their cities. Unfortunately, now they think that we have a former rogue cop looking for revenge for the murder of his old partner right here in our community."

"Dammit Hillsmeier, that's not my concern!" the mayor expressed. "This felt like a personal attack. This was the governor's way of saying that I was not getting her job any time soon. The TBI, DEA and ATF were there to let me know that if we don't solve this issue soon, one of these agencies will take over the investigation, and then I can say *fuck it* to a run for governor...or even to other run for mayor."

Cal didn't respond. He didn't give a damn about the mayor's political assessments at the moment. He had his eye on the bigger picture, which meant ensuring that his friend, Zachary Brick, didn't destroy his adopted city or have every federal agency send numerous agents to Memphis trying to make a name for themselves.

"We need to change our strategy," said Director Wanamaker. "None of us expected a federal presence and even after we were briefed, we disregarded the possibility. Now we can't afford to take their presence lightly. We need to capture Brick and bring him to justice. If not, he may take all of us down."

"That's easier said than done, Director," Fontaine stated. "Half the force wants Brick to bring down the Harvey family, and the other half wants to get the award the Harvey family is offering for Brick, found dead or alive."

"What?" The quizzical look on the mayor's face spoke volumes regarding his level of shock. "We can't have a fucking bounty on a former cop's head. What in the fuck is wrong with these people?

"Dammit, Sam, you need to talk to old man Harvey and tell him that this is fucking unacceptable. This is not fucking Dodge City or Tombstone in the old west. What the fuck is going on? Does anyone think this is acceptable behavior?"

"Mayor, that's not our call," Wanamaker replied. "We can't control the Harvey family. Even if I question them, they'll just deny it, and then what can we do about it? Do we threaten to arrest them, if we do find out that it's true? How do we ensure there is veracity to this rumor? It may be the word on the street. But hell, there are a lot of words on the streets of our fair city and we can't verify or validate the veracity of any of these rumors."

"Sam, I don't believe that we should do nothing," Archibald countered. "We are the law in Memphis and we need to stop kowtowing to the bad elements in this city. You and your guys need to come up with a viable strategy. Something I can take to the governor to ease any potential pressure she may receive from those in Washington."

Cal Hillsmeier didn't say anything. He knew, just as he thought Director Wanamaker also knew, that this was about two unmovable forces going head-to-head. One was light years smarter than the other. But Hector Harvey Senior had been in the criminal business for a long time and the man had survived. He was still the patriarch of his family and more importantly, he was a man of connections.

For Cal, Brick was the ultimate weapon, a creature of death. The CIA was full of creatures of death. However, there used to be a time when the top ten officials in the Company's chain of command all had the same number on their speed dial...and it belonged to the man presently known as Zachary Brick.

CHAPTER 34

HEARTBREAKS AND DIARRHEA OF THE MOUTH.

"My family is in danger," said Kendra Harvey. Her navy blue, pinstripe gray suit and off-white blouse represented power. A power she knew how to wield. Her Jimmy Choo custom-made pumps were the exclamation point that accentuated her strength.

"What do you want from us?" asked Lieutenant Jody Fontaine. He tried to come across as full of confidence. However, it was false bravado. He wasn't afraid of the man in the physical sense, but mentally and intellectually, he was outclassed and he knew it. The woman was intimidating—from her intelligence to her quiet confidence to the clothes she wore, most men didn't stand a chance against Kendra Harvey. Unfortunately, Jody Fontaine was one of those men.

To add to his stress, Hector Junior stood next to the sofa his sister sat on. Her legs were crossed. She had a glass of wine in her hand. Junior, on the other hand, had both hands in front of his body, with a Glock 37 automatic pistol in his right hand. The man was stone-faced, with his eyes focused on Fontaine.

Fontaine stood in the middle of the room. He wasn't visibly worried. He was sure Junior was just adding his version of intimidation. However, he was glad he had on a lightweight jacket, so that the Harveys wouldn't see how grossly his underarms were sweating.

Kendra asked, "You know the first time I saw you?" Before Fontaine could respond, she answered her own question with a slight smile on her face. "It was at the JSL in Jackson. I assume you were providing security support for the mayor and his girlfriend. I smile because both the mayor and mayor of Jackson had their girlfriends with them, but I'm sure the perception was that they were with their wives." Her smile widened. "You sat two tables over from me. It was so funny at the time. The JSL has a restaurant with twenty private rooms and only one open area, and the most important men in their respective cities could only afford to sit in the open area of the restaurant. There was one bodyguard for each, including you for Mayor Archibald, plus a female detective with the Jackson Police Department adding security for the Jackson mayor.

"You and she made a strange couple, Lieutenant. Your lily-white ass and a black woman just a shade lighter than midnight. Such an unlikely couple."

"I didn't come here to talk about the past or about a fucking dinner," said Fontaine. The anger was obvious in his tone.

"Watch your voice, detective," Junior stated.

Their glance at each other was quick for Fontaine. As quickly as he lifted his head to look at Junior, Kendra said, "I sized you up as exactly what you are Lieutenant Jody Fontaine...as a little bitch of a man. An errand boy, who does as he is told."

Kendra sat her glass of wine on the coffee table in front of the sofa, before she arose and walked over to the detective. Junior repositioned himself, so that his line of sight was completely on Fontaine. His sister was only a couple of inches from the detective. He had a couple of inches on her. Without shoes, she stood a tall five-seven, with long legs that made her look taller. With her four-inch pumps on, she was five-eleven.

"You are a little man, a small parasite of a man, Lieutenant Jody Fontaine." She liked using his rank and full name. The detective knew that in his world, this was a way of telling perps he had more information on them, whether it was personal, professional or both. He had never wanted to identify with the criminals he had arrested or questioned in the past, but now he did...and he didn't like the feeling at all.

Kendra sniffed a couple of times and frowned. "I smell your fear, detective. You are the law. You don't have anything to be afraid of. Be a man. Be the law. Stick your chest out, grab your cock and tell me how badass you are."

Fontaine didn't like this. He wasn't sure if he would live or die today. It was daytime. The building had people in it. He knew there were only two names on the law office door, but Kendra and her partner had other attorneys and office personnel that worked for them. However, in his mind, she was the attorney for her criminal family and she knew the family business better than anyone. If they killed Alaina Rivers, they could easily kill him as well.

"Tell me detective, what in the hell is the law doing to find your former co-worker, Zachary Brick?"

"We have feelers out," stated Fontaine in a very weak tone. He wanted confidence to be on his side, but his voice failed him.

"Speak up detective!" Junior yelled.

"We have feelers out," Fontaine repeated. His voice was stronger and with only a minor crack this time. He swallowed and took a second to allow his composure to take hold. "Every cop in the city and CI are keeping an eye out for Brick. If he is still in the city, then we'll get him."

Kendra smirked. She didn't like his answer and quickly let him know. "Dumbfuck! Half of your force is hoping Brick will wipe my family off the map. And confidential informants aren't worth a damn in this matter. How in the hell does a police department not have one photograph of a former employee? That's just asinine to me. I have no idea why we pay you incompetent assholes so much money to assist us. Totally fucking worthless."

Fontaine could think of a thousand and one things to say in response, but dared not with Hector Junior holding a gun and monitoring his every movement. No. The best plan of attack was to just take the abuse.

"Well, detective, tell your boss that my family has decided to help the Memphis Police Department. As we speak, my brothers and their crew are putting the word out on the street that we will pay twenty thousand dollars to anyone who sees Brick and calls us immediately. We'll pay a hundred thousand dollars to anyone who can tell us where Brick lays his head every night. And the money is coming out of the coffers we pay your boss and your fellow co-workers."

Fontaine didn't respond. If there was a such thing as a cat having his tongue, it would certainly be true in this instance. He felt catatonic, yet his mind was racing, and thinking about how bad an idea this was, but he couldn't...no, he wouldn't say anything.

He was so stunned by the news that he hadn't even noticed Junior had walking up to him. That is, not until the man whispered in his ear, "Now get the fuck out of here."

When the detective departed from the man, Junior looked at his sister. "No one authorized you to say it was coming out of the cops cashflow."

Without hesitation, Kendra responded, "I made the decision, Junior. Mother wants her baby boys to run the business and Father just wants to keep his wife happy. You and I are the oldest, and we know what's best for the family. I hate to say this, Junior, but trust me on this, there is nothing in the world that will keep Brick from killing Ronaldo and Damian. I love my baby brothers, but they committed the ultimate fuck up. He is the *tigre silencioso,* the silent tiger."

"And the silent tiger brings death."

CHAPTER 35

...A<small>ND MY HEART SHEDS A TEAR</small>
FOR THE WOMAN I LOVE.

I was sleeping well. The winter time does that to me, makes me sleep well. I have always possessed an active imagination. But not lately. Alaina had taken over seventy-five percent of my brain matter, Sondra fifteen percent and the remaining ten percent belonged to the Harvey family and the current situation in Memphis.

I had always considered myself an extremely logical man, but emotions had kicked my ass recently. That wasn't a good thing. The act of killing, seeking vengeance for a loved one, was an emotional act. However, it took a logical person to create a viable game plan and keep a calm and cool demeanor in order to execute that game plan. So, logic has been my friend and ally. Emotions without logic were reserved for my bedroom, or more specifically, my bed—and only while I slept or closed my eyes to rest. Once my feet hit the floor, it was back to the grind.

The text from Sondra changed my current mindset: *Let talk. I'm on the computer, waiting on you.* I put on some clothes and made my way to the computer room. This was my command post.

She had a smile on her pretty little face. Her hair was unkempt, which actually made her prettier. She was her mom's child, Alaina's likeness, but with more hair and two decades younger.

"What's on your mind?" I said to the monitor.

"Good morning to you too, Mr. Grouchy," she said as she held up her coffee cup, as if she was giving me a toast. "I see you woke up on the wrong side of the bed."

She still had a smile on her face. That actually made me happy. I wanted her in a good place. Even so, I wasn't crazy about her coming back to Memphis within a day or two. I got it though. That was important. I needed closure, but so did Sondra. My thoughts of her lately were consumed with fears of losing her. But not to death. It was more about losing her to a dad who was anything but a dad. He was just her sperm donor. Alaina was both mother and father to her. But like every child, she wanted both a mother and a father, even if that sperm donor wasn't much of a parent.

"It's funny that you are in a grouchy mood, because I have never seen you this way," said Sondra. I understood what she was implying. She was right. Alaina and I had a golden rule: never wake up without a song in our hearts.

"I'm sorry."

"Don't be. You have never treated me like a baby or little girl. Not like Mom. Please don't start now."

I actually smiled at the comment. "Your mom was worried about you." I smirked at my reply. "You were all she had. Like her mom, you were her world."

"No, we were her world. She loved you. When you came into her life, her life changed. She changed. She was still hard as nails, but you brought out a softer side. That bugged the hell out of her when she realized she was changing. It was hard for her to accept.

"I can remember us having a conversation last year and it was clear to me that she really liked talking about and letting me know how much you changed her life and how much she loved you. Every time you guys hooked up on one of your trips, she would come back to Memphis with a smile on her face, but within a week, that smile would change to a frown. She missed you. I used to think that with every visit, she would come back and tell the MPD to go to hell and that she was quitting."

"I wish she would have," I said weakly.

"I do too," Sondra responded immediately. "Unfortunately, she was a woman of the people." I saw Sondra's eyes get glassy with tears. "People needed her and after your departure, she felt like she was the only one who could right the ship. I really do believe she wanted to leave the city, so you guys could start a life together, but crime never stops in that fucking city."

She half-heartedly smiled. She drank some coffee, then took her napkin and dabbed at her eyes. I smiled in turn. We were two people with wounded hearts. The pain would cease one day. But we were months, possibly years away, from that day. We were both grieving and trying to navigate our way to a good place. My way was vengeance. Not the best method to grieve, but for me, not the worst. For Sondra, I was her method. She needed me. I knew that. That's why I didn't complain or disagree when she said that she and Max were coming to Memphis. Dad or not, we were family. We needed each other.

"It was her city," I said. "She loved the city and the people. She was leaving. This was her last case. She wanted the Harvey boys. But more importantly, she wanted who the Harvey boys worked for."

Sondra's facial expression changed. The gears in her brain were turning. I wasn't sure if she knew something or thought she knew something.

"What's wrong?" I asked.

"We talked about walking away. She told me she had to do this before she walked away. But she didn't tell me what *this* was.

Then Miss Lucy told me the same thing at the homegoing…that she was walking away after the case was closed."

Lucy and I had talked about this. She was convinced as well that Alaina would walk away from the MPD after she put the Harveys away and put the real boss behind bars. She, like me, knew the *big* man was not a Harvey man. Their operation was bigger than them. Only the old man had that kind of juice, but he really wasn't the leader of the pack either.

But in watching Sondra, I realized something. She had a lot on her mind and I was the person she wanted to talk to. "So, talk to me, young lady. What's on your mind? I can see the gears turning in your head. What's up?"

She smiled. "You have always been able to tell when I had something on my mind. Some things never change, I guess." She was stalling. I was patient. I didn't have any place to be. "When I woke up this morning, Cheryl Lynn's *No One Else Will Do* was playing on my playlist, and I remembered the first time I had ever heard that song. You and Mom were slow dancing… getting your bump and grind on." We both laughed at that comment.

"It was night and I had gotten up to use the bathroom. I wasn't used to you guys playing the music low. So, I peeped in the living room and saw you guys dancing. I can still see my mom's face. She was so in love with you. I could see it in her eyes. I could tell how she touched you, how you guys danced and how she put her head on your chest. I don't know how long I just stood and watched you guys. It was crazy. I was probably about twelve or thirteen, and I couldn't take my eyes off you and mom. She was happy. So happy. I wished that day had never ended. In my head, Zach, that day will live forever."

I didn't know what to say. Words escaped me. I remembered the day like it was yesterday. Alaina's playlist consisted of ten of her favorite slow songs. Her slow jams. We danced until the last song ended. It was a Saturday night in December, close to Christmas, just like now. We were enjoying life, enjoying each other.

"I said to myself then, that that was what I wanted. I wanted someone to love me the way you two loved each other. And how I knew you guys were deeply in love...that was the only time ever that I was able to sneak and see what you guys were doing. It was like Mister and Miss Observant had only one thing on their mind: each other."

She was right. Of course, she was right. That night was special. It was really the first holiday season that we were truly a couple.

Sondra was in a groove. She needed to talk...and I let her do just that—talk. We were on the computer for another couple of hours. The entire discussion was about her mom and me. I got a word in every now and then. But it was nice to hear her thoughts.

Internally, my heart was truly broken. Through the smiles and occasional laughing, the pit in my stomach was saying kill, kill them all. That would come.

For now, it was about ensuring a young lady that she was not alone and she would never be alone.

CHAPTER 36

Said the Lioness to the Lion...

"Who do I see about my brother's death?" Kendra Harvey asked Director Sam Wanamaker and Major Cal Hillsmeier.

"You see the Tennessee and Mississippi Bureaus of Investigation, the FBI and ATF," Cal answered immediately, without hesitation. The men had come to Kendra's law office to compel her to retract the various rewards being offered for Zachary Brick.

Kendra retorted, "See, that's my problem and my family's problem Director Wanamaker. No one wants to accept responsibility. Everyone wants to pass the buck and here you are asking my family to make concessions."

Kendra sat behind her desk, a traditional marblewood executive desk situated in a large office, which included a small dark gray sofa, three matching armchairs, two end tables and a coffee table that sat to the right of Kendra's desk. In the back of the room there was a small conference room table with seven chairs, one at the head of the table, and three chairs on each side of the table. To the left of Kendra's desk, next to the door was a small bar area with a five-shelf bookcase full of books next to the bar. Three armchairs sat directly in front of the attorney's desk.

"No, Miss Harvey, we are not asking your family for concessions," Wanamaker stated. "We are asking your family to obey the law and let the legal system do what it does. Whoever killed your brother and his bodyguards will be brought to justice."

Kendra actually laughed. She refused to allow the two cops to see her show any emotion. She wasn't happy. But that wasn't their concern. "From what I know, Director, my family is very law abiding," she said, as she leaned forward and allowed her chin to rest on both of her hands. "My brother died, along with some of his friends. I do not know why you refer to Arturo's friends as bodyguards, nor does my family Maybe you know something we don't know. Or maybe you just want to disrespect my family."

She had to restrain herself from calling out Director Wanamaker. He was one of a number of cops and city officials on her family's payroll. She knew he had to put on an act for his chief of detectives. She didn't know much about Cal Hillsmeier, but it wasn't from a lack of trying. She had put out feelers before and none of her connections in local or federal government circles were able to help her out, and that bothered her. It was the same result that had come back on Zachary Brick.

"Miss Harvey, we are not disrespecting your family," countered Hillsmeier, with a voice of confidence in his voice. "As much as I wish our department had facts, Miss Harvey, we just don't. Other government agencies investigating Arturo Harvey and his friends' death informed us that those who perished with Arturo were his bodyguards. So, I do apologize if we got it wrong. Additionally, we have received reports from fellow officers and local residents that your family...specifically, your brothers, Ronaldo and Damian, have offered money for Zachary Brick's body, alive or dead, or information on his whereabout.

"Basically, Miss Harvey, we come to you because you are an attorney, and we need your assistance. We don't know what's true and what's not true. However, we do know one thing, Miss Harvey. If it is true that there is a bounty on Brick's head, it won't be received well. And the Director and I have worked with Brick.

We know Brick. If it is Zachary Brick who is wreaking havoc in our fair city, I promise you, he won't appreciate being threatened and certainly won't like having a bounty on his head."

Kendra Harvey stood and stated in a powerful voice, "You think I give a damn about what Zachary Brick likes or doesn't like?" She walked around to the front of his desk and sat on the edge of the desk. "My fucking brother is dead. Killed by your former detective. And you come in my office and tell me that he won't be happy! Fuck him, Detective, and fuck you too!"

"Cal, please excuse us," Director Wanamaker intervened, as he stood up. "Wait for me in the waiting room." His chief of detectives did as he was told. "Thank you, Cal."

Hillsmeier didn't press the issue. He knew the possibility of his director of police being on the Harvey payroll was probably more of a fact than a rumor. He didn't care. They came here for a reason and that reason was to warn the attorney that Zachary Brick would probably kill her entire family if he heard about the bounty on his head. To Cal Hillsmeier, that was definitely more fact, than fiction.

"Kendra, what are you guys doing?" Wanamaker asked, as soon as Cal closed the door. "You are the attorney, and a cooler head needs to prevail in this situation. What Cal told you is true. You and your family may not give a damn about the Pandora's box you just opened, but you should. What your brothers have done has placed the largest bull's eye in the world in the center of their chests. Is this what your family really wants?"

"Damn you, Sam! That son-of-a-bitch killed my brother and you of all people should know that my family would be seeking some kind of retribution."

"Kendra, what in the fuck did Ronaldo and Damian think was going to happen once they killed a cop and the worse part, killed the love of the man's life?"

The attorney didn't say anything. She walked around her desk and took a seat. She needed to decompress. She had warned her father on many occasions that one day her younger brothers would cash a check that would end their family. The name on that check was Zachary Brick. She had heard about his exploits, but Arturo's death was the real deal. However, instead of being the cool, collective one, she felt irrational and wanted vengeance just as much as the rest of the family. That wasn't her role though. Her role was to be the smarter one, the one who made the low risk, high calculated decisions. The director was right and that was hard for her to say. So, thought it, but refrained from sharing it.

"You know it's too late to call off the bounties," she said in a low tone. As much as she loved her father, she was closer to her mother. The thought of consoling her mother if her younger brothers were killed pained her heart. Mariana Harvey loved all of her sons, but her two youngest boys were her heart. She took the death of Arturo hard, especially since they still hadn't had a funeral for him yet. Kendra knew if anything happened to Ronaldo and Damian because of the bounty, she would be complicit.

"To be on the safe side, Kendra," Wanamaker interrupted her thoughts. "I would recommend that all of your brothers stay at your parents' house. Brick is a lot of things, but a killer of old women, he is not. As much as he probably wants to kill your brothers, he will not hurt your mother. That's just the kind of person he is."

"Sam, you know that's not happening." Kendra folded her arms. She was exasperated and had a headache. She was a planner. She didn't believe in being rash and didn't like being unprepared. That summed up her last two days—making rash decisions and being anything but prepared. Now it may cost her the lives of her family...and she hated to think about that.

Director Sam Wanamaker had walked to the door and had placed his hand on the doorknob. "I will say a prayer for your family."

CHAPTER 37

No time like the present.

The phone call didn't surprise me. However, the information that Brownleaf provided for me did catch me by surprise. Lydia Brownleaf was the manager at one of my favorite barbeque restaurants in Memphis. She informed me that my favorite family had put a bounty on my head, dead or alive. They were also offering money in real time to anyone that spotted me and called the Harvey brothers.

It was laughable.

One of the traits of a good CIA officer was situational awareness. Evidently, the Harveys were willing to pay people $20,000 each, just for information about me. As much as I wanted to test the concept that Ronaldo and Damian would actually pass out money to local residents or even their own men, I decided not to test my luck.

Fortunately, this grandiose gesture by the Harvey brothers had created an opportunity for me to capture or kill them whenever I wanted. They had made it much easier for me to organize and plan their demise. I shook my head and wondered how in the hell this family had control of anything. It was a rhetorical thought on my part. I knew the backstory.

The Harveys came to the city and struck lightning in a bottle. That lightning included a death squad from Mexico and the subsequent killing of the so-called bad or criminal element in the city. As rumors have it, within the first three months of the crime family arriving in the city, they had murdered the top six drug dealers, as well as many members of their crew. From there, the Harveys ran roughshod over the city and enticed cops and city officials to jump on their criminal bandwagon.

Now I was the obstacle who threatened the hold they had on the city. I studied the family, I knew the family. This was about money and drugs to them. Old Man Harvey just needed one son and his daughter to keep the family business going. He preferred the son with his namesake, Hector Junior to fill this role. I had gathered that much from the listening devices planted in his house. The unfortunate thing was that I think Ronaldo and Damian knew this, and that probably made my job easier.

I knew what I wanted to do, but it wasn't the smartest thing to do. The last time I wanted to act a fool and hurt the Harvey business interests, Sondra talked me off the ledge. I now imagined she was getting some sleep before she and Max began driving to Memphis tonight.

It was cold outside. You could never fully predict the weather in Memphis in December. It had been raining all day, a freezing rain. I had parked at the intersection of two streets, making sure I had an eye on the residence of Cal Hillsmeier. Cal had company.

This was actually funny. There were three separate vehicles. One vehicle belonged to the MPD. It was a black four-door sedan, with dark tinted windows. I wasn't sure if it was for Cal's protection or if someone within the department was spying on him and his family. The second vehicle was a dark colored mini-SUV. All three vehicles had one thing in common—dark tinted windows. This stakeout was sanctioned by Brice Sloane, CIA officer, a man who hated me more than he hated enemies of the country.

I wanted to say Brice's hate was his downfall, but that was the furthest thing from the truth. The man's downfall was what it had always been—money. Every operation I had interrupted years ago in South America had hurt Brice financially. He had an arrangement with several cartels in South America and his front was running an operation for the CIA. The man was once an operations lead for my assignments. He had set me up and made me a pariah in the Company. I had numerous opportunities to kill his traitorous ass, but felt that his death wasn't worth it.

Until now.

The third vehicle was my target. Amateurs. It was an old white Mustang. Smoke was coming out of the tailpipe. Even with the tinted windows, I could tell that the windows were frosted from the two idiots probably talking non-stop. They worked for the Harveys, and they were making it too easy to kill them.

Two minutes later, I was walking in Cal and Deb's backdoor. "Y'all should probably lock the damn door," I said.

"We'll make sure we do that the next time you call and say you need to drop by," said Deb, as she looked up from cutting her salmon. "I told Cal this is about the time you start going crazy and killing everyone."

Cal was sitting next to his wife. They were having salmon, baked potatoes, green beans and garlic bread for dinner. There was a plate that sat across from them on the table. It was my place setting and the food was still hot. It was perfect timing because I was hungry.

"Talk to me," I said, as I stuffed my mouth with fish and took a sip from the glass of red wine being served with the meal.

Cal answered, "There is a hefty bounty for your ass. Dead or alive and money offered just for your location, a recent photograph of you or whatever else they can get. The Harvey crime family is finally tired of your black ass interrupting their business, their cash flow. Is Deb right, are you about to turn loose and transform Memphis into the wild west?"

"Yes I am. I'm tired of this shit. The lady I love is dead. I came here to see why she died. But honestly, Cal, I don't give a damn. Or I'm tired of giving a damn. Her partner, Smokey Franklin, set her up. She tried to help his nasty ass and instead of having her back, he set her up and contributed to her death. He is big in the Harveys' pockets and is one of many on the MPD. When I was Alaina's partner, I did as she wanted me to do. As much as I wanted to clean up the city and just kill everyone that pissed me off, she wouldn't let me.

"Now, I'm dealing with my own dilemma. She told me that if anything ever happened to her, she knew that she couldn't stop me from killing people, but made it crystal clear that she didn't want me killing cops. Honestly, Cal, I don't give a damn anymore. I don't know who is a part of this shit. I only have an idea. But yes, Cal, I'm ready to seek some vengeance. Patience is a virtue, but not a quality of mine."

Deb knew me well. She was my handler for a good number of years. I missed her voice in my ear. She was one of the best. She had my back and she knew what I was capable of doing. I wasn't sure how in tune she was with me at the moment though. Years had passed since we were a team of two, working for the Company. My demise occurred when she and Cal decided to live a normal life. Thanks to Brice, the CIA decided to come after me. Why? I'm not completely sure...nor did I give a damn.

This was my life. A series of events that occurred that I didn't have control over. Now I was here, trying to get vengeance for events that I somehow created by becoming a detective, and because I saw a woman that I instantly fell in love with. A woman who may have been living today, if I had just adhered to protocol and completed my job.

"What's your plan?" asked Deb. I saw it on her face and I hadn't seen that look on anyone's face in a long time. She was worried, concerned for me.

"I miss her, Deb," I said. "You know the discussions you and I had over the years. Did you ever imagine I would feel this way about anyone?" I half-heartedly smiled. Cal was playing with his wine glass, swirling the wine around in it, while Deb was taking occasional sips from her glass. "I can't get her off my mind. So, Deb, to your question, 'what's your plan?', it's to inflict pain on those who are responsible for her death. Every single one of them."

I took one last swallow of wine. Then I took the phone out of my jacket pocket and hit a couple of keys before hitting the send button. The Mustang with the two thugs who worked for the Harvey family was one of four locations within the city where the bombs exploded. The other three places consisted of two warehouses and a dope house.

Neither Cal nor Deb jumped at the sound of the car exploding outside.

I got up and left the way I came in.

CHAPTER 38

I'M HORNY, BOY SCOUT, HOW ABOUT YOU?

That's how it started. Those were the words Detective Alaina Rivers said to me, while we were on a stakeout. I had spent over two years being her babysitter when she went on dates with guys that I considered undeserving of her company. She had treated me more like the proverbial redheaded stepchild than the man who had loved her before we actually officially met. I never thought in my wildest dreams that I would become like the close uncle or second dad to Sondra.

But to Alaina I was the damn girlfriend with a penis. This blew my mind. However, I laughed at that thought.

I was lying in my bed, on top of the cover. I only had on shorts and my hands were behind my head as I was looking up at the ceiling.

In. The. Dark.

With thoughts on my mind.

One evening, we were in a Chevy Suburban, with dark tinted windows. It was past midnight, a nice spring night. Alaina hadn't been on a date in six months. We were closer, which was a huge jump from my first day on the job.

Now sex was on the table. No. On the front seat of an SUV.

"I'm a damn man, hell yeah I'm horny!" I exclaimed.

She was in the driver's seat. She leaned over and kissed me. Fuck! If I hadn't had strong feelings for the woman, this would have done it. Her tongue playfully teased at my lips, as she placed her left hand behind my head. Then our tongues merged as one, as we kissed deeper. It was a long kiss. I opened my eyes, because I didn't know what was going on. Damn. It felt great. I reclosed my eyes and pulled Alaina closer.

She said, "You know I have been wanting to do that for the longest," as our lips disengaged. "And you didn't disappoint, Boy Scout."

Gazing into each other's eyes, I saw what I wanted to see—desire, sex, want. We kissed again, just as sensual, just as hot.

"You...want—" she was trying to speak while we were still kissing. "Want...to...get into the back seat."

I didn't speak. Alaina was already lifting my tee shirt over my head and grabbing at my belt buckle.

"Get your ass in the back seat," I said. She gave me another hard kiss, before jumping in the back seat. I immediately followed her. I think we set a record for getting out of our clothes. I don't think either one of us gave a damn about the stakeout at this point or maybe we just hoped for the best scenario—that nothing would happen.

Even with dark tinted windows, the wash of the moonlight and street lights provided adequate lighting, enough light to see Alaina's nice breast. Her nipples were big, inviting, and I didn't waste time. I attacked them with my hands, tongue and mouth. Alaina's right hand was rubbing the back of my head. I wasn't completely bald, but damn near bald. Her touch was soothing, yet, stimulating. Her left hand was teasing my nipples with slight pinches, which was driving me crazy, making me suck even harder on her breasts. Then she would slightly scratch her nails from my nipples down the middle of my torso.

I was ready for action. Then Alaina pushed me forward, so that I was lying on my back. She kissed me again, then worked her way down to my nipples. Her tongue drove me crazy, as she gently bit and licked them. Then she kissed and licked her way down to my cock. When her mouth engulfed my organ, her hot, wet mouth pushed me to another level. She was focused, determined, and I was a willing participant.

The pleasure was intense, biting. As much as I loved what she was doing, I took it as a challenge to do the same for Alaina. I pushed her head away, placed my hands under her armpits and repositioned her. She was reluctant to move, gently resisting my efforts. When she was on her back, I took my turn at pleasing her. I didn't waste time with more foreplay, but went in for the kill, putting my face between her thighs.

I went full blast, sucking on her clitoris and sticking my tongue deep in her love canal. She jerked and moaned, as her body shook from what I imagine was both surprise and pleasure. She then put both her feet on my back when a thought raced through my mind—that we were in a neighborhood on a stakeout and we were butt ass naked having unadulterated sex. However, it didn't stop me from my assault on her pussy. I licked and sucked her clitoris, and up and down her pussy, occasionally, sticking my tongue and fingers inside. I loved her legs and whole body shaking, the feel of her hands on the top and back of my head, and the moaning and groaning from the woman's mouth. I was thinking I was the top dog, pleasing her more than she pleased me. It was a mentality thing.

"Fuck me," Alaina voiced. I proceeded to do what she demanded.

I repositioned my body and as wet as she was, she was still tight. I took that as an indication of no recent action, as well as nervousness. It didn't stop me as we both worked our magic. It didn't take us long to get in a rhythm. Sometimes, you don't know how competitive a person really is until you engage in sexual activity. It was funny, yet, ironic and truthful.

As I continued to move to our rhythm, Alaina pinched my nipples once againn. When she realized how much it turned me on, she raised her head and her mouth greedily came down on one. The woman was relentless in her pursuit to move me to come. Equally, I became just as obsessed to do the same. I increased the intensity of my strokes, playfully making a harder, surprising push every five or six strokes.

Alaina said, "Let's turn on our side. I like it from the back." That's what we did.

Initially, we were in a spoon like position, as much as the back seat could provide us. I repositioned myself several times, as I kept Alaina in the same position. Everything I thought about the woman was true. She had a sweet ass, as nice, smooth and perfectly symmetrically round as I thought. This was my play time or as every man won't admit to, that break time when you intentionally go slow, pulling the head almost completely out and then sliding it back in with an extra thrust when it was almost fully in. I did this for several minutes, before Alaina told me she wanted to get on top of me.

Her knees were on each side of my waist and her feet were positioned by my knees. Alaina's body was taut, tight. Although this was our first sexual encounter, everything seemed familiar, felt right. We had occasionally flirted, teasing each other, but due to her serious demeanor, I wasn't always sure if she was being playful or serious. As time went on, I realized how comfortable we both had become with each other.

Tonight was the apex of that comfort level. As she positioned herself on top of me, our eyes met. I was nowhere near an expert or too knowledgeable about love, but that's what I saw in Alaina's eyes. I was sure that this was what she saw in my eyes as well.

We kissed. As much as our previous kissing had revealed how much we cared and had feelings for each other, this particular kiss was recognition of something more. *Love.* That's what drove us. Our intensity increased as Alaina rode me, moving up and down, while continuing to kiss me. Our tongues meeting made the sex hotter. A certain sensuality overcame my body and I began pumping harder. My hands were on Alaina's buttocks as I made her ass move with my faster, harder pumps. Within seconds, Alaina was saying, "Fuck...fuck...fuck!" which equaled my "Shit! Damn, keep pumping."

She collapsed in my arms. She was drained. I was drained. I was still inside Alaina. We didn't immediately speak. I didn't know what Alaina was thinking. I could feel her heart, feel my heart. It was as if we were synchronized. Her beat meeting my beat.

"You know we are on a stakeout," she finally stated. I could hear the laughter and smile in her words.

"We're not on company time," I retorted. "This is your op, completely off book." This wasn't the first stakeout we had pulled off book and I knew it wouldn't be the last.

"What do we do from here?" she asked.

"You be Detective Alaina Rivers and I'll continue to be Detective Zachary Brick. We live our lives. We continue to be a team. The only thing that will change is knowing how we feel about each other. We keep our love private. Only you and I know about this."

"Sondra knows." Her omission surprised me.

"How, we just did it?"

Alaina didn't immediately respond. She gently put her tongue in my ear, followed by a kiss on my ear. Then she said, "She told me over a year ago that we should be together—that she saw how you looked at me and...how I looked at you. She told me I was stupid for going out on dates with guys I didn't like, when one was at the house who clearly loved me."

I smiled. "She's twelve."

"And has more knowledge and clarity than both of us," she responded. I was hard again and evidently, Alaina liked it, as she slowly gyrated her hips. She raised up and looked at me. "I haven't had sex since she told me that. She was right."

She leaned back down, placing her mouth on my ear. She moaned between statements. "I went on those dates, because I didn't like myself. I was afraid of how I felt about you."

She softly shrieked. Then she stated, "I said fuck it. I'm not stupid, Boy Scout. You had busted heads in my name, kicked asses and threatened many because of me, even those above your rank. Now, I realize that I have a man who has good dick, a righteous tongue and loves the fucking ground I walk on and more importantly, gives a living fuck about my daughter. Friendship is underrated, love is overrated. What we have is perfect. What we have is special, Boy Scout. What you have is what you've always wanted—me and my daughter."

Then she kissed me and moaned again. With every pump, we became one.

It was only a memory.

But I turned on my side and succumbed to the sleep that called my name.

CHAPTER 39

STUPIDITY BEGETS A QUICK DEATH.

"What locations did we lose and what was the final count?" asked Hector Senior, as he sat at his dining room table. Each of his children were in attendance. The old man sat in his wheelchair at the head of the table with Junior sitting next to him in a chair. Kendra sat on the left of her dad, opposite Junior. Ronaldo and Damian sat across from each other, with both occupying a chair at the other end of the table, away from their father.

It was late and cold. Only three hours ago, the city had been rocked by four explosions. Regardless, every member of the family felt safe in the Harvey's main house, which was being protected by over twenty bodyguards. The city was on edge...which included law enforcement, powerbrokers and unfortunately, the Harvey family. Every inch of the house, the surrounding grounds and every car on the property had been inspected and re-inspected for explosives. This was real. Death was always real.

Ronaldo said, "Two warehouses near the Mississippi – Tennessee border, one past Shelby Drive and the other past South Third got hit. Altogether, we lost over two million in cash, a thousand pounds in coke and heroin, and about twenty men. The dope house was in the Hollywood area. The good thing is that there was no one at the house, and no drugs."

"And the fourth bomb?" asked Kendra.

Ronaldo looked across the table at Damian, who reluctantly responded, "We lost two soldiers that I had watching Major Hillsmeier's house. Supposedly, the major and detective were good friends, so I thought it would be smart to station soldiers at the homes of people he was cool with."

"That actually makes sense," said Kendra quickly. She didn't want to discourage her youngest brother. Her mind was moving a mile a minute. There was good and bad in that decision. Her father's influence was taking control. The man was wise, intelligent beyond belief. He raised his sons to seek education and combine their book knowledge with street smarts, and become the best criminals in America. It sounded good. But everything that sounded good was not always good for you.

"We made a mistake," Kendra continued. "We never should have taken out the bounties on Detective Brick. We have made two major mistakes, both overestimating and underestimating Brick. We didn't realize how much he loved and cared about Detective Rivers. Additionally, we failed when we didn't listen to Arturo and Junior years ago. Arturo tried to tell us all that Brick was the smartest person he had ever encountered and that we needed to be careful in how we dealt with the man. Unfortunately, we didn't listen."

"I did listen to my boys," retorted Senior. "That's why I told these two dumbfucks to leave Detective Rivers alone." Senior's eyes bored into his two youngest sons. "The deep love that I have for your mother is the same type of love this Brick had for his lady detective. The best thing we could have done was to have left both of the detectives alone. What these two jackasses didn't understand was that a man like Brick just doesn't die that easily. Men like him are hard to kill and they may be out of sight, but certainly are not out of mind."

"Pop, that's water under the bridge," said Kendra. She would never say it out loud, but she noticed how much her father had aged since the death of Detective Rivers and the reemergence of Zachary Brick. Memphis represented peace and serenity and more importantly, a long life. Now Ronaldo and Damian had screwed that up.

"We need a new strategy," she continued. "We need to make a concession with the detective. We need to come up with something that will keep you two alive and send Brick back into hibernation."

"I already have a plan," said Senior irritably. "I directed Junior to make a phone call for me. I have hired the Ramirez brothers to eradicate our problem. They will be here soon. I'm paying them damn good money to do what we can't do. We haven't been aggressive enough with Brick. We haven't deal with him directly. Yes, we have been proactive in looking for him, but he is the one who's been in charge. He is the one that's been pushing all of the buttons."

Kendra didn't say anything. She knew of the six Ramirez brothers. They were hitmen for hire. They primarily did work for the various cartels and criminal elements. They had a reputation for being ruthless and murderous. She was hoping that their paths never crossed. Now that hope was just a bad thought.

Ronaldo said, "We don't need the Ramirez brothers, Pop. We have never allowed the Death Squad to track this psycho, but they are now. I told them to get to work."

"Good for you, Ronaldo," snarled Senior. The old man began standing and Junior stood up to help his father. Senior put his hand on the table to balance himself. Junior stood behind him, ready to catch him if he fell or possibly to help him sit back down in his wheelchair. Kendra also stood up to be there for her father.

"Death Squad!" Senior directed his comments to Ronaldo. "The overpaid, underworked assholes who are happier with hanging out at that damn club, then doing actual work?"

Ronaldo leaned forward in his seat and said incredulously, "Pop, every job that we have given them, they have done what we needed them to do. You said to keep them out of the city, because you didn't want the city running red with blood. You didn't want them randomly killing people. Well, guess what? This fucking Brick is killing our soldiers and setting off bombs throughout the fucking city. We need him gone. We have the Feds...the DEA, ATF, FBI and who knows how many more alphabet agencies coming this way. Even though they may be coming after Brick, guess what? We will all get caught in the crossfire."

The father traded a glance with his son. Hector Senior was mad. He realized that he was too old for this junk. He truly wanted to turn the whole operation over to one of his sons, but they all had disappointed him, especially his two youngest. Senior knew he had messed up. He punished Arturo and Junior for not killing the monster named Zachary Brick.

The toughest thing for him to admit to himself was that he acted irrationally with the most dangerous man he had ever encountered. That's why they were at this detrimental point. His youngest had entered into an arrangement that was suicidal.

Now death was at his door and like five years ago, death still had the same name . . .

. . . *Zachary Brick.*

CHAPTER 40

MOST OF THE WORLD WOULD
PREFER TO PLAY TIC TAC TOE...

They had been in the mayor's conference room for fifteen minutes. The silence was nerve-racking for a few in the room. Police Director Sam Wanamaker was accompanied by Robert Turner, his Chief of Internal Affairs, Jody Fontaine, his Deputy Chief of Detectives, and Major Cal Hillsmeier, his Chief of Detectives.

The mayor had called the meeting on this cold night. It was in response to four bombs going off in his city. Mayor Archibald conveyed to his police director that he and his chief of staff were called into a meeting with the DEA, FBI, ATF and a division chief from Homeland Security.

Fifteen minutes.

No one spoke. Director Wanamaker sat in the first chair to the left of the mayor's seat. Fontaine sat next to him, on his left. Major Turner sat a couple of seats down from Fontaine, while Cal sat across the table, four seats down from the head of the table.

Wanamaker didn't know what to think. Truthfully, he didn't want to think. He noticed that both Fontaine and Turner were on their phones, surfing the net or playing games, or doing whatever grown men do on their cell phones for fifteen minutes. He could never wrap his head around the fact that grown people were on their phones just as much as their children or grandchildren.

However, he was worried about Cal. The man had kept his eyes on the director and his deputy chief of detectives for most of the time that they had been in the room. Wanamaker knew his chief of detectives didn't trust him. However, Cal didn't make waves or cause trouble. The man kept his head down and just solved cases. He was also there for his detectives, giving them clues or ideas on their own cases. Wanamaker liked the man. He was by far the best chief of detectives he had ever been associated with, and in fact, better than himself. But he probably distrusted Cal just as much as Cal distrusted him.

Ten minutes later, Mayor Archibald and his chief of staff, Ryan Robison, walked in the room and went directly to the head of the table. Ryan sat to the right of his boss.

"It's late, and this may or may not be a quick meeting," stated Mayor Archibald tersely. He looked at those in attendance, not saying a word, as he stared at each one of them. He finally rested his eyes on Cal. "Major Hillsmeier, a car blows up on your street, not far from your house, and I'm told by Homeland that more than likely, the car was on your street because of reports that former detective, Zachary Brick, used to be a regular guest at your house. You care to explain?"

Cal didn't speak immediately. He and the mayor exchanged glances. He diverted his eyes for a quick second to look at his boss. Then he returned his glance to the mayor. "Mayor Archibald, I certainly don't mind answering your question. But let's make a deal." Before the mayor or anyone else could say anything, Cal continued talking, "I will tell you how Brick and I had a very good relationship. Even a friendly relationship. I'm happy to answer any question you may have. Then, we can discuss why Brick left bodies in your front yards."

"He also left a body in your yard!" the mayor yelled with vigor.

"True, Mr. Mayor. However, I'm sure it was just Brick's way of informing me that hell was about to rain down on the Bluff City."

"Counterproductive." It was the only word Sam Wanamaker needed to say to get everyone's attention. His hands were grasped together on the table. He looked at Cal, then back at the mayor. "Mr. Mayor, you called this meeting for a reason. I'm sure it had everything to do with your meeting tonight with the federal agencies.

"I think we all are a little exasperated and anxious for this to be over. I, for one, don't care about Cal and Brick's relationship." He looked at Cal when he made this statement. "I think we just need to be briefed and find out where we stand."

The mayor didn't immediately speak. Then he nodded his head at his chief of staff. With that, Ryan Robison began back briefing his fellow law enforcement officials.

"The mayor was summoned to the federal building," said the chief of staff with a voice of confidence. "I guess you could say I was his plus one. We were surprised with the presence of representatives from the FBI, ATF and DEA as well as the Shelby County mayor and our briefer, Special Agent Seth Painter from Homeland Security."

The CIA taught Cal how not to act surprised when he was actually feeling that way. He learned the true meaning of a poker face, or one with no identifiable facial expressions, like a raise of the brow or the growing effects of the eyes. He knew Seth Painter when he was in an official capacity at the CIA. Seth was a good man. He was a man who lived and bled CIA. Yes, he was now a man of action with Homeland Security, but Cal knew, the man was also, unofficially, still associated with the agency that taught them both.

"We were sure they summoned us to tell us they were taking over the case," continued Robison. "However, instead, Special Agent Painter told us that the federal government does not like bombs going off in a major city and scaring people into thinking we are under attack from terrorists. They deem this as a local challenge and felt it necessary to assign an FBI agent to team up with the MPD's team. Additionally, the ATF, in coordination with the DEA, will be conducting an investigation into the possible procurement of explosives and dangerous weapons. Their words. The DEA is involved because of the possible involvement of the Harvey family. Homeland Security is giving us three days to find Zachary Brick. If we are not successful, then they will... indeed, take over the investigation.

"Lastly, we did have one contentious area. Agent Painter wanted to know why we haven't arrested or brought our former detective Brick in for questioning if he is, in fact, the person responsible for this carnage. Also, his words. When I explained that we didn't have enough evidence and weren't one hundred percent sure it was Zachary Brick, he wanted to know if we knew of his whereabouts and if not, did we at least distribute a photograph of Brick. The agent turned two shades of red when I told him *no* on both accounts...and I thought he was going to blow a gasket when I told him that we didn't have any photographs of Brick."

Mayor Archibald intervened, "Then he wanted to know why we suspected former Detective Brick for the mess we had on our hands." The man was visually upset. "And that is a great question. No one has seen Brick nor has he communicated with anyone."

All eyes rested on Cal. "This is funny," said Cal. "If Brick had contacted or communicated with me, I would have let it be known. Or worst-case scenario, I would have asked him to come in for questioning. But I haven't heard from or seen the guy. I was checking on Detective Rivers' daughter, Sondra, but she is no longer staying at home. I do know that at one point she thought she was being followed or watched. She may be staying with friends or family, in a hotel or may have left town for a few days or a few weeks. Who knows?"

"We can no longer let this play out," added Mayor Archibald with tenseness and anger in his voice. "We have to bring Brick and the Harvey family to justice. Sighting or no sighting, I'm convinced that this motherfucker is running amok in our city. But Hillsmeier brought up a very good point. We can all play dumb, as if we don't know what he's talking about, but we do. Brick thinks that one or even all of us may be involved with the Harvey family, hence, the bodies in our yards...and he wants his pound of flesh. What I know of former detective Zachary Brick is that he is the most dangerous man I have ever come across. And he is equally smart and conniving."

The mayor left it there as he walked to the door with Ryan Robison in toll. Then he stopped at the door and turned around to face his law enforcement officials.

"Three days people. I don't want the Feds to take over this case and more importantly, I don't want Brick killing any of us."

CHAPTER 41

I KNOW THE TRUE MEANING OF FEAR...DO YOU?

They had been on the road for four hours. Max was driving a five-year old Mercedes-Benz GL-Class SUV. She had awakened Sondra at two in the morning, told her to finish packing and be ready to roll in an hour. Forty minutes later they were on the road. The young woman had been asleep since their departure.

"Why did we leave so early?" asked Sondra, as she had been drifting in and out of sleep for the past thirty minutes. "I thought we were leaving tonight at eight or nine o'clock."

"Brick needs us," replied Max. She was focused, but her mind was elsewhere. She and Brick were a team. Throughout their time together, each had accomplished individual assignments and the occasional assignment together. But truthfully, none of their missions were an individual effort. They were a team. It didn't matter who got paid. They worked together and they killed together.

But this was different. She knew that from the start. She saw the same video that the rest of the country saw. She knew he would go it alone.

However, she had to be realistic. She loved the man and she was the one who had to be his rock and his conscience. Hearing about the explosions in Memphis meant one thing—Zachary

Brick was the man in love with a woman who was brutally murdered. Now, Hunt Collins had reemerged and he would seek and get vengeance.

And she had to be there to save him from himself.

"Max, you okay?" asked Sondra. She was fully awake now.

"Yeah, I'm good."

"Are you going to let me drive?" the young woman asked.

"Definitely!" said Max, with excitement in her voice. She looked at the girl, who smiled. "Brick told me that when he first met you, you were suspended from school for kicking the shit out of three boys that were bigger than you."

Sondra had picked up a container containing grapes and fresh pineapple from the small cooler in the back seat. "He told you the truth," stated Sondra, as she picked up some grapes and put them in her mouth. "Did he tell you everything?" Sondra asked.

"Everything like what?"

"I was suspended for three days. This happened on a Tuesday. My mom took the rest of the week off. The parents wanted me to be charged with assault. It didn't matter that I was nine and every last one of them outweighed me by twenty or thirty pounds."

Max didn't respond. Internally, her heart was warm with laughter. She waited patiently for Sondra to resume her story. Although there was no blood between them, she looked at the man with many names and the girl named Sondra as father and daughter. Yes, the two of them would never look at each other that way, but Max knew without a doubt, these two were truly kin.

"The next day, something crazy happened," continued Sondra. "My mom received a phone call to turn on the evening news. When she did, there was a news crew talking about a little girl at my school who had beaten up three boys who were trying to rape her. The reporter said that the kids' names would not be released because of their ages. But supposedly, I exacted revenge on the three of them for molesting other little girls in my school.

"Just like that, the tables had turned. The reporter said the three had been bullying little girls at the school the entire school year...which was true...and should be sent to juvenile court."

"I don't get it. What happened overnight?" Max asked. Her interest was genuine. Brick hadn't told her the rest of the story.

Sondra smiled. "You know what happened. Zachary Brick happened." She reached for more grapes. "Four mothers gave an account of what the boys had done to their daughters. The Board of Education suspended the principal and assistant principal of the school. The next day, it was on the front page."

She then put some pineapple in her mouth. "That afternoon, someone from the Board of Education came and gave my mom a check for $100,000 and some papers to sign that said she wouldn't sue. My mother wouldn't sign unless the other mothers received the same amount. They did."

"What did Brick do?" Max's curiosity was getting the best of her.

"I don't know for sure. My mother and I never talked about it. The more I got to know Zach, the more I realized that he was the one who made things happen. In less than twenty-four hours, whomever he had talked to or whatever he had done made the city spend a half million dollars and the only thing I had done was bait three boys into the girls' restroom, so I could kick the shit out of them. That's what I did.

"The true gist of what Brick had done was put a smile on my mom's face. Made her believe in others. For my mom, that was a win. Plus, he did something my father never had. He showed a woman and her daughter what love was about."

CHAPTER 42

Words from the grave will re-kill dead souls.

Since receiving Alaina's laptop and thumb drives from Lucy Bankwell, I had looked at them for hours on end. I had left the house several times and had come back to see the laptop and thumb drives sitting on a small side table on the left side of my computer station. I felt strange. There was a finality to both items. A finality that I didn't want to think about.

I inserted the thumb drive into my desktop computer. It was a 27-inch monitor with a built-in hard drive. There was only one file on the thumb drive titled, *My Love*. I reluctantly clicked on the file.

"First, I love you," stated Alaina. She was wearing a see-through black lingerie slip that fell down just below her crotch area. She was beautiful. Her short, reddish-brown hair was unkempt and it made her look sexier than she already was. I stared at her eyes and once again, she melted my heart.

She had a hairbrush in her right hand and started singing Teena Marie's *If I Were A Bell*. It was the first song she had ever sung to me. Unfortunately, it would be the last.

Her eyes were sparkling. Her face and smile...glowing. She had a beautiful voice. I missed her voice, missed her singing. I missed the way she moved, as if she was performing, as if she was singing to me. She was...singing...to me.

While she was singing, the computer was flipping back and forth between her and a collage of photographs of us. With every song, with every photo, my heart broke just a little bit more. There was a reason I hadn't looked at the thumb drive or the lap top. I knew the emotions it would stir within every fiber of my body.

I had been fighting the urge to kill everyone I thought was responsible for her death. I knew if I had done it my way, I would have been in and out of this city within three days. But I would have endangered Sondra's life.

That was a deal breaker.

I loved Alaina's facial expressions when she sang. She was full of emotions and it showed on her face. From joyous smiles to serious grimaces, each note, each lyric brought an emotion to her face.

I loved this woman.

I missed this woman.

After the song was over, she was still full of emotion. She had to take several deep breaths before she could fully engage and communicate to the camera.

"The crazy thing, the thing I know that's not true," she began. "Is that we are looking at this together and laughing at me for putting this video together." She smiled. I could tell she had a lot of thoughts flowing around in her head. That smile. It was breathtaking.

"I honestly don't know how many of these thumb drives I have made, but this one was the hardest to make. I was thinking that this was it, that I had finally broken the case, but everyone I should be able to depend...and expected to depend, was not there when I need them."

She paused again. "Honestly, babe, I don't know how that sounds, but I freaking love you and I'm kicking myself in the butt for having so much pride in having to see this case through, instead of just giving it up to spend my life with you. Zachary, I apologize to you. If you are watching this, I truly apologize. I got so obsessed with cleaning up a city and bringing a family to justice, despite knowing that I'm probably the only one in this damn city that even gives a damn.

"But the bottom line, my last eight years have been great. I thank you for that. Before you came into my life, I had Sondra and I had work. I was a piss poor mom. I preferred work over my own daughter. I raised her like my mom had raised me, to depend on herself and no one else, including me, her mom. You made me see how stupid that was. At times, I was jealous of you and Sondra. While I was out there acting a fool, you were home bonding and taking care of my daughter. You were the parent she didn't have."

I saw a tear roll down her face. "Thank you for making me be the mom I needed to be...the mom I wanted to be. For everything you did for me at home, you did for me at work as well. I owe you so very much...and the only thing you wanted was me."

She held her head down. She was crying. I felt bad. Then I was mad. I could see how distraught she was, how hurt she was. I so wish I could have been there. I wish she had called me and just told me to come back to Memphis and kill everybody.

Another collage of photographs flashed on the monitor. It was a collage of Sondra, from her as a baby to the here and now, the present. This was followed by a collage of me, then a collage of Alaina, and lastly to a collage of all of us in various photographs.

Then, she was back on the screen. She was together. Her hair was in place and she had on a little makeup. Now she was wearing a red bra with white hearts and matching panties.

More importantly, she was smiling.

"Ok, I love your black ass," she said. "First, take care of my daughter. I love her. And she loves you. Maybe my death will bring her and her father closer, but I doubt it. I don't give a damn. I love and care about you, and I know how much Sondra loves and cares about you. I pray that the two of you are father and daughter one day. She is a grown woman now, so you don't have to raise her, but be there for her. Keep her focused and if that means you getting and staying on her ass, then do what you have to do."

She paused again. She took in a couple of deep breaths. "I love you, Anton Hargreaves/Hunt Collins/Zachary Brick. Whatever name you call yourself, I love you. You have made my world special. You have filled my heart with love and hope. You have been the man I have always wanted in my life. As much as I want to say that there is so much to dislike about you, I can't. You opened my eyes, made me realize that there are good men out there. I know your flaws, but the good in you far outweighs anything else.

"When we are together, I feel love. When we are apart, I miss your touch, I miss your presence, I miss you."

Her eyes were sparkling again. She was still trying to keep her composure. "Be mad at me Zach. Be upset with me. But know that I love you. There are a million and one things I want to say, but I can't. When you met me, I didn't do emotional. That was a sign of weakness to me. You, Mr. Man, changed all of that. When it comes to you and Sondra, my emotions runneth over. I thank you for that."

Her smile got bigger. Then she blew me a kiss. "You are my love. You will always be in my heart. And you became my life, became my light and will always be the love of my life."

She threw me another kiss. I froze the frame. I don't know how long I had looked at Alaina's photo. I allowed my feelings to overtake my heart. So many thoughts, so many memories invaded my head. I smiled both inside and out.

We had a great run. I did blame myself. She was an independent woman and I never forced my hand or pressured her to make me a priority. I accepted her for who and what she was, and now, I was hating myself. I had options. I chose the wrong one.

I looked at the video two more times. I had new memories that flooded my mind, but also the same regrets.

Damn, I really love this woman.

CHAPTER 43

A LIE TOLD, IS A LIE REVEALED.

This whole undertaking was way too much for one person. But if one person had to tackle it, Detective Alaina Rivers was the right person for the job.

The name of the file was *Gotcha*. It was revealing. The file was huge, consisting of over two hundred written pages with fifteen headings and numerous videos, photographs and audio snippets. I read every word, listened to every audio, examined every photo and viewed every second of every video.

She was thorough and meticulous. She had been very busy, especially with Sondra being in college now. She had a list of every stash house, warehouse and storage location. Plus, she had a list of every gang, gang member and thug associated with the Harvey family. She had clearly done her homework, as she also had a list of every business location that sold drugs and the passwords for each location. If you patron Peterson's Camera Store in North Memphis, the passwords were *Mariana's Zoom Lens*. At Riverside Bookstore downtown, it was *Cynthia's Web*. Of course, there was no such thing as *Mariana's Zoom Lens* or any book named *Cynthia's Web*. It was laughable in some aspects, but it got the job done.

It was pure genius regarding the information she had obtained and accumulated. Of her many lists, one included a list of cops and local city officials who worked for or who were involved with the Harvey family. At the top of this list were the names Jody Fontaine and Smokey Franklin. Mayor Archibald and Director Wanamaker also made the list. Both had question marks at the end of their names. Major Robert Turner, the Chief of Internal Affairs and Ryan Robison, the mayor's chief of staff were on the list as well. All had their own heading, except Wanamaker.

I read it all. Fontaine and Franklin were in deep with the Harveys. If Alaina was right, Fontaine was also the intermediary between the Harveys and the mayor. She had fifteen pages of information on Fontaine, as well as several videos, photographs and audio recordings of Fontaine with Harvey crime members. She had illegally bugged Fontaine's work phone, as well as other members of the MPD, including the director, chief of internal affairs and the mayor's chief of staff.

I wasn't surprised, but I wondered how in the hell Alaina got access to every office long enough to plant listening devices in their phones.

She had done the blue-collar work. The dirty work.

Fontaine was a busy man. He had his fingers in a little bit of everything. I understood why Alaina bugged the office phones. Major Turner was the chief of internal affairs and he was in deep as well. If anything came back on any of the other law enforcement types, Turner could kill the inquiry. Therefore, using the office phones was safe for anyone working for the Harveys. Lieutenant Jody Fontaine took full advantage of that luxury. He talked to the Harveys every day. From his conversations, I surmised that he had three cell phones.

Fontaine and I needed to have a conversation.

I was surprised Alaina had anything on the Garsay crime family. That section was riddled with question marks, which I knew was promising, but it was difficult trying to establish the connection between the Garsay family and the Harvey family. I was proud of the woman I loved. But it was crazy as I considered the amount of information she had on everyone and everything.

I saved the information on Detective Smokey Franklin for last. Although I thought that Alaina had trusted Smokey, I was completely wrong. Franklin worked for the Harveys, but he also worked for himself. He had several women who worked for the MPD working as quasi prostitutes for him. It was an extortion ring. They would set up dates with city officials, and movers and shakers throughout the Mid-South region, which included neighboring towns outside of Memphis in Arkansas and Mississippi. Conveniently, Smokey would be outside with his long-range zoom lens taking pictures. It was a good racket, and a lucrative one.

I was mad at myself again. I should have called on Lucy Bankwell as soon as I hit the city. Additionally, even after I received the laptop from Lucy, I should have looked at the *Gotcha* file. It had everything I needed. It detailed the inner workings of the entire Harvey enterprise.

I knew everything I needed to know now. Except one thing. On numerous pages, she had the words *federal official* double underlined and circled. On the last page, she had written in red ink and tripled underlined *Point man – federal official – Who is the federal official?*

Federal was my territory. I knew the federal official. Or, at least, I thought I knew the federal official. We had history. He wanted me dead. I used to know his secrets, but that was years ago. Evidently, he had new secrets.

If he had anything to do with Alaina's death, I planned on putting him six feet under.

Part Three

GAME ON

CHAPTER 44

DAY ONE.

I wanted to hate this spot. Hell, I couldn't. How could I? It represented so much to me...and to so many others. I was in the parking lot of the National Civil Rights Museum on the outskirts of downtown Memphis. Those in the city called it the Lorraine Motel, the original name of the motel where Reverend Dr. Martin Luther King, Jr. had been assassinated.

It was Alaina's favorite place. I got it. How could I not get it? I had the heat on low in the car. Mentally, I was in a place. There was indifference on my part. I wanted to be here, yet, I also didn't want to be here. But I realized it was about Alaina. Or better yet, it was the thoughts about Detective Rivers. Thoughts of her usually put me in a great mood, like this morning. At other times, sadness gripped my heart. Made me hate life. Made me want to burn this damn city to the ground.

But it was a passing thought. A stupid thought.

I wasn't sleepy, but I still closed my eyes and allowed my mind to relax and my thoughts to take me to another time...but the same place.

"Tell me about Zachary Brick," Alaina asked me, as we walked around the museum. We were a couple now and I had always been able to escape this type of conversation. We were on-duty, but coming to this place had become our lunchtime ritual, if we happened to be in the area.

We were in the slavery exhibit. We were regular customers, but Alaina more so than me—the staff knew her by first name and title. Regardless, I loved spending time at the museum. One of the staff members once said to us, "You guys are a helluva pair. What a contrast." I knew what she meant. I was black and Alaina looked white. During that time, she had just chopped her usually shoulder length red locks into something shorter. As with most natural redheads, she had some freckles, but not many. She was the truest sense of the word redbone. I had seen photographs of her father and though both of her father's parents were African-American, he was the whitest black man I had ever seen. Alaina was the spitting image of her father in so many ways, including her skin tone.

In many ways, I was afraid of Alaina. I was definitely afraid to get too close to her. We were partners, but we had established a friendship as well. We had crossed the threshold, and as much as I tried to stay out of her life, I couldn't.

I knew that it was because I didn't want to. At that point in our partnership...our relationship, I had been in Memphis for three years. Alaina and Sondra were now family to me. They both had my heart.

That was the problem. We did feel for each other. It was new territory for me. Uncharted waters. I was trying my best to tread lightly.

"Not much to tell Laney," I lied. "Just another man, another detective with a boring life. Nothing spectacular about my life. Equally, nothing too devastating."

I lied on both counts. My life was one of excitement. I knew plenty of guys who wished they had my life. I wasn't one of those guys. I would have easily traded it all for love, a woman of my own and a family. Hell, I didn't like dogs, but wish I had the wife, two and a half kids, a dog and the big white house with the picket fence. It was good enough for most average Americans, so why couldn't it be good enough for me?

I realized I was thinking about telling Alaina my pipe dream. For most CIA officers, especially those in my line of work, the excitement wasn't worth a damn after the second or third adventure, and likewise, risking your life is never good. I was a wanted man, and after defecting from the CIA, I still didn't know why they had wanted me dead.

I guess I should say that I really didn't know the original reason they came hunting for me. I knew all too well now though. I didn't, or couldn't, blame them now. With the exception of Max, I had killed all the assassins who had hunted me, all who had come to deliver me home.

"Brick, you had a life before Memphis," Alaina stated. "It's a life you may never share with me. But boring. No, Detective Brick. There is nothing boring about the man with the fake name."

She stunned me with that statement. "What makes you think my name is not Zachary Brick?"

"I can recall on at least three occasions, where someone called out a name and you turned your head as if they were referring to you," she declared. "And it wasn't just one name, it was different names. Brick, if you are CIA, I know about the thing called *legends*. Every time you take another name for a mission, that new name becomes your next *legend*. I say CIA, but you could be MI-6 or Interpol. Hell, there are probably a dozen agencies you could be a part of."

"Sorry to disappoint, Laney, but Zachary Brick is my God-given name." Every word was spoken with confidence and every word was a lie. My life was one full of lies. Hell, I could lie even before I became a member of the Company. It was a natural part of me. The lies flowed and I could tell a story or two or three without missing a beat. Without mistaking the facts.

I knew of every incident she had mentioned. It was human nature to succumb to being a human being. She was right. I reacted to someone calling a name, an old legend. She was equally right that Zachary Brick was a legend I had made up.

As we continued to walk around the museum, it was somewhat awkward. The lady knew she was right. That was her superpower, her quiet confidence. She was as observant as anyone I had ever known.

We stopped walking. I looked at Alaina and she looked sad. "What is it?" I asked.

"Hold me," she replied. I did as she requested. This was unusual for us. We didn't do public displays of affection. Plus, we were on duty. But if she asked me to hold her, something was going on.

"What's going on? You okay?"

It took her almost a minute to reply. During that time, I kissed the top of her head a couple of times and gently rubbed my hands over her back.

"I never really told you why I like coming here," she said. "My father's uncle was a sanitation worker here in Memphis. He is one of the men that Dr. King came to Memphis to fight for. Plus, my grandfather lived in Mississippi during that time, and he and his brother, that same uncle, were at Dr. King's last speech, *I've Been to the Mountaintop.*

"I remember my grandfather telling me that many in attendance that night realized Dr. King knew the end was coming soon. I loved my grandfather, Zach. He talked to me like I was somebody. Yes, he saw me as his granddaughter, but he saw so much more. He saw me as a little girl who would grow into a young woman, someone who would one day have to make a decision on her race. He knew it wouldn't be easy. He told me that both he and his wife, my grandmother, as well as my father had dealt with the same issue. All three of them could have easily passed as white, but they each identified as black."

She looked up at me. Her eyes were glassy, but I knew no tears would be released. She let me go and her hands went to my hands. "I made my decision as well, Zach. I was a black woman and as such, put black or African-American down on every form or application I have ever filled out. But I didn't shout it from the highest rooftop or put out an ad in a newspaper, I just accepted it. There are those in the department that know and with some, it's a big deal, with others, not so much.

"But I come here because it keeps me connected to my family. My great uncle had a light brown complexion, like you, and he and my grandfather were so close, as close as two brothers could be. I remember the stories they used to tell, or I should say, the shit they used to talk, when they were together. Regardless of all of the racism and hate they had experienced, they had endured and survived. That's why I love this place. That's why I love being a detective. I want to help people to endure and survive."

The conversation had ended. The love I felt for the woman grew exponentially that day, and at that moment. The woman I occasionally called Laney was indeed one hell of a detective, but even more telling, was a very good woman. She had the qualities that any man wanted in a woman. She was my saving grace and she loved me. And I loved her.

The lies I told, like being named Zachary Brick, she would let go—for now. The next time the subject would come up in conversation, it would be me who would bring it up.

It went without saying that I couldn't get my mind off Alaina. We had tons of unfinished business. That was on me. It would always be on me. However, that day was special to me. It was as if I was seeing her for the first time. It was that thought that haunted me day and night. She shared with me and eventually I would share my life with her. But we would never call each other husband and wife. That was disappointing and painful.

I loved a woman. That woman loved me back.

As partners, she saw all the bad traits of my legends. I had prayed that she would never see the worst of my legends. I don't believe she ever did. I was happy for that.

Tonight, the city would bleed red.

CHAPTER 45

OLD LIES DIE HARD...SO SAY THE TRUTH TELLERS.

"Fuck, it isn't supposed to get this cold in Memphis," stated the tall man, who had just sat down in the passenger seat of my SUV. Seth Painter was once my chief in two directorates in the CIA and the lead officer on most of my assignments. Deb Hillsmeier was my handler for most of that time, and both Deb and I reported to Seth Painter.

Seth was always funny to me. Throughout our years together, his distinguishing features were always his hair and glasses. One would think it was his height since he stood six three. Another aspect about the man that made him stand out to me was that he was the direct opposite of his northeastern upbringing. His New England accent had abandoned him years ago, as well as his *clear* complexion—as he used to refer to it. At our initial meeting, I thought the man needed sun worse than the rain forest needed water. Plus, his hair was dirty blonde and curly, and as high as any Afro. His glasses were brown rimmed and big. Looking at old photographs today, the younger generation would call them coke bottle glasses.

But now, Seth was a different person externally. His head was bald and he wore small, rectangular, gold-rimmed framed glasses.

"Stop being a baby, Mr. D.C.," I stated. Seth was wearing a long, dark blue overcoat. I was sure there was a fur liner inside. He was official today, as he had on a suit under his overcoat. I knew the man very well, which in my mind meant he had at least three guns on his person, two underneath his suitcoat and one on his ankle. "You leave D.C., where it is colder, then become a wimp of a man."

"Fuck you...Zach," he smiled as I looked at him. "Yeah, even after all these years, it still feels funny calling you Zachary Brick or even to hear anyone refer to you as Zachary Brick."

I never thought I would adapt to the name as I had. But it was a part of me now. I more than accepted it. I relished in the name. It was the name both Alaina and Sondra knew me by—and that meant something to me.

"Bombs...really?" We were still looking at each other. Seth wasn't happy. "Every fucking body who is somebody in D.C. wants to know what in the hell is happening in Memphis, Tennessee. Do we have a case of international terrorism or domestic terrorism, or is it just some damn fool, like a distraught ex-cop wanting revenge for his girlfriend's death?"

I responded, "You know better, and come on, Painter, I know you, I'm sure you have briefed the White House, Capitol Building and all the powers-to-be what the score is here. Most likely, you informed everyone that what needs to happen is for you to come down to support the local officials and run roughshod over several alphabet agencies, while taking advantage of this time away from the wifey to pig out on good barbeque.

"And play the short con. Tell the governor and mayor that this is their issue for now and they have three days to solve their issue. Then, after three days, when they come begging for more time, you will give them another three days to bring this to closure."

Seth was back smiling again. "Two additional days. I have to get back to Virginia. You know, Christmas and gifts and all that jazz."

"You are still a dick, you know that?" I shook my head while smiling. Our history was deep. The man had taught me a lot over the years. More than that, he had been there for me. Our relationship was truly mutual.

"I talked to Max," said Seth. "She was leaving tonight, but she is already on the road. I didn't ask her why, but I'm asking you."

"Sondra wants to come home," I said before he expounded on his thought. It was a lame answer. It really was a topic I didn't want to broach. But that was the Seth I knew. He solved problems. It didn't matter if it was professionally or socially, he was good at what he did.

"Your baby girl wants to be close to the father she knows," he retorted. "She is also afraid that she will lose you too and wants to spend as much time with you as possible. But you know . . ." He looked at me with his head cocked towards the window. "She shouldn't be in Memphis. You really don't need Max. Hell, I know you have five or six men here in the city already."

"How do you know that?"

"Makes sense. You placed eight bodies in the yards of five city officials. Only a damn fool would think you did that by yourself."

"Stop it, Painter! You know Cal would have nipped that in the bud from day one. He has my back."

"Cal didn't bring it up, but it doesn't mean someone else couldn't have."

Seth was right. The police department wasn't overwhelmed. They just had too many agendas. At least half of the department was corrupted by the Harveys and the other half was trying their best to keep the stink away. That's how the loyalty to Detective Rivers fell—half thinking she should have minded her own business and the other half hoping justice is served in the name of Alaina Rivers.

"The FBI sent two profilers to work with the locals," Seth stated. "I laughed to myself when they were describing the former detective who came back to the city to seek his vengeance on the Harvey crime family. They said that you, without question, loved the female detective, but that you are a narcissist and blame yourself for her death. And because you left the department prematurely, it was your fault.

"Then I realized my laugh was premature as well. There is a lot of sense to everything they are saying. You need to tread lightly sir. A good profile is half the battle, right?"

I didn't say anything. I allowed my mind to travel. I heard Painter. Loud. And. Clear. It wasn't anything new. The FBI profilers probably mimicked the same thoughts of the MPD's profilers. The Bureau gave more credence to the analysis, however. Hell, I didn't care. I had my issues. The man sitting next to me knew those issues all too well.

Max, Painter and I were all connected now. However, Painter was there from day one. He was the one who recruited me and paved my way in the CIA. He was my boss and the one who taught me how to navigate life in the Company, as well as how to find the true me. When the Company decided to come after me, Painter stepped aside and let the CIA send killer after killer to eliminate me. When that didn't work, they went back to Painter and he sent Max to take me out. He knew something I didn't know—that I would like the lady and that I wouldn't take her out like I had taken out the previous operatives sent to kill me.

Painter had a plan. That plan included he, Max and I forming a team and working out of the hometown of his paternal grandparents, Shelbytown, Texas. The business was still death. Seth kept his government job in D.C., and Max and I would live a normal life in Shelbytown, while accomplishing the occasional kill throughout the world. During this time, I took a five-year semi-sabbatical working as a detective in Memphis. I still did the occasional job for Painter, but he allowed me to do what I wanted to do—to become a detective and fall in love.

I was assigned a job in Memphis. Prior to accomplishing my assignment, one of the detectives assigned to the case was a beautiful redheaded detective named Alaina Rivers. I made a request to Painter to allow me to be a detective in Memphis. He granted me my wish. For five years, I was a detective. Now I felt bad for leaving...and felt worse for coming to Memphis and becoming a part of Alaina and Sondra's lives.

"I don't need to tread lightly," I said. My tone was calm. "Cal told me that they have ten to fifteen artist depictions of me, but no actual photographs. Every sketch is different and no two sketches look alike. You are giving me five days to do what I need to do. I just may do it in three days. But you can expect several more bombs and multiple deaths.

"That, I promise you."

The tall man didn't say anything. He was looking straight ahead. I knew there was a lot he wanted to say, but he kept his thoughts to himself.

He was right, I had six guys in the city, but this wasn't their fight. It was my fight. They were there in case I needed them. They too lived in Shelbytown. Although I had told them to go back home, they refused. They were in touch with Max. She too knew this was my battle...my battle alone.

Painter opened his door and slid his right foot out. Then he looked at me. "You don't have to do this alone. I'm here if you need me."

"I know. I will need you. It will turn the city upside down, but I will need a favor on this one. Huge favor."

"I love my wife, Brick," said Painter, as he held the door open, looking at me. "Easily, she is the best thing that ever happened to me. But I don't think I have ever known anyone to love anyone as much as you loved Detective Rivers."

I didn't say anything. "I got you, Brick. From day one, I have always had your back. I can't imagine that ever changing. Tell me what and when, and I will be there or I will make whatever happen. Just let me know." With that, he was gone.

I sat there for another five minutes wallowing in my self-pity. Then I got out the car and made my way inside the National Civil Rights Museum. I wanted to feel the energy of Alaina Rivers one more time, before I hit the start button on my three-day countdown.

CHAPTER 46

Pᴀʀɪꜱ ɪꜱ ʙᴜʀɴɪɴɢ.

It wasn't the answer Sondra was looking for. Internally, she smiled. She recalled her mother providing long replies to what she thought were short questions, and she would start every answer the same way, "I remember when." She missed that, just as much as she missed her mom. One more story. One more lesson. Even if it was just one more syllable, she wished Alaina Rivers was there to give her a kiss on the forehead before she went to bed, or school, or came home from work.

She thought her question to Max was simple. "How does Zach do the things that he does?"

Max's answer was immediate. "Paris is burning," followed by silence.

Sondra was now driving and had allowed Max to get some sleep. During that time, Sondra had allowed her thoughts to drift to happier days. She loved the holiday season, as her mother had, who ingrained in her the true reason and joy of the season. She missed so much about her mother and something as simple as spending a night together in pajamas and watching Christmas movies was not lost on her. Then her mother would tell her about her childhood and she would learn about her grandmother and grandfather, followed by stories about her grandfather's father.

She learned a lot about her mother during this time of the year. That was heavy on her mind.

That was why she was happy when Max woke up—to keep her from weeping and reminiscing.

"That was my danger phrase when I was in trouble," said Max as she looked at the road. She knew Sondra was a captured audience and the young woman was mesmerized by stories of her pseudo father.

Max continued, "I had accepted a job in the Netherlands. However, within a couple of hours of being in the country, Zach had called me and told me that it was a set-up. I was stunned. I knew the CIA was not happy with me, but I don't think I truly understood what that meant...until that moment. Zach told me where to go, whom to ask for and sent me a couple of photographs of the couple that would hide me out. As skeptical as I was, I followed his directions and within a day he was there to save me, to rescue me.

"And Sondra, I wanted to know what you want to know, 'how does he do the things that he does'?"

Laughter filled the car.

"Bottom line, Zachary Brick is so many things," Max continued. "But the one thing he is for sure, is a good man, a good person, with a big heart. I promise you, the ratio of those he has helped to those he has killed is probably ten to one. Trust me, he has killed his share of men."

Max suddenly felt bad at her comments. Yes, Sondra knew the business Zachary was in, but not to what extent. She looked at Sondra, who was focused on the road. Her facial expression hadn't changed.

"I'm good," stated Sondra, as she turned her head quickly to show Max that she was indeed, alright. "Both you and my mom have told me things, but even so, you try to sugar coat the stories and paint a cleaner picture of Zach. I do know that it is a true picture though, when you both describe the kind of guy he is. He is one helluva man and so good in so many ways. But his love for my mom, for me...and for you probably make him the most dangerous man in America, if not the world.

Max kept her eyes on the young woman. "Damn, I wish I had been that mature when I was your age. I wish I had viewed life through your eyes when I was nineteen. I didn't know if I was coming or going at that age. Hell, I had wished I had a father like Brick when I was a kid, while trying to learn and figure out this crazy thing called life."

"Your dad wasn't there for you?" asked Sondra, as she took the coffee thermo mug from Max. She took a small swallow. "Mmmm. That's good. You're right, these mugs are good. It's still hot after all these hours."

"Yeah, they are pretty good." Max looked away, looking out the window as they were making their way through Oklahoma. "Like you, Sondra, I knew my father, but he really wasn't in my life." The words were slow and methodical, and said with a tinge of sadness, or maybe remorse.

"I'm sorry to hear that," Sondra said politely.

Max liked the young woman. She knew her words were true. She knew that the time Sondra had spent with her had been educational. Not only to the young woman, but to Max as well. She hadn't directly told Sondra she was an assassin, but she had implied as much in the many stories she had told the young woman.

Max debated on whether she would tell Sondra her story. Her thought was that maybe her story would shed some light on Zach's story. It was a quick thought before she said, "My mother was French and she was an au pair for the France ambassador to the United States. The ambassador was a widower and had three children. My mom was in her early twenties at the time. She loved those kids and preferred to be in the United States.

"Then one day, she met a business colleague of the ambassador. They secretly saw each other for a couple of years before my mom got pregnant with me. Well, the ambassador didn't like that, and to say it was an awkward situation would be an understatement. So, she was shipped back to France and resettled in her hometown of Dijon, in the Burgundy region, which was southeast of Paris. A beautiful area."

Still looking out the window, she allowed her mind to wander back to Dijon and the three-bedroom flat she and her mom lived in for a while. "I met my father when I was three years old. He was a tall man. Of course, when I was a kid, I didn't have a clue about age. My mom was still in her twenties and my father was in his forties. He was one of those people who aged young. He had silver hair, with a silver mustache and facial hair. I wish I could say that I really remember that first meeting, but I don't. My mom told me it though. I remember but my father visiting us three or four times a year for seven years straight before he moved us back to the United States. We didn't live with my dad, but we usually saw him a couple of times per week. But my mom was happy, so I was happy."

She finally turned her head. Sondra saw the seriousness on her face. "My mom never wanted me to ask questions. So, I never asked her questions. But my dad...we were close and he talked to me. There were no secrets between us. He told me that he was the lead special agent at the State Department and was married with two sons older than me. I didn't care. He loved both me and my mom, and that's all I cared about.

"We were happy for ten years, but then one day my father appeared at my apartment in Reston, Virginia and whisked me away with just the clothes on my back. He took me to a plane at Dulles Airport and from there we flew to Paris. He told me that his oldest son had learned about me and my mom, and had killed my mom. He was truthful with me. He also told me that he couldn't see his son in jail, but equally, he just wanted to get me away from the States."

Once again, Max turned her head to look out the window. She wished she could say that these thoughts had been suppressed for years. But that would be a lie. Her mother's death and everything that followed afterwards would always be in the front of her mind.

"Life can be crazy, Sondra. After my father told me about my mom, I didn't shed a tear. Instead, my father teared up and quietly cried for the next hour. I was so catatonic, and in shock, that I just didn't know what to say, or what to do. Maybe that was the first time I knew I was different.

"My father took me to a safe house and within a couple of days, I had my own place in Paris. Over the years, my father had taught me how to shoot, how to use a knife and how to be observant...essentially, how to be a spy or badass or whatever I needed to be. In other words, I could protect myself. He knew that. He set up an account for me with a $100,000 and sent my mom's body back to be buried in her native Dijon."

She then turned her head back around. "Remember how I told you that my father and I had this great relationship."

Sondra answered a barely audible, "Yes."

"I lied. He didn't tell me everything. His son was also an agent with the State Department—like father, like son. He had cut my mom's throat and shot her four times in her upper body. Disappointing, to say the least. However, within a couple of weeks of burying my mom, I saw on television that my dad had committed suicide. As soon as I heard, it, I knew it was a lie. It was a couple of days later when I had officially received the money

254 | John A. Wooden

from my mom's life insurance policy. A half million dollars. I had talked to my dad the night before and he had handed in his retirement papers and was calling it quits. Then he supposedly committed suicide. This time, I did cry and felt bad. Everything my father had taught me, came back to me. I realized why he had trained me like I was one of his agents."

Once again, Max got quiet. This time the silence was long. Sondra looked at Max several times, but didn't want to disturb her thoughts. She got it now. She knew why her mother and Zach had steered her to Texas to stay with a woman that she didn't know. If Zach knew Max's story, and she was sure he did, then she was sure that her mom knew as well.

"You okay, Max?" Sondra asked.

"Yeah, I'm perfect, Sondra." The young woman had noticed the change in Max's voice. Her voice had been somber and sad while she told her story. Now, she was back to normal, full of confidence and full of fiber. Sondra didn't get it...and she hoped that the story wasn't over.

"Back to your original question," Max said. "How does Zach do the things he does? Easily. Connections. My father had a couple of new identities for me, the insurance money and three places throughout France that I could call my own. Oh, and the weapons. Plus, in France and here in the States, I had people I could reach out to.

"And that's the magic of Zachary Brick. That big heart he has is magnetic. People gravitate to him. He has done so much for so many. Even when he was a detective, most of the force had loved him just as much as they had loved your mom. As long as I have known him, he has been good at winning people over. Not with his winning personality. But with his actions. In some instances, those actions included dishing out money. Other instances may have included finding a son or daughter, a mother or father. Then occasionally, he may have had to beat down an abusive father or husband. Whatever you needed, Zach was your man. Then, you owed him. But often times, you never had to pay him back. If you did pay him back, it was with a favor here or there, and guess what? Then he felt that he owed you back."

"He is pretty special," stated Sondra, with a slight smile on her face.

"Yes, he is very special," Max agreed, with a bigger smile on her face.

CHAPTER 47

THE BURDEN OF PROOF!

Gloria Berkley was a beautiful woman. She and I had never officially met. I wasn't sure if she knew me or not. I knew her. She was a uniformed cop who worked out of the Tillman Station. Memphis believed in police stations, instead of precincts.

She and her partner, Officer Sherman Robinette, had been having lunch at a small burger joint in a strip mall on Poplar Avenue, across from East High School. Her shoulder length brownish locks were up in a ball. Her dark blue uniform was tailored for a tight fit on her slender body. She looked more like a sexy police officer on a television show than the real deal. Most female cops were light with the makeup. Officer Berkley was not the typical cop.

She looked different than on the night I had seen her on the balcony. That was the night she had been having sex with a city commissioner, while Smokey Franklin took pictures. She was Smokey's main lady in his extortion ring of city officials and power brokers in the local metropolitan area, which included Memphis, the county and the outlying Arkansas Mississippi towns that bordered Memphis.

Her back was to the door. Sherman knew I was in the small diner. The burger joint only had five tables and a bar. It was reminiscent of the old-time burger and malt shops from the fifties and sixties. The grill and workers were visible to the customers at the bar. I knew the owner and the staff, and they didn't have an issue with me hiding out in the kitchen until Officers Berkley and Robinette made their entrance and sat down.

Sherman and I had agreed that they would sit at the end table. They were the only patrons for now. That detail was also planned. Sherman kept his eyes on the menu as I walked up. Berkley was also looking at her menu.

I put my gun to Berkeley's head. Sherman didn't say a word. "Slowly with your thumb and index finger, take your piece out of the holster and give it to me," I said.

She looked at me with her peripheral vision and I saw the tears forming in her eyes. Then she looked at Sherman.

"I don't usually repeat myself."

She did as I told her, as Sherman got up and picked her phone up off the table. Then he got on one knee, pulled up her left pant leg and secured her side piece from her leg holster. Then Sherman sat at the bar as I took his place at the table.

I said, "Place your hands on the table, so I can see them." She complied immediately. "Officers Allison Glasgow and Pearl Bake, Detective Abigail Richmond, and Lizzie Osman, an executive assistant in the Internal Affairs office, and one Officer Gloria Berkley." I let the names linger. I wanted her to think. The more the thoughts danced in her head, the more afraid she would get. Additionally, I wanted fear to kick her in the ass at that moment.

I could see the fear in her eyes. Equally, her eyes were also dancing and I could see her thoughts running amok. She was formulating a plan, trying to get the right words to say to me to clear herself. To make this go away.

"So, what do you have for me?" I asked.

258 | John A. Wooden

"What do you mean?" she answered my question with a question. She was still formulating her thoughts and with every second, I could see and feel her nervousness.

"Gloria, I don't give a fuck about you and Smokey's extortion ring. As far as I'm concerned, he can be a pimp and a detective, and you can be his number one girl, his recruiter and a police officer. I don't give a damn. But what I do give a damn about is Detective Rivers and how she died."

"Detective Brick, I don't know anything," Gloria said, as a few tears flowed down her face. She grabbed a couple of napkins out of the dispenser and blotted her eyes.

I gave her a halfhearted smile. I was good at reading eyes. I was convinced that the only time Officer Berkley had correctly read a person's eyes was when someone wanted to have sex with her.

"Okay, I will buy that," I responded. "I guess twenty or thirty years in jail will do you good."

"I'm not going to jail," she said incredulously. "We have photographs and recordings of some of the biggest names in Memphis. Not just recordings of sex, Detective. I personally have recordings of some of these assholes telling me things they would never want released."

"No, Gloria, you do not." Once again, I allowed my words to linger, to register in her mind that she just may be trouble. With the other four women, they had known they were in trouble when they first saw me. Each and every woman then told me that Gloria would be hard to break. I laughed then, and internally, I was laughing now.

"I have the recordings and the photographs. Look outside."

She slowly turned her head. What she saw made her turn a shade whiter. It was as if the blood had escaped her body. Beads of sweat formed on her forehead and her eyes were full with tears.

Cal was outside with three other detectives—detectives I knew. More importantly, they were detectives who knew and cared for their fellow detective, Alaina Rivers.

"Smokey was stupid...wanted what he couldn't have," she said, returning her gaze to me. "He wanted Alaina. She didn't want him. Plus, she still had her own things going on, like her secret cases that she didn't share with him. So, when the Harvey brothers approached him to feed them information on his partner, he agreed. In turn, they made him a rich man."

I didn't say anything. She correctly assumed that I wanted her to continue. "As far as the extortion ring—"

"I don't give a fuck about that," I interrupted. "Tell me about that night."

Her eyes were full of fear. She probably thought I wanted to kill her. I didn't. She was a cop. Alaina didn't want me to kill cops.

"Smokey told Alaina that one of his confidential informants had some information on a big deal going down at a warehouse on South Third. He said he didn't want anything to do with it, so he connected Alaina with his CI and he told Alaina what was up."

More tears formed in her eyes. "The CI worked for the Harvey brothers. They paid Smokey $250,000. That night, we kind of drank the night away. He felt guilty, but knew that if he didn't do it, they would kill him. He didn't have a choice."

While still looking at Officer Berkley, I signaled for Cal and his guys to come in and arrest their corrupt comrade. The game plan was simple. Cal would sit on the five females until he arrested Smokey later that night. For the time being, Cal had a couple of his detectives with eyes on Smokey. Equally, I had two of my guys with eyes on him.

I stood up and kept my eyes on the officer. "I remember when your mom died. Detective Rivers was there for you. She helped raise money, checked on you daily and even sat with you on several days. She was an amazing woman, one who stood up and went to bat for the other women on the force."

I didn't give a damn about the words lingering this time. There was a lot more I wanted to say. But chose to walk away.

As I walked out the door, Cal and his men walked in.

CHAPTER 48

THE POWER OF THE BADGE DOESN'T EQUAL
THE POWER OF THE GUN.

Sam Wanamaker was silent. If he had been Caucasian, he was sure that his complexion would be white as a sheet. He was hating the Harvey family, just as much as he was hating former Detective Brick. These were the days that he had been dreading, starting from the first day he ever heard of the Harvey crime family. Worst of all was he getting in bed with the family.

"Major, I miss simpler times," he said to Cal Hillsmeier. The two men were sitting in his office in two chairs that sat in front of his desk. He had brought out what he considered to be the good stuff, his favorite alcoholic beverage—Johnnie Walker Black.

"Don't we all," responded Cal, as he threw back the half full shot glass of alcohol. The Director immediately refilled his glass, along with his own glass.

Wanamaker said, "So, basically Cal, you are telling me that I'm shit out of luck, that good old Brick has my pants around my ankles and a noose around my neck."

The two men exchanged glances, while playing with their shot glasses, and without taking another shot. A subordinate feeling bad for his boss. A friend feeling equally bad for another friend.

262 | John A. Wooden

"Explain it to me again," demanded Wanamaker tersely. "Tell me about this elaborate plan of Brick's and why I should just sit on my ass and allow him to kill people at his leisure."

"Simply put, you love your life and your job," Cal retorted immediately. He couldn't avoid the smile on his face. "Sam, we allowed this to happen. We screwed up. I messed up by allowing Rivers to do her thing unchecked. I should have supported her more. I played the game. I didn't want to step on toes...didn't want to piss you or others off."

Wanamaker didn't respond. He drained his glass in one deep swallow and poured himself another shot.

"You screwed up, sir, by giving Jody Fontaine, Smokey Franklin and the Harvey family too much power without checks and balances. You gave the Harveys carte blanche as long as they kept the body count down. Truthfully, Sam, I don't know if you received any money from the Harveys, but we should have made life hard for them in the city. We didn't. We allowed Fontaine and Franklin to be puppets, as well as many other officers and detectives. Now, the roosters are crowing loud and Brick is the gatekeeper."

Wanamaker still didn't respond. Thoughts were twirling around in his head. Cal was right. He knew he was right. He wasn't sure if it was truly Cal's words or the words of Zachary Brick. As much as he wanted the rogue detective to be his enemy, the man wasn't. More than anybody, Brick and Rivers were more responsible for him being in this position than anyone else. They solved crimes and he knew Brick did many off the book operations. No one could officially prove any of the thousands of rumors that floated throughout the Memphis metropolitan area, but it was just too coincidental that the city became a better place to live after the arrival of the transferring detective.

Now, he didn't want the man coming after him. Cal was right, *he did love his life and his job.*

Cal continued, "We have Detectives Gloria Berkley and Abigail Richmond, and Officers Allison Glasgow and Pearl Bake, and Lizzie Osman, an executive assistant in the Internal Affairs office in a secure place. We are arresting Detective Franklin tonight. Brick is going to rid the city of some bruising thugs who work for the Harveys."

"The Harveys' vigilantes, their hit squads?" asked Wanamaker.

"Yeah. Brick has his plan. As bad as it sounds, it works to clean up the city, while we take credit for it. It's as if we are responsible for ridding the city of the Harvey stink once and for all."

"True," said Wanamaker dryly. Cal didn't speak. He knew his boss had more thoughts on his mind. He was patient. After all, he was still several hours from arresting Detective Franklin. "Arresting cops. Never a good thing Cal. I expect our boys in blue to be impatient. Not sure this will solve anything."

"Sure, it will, Sam. He will keep the FBI off our asses, as well as make D.C. happy. The last thing we need is the Bureau, ATF, DEA and Homeland camping out for an extended period of time in our backyard. It just doesn't bode well for us as a city. It certainly doesn't bode well for you as a police director or for our mayor."

"I'm surprised you didn't mention Mayor Archibald."

"Not my place, Director," Cal replied. "Primarily, because Brick didn't. I don't know if he has plans for the mayor, or if he even has a reason to have plans for the mayor."

Cal played dumb, somewhat. He was telling the truth about Zach's omission of the mayor. However, if he was a betting man, he would roll the dice on the mayor's involvement with the Harvey family.

"Tell me the truth, Cal. How long have you and Brick been in contact with each other?"

"Just today," lied Cal. "He trusts me. Plus, he knows I love my family and I could care less about the Harvey family."

264 | John A. Wooden

"Tell Brick I won't get in his way," Wanamaker surrendered.

The director refused to allow dumb pride to get in the way of a golden opportunity. He could fight Brick, but the man was smart and conniving. Hell, they didn't have any real, hard and fast proof that the man was actually in the city anyway. He really was a ghost. For Sam Wanamaker, this was the most cautious and strategic move he could make. More importantly, it was a win-win for him and his police department.

"I'm hoping it's not too bloody and that I don't have too much mud on my face after this is over with, Cal."

"It's Brick, sir. We can only hope for a lake full of blood, instead of an ocean."

CHAPTER 49

SILENCE IS THE DEADLY STRANGER.

"Do you have to leave now or do you have a few minutes?" Director Wanamaker asked his chief of detectives.

Cal was standing, looking down at his boss. He sat back down and stated, "Sam, you pay my bills and make my wife and kids happy, so of course, I have time for my boss."

Wanamaker refilled both glasses and while he turned his glass upright, Cal didn't drink. He was wondering what was going on in the mind of his boss. He was convinced the director asked him to stick around for a reason. As much as Cal didn't want to be paranoid, it was just a part of his past. That past included survival.

"Tell me about Brick." Wanamaker's voice was relaxed, yet full of confidence. "I have never met anyone like Zachary Brick. Maybe I'm intrigued, or like a child who is experiencing his first crush, but the man has always piqued my interest."

Cal smiled. Although his mind was racing, the look in Sam Wanamaker's eyes told Cal that the director was genuine. "Yeah, you, me and a thousand and one other people," Cal responded. "One of the lessons I learned from Sam in another life was that there are two types of people in this world—those who push the buttons, and those who are the button...and some buttons are more dangerous than others."

Wanamaker's stoic expression changed. His eyes got a little bigger, and then a half-hearted smile graced his face.

Cal began, "I first met the man known as Zachary Brick at a dinner party." From Wanamaker's busy eyes, Cal could tell that the statement had caught his attention. "The party was thrown by an operations supervisor at the organization we both worked. The party was on the organization's four-deck, football stadium sized yacht that sat on a pier in D.C. My wife also worked at the organization. There were probably about thirty people total in attendance, mostly co-workers, and maybe a few spouses.

"It was pretty cordial for the most part, until the ops super called a little impromptu meeting with six of us on the lower deck. When we reached the bottom deck, the ops super was playing pool with a guest I didn't know and actually was seeing for the first time that night. We had already been on the yacht for over two hours and had drifted maybe a good mile away from the pier by this time. I could only assume he was on the bottom deck the entire time.

"Anyway, the ops super didn't introduce the man, but others, including my wife, seemed familiar with him. The meeting began with the two of them still playing pool. I was surprised to be the lead briefer. I was an analyst at the time, and I had been collecting and analyzing data from one of our allies."

"As in foreign allies?" Wanamaker asked.

"Yeah."

"What kind of data?"

Cal smiled again. "That's not important, Director. Let's just call it marketing data that affected our gross national product. We discussed my data for about fifteen or twenty minutes, before the ops super asked for solutions to resolve this issue. Throughout the discussion, the pool game continued and not once, did Brick guy say a word. Then the super asked me what did I think we should do? Jokingly, I said, 'A regime change.' And fuck Sam, the whole damn room got quiet. You could probably literally hear a pin drop.

"Then the ops super asked the question, 'Is that possible'? You would have thought that the question was for everyone, but he was only looking at Brick when he asked. Still, he didn't say anything. Amazingly, the conversation went in another direction after the comment I had made in jest."

Cal finally took a sip of his drink. He could tell by Wanamaker's expression, that he had piqued his boss's attention. "After the dinner party, Deb, Brick and I went to a jazz and blues spot in downtown D.C. for drinks. It was a nice, small, quaint place with good music and great buffalo wings. I couldn't help myself, I kept my eyes on Brick. Like you Sam, I was intrigued by the man. There was just something about him that I couldn't put my finger on.

"At one point, he asked me how I felt about having a party in my honor. I looked at him, kind of dumbfounded, and then looked at Deb. The two of them had a very close working relationship. They worked in the same division, and often on the same assignments. Evidently, our ops super had put together this dinner party just to talk about my findings and possible solutions. I didn't know that.

"But in talking with the man, I realized that Brick was just that—a man. He was entertaining, interesting, engaging and had a good sense of humor. He was smart and knowledgeable. Sam, after a couple of hours of talking with the man, I still had no clue that I had been the reason for the dinner party and that he was the solution."

"How so?" the director asked.

"A couple of weeks later, that same ops super told me the case was closed, to box up my data and file it in the organization's vault. No questions asked. Several months later, we were briefed that the head of state and the next five people in succession were no longer in the picture. The new head of state had signed a new import/export trade agreement with the United States."

Sam Wanamaker's eyes got bigger. "Are you telling me that Brick killed a head of state and the next five people to take his place?"

"No, Director, I would never tell you anything like that. If I had—one, it would be classified, and two, I would have to kill you." Wanamaker cracked a smile, whereas his subordinate did not. "The head of state and one of his successors died from natural causes. While the other four successors were killed by the head of state."

Wanamaker stated, "Is that the official story?"

"You could say that Director." Cal picked up his shot glass and threw back the rest of his drink. "That's when I really learned that some buttons are way more dangerous than other buttons. Unknowingly, Sam, I had met the most dangerous button of all."

CHAPTER 50

H<small>ONESTY IS THE FIRST LAW OF DIGNITY.</small>

I didn't completely know Jody Fontaine when I was a detective in Memphis. He was a detective sergeant in the narcotics division. There was nothing special about the man or any of his accomplishments. The rumors ran rampant that the sergeant had secrets, but more importantly, connections. His fast promotion to lieutenant and deputy chief of detectives validated the rumor of his perceived connections. I don't know if anyone had ever investigated any other rumors surrounding Fontaine. Nor did I care...until now.

Looking into Fontaine was easier than I thought. He had been a lieutenant for three years and had surpassed numerous more qualified candidates to get to this position. Cal did not select him as his deputy chief of detectives. That had been Director Wanamaker's doing. It made me wonder about Sam Wanamaker's relationship with the Harvey family, since I knew Fontaine was in the Harveys' pocket deeper than anyone.

The lieutenant carried three phones. He had one for business and another one for personal use. This practice was commonplace for cops and many professionals that had phones issued by their companies. However, his third phone was a part of his secret life. This was the phone I wanted to know everything about—what he had been using it for, who had called him, who he had been calling, as well as any other information he had on his phone?

It all sounded so enigmatic and mysterious, and it was. The obvious answer was the correct answer, which consisted of the information I already knew was there—the phone calls from the Harveys, along with all the files associated with their ongoing communication. Knowing that I would find all this information was encouraging, but I still needed to know about everything else that was on Fontaine's tertiary phone.

I needed an expert and someone who didn't work for a phone company or government agency. I knew the right person for the job. She wasn't that far away either. The three hours that I spent in her office was worth every second.

Lucy Bankwell knew people. Her dynamic personality was more suited for Hollywood or a Washington, D.C. news channel than for a Memphis bank. She made a series of phone calls and within forty-five minutes had video, audio, photographic and written files of everything on his third phone. For the next two hours and fifteen minutes, I spent every second reading about the torrid affair between Fontaine and a married woman, in the form of text messages. This explicit dialogue was accompanied by compromising videos and photographs of the two.

During my time in her office, Lucy had occasionally looked over my shoulder and shook her head at the craziness of the affair. She actually knew the woman. It was hard for Lucy to process this affair. Although Lucy had a history herself of doing idiotic things, like cheating with married men, this situation truly disturbed her. Maybe it was because the woman in the videos, photographs and the author of the texts was having a sizzling affair with her brother-in-law.

Lieutenant Jody Fontaine was sleeping with his brother's wife.

Marcus Fontaine was one of the top councilmen in the city and one of the top hospital administrators in the country. The man had done a lot for the city. The worst thing that he had probably did was assist his brother in moving up fast in the ranks of the MPD. His wife, Caroline, was a beautiful lady, who was also one of the top realtors in the city.

I thanked Lucy for the information. She volunteered to check out everything else on the phone and more importantly, to have it cloned. We had agreed that she would contact me when Caroline and Jody Fontaine would be seeing each other again.

That was three days ago.

I was still on day one of Special Agent Seth Painter's three-day suspense to wrap *this* up. *This* being my vengeance on the Harvey family and any others involved in the death of Detective Alaina Rivers. I liked the three-day suspense, as it established a goal and timeline—things that used to control my life as a CIA officer. Fontaine was on my day one to-do list.

The lieutenant and his sister-in-law had late lunch plans at a restaurant located off the beaten path in Tunica, Mississippi. Tunica was famous for their riverboat casinos in the northern part of the state. The town was less than an hour from Memphis. The restaurant, *The Hungry Alligator,* was five miles from the casino area, down two side streets off the downtown area. These details confirmed something for me. The two had a sexual thing, but they also had a genuine love for each other. I had thoroughly reviewed every text that the two had sent each other for the past three years. But that was all I could take. The phone contained at least another four years of texts, photographs and videos.

The Hungry Alligator was one of three places in Mississippi towns on the outskirts of Memphis that the two patronized. From the texts, I surmised that they had hooked up at least once per month for a late lunch or early dinner. It was their commitment to each other. However, occasionally, one of the two would throw a curveball, which included calling off their appetite for food and instead, choosing their appetite for each other, fulfilling their sexual desires.

Caroline was the third partner in Jones & Jetson Realtors. She was a silent partner, but she brought in the right customers, the deep pocket clients who wanted ritzy homes and quality commercial property. Lucy had made the connection for me. We decided to meet in a small warehouse in the hospital district in the midtown area of the city.

The entrance to the warehouse was in a narrow alley that ran from a side street to Jefferson Avenue, not far from Regional One Medical Center. The warehouse used to be owned by one of the hospitals in the area. That's how Lucy Bankwell had represented me to Caroline Fontaine, as an up and coming medical supplier looking to do business with hospitals in the local area. Lucy's computer person had created a fake website for me, with phone numbers and fake reviews from legitimate hospitals. The website also included fake pictures of the president and vice president of the company. It was a long con to procure the information I needed.

As soon as I opened the warehouse door, I greeted her at the door with a chloroform handkerchief over her nose and mouth. She was instantly knocked out. I put her back in her car and drove her to Lieutenant Jody Fontaine's house in the White Station area of the city. The two-story house had three big bedrooms on the second floor, with a bathroom in the master bedroom. The two spare bedrooms were around the walk from the master bedroom, with the second bathroom sitting across from the bedrooms.

I had kept with Jody and Caroline's trend of sending sexually, playful photographs that got the two of them aroused and lustful for each other. I had sent the lieutenant a series of pictures, which consisted of pieces of clothing on the first floor, the spiral staircase that led to the second floor and master bedroom, and the bedroom floor and bed. From her shoes to her panties, every piece of clothing was photographed and sent to Caroline's brother-in-law and lover.

I didn't have to imagine what was on Lieutenant Fontaine's mind. His texts were intimate and very sexual. He wanted to lick every part of her body and basically, screw her brains out. The man was dealing with an insurmountable amount of stress and was dying to relieve that stress with his sister-in-law.

I had followed their modus operandi to the tee. I had sent Jody almost ten photographs of every piece of clothing Caroline had on. I created a trail from the bottom of the staircase to the bed in the master bedroom. The first photograph included a shoe, followed by the second shoe, until the last photograph of her panties on the bed. Sometimes the photographs were very graphic, with Caroline's selfies of her naked body parts, including close-ups of her groin area and breasts.

I bypassed those photographs.

His drive would take at least forty-five minutes from *The Hungry Alligator* to get to his place. I took that time to talk to Caroline Fontaine.

Although I had undressed the woman and used her clothing to entice Jody to come home fast, I had then put a robe on her and tied her up to a computer chair that was in another bedroom. I had also rolled Caroline in the master bathroom and placed tape over her mouth.

She had been out less than an hour and a half. I sat on the bed as I situated Mrs. Fontaine in front of me.

"Mrs. Fontaine, before I pull the tape off, I need to let you know that if you scream, I will kill you." Her eyes were excitable and big. My statement made them bigger and brought tears to her eyes. She had only been awake maybe a minute or two, and she was still discombobulated. "Do you understand what I'm saying?"

She nodded her head. That was a good start. I pulled the tape off with one quick pull.

I know it hurt, but she kept quiet. I then grabbed a water bottle I had, opened it and put it to her mouth and allowed her to drink.

"I know you," she said warily. Her eyes had settled down. She was searching for something. Probably my soul. "You are the one... the one the cops and the Harvey family are looking for."

"You got me," I said.

"You are making a mistake. My brother-in-law is going to kill you. You crossed a line." I thought it laughable that she was trying to admonish me.

"Yeah, I guess I should be afraid of your *brother-in-law*." My statement was in jest, full of sarcasm. From the numerous texts, I knew where Caroline had got the idea that Jody Fontaine was the badass of the Memphis Police Department. I wasn't sure if she really knew the truth. Jody Fontaine had been very fortunate to have a brother who was a mover and shaker, and loved being his brother's protector and provider. This was also the same brother Lieutenant Jody Fontaine had no qualms about betraying.

"Is this funny to you?" Caroline was still incoherent. She was drowsy, trying to get her bearing. I think I had probably put too much chloroform on the cloth I had placed over her nose and mouth to knock her out. Additionally, I was pretty sure that waking her up earlier than I should have was a factor as well.

I didn't respond, which seemed to irritate her. "Did you like what you saw?" I still didn't respond. I knew the reference was to her body. She had noticed that she just had a bathrobe on and was completely nude underneath.

"I know you like white women," she said. That one caught me off guard. But still, I didn't respond. "I heard Detective Rivers was half-black, but I didn't believe it. Black women don't have that kind of tenacity. Then again, maybe she got her hardheadedness from the black side of her family and the tenacity and smarts from the white side."

She smiled at her comment. She was trying to bait me. Why? I didn't know. Maybe she thought that by getting me upset, she would get me off my game. But I wanted her to talk. I knew that it was her nervousness and the fear of the unknown that lead to her chatter. She knew of my reputation and my exploits, I was sure of that. But it never surprised me when people you would least expect to challenge you, do exactly that, challenge you.

"What do you know about your brother-in-law's illegal business interests?" I asked. The question wiped the smile off her face. From the look of confusion on her face, I had the feeling she was searching her mind for a response. This was the time for a fast "I don't," but that may have been the chloroform talking.

"I don't...I don't know what you are talking about," she finally got out.

"Okay," I responded. "Let me take you back to the bathroom."

"No!" she stated before I could completely rise from the bed. I was surprised that she hadn't screamed out. Although I had threatened her, I thought she would still try me. With every minute that had passed, she was getting more coherent, which I was good with. I had a person parked down the street who would tell me when Jody Fontaine was approaching the house.

"Let's talk about Alaina," suggested Caroline. I wasn't completely sure about her strategy. I thought that maybe she wanted to stay in the bedroom until Jody got home, and then yell out to warn him that I was in there. She knew that he would show up soon, based on the last text messages she had received from him, which clearly indicated that he was very horny and desired her affection.

I estimated I had another minute or two.

"Let's not," I said. "We can talk about his business interests and I may allow him to live, or I can kill him as soon as he hits the top of the staircase."

Her face turned pale, as if all the blood had drained from her body. She must have suddenly realized how dire the situation was that she and her brother-in-law were in.

In my ear, my lookout, Lucy Bankwell, told me that Jody was pulling up and parking the car.

I immediately grabbed the roll of tape and pulled off a fresh section. I had just enough to cover the mouth of Caroline Fontaine. It caught her by surprise, as I rolled her back into the bathroom.

The look on her face told me she thought she would not see tomorrow.

CHAPTER 51

T ELL ME A LOVE STORY . . .

I heard Jody Fontaine running up the staircase. The man was excited. That was exactly what I was hoping for. He was making this too easy.

As soon as he hit the door, I had a clear path and pulled the trigger of my Glock 40 with a silence suppressor. The first shot hit him in his left shoulder. He was caught completely off guard. He wasn't expecting me and I think the attached suppressor surprised him as well. He fell back on the door and my second shot hit his right shoulder, causing him to slump down to the floor. Sitting on the floor with his back to the door, I had taken my time walking to him with my gun pointed at his head.

"Damn." Maybe it was the only word he could muster up. Maybe this was the ending that he never saw coming. Whatever he was thinking brought tears to his eyes.

"You got me, Brick," he said. "You got me good." He couldn't move his arms. As cool as he was trying to be, the pain could still be seen by the grimace on his face.

"Who do you work for Lieutenant?"

His head was down. He slightly lifted it up to look at me. "Where is Caroline?" I didn't immediately respond. "Was she ever here or did you just bait me with the texts."

"She's in the bathroom sitting down in your computer chair. Tied up. With tape over her mouth. But safe enough."

"Don't hurt her. She has nothing to do with this."

I said, "I agree. As long as you tell me what I want to know, I won't hurt her."

"She is a good woman."

A good woman. I didn't want my mind to wander to Alaina. I knew if she had captured my thoughts, I may lose it and do what I promised her I wouldn't do—kill a cop. She was my epitome of a great woman. And at that moment, so many memories flooded my mind. I was trying to completely regain my composure, while keeping the struggle from Fontaine.

"So was Alaina." His eyes dropped. He didn't expect that. Maybe he felt an element of remorse. Maybe he didn't. I didn't care.

Before he could say anything again, I reengaged. "Who do you work for?"

"I feel bad about Alaina."

I shot him above his right knee. He yelled out. He was in deep pain as he tried to reach his bloody leg. However, with bullets in his shoulders made that hard to do. "Who do you work for?"

Lieutenant Jody Fontaine was afraid for his life—and probably for Caroline's life as well. I saw death in his eyes. He had given up. He didn't want to give up, but he was defenseless. I walked up to and hit him in the nose with the butt of my gun. I then reached in the left side of his jacket and secured his police-issued Glock 22 semi-automatic pistol from its holster. I then proceeded to secure the .380 semi-automatic pistol from his ankle holster. Lastly, I thoroughly searched him and found two of his phones. I threw it all on the bed.

After dealing with him, I went to the bathroom and rolled a wide-eyed Caroline into the bedroom. Tears rolled down her face, as her eyes widened in response to seeing his bloody state. I looked back and forth at the two lovers. Jody teared up as well. The two really did love each other. That was all I needed to know.

"Who do you work for?" I asked again.

"You know who I work for!" he yelled.

I put my gun against her head. "I don't give a fuck about the Harvey boys," I stated. "Listen, Lieutenant, I could easily go an eye for an eye and kill your sister-in-law. I really don't like killing innocents, like the people you work for do."

I allowed that to linger. Caroline's face was a mess. The tears had completely smeared her mascara. If she had no idea of what was going on before, she did now with a gun pressing against her head.

He mouthed the words "I love you" to Caroline. Then Jody said to me, "I work for the mayor and I know he works for someone else, beside the Harvey boys. It's a federal government official. I promise you, Brick, that's all I know. As God as my witness, that is all I know."

"You ever see this government official? Man or woman? Black or white? Asian or Hispanic?"

"No, I never did." Fontaine was writhing in pain. I could see him fading. Caroline wasn't in the best of shape either. I didn't give a damn.

"Tell me how deep the mayor is in with the Harveys."

"Very." His eyes got sad. I knew he was getting weaker. I needed to wrap this up fast. "You can call him the lead motherfucker in the city, if you'd like. He has others like me on the force and other city officials as well. He has an account in Switzerland. He pays the guys on his payroll, who also have accounts in foreign lands, but the Harveys pay me and Franklin."

I was surprised. I didn't expect that. Then I got it. This was a man truly trying to save the woman he loved. Admirable. I guess whatever chivalry resided in the body of Jody Fontaine, he was mustering it all up for his sister-in-law and lover.

"Keep talking," I said. "How deep is Wanamaker in?"

"Not deep at all," he replied weakly, as he coughed several times. "He received money at the beginning of every year to just look away. Initially, he didn't play their game. But on three occasions, his wife or kids had flat tires and guess who was there to fix them. They didn't hurt his family, but they sent him photographs. He got the message...accept the money every year. The important thing—his family is still living."

"How about the government official? What's his role?"

"I don't know." Tears were streaming down his face. "Let her go, Brick, I'm cooperating."

I responded, "Keep cooperating. Keep talking. The government official."

"The only thing I know about him," he coughed some more. "Is that he knows you and wants you dead...said he owes you. That's why Archibald ordered Alaina's death. The government official wanted you back in Memphis. He has been looking for you for years. He was tired of looking. In the meantime, he made a deal with the Harveys. He gets a very nice monthly stipend from them."

"How do you know all of that?"

"Mayor Archibald. He gets talkative when he gets drunk and stressed. Alaina was getting too close to the mayor and the Harveys. The government official loved the money, but wanted you. He ordered River's death to appease the mayor and his cash cows. Since both me and Smokey were on the Harveys' payroll, it was easy to get Smokey to set up Alaina. He wanted her for himself, but she loved you. No one in the department knew that, but she told Smokey. I believe that he loathed you for having the one woman that he really wanted."

He smiled. He was evil. Unfortunately, it was telling. It was about me. He knew that.

"Life's a bitch, Brick. It was a perfect storm," he said, still coughing, looking weaker and defeated. "The government official wanted you. The mayor and Harveys wanted Alaina."

"Well, I don't know what you and Smokey wanted," I stated. "And I don't give a damn. But thanks for the information."

I walked toward the bedroom door, and looked down at Jody Fontaine for the last time. The man was no longer a threat to me or anyone else. If he survived this night, he would need plenty of rehab. I looked back at Caroline. She was a distraught woman with tape over her mouth.

I said, "I sent Marcus the tapes, videos and photographs of the two of you together." My eyes had returned to Lieutenant Jody Fontaine. "You are right, Alaina Rivers was more than just my partner. She was the woman I loved. The last time I saw her, she made me promise to not kill any MPD personnel if anything ever happened to her. So, I'm letting you live."

The lieutenant didn't say anything.

"I just hope your brother feels the same way," I said, as I disconnected the silence suppressor and threw the gun on the bed with the other guns and phones.

I went out the backdoor and within a minute I was on the next street getting into Lucy's car.

CHAPTER 52

THEY LOVED EACH OTHER.

It was a statement. Sondra was sitting in the passenger seat as she and Max worked their way toward Memphis. In the week or so that she had been in Texas, she had had the time to reflect and gain perspective. In so many ways, she was the catalyst for the love two people shared. The two people that she loved most in the world.

"What're you thinking?" asked Max, keeping her eyes on the road. They were making perfect time. Max had taken over the driving as soon as they hit Arkansas. She had preferred that the majority of driving was done at night, since she was more nighthawk than daylight dweller. To her, night represented abnormality, the sinister and destruction of light, which were all elements of her make up. But the man of too much pride needed her...needed them.

Sondra said, "While sleeping in Zach's bedroom, I saw and felt the love."

"Pardon me," said Max, the statement caught her by surprise. Primarily, because she wasn't sure what Sondra was referring to.

"When I was sleeping in Zach's bed, I realized that it smelled like my mom," replied Sondra, wiping the tear from her eye. "Actually, I smelled both of them. I felt the love they had for each other. It reminded me of home. It was also just so funny."

"What's funny?"

"Well, when they started sleeping together, or I should say, when they started sleeping in the same bed, Zach would get up early and go lie down on the sofa. They didn't want me to find out that they were doing the do." Both women laughed at the reference, *doing the do.*

"What they didn't take into account were the times when I got up early and would sleep on the sofa with Zach. So, one night, I got up and saw his shoes and shirt by the sofa, but he wasn't there. I laid down thinking that he may have just gone to the bathroom, but he never showed up.

"So a couple of days later, I got up early again and the same thing happened, he wasn't there but his shoes and shirt were. It was about two or three in the morning, so this time, I decided to do something different. I opened my mom's door and was surprised it was unlocked. Then I took off running and did a kamikaze jump between the two of them. Oh, Max, you talk about surprised. I had never known Zach to be a sound sleeper, but he was knocked out, and I heard my mom actually snoring before I jumped on them."

Sondra couldn't stop laughing. Max thought it was funny too, but her laughter could not compare to Sondra's. When she finally stopped laughing, she continued, "My mom was so pissed off, but Zach just told me to get my butt under the covers and get some sleep. That next morning, I jumped in both of their stuff. I let them know that they were too damned old to be sneaking around like little teenaged kids."

"How old were you?" asked Max, with a smile on her face.

"Eleven or twelve. My age didn't make a difference. We were already family. They just didn't know it yet. After that, life was good or maybe I should say, life got greater."

Ten minutes later, Sondra still had a smile on her face. The car was quiet, with the exception of music softly playing in the background. Max was focused on the road. She liked Sondra. She thought she was a good kid. Although the young woman was almost twenty, she didn't know what kind of relationship Zach and Sondra would have now, since Alaina was no longer around.

"So what was the urgency to leave eighteen hours early?" asked Sondra, as she glanced closely at Max. She liked the mysterious side of Max. She laughed internally at how Max and Zach tried to keep their true professions from her. Her mom tried to do the same thing regarding the dangers of being a Memphis detective. It was sadly funny then, and it was sadly funny now. She had a history with Zach, but she knew he would always treat her like his *lil' lady*, which was the moniker he beset on her years ago.

"I overheard a conversation between the Harvey boys," Max began explaining. "They have two groups of hired killers who work for them. One is a local group that act more as enforcers than true killers. However, they have killed their fair share of Memphians over the years. Call themselves the Death Squad."

Max glanced at Sondra through her peripheral vision. The young woman had an indifferent look on her face, as if to say, what the hell. "I thought you would like that," Max added. "Well, you will like the second group just as much—the Ramirez brothers, who work out of Mexico and throughout South America. The Harveys want Zach eliminated, once and for all. He is that headache to them that you just can't get rid of."

Sondra said, "I didn't think we had anymore operating listening devices in their vehicles or houses. Guess I was wrong."

"Not really. I think they had tried on numerous occasions to get Zach to be at certain places and when he didn't show up, they concluded that they had found all of the bugs. But they didn't."

"Are these guys dangerous?" asked Sondra, with concern written all over her face.

"Yes, they are. But no one is more dangerous than Zach," replied Max, with a smile on her face, as she turned her head to glance at her riding partner.

"So how are we going to do this?" asked Sondra. "You told me that Zach didn't want you to leave me alone. Now, we are in the belly of a whale named Harvey. So do I go with you or will you stash me at his secret hideaway."

"You stay with me. You stay in the car and I will give you a couple of guns to protect herself. But when we get closer to our destination, I'll want you to get in the backseat and lie down."

It was at that moment that Sondra truly understood that this wasn't a game of hopscotch or hide-n-seek. This was the world of death and she just hoped that she would still be living and breathing after the streets of Memphis ran red with Harvey blood.

CHAPTER 53

THE CIRCLE OF COMPLACENCY.

Sam Wanamaker did not like being summoned to his office. He was the director of police, and only the mayor was above him. However, it wasn't the mayor demanding that he come back to his office. It was his subordinate, his employee, and a special agent with Homeland Security. It just didn't sit right with him.

He remembered the days when he called the shots, when he was the big man on the street. He had been thinking a lot about those days recently, when he clawed his way up that proverbial ladder of success. Hence, he deserved to be the director and he deserved to be in this position. He was chosen over six local deputy chiefs, a deputy director and numerous external applicants for this position. Now he was dealing with a level of disrespect that seriousy ruffled his feathers.

He was trying his best to keep his cool, as he approached his office. It was nightfall. It had been a long day.

He knew the day was not over.

He opened the door and held it open. The special agent sitting on his sofa didn't say anything. As a matter of fact, he was reading a newspaper as if he didn't have a care in the world. Of course, he knew better. He knew the man. He didn't like him. He was smug. No. He was an asshole. He kept his eyes on the man, as he stood in the doorway. He wanted Special Agent Seth Painter to look up, to acknowledge him, and to give him credence and respect as the director of police for the Memphis Police Department. He wanted to keep his cool, but the agent was getting under his skin...and he wanted to kick his ass.

"Director, how are you doing?" he heard his chief of detectives, Cal Hillsmeier, ask. He saw Cal out of his peripheral vision. Two days ago, he had felt unconditional trust in his chief of detectives. Now, two days later, it seemed like a lifetime ago.

He finally closed the door and walked to a seat in front of his desk, which was in the same location where Cal was sitting. His chair was positioned in front of Cal and faced the sofa where Special Agent Painter was seated.

"Where do you want me to start?" Painter asked the director.

"If I knew where to begin, I would have started this conversation as soon as I had opened the door," stated Wanamaker. "I don't know who to trust." He glanced at Cal as he made this statement. "My city is in full-fledged chaos and I don't even know what my role is now. That's a fucking shame considering my position. Somehow, I have disgraced this office, this position, and that pisses me the fuck off!"

"You don't have to raise your voice, Director," Painter retorted as he placed the newspaper next to him on the sofa. Then he leaned forward. "You are insulated to a certain extent. This is not about bringing you down. This is about justice and cleaning up your city. We could have completely blown up this entire city and taken you down, along with the mayor and over half of your department. But we are not going to do that, Director. My job is to ensure that you come out as the hero in all of this mess."

"Who is *we?*"

Seth Painter didn't immediately answer. The two men's eyes met, with one wanting to tell a story that could possibly shed light on this dire situation, and the other wanting answers and clarity.

Out of nowhere, Cal answered the question. "Sir, *we* are Zachary Brick and Special Agent Painter. Director, we can pretend that this is not about Detective Rivers, but it is. Brick and Rivers were more than just partners. They seemed to have loved each other unconditionally. Somehow, Sam, we have allowed our city to be held hostage. Brick is doing what we should have done years ago."

Sam Wanamaker didn't like the speech. For one, it was too honest. Two, Cal had owned up to being part owner of the city's dysfunction. Regardless, he knew if he had given the order, Cal and his other subordinates would have cleaned up the city and the department. All he had to have done was say the word. Cal was loyal. As much as he wanted to think otherwise, he knew the man had his back.

"What happened with your deputy?" Wanamaker asked Cal.

"Love triangle, Sam. His brother, Marcus, killed both Lieutenant Fontaine and his own wife, Caroline. Seems as if Jody and his sister-in-law were having an affair. Councilman Fontaine found out about it and caught them in a compromising position. He shot Jody multiple times and shot his wife in the head. He had photographs of the two of them together, along with a ton of texts, pictures and videos that he found on their phones."

"So, it had nothing to do with Brick or Rivers?"

"Just a coincidence," Cal replied. "I'm sure he was probably on Brick's radar, but Councilman Fontaine beat him to it."

"What about everything else?"

Painter added, "Everything else was about cleaning up your city, Director. A joint task force that consisted of the ATF, DEA and TBI, and led by your police department took down over thirty business organizations that worked for the Harvey crime family. Plus, they officially raided warehouses, stash houses and storage locations. Lastly, we arrested your internal affairs' chief, Major Turner, the mayor's chief of staff, Mr. Robison, another thirty plus detectives and officers on your force, and several cops extorting city officials and local businessmen."

The two men continued to exchange glances. In one night, the world had changed for Sam Wanamaker. He knew that if his world had changed, then the mayor's world was equally as chaotic. Ryan Robison was the mayor's right hand. If he was arrested, that meant the mayor was culpable. He also wondered if the deputy mayor was ready to step up and take his position.

"I take it we are good, Director?" asked Special Agent Painter.

"No," replied Wanamaker. "Who in the hell is Zachary Brick?"

Seth Painter put his face in both of his hands, then rubbed his hands over his head. "That's a long and complicated story, but I could probably make it a very quick story, Director, if you have the time."

"I do."

"I used to be an officer in the Army," Painter began. "Once upon a time, the Department of Defense used to have a joint military exercise called the Killer Experience. For political correctness, the Killer part was dropped and it was renamed the Experience. Anyway, the exercise included the best new recruits from each branch's special operations units. You know, Navy Seals, Delta Forces, et cetera.

"The exercise had an established time limit, which is classified, and the purpose of the exercise was to complete six out of eight training scenarios, with one major stipulation—you couldn't use the same killing methodology more than once."

"So the training scenarios were about killing?" Wanamaker asked.

"The long and short answer, Director, is yes," Painter replied. "However, there was a problem-solving element to each scenario. The best time ever recorded for completion of the exercise was six hours before the time limit and that was just for six of the scenarios. The exercise was mentally grueling and physically challenging. Many men had been broken trying to complete the exercise.

"However, it had been several years since I had last attended this exercise…and I was pleasantly surprised. There was a two-man team, actually, a man and a woman team. Delta Forces trained. Master sharpshooters. Master knives-men. They were supposed to be the best. Singularly, they were both deadly. Together, they were unstoppable.

"This exercise set a new record—they completed all eight scenarios and with twelve hours to spare. Simply amazing. I was impressed. Their performance blew me away. I recruited them as a team for an operation in the Middle East. They became a part of a twenty-man team. Quite honestly, Director, I screwed up. They were my main attraction. The other eighteen team members were just there to provide support to my special killers.

"Hell, it went well for two or three years. Never had one complaint, and the team got along well. Whatever they needed, they got. Then, we messed up. We swapped out some team members and overall, everything changed.

"The man on my special team was quiet and very likable. He was a warrior and a true leader of men. The woman was another story. She was the better of the two, but not the most personable person. The new team members were all men and were not crazy about supporting a woman. It was bullshit, but the male's ego has always been about bullshit. I'm sure you would agree with that."

The director nodded his agreement.

Painter continued with his story. "Regardless of her so-called shortcomings, the two were a formidable team and had a true friendship. Nothing romantic. If anything, they were more like brother and sister."

Seth Painter stood and walked toward the door. "One day, the man had gone on a mission for three days. He came back and his partner was dead. Five members of the team had raped and killed her. As I said, she wasn't very popular and was probably more manly than any of them were. Within those three days, the men had been transferred out of the country. Well, the man was quite unhappy. He became reserved, withdrawn.

"He was released from duty six months later. He was then recruited again by me for an alphabet agency. He served his country well. Within a couple of years of being released from the Army, all five soldiers died some very gruesome deaths. His partner's death had changed his life. He had lived with that death for years. She had been a great friend and had changed him. Then one day, he met a female detective and created a new legend for himself."

He turned the doorknob and opened the door. He looked at Cal. Although he was surprised at the story he had just heard, his facial expression hadn't changed. Then he looked at the director. He knew Sam Wanamaker was in another world. Seth Painter had never told anyone the story of the man now known as Zachary Brick.

He concluded his story by saying, "Director, the name of the young lady was Brittany. Brittany Zachary. We called her Brick, because as nice as she looked, and trust me, she was a beautiful lady. Brittany just didn't seem like the most appropriate name for her."

CHAPTER 54

THE PRUDENT MAN LIES THE GOOD LIE.

Memphis was under siege by local and federal law enforcement agencies. It was a coordinated effort orchestrated by Special Agent Seth Painter. As much as I wanted to say that I owed the man, I didn't. He, Max and I had a relationship that would probably last until two of the three of us were buried six feet under. If we were lucky.

Seth was officially with Homeland Security. However, the man was unofficially an advisor to several alphabet agencies and the White House. I had known the man for more than twenty years—first, as a soldier, then as a CIA officer, and recently, as a mercenary, an assassin for hire.

Cal had called me and told me about Seth's conversation with Wanamaker about everything that had occurred in Memphis and his free pass. The director had been complicit in looking the other way. But I got it. I was sure that the Harveys had threatened his family, while he took money on an annual basis to be a good steward and to pay no attention to the illegal wrongdoings of the Harvey family.

Family trumped all. Even for law enforcement types.

The disturbing part was that Seth had told Wanamaker about my dear friend, Brittany Zachary. Evidently, the story had caught Cal by surprised. He had wanted to talk about it, but I let him know that that was a conversation he and I will never have. Brittany was off limits. Alaina was the only person I had ever talked to about Brittany. She was special to me. We were a team, but many had looked at us as just a couple of killers. We were more than that. We had more than that. I loved my sister, but Brittany and I were just closer.

Before Alaina had come into my life, I had thought about Brittany at least once or twice a week. We had a connection, based on mutual respect and admiration for each other. We had a beautiful friendship, a great partnership. We often laughed that our relationship was based on killing, but at the end of the day, our relationship was far more about friendship, honesty and a commitment to each other. Her death made me want to kill myself. In a crazy way, I felt that those who killed her, saved my life. I wasn't going to die, until they died first. That thought had saved my life.

But that was another day, another life. I had told myself that if I had ever found a woman I loved, I would adopt the legend Zachary Brick, in honor of Brittany's surname and nickname. That woman was Alaina Rivers.

She was my here and now. And now, she was gone.

In my mind, I had killed the Harvey family, all of their minions and half of MPD a hundred times over. I often imagined myself riding on my black stallion as if I was in the wild west, slinging my six shooters and killing all the bad guys. Another common thought that I had was showing up in a fiery red SUV or Lexus sports coupe, both loaded with guns, grenades and numerous other weapons, and with the same ending that I had when on my horse, the killing of everybody.

But I was in the here and now, and that meant running down leads and coming up with a plan. It was a stupid plan, but still, it was a plan nonetheless.

When the door opened, the first thing he did was pull his firearm. That was smart. He was on alert. Not hearing his alarm beeping when the door opened, meant one thing—someone had already disarmed it.

"You don't want to do that," I said to Detective Smokey Franklin. He was startled to have a houseguest. Hell, I would have been startled and just as upset as he was, if I had come home and had someone I thought was a friend pointing a gun at me. "We can solve our differences without guns or knives Smoke. We can do this the old fashion way, just plain old fists. Either you beat my ass or I beat your ass."

He smiled. "I like that," he said. Then he put his gun on a small table that sat near his doorway.

I nodded my head toward his right ankle and he slowly bent down, pulled his right pant leg up and pulled the .380 Saturday night special out of its holster. Then he placed it on the table. Next, I raised my eyebrows, indicating that I knew him, that I was familiar with his tricks of the trade. He took his light jacket off and turned around. I saw the serrated knife. He started to reach around with his right hand, before I stopped him.

"Are you really that stupid?" I asked.

He turned his head towards me and smiled again. He then reached around again, but this time with his left hand and removed the knife. This was followed by him turning back around to face me.

Smokey was playing it cool, but I knew he wasn't happy. This was his second home...the one that nobody was supposed to know about. It was in the Bartlett area of the city, and was a nice four-bedroom house not far from Interstate 40-East. It was a great getaway.

The city had imploded, but it seemed that Detective Smokey Franklin had escaped the craziness. Cal had assigned detectives to watch Smokey's every move, and the women of his extortion ring were told to act as if nothing had occurred. Smokey wasn't the wiser. But the man wasn't stupid. He knew it was only a matter of time. Why go to your home of record in South Memphis and be arrested at your house, when you can go to your new place and come up with a plan?

"I see you dressed for the occasion," said Smoke. He was right. I had on a white T-shirt, a wife beater, with military-grade camouflage pants and combat boots. I was actually cold from the weather outside. Plus, Smokey didn't keep a warm house. "You think you are fucking G.I. Joe or some motherfucker?"

"Yeah, I'm some motherfucker," I said, as I put my gun down on a nightstand. Smoke was already walking toward me. When he was sure that my piece was on the nightstand, he rushed me. He was less than ten feet from me, but it was enough space to build up some steam.

It was on...and it was real.

He hit me hard, like a linebacker tackling a running back, but I was able to maneuver my body and somewhat catch him in a spinning motion. Our bodies turned slightly, and we went flying into his wood, rectangular coffee table. The table was completely destroyed. My body ached. I landed on my right side, while Smokey landed on his left. His body probably ached as well. However, it didn't stop him from swinging at me with his right hand. I ducked my head and the blow hit the back of my neck. It still stung.

I could tell that Smokey shared my pain and I immediately got on top of him. He countered my move by picking up a leg from the table and hitting me over the small of my back. It wasn't a solid hit. He hit me again and this one was more painful. I gathered my strength, raised up and grabbed hold of his right hand before he could hit me again. Then I hit him hard with my right hand, followed by another punch and a third. Then I screwed up. I let go of his right hand and put my left hand on his throat. He countered this move by hitting me hard on my arm with the table leg, followed by mustering enough strength to push me off of him.

I rose and allowed Smokey to get on his feet as well. This time when he rushed me, I stepped to the side and led with a right fist to the left side of his face. It hurt him. He turned around fast to face me and I kicked him in the balls, followed by a quick right, left, right combination to his face. The last hit knocked him on his ass. He looked disoriented as he struggled to get to his feet too fast. I kicked him in the face, a solid kick to his nose. The blood gushed out of his nose. I leaned down and grabbed him by the shirt with my left hand, then hit him hard repeatedly with my right. The more I hit him, the more I realized that Alaina was on my mind. The more I thought about her, the more I wanted to kill Smokey Franklin.

Instead, I said into the earpiece of Major Cal Hillsmeier, "Give me a minute to walk out the backdoor, then you can come arrest this piece of shit."

The news the next morning would report that on top of the numerous arrests that had already been reported, Detective Smokey Franklin, a homicide detective with the MPD was implicated in the death of his former partner, Detective Alaina Rivers, and was a member of the Harvey crime family, as well as the leader of an extortion ring.

CHAPTER 55

MY BODY WAS SORE.

I had bested Smokey, but regardless of how great of shape I was in, it had been years since I had actually fought anyone. My kills were quick and fast. Sometimes I used a long-ranged rifle, other times a knife or syringe. In my line of work, discretion and covert operations were my calling card. I still felt good.

I noticed that one of my boots was untied, so I bent down to tie it. Initially, I didn't hear the shot, but the bullet hit the backdoor. I quickly pulled out my piece and took cover behind the only thing in the backyard, a big, green plastic trashcan. I heard what I thought were three shots. Whoever was out there had a silence suppressor. Depending on the size of the weapon, you had to be trained on the slight sound of a silence suppressor, which drastically cut down on the sound of a fired weapon. Of course, the ultimate goal was that no sound could be heard at all. I knew the sound well and had counted five shots, but no more directed at me.

It was dark outside. Cold. My jacket was in my car. My adrenaline was flowing. My senses were hypersensitive. I knew a shot could easily penetrate the trashcan. However, it was providing some type of cover. The backyard was big, but bare. The trashcan was close to a gate near the house. There was also an opening at the back of the yard, which led to the next street over.

The area was heavily populated with trees and bushes. This was a part of the Bartlett area where houses were properly spaced, with big back and front yards. Basically, the wooded area behind the house had enough trees and bushes to provide very good cover for anyone looking to surprise me.

I still had my earbud in and was hoping that Cal had his earbud in as well. "Cal, you there?" There was no answer. I was sure Cal was busy with Smokey.

Then I saw the silhouette coming toward the house. The closer the person came, the more I recognized the silhouette.

"You okay?" Max said to me. She had on a dark colored jacket. She actually had on more than one, as it looked tight. I knew the woman, and normally the jacket was one size too big. She had a nine mil in her hand, and knew that she had two others with additional clips under her jacket.

"Yeah, I'm good," I replied.

She said, "Come on, there is one more out there. We need to get him fast."

"Get who fast?"

We cautiously trotted to the back opening. I had been here on two separate occasions and knew about the wooded area. Both Max and I surveyed the area before we proceeded. She was situated behind a tree and I was stooped down behind a bush. Even though it was December and several days before Christmas, the bushes still had an ample amount of leaves.

"The Ramirez brothers," she stated.

I looked at Max. She was still surveying the area. Then I realized that she was purposely not making eye contact. "I killed five, but there is still one out there. I killed two with a knife to the throat and shot the other three. The other two shots came from them."

I asked, "Where is Sondra? At the house?"

Max didn't immediately respond. Then she looked down. When she looked back at me, I knew the answer.

"Where is the fucking car, Max?"

"Two blocks over."

"Fuck." I was not happy. My best friend knew it. But she saw in my eyes what our next move would be.

We took off running toward the car.

Then I stopped in my tracks when we made it past the first street when I heard three shots. Max was still running. I picked up my pace again and we ran through another wooded area to the next street.

When we got to the street and looked at the car, we stopped immediately. The back door was open. I was speechless. I was still pissed. My eyes didn't believe what I was seeing.

Sondra was lying on the floor in the backseat of the car with a smoking gun in her hand. And on the street lay the sixth and remaining member of the Ramirez brothers.

"Hey, Zach," Sondra said to me. "I think we need to get out of here."

I closed the back door. Max was already in the driver's seat. I made my way to the front passenger seat.

I looked at Max. She smiled. Then she put the car in drive. I shook my head as I looked at her, then at Sondra.

CHAPTER 56

Life can be a box of bad decisions and results.

Kendra Harvey was remembering a time when she was younger. She had been a junior at UCLA and had done something that some in her family circle considered to be stupid—she had brought home a young man. He was supposed to have been the love of her life. His name was Travis and he was Caucasian with dark hair and dark features. He was from Napa Valley and his family owned four vineyards in Napa Valley and Orange County.

She was shocked when she went to a fraternity party with him and became the woman of the night. She didn't remember the whole night, nor did she ever want to. She had sex with Travis, but this was followed by others in his fraternity using her. Basically, raping her. The most shocking part was that Travis had met her mother and father, and knew her father was an attorney.

She knew what he was thinking. His family's wine money and status out-trumped and were more powerful and important than an attorney of Mexican heritage. But Travis really didn't know her family. Yes, her father was an attorney. However, he was an attorney for the most powerful cartels in Mexico and South America. It was at this moment that she realized the love and essence of having brothers.

Arturo and Hector Junior were her protectors. For years, she had kept her brothers at a distance. She loved them, but they were very over-protective. If it were up to them, she wouldn't be allowed to leave the house without an escort. They didn't like her dating or even going to college on a daily basis. But when it came to Travis and his fraternity brothers, Arturo and Junior were the remedy. She didn't blink when she heard the news about the deaths of six of the frat brothers, including Travis, and the serious injuries of ten other frat boys.

That was the day she realized she needed her brothers—the day she realized how much she loved her brothers.

Arturo was gone. In her mind, Junior was the only one left. Ronaldo and Damian were brats. As much as she loved them, she knew they were dead men. The only issue now was relaying that knowledge to her parents.

"What the fuck happened today?" asked Hector Senior. He looked frail and defeated in his wheelchair. The luster and energy he had felt in his heart just a day ago, had disappeared. He was drained and disappointed. Once again, he wished that his wife had aborted their two youngest sons.

Kendra knew Junior had briefed their father on today's events. As bad as he looked and probably felt, she knew that he would still want to hear the news from her. After all, officially, she was the Garsay Cartel's attorney. Therefore, she was the de facto crime boss in Memphis. She knew that. Her father and Junior knew that as well.

Ronaldo and Damian probably knew it as well, but didn't want to accept the truth. Now, it had hurt the family and more importantly, hurt them financially. They had lost money and property that belonged to Santana Garsay. That was never a good thing.

"Dad, we lost everything," stated Kendra, as she sat next to her dad at her parent's dining room table. Junior was sitting on the other side of their father. "The feds came in and took down our whole operation. They emptied out the warehouses, storage units, stash houses and everything from the most minor of locations to the largest. No place was safe."

The old man sat quiet. Tears welled up in his eyes. Junior put a hand on his father's arm. It was a hand of condolence. No father, regardless of age, should be mentally weak around his children. Losing his oldest son could not break him. Losing part of the Garsay fortune could...and did.

"Tell me about our protection?" Junior inquired.

Kendra's eyes dropped to the floor. This conversation was about keeping it together and unfortunately, passing bad news on to the people she loved.

"Junior, everything is gone," she began. "Santana wanted his money. All of the local and offshore accounts have been emptied out...by me. All valuable assets, including all of our houses, vehicles, paintings and any other valuables will be sold off and the money will go to Santana."

"Santana! Santana! It's fucking Santana now!" screamed Junior in Spanish. "You chose fucking Santana over your damn family! How could you?"

"I chose life, Junior," retorted Kendra in a calm voice. "Santana Garsay gave me something my family didn't give me. Respect. Honor. Consideration." She and Junior looked at each other. She didn't fear her brother. But she wished she could do more for him. She couldn't. She also answered to the man who had given her opportunities.

"How did Garsay know about everything that happened today?" Senior asked as he looked at Kendra with hard eyes... eyes that were full of hate now for the daughter he had loved.

"Dad, it's been on every national news station, the internet and every social network out there. It wasn't hard to figure out what was going on. Garsay has federal officials on his payroll, just like we have local officials on our payroll."

"This is bullshit!" he exclaimed. "Fuck Garsay! We all can leave here together. We just need an hour or two to get our shit together."

Kendra glanced at Junior. He knew the look. He knew how this story would end. Still looking at her brother, Kendra said, "No, dad. No, we won't. Mother and I will be out of town before daybreak. Santana told me to tell you that this is the day the bough breaks."

Her father smiled. His eyes softened. He recalled the saying well. When he was allowed to move his family to California, and then from California to Tennessee, both times Santana told him that one day his bough would break...for good.

He signaled for his daughter to come closer. They hugged and he held her tight, as if it would be the last time he would ever hold her this tight again. She tried to hold back the tears, but she couldn't. She loved her dad. She wished she could help him, but her boss gave her a choice. She chose her mother.

"Did Santana run off the servants as well, Kendra?" asked Junior, as he was still coming to grips with his ultimate destiny. "Mother has been asking about the servants the whole day and I haven't been able to get any of them on the phone. Plus, when we sent guys to their homes, every home was cleared out, as if they had never lived there."

"No, Junior, that wasn't Garsay," responded Kendra, with a perplexing look on her face. "Fuck! Brick!"

"He really is a cunning son-of-a-bitch," stated Senior. Father, son and daughter exchanged glances. Kendra realized that there were zero players in this game. Former Detective Zachary Brick controlled every move and put the onus on Santana Garsay to close the door.

"Ronaldo and Damian, their whereabouts—you know?" asked Junior. He glanced at his sister. However, her eyes were back on her father. He was smiling. For her.

Internally, Kendra recognized that she was serving two fathers. The one who gave her life...and the one who paid her bills and ensured she had life. She loved Senior. It was the business they chose and that business created strange bedfellows. Her bedfellow had spoken. But she knew that the two men she loved most in her life, shared the same name and would probably share the same fate...soon.

"There is no sign of Ronaldo and Damian," replied Kendra. "I seriously hope they are long gone from Memphis. If not, I expect Brick will make them pay for Detective Rivers' murder or worse, the cartel will make them pay for losing millions of dollars."

"Will our own bodyguards be our assassins?" asked Junior.

Kendra replied quickly, "No, but both of you need to leave now. Take half the money in the safe. The other half is for mother. Please get out of here now. We will be leaving in a few hours."

"Can you tell us where you guys are going?" asked her brother.

"Yeah, Junior. Southern California."

She hugged her brother and knew in her heart she would see him again. She didn't like her life or her situation at the moment. Her family didn't get the chance to have any kind of funeral or burial service for Arturo and now, it would probably be the same result for both Senior and Junior.

She wished Detective Rivers was still alive...then the man named Brick would still be hibernating in his hole, hopefully far away from Memphis.

CHAPTER 57

IT'S A FAMILY AFFAIR!

Max and Sondra followed me to the house in Olive Branch. Max knew the place well. She had been here on numerous occasions. She had probably stayed in the house longer than I had. During my first six months in Memphis, Max stayed at the house, hoping I would come to my senses and leave the MPD behind. But she realized I loved a woman, who at that time, couldn't care less about me. As much as it pained Max to see me love someone else, she remained loyal to our friendship and whatever crazy relationship we had.

She knew I wasn't happy. I didn't want Sondra anywhere near the scene outside Smokey's house. Worse, I certainly didn't want her shooting anyone.

That's why I wanted her to ride with Max. I was too pissed off to be in the car with either of them.

I took all the bags in while the two went in the house. I could tell Sondra was expecting a hug or something affectionate from me. She didn't expect me to just get the bags.

When I came in the house, Max was showing Sondra around the house. I knew what was going on. Max was giving me time. Probably giving us time. I was sure Sondra was just as upset as I was disappointed.

I went into the kitchen, washed my face in the sink and grabbed a cold beer from the fridge. I then sat at the table and thought about how I would have felt if something had happened to Sondra.

When I looked up, she was standing in the doorway. "This is not your life, young lady," I blasted. "Unlike me, I want you protected and unscathed from this kind of life. Dammit, Sondra, this is not your world."

I took another swallow of my beer. I was surprised she hadn't said anything. I looked at her and saw the tears in her eyes. I got up and she walked quickly over to me.

We hugged and with her head in my chest, the tears endlessly flowed. No, she wasn't my daughter by blood, but she was my little girl. I kissed the top of her head.

"I'm sorry," I said. "I just want you safe. I love you. I told your mom that I would always protect you. And you come back to Memphis and kill somebody."

"If I hadn't, he would have killed me." She giggled at that. I slightly shook my head side to side and had to smile myself.

"Are you alright?"

"Yes, I'm fine," she replied. Sondra was holding me tight as if to make sure I didn't get away. I got it. She was happy to see me and I, in turn, was equally happy to see her. I could also tell she had something on her mind.

"Talk to me, what is it?"

"I miss mom."

We both got silent. It was a double-edged sword. Alaina was surely the epicenter of our lives. In so many ways, she fortified our lives. For Sondra, she was the mom who taught her more than the regular things mothers teach daughters. I used to joke with Alaina that Sondra went from a rattler to a gun and could throw a knife by age ten. Sondra's computer prowess was her mom's doing. She taught Sondra survival skills, while also teaching her to be a little girl, an adolescent and finally, a young woman.

When it came to me, Alaina did one thing—love me. That's all I needed from her. That's all I wanted from her. Her remarkability and penchant for fairness and righteousness taught me how to care and be compassionate toward my fellow man. Feelings that had failed me over the years.

"We both miss your mom," I said numbly. My mind was in two places: here with Sondra and elsewhere with Alaina. Elsewhere meant bouncing from one thought to another. From riding together as partners to sitting on the floor watching television to making love, I couldn't stop thinking about Alaina.

I was trying to stay away from a heavy heart. It was hard. It would always be hard...now.

"We have a lot to catch up on," said Sondra quietly. "And talk about the future."

I didn't say anything. She was my baby girl, but Sondra hadn't changed since the day we had first met. She was the young princess of distraction.

"The last Ramirez brother was running to his car down the street from Max's car, how did he end up at your car?" I asked out of curiosity. I put her at arms' length, while still holding her hands. "What did you do, young lady?"

She looked at me with her mother's eyes. I was putty in her young hands. I was so conflicted. As much as I wanted to say she was a daddy's girl, she was another man's daughter. However, blood or not, we were as close as any father and daughter.

"I left the backdoor slightly ajar," she admitted. "Although Max had told me to stay in the car, I followed her, just in case she needed back up. When I realized she was good, I went back to the car, and then I heard someone running. So, I slid down in the back seat, left the car open and waited on him to open the door. I kind of figured that he wouldn't be able to resist."

I smirked and shook my head again. "You are indeed your mother's child."

"She was my mother, and it just didn't seem right that you and Max had to do all the heavy lifting."

"Sondra, that's not true," I said briskly. "You are the computer person and that's where I need you. I don't need or want you handling a gun. Whether you can or not is irrelevant. I don't want you in my world. I want so much more for you. And your mom wanted the same for you. The moon and more. Not the world we live in."

"I'm tired, I'm going to bed."

I knew that move too. She had pulled it a lot on me in the past. Alaina never fell for her bed excuse. I wasn't her mother. I was the pseudo father who could be manipulated by his pseudo daughter.

I pulled her closer. Another hug. "Although you could just be lying, you may actually be sleepy after this long day. You shot someone and stuff like that stays with you."

She held me tighter. I kissed the top of her head again. "My first thought every morning is of my mom. My last thought every night is the same. I'm not losing sleep over killing someone who probably had something to do with my mother's death."

I kissed her again.

And wondered how real fathers dealt with the pressure of being a good dad.

CHAPTER 58

T HE FEAR OF BEING EATEN BY THE L WORD...

I wanted to have a conversation with Max. When I went into her bedroom, she was sprawled out on the bed, knocked out cold. It had been a long day for her. She was truly amazing in her own way. She saved my life tonight, but that was nothing new. I was used to it.

It was already the wee hours of the morning. Daylight would break in a few hours and this night and the night's events would be officially over. In the morning, I would hug Max and give her a speck on the forehead and she would know that would be my thanks for saving my life.

I made a pallet at the foot of Sondra's bed. She was also knocked out as soon as her head hit the pillow. She was sleeping in the master bedroom. I had lied to her and told her I would be sleeping in the spare bedroom. As much as I thought she was okay, I wanted to be close...just in case.

I had tried my best to keep my mind off Alaina, but it was virtually impossible to do. All day and night my mind had been wandering back to Panama City Beach, Florida. It had taken an arm and leg to convince Alaina to take a vacation. She was a workaholic. When she wasn't working, she was trying to spend time with Sondra. As Sondra aged into a teenager, she had less time for her mother, which meant either more work for Alaina or more sleep.

We had a beachfront room. The view was absolutely beautiful. A sandy beach, with blue green water for endless miles to see. The pier was also a part of our view from the room. We were on the twenty-first floor and it was a nice breezy, but warm April morning. Alaina had slept for twelve hours the first day.

We were lying on a lounge chair outside on the balcony when she said, "Do you think my ass is big?"

I laughed. She looked at me with big doe eyes. Her look was sad. My laughter stopped. I thought she was joking. When we were partners, we used to talk about a myriad of subjects. The conversations regarding self-conscious women issues always garnered a laugh from me. Now I was afraid I had overstepped my boundaries.

Then she laughed. "Gotcha, boy scout."

Our trip was two years ago, three years after I had left Memphis and the MPD. Our relationship was full blown and our love was deep. This trip was different. This was not the three or four-day trip we occasionally took. This was ten days of hanging out and enjoying life.

"Well, woman, I love your fat ass," I joked. "Fat as in P-H-A-T."

"Nice try, Zach. Comebacks aren't funny if they are not quick. Your slow ass will learn one day."

I laughed again. She was right. My sense of humor could be slow at times. In many ways we were alike. In many other ways we were totally different. She had her moments of being serious and so did I. The same applied for us being laughably funny. I think I had the better daily sense of humor. When we initially partnered up, Alaina only laughed occasionally when we were off duty. Once we became comfortable with each other, she smiled and laughed more.

"You can begin whenever you are ready," she said, as she looked at me with a slight smile. I knew what she meant. I knew what she wanted to know. The only reason she had decided to come on the trip was I promised to tell her about me. The real me.

"Where do you want me to begin?" I kept looking at the water. It was soothing, a beautiful sight. It reminded me of the many beaches and waterfronts I had been on over the years. I was addicted to the Mediterranean Sea on the island of Sicily, Italy. I had a villa on the outskirts of Siracusa, a province on the southeastern boot of Sicily. The province was full of ancient Greek history and architecture. My villa was quiet, provided me peace and serenity. I could sit on my first or second floor balcony and just enjoy the smell of fresh water and the breeze. I told myself that one day I would go back there and retire, then I ended up killing a team of four assassins who came looking for me. I gave my villa to a nice young couple who had just gotten married on the beach by my villa.

Maybe that's why when I was around water, I thought about that villa, imagining Alaina and I were just chilling on the balcony as we were doing in Panama City.

Alaina asked, "Is Zachary Brick your real name?"

"No."

"Don't be like Sondra and one word answer me, mister."

I turned my head towards her and smiled. She wasn't smiling. Then she stuck her tongue out and we both laughed.

"Remember what you told me when you asked me to tell you about my life, about who I am?"

"Yeah, I remember," she replied. "That I wouldn't get mad or upset, and I wouldn't pack my bags and go back to Memphis."

I was still looking at her when I responded, "I was born Anton Hargreaves. When I was twelve, my father killed my four-year-old twin sisters. My father and his father became my first kills. After that, my eight-year-old sister and I relocated to Arizona. She was placed in the foster care system and eventually adopted by a nice family."

"Are you for real," she asked. She repositioned her body, turning on her side to look at me. In turn, I got up and sat down on the lounge chair looking at her.

"Yeah, no lies, no fairytales. My story and my life are not good ones, Alaina. I have made my version of lemonade out of lemons. But it wasn't easy. I like to think that maybe I made it look easier than what it really was."

"Why weren't you adopted by a foster family?"

"Because I was never a part of the foster care system. Only my sister. She was signed up as an only child. I lived in the streets. I was by myself from age twelve until I went into the Army at age seventeen. I lied about my age, paid to get a fake birth certificate that said I was eighteen. By that time, I had changed my name at least a couple of times."

"How did you survive?" I had piqued Alaina's interest. Her eyes were big, her face intense.

"I did whatever I had to do. I stole, I lived in abandoned houses and cars. I stayed with friends every now and then. And yes, I sold drugs. Amazingly, never took drugs, but I would buy weed and cut it with sage or bay leaves, and resale it to others. I would break into cars in some of the better neighborhoods in Phoenix and sell the things I stole to the folks in the 'hood. Then I got a part-time job as a mechanic at an automobile repair shop and kept that job for two years. After I graduated from high school, I enlisted in the Army."

"Hold on, I was wondering about school. So, you did graduate from high school and didn't get a GED?"

I smiled. "Yes, I graduated from high school, enlisted in the Army for six years and became a sharpshooter. From there, I was recruited by the CIA and spent eight years with the Company. Then I spent a couple of years doing *private consulting* and *wetwork* with Max."

"You did all of this as Zachary Brick?"

"No. My name with the Company was *Hunt Collins*."

She smiled. "I like that name." We just glanced at each other. I knew what she was doing. She was searching my eyes for something. Anything. She had done this so many times before. It was about connecting. It was ironic. I thought we had a great connection. But it didn't matter what I thought. I was only one-half of the relationship.

"How long have you been Zachary Brick and why Zachary Brick?"

I told her about Brittany Zachary. About how we met and our friendship. I told her about Brittany's death and how it affected me. And then I told her what I had promised myself years ago, that I would take the name Zachary Brick when and if I ever found a woman I wanted to be my own.

"So, you came to me because there was someone you wanted to be your own?" There was a expression of curiosity on her face. She placed her feet on the ground and we were sitting within a foot or two from each other.

She wanted an answer. I wanted to provide her an adequate, but truthful response. But it was hard...and I was afraid.

Although hesitant, I continued, "I had an assignment in Memphis. I was tasked to take out Hector Harvey Senior. I had surveilled Harvey for almost two weeks. Then the day I had planned on taking him out, he was visited by two detectives at his favorite restaurant he patron every three days for breakfast. The female detective caught my attention. Your hair was longer then. You had on a dark red shirt with black slacks. Hector Senior was with one of his bodyguards. I liked how you sat in the booth next to the bodyguard, forcing him to get over."

Alaina still had a perplexed look on her face. I was sure I sounded like a stalker now, but she wanted to know and I wanted to be honest with her. "I listened to your conversation and I heard you tell him that one day him and his family's luck was going to run out, and you would be there to take him, Arturo and Junior down. I loved your spunk and confidence."

Her expression didn't change. "I called my benefactor, told him it was a no-go on taking out Senior and that I wanted to be assigned to the MPD as a detective. I wanted to partner up with Detective Alaina Rivers...and make my legend Zachary Brick."

She didn't say anything. After sitting across from each other for a few minutes, she kissed me. A deep kiss. Then she went inside. We didn't talk for several hours. She actually went down to the beach and walked the beach for a while. I didn't disturb her. I wasn't sure what she was feeling or thinking. I didn't want to be the stalker guy. But in so many ways, I was the stalker guy. I had done the craziest thing I had ever done. It was even sick by my own standards.

"I don't know what love is," Alaina said to me. I had fallen asleep on the sofa. It was afternoon. I had no idea how long she had been gone or how long she had been back. I wasn't a sound sleeper, so I had to be pretty tired or full of anxiety.

"What do mean?" I asked.

"I know you love me," she said. "From the time you came into my life, you have been there for me. Even before you knew about or met Sondra, you gave me respect and honored me as your partner and your equal. As a female cop in Memphis, respect from our male counterparts was hard to get. But then you and Sondra hit it off and the whole world kind of changed for me."

I didn't know what to say. So, I did what dumbfounded men do—I said nothing.

"Anton Hargreaves, Hunt Collins, Zachary Brick. Army, CIA, MPD, assassin. I don't give a damn. We are both kind of fucked up people. I actually think you may be more fucked up than me. But I know one thing...regardless of what bad qualities you may have or think you have, you are a good man and I love you Zachary Brick."

That was the last thing I remembered before I closed my eyes and fell asleep.

CHAPTER 59

Day two.

Hector Junior wasn't a happy man. However, he was content. After all, he was still breathing and able to wake up on this side of the grass. He laughed at the comment. He never thought he would be thinking this way or about that particular phrase. He actually heard the phrase from former Detective Zachary Brick.

He hated that he remembered the saying and the moment he heard it. Unfortunately, both he and Arturo were getting their asses handed to them, and the thing that really upset him was that Brick was talking shit the whole time. When he said, "Gentlemen, the thing I really like is waking up every day on this side of the grass," he knew he and Arturo were dead men. Why the rogue detective spared their lives, he didn't know or understand. He was just happy they had survived to see another day.

Now he and his father were driving on Interstate-55 North, headed to Canada, trying to escape sure death. Junior knew Santana Garsay had a long reach and maybe Brick had a long reach too. But no way they were going to make it easy for anyone to kill them.

He wanted to blame his sister. However, he couldn't. He knew Kendra probably saved his life, by giving them a heads up and a head start. If she had kept her mouth shut, he was sure this was the day they would die. Kendra did the right thing, in his mind. She would protect their mother and he would protect their father.

They had been on the road for almost three hours. They were in a Chevy Suburban. His father needed the space, as he sat in the passenger seat with the seat pulled back and the back of the seat leaned all the way back. Senior was asleep within five minutes of them taking off. Junior was glad he was. It was hard for him to say goodbye to the woman he had loved for over fifty years. Maybe one day they would be back together. It was a hope Junior wished came true.

He couldn't help but think it was his fault the family was in this predicament. He was the hothead five years ago, who challenged Brick and convinced Arturo to go to war with the detective. The man wanted one thing—a guarantee from his family that his partner, Detective Alaina Rivers, would be safe. Hell, they could have lied. Instead, he wanted the detective to know that the Harvey family didn't take orders—they gave orders.

He also wished Ronaldo and Damian had listened to him years ago when he tried to tell them to learn from he and Arturo's mistakes. He could have been more forceful, made them listen. Instead, he didn't push the issue. He allowed his younger brothers to learn the hard way. Unfortunately, that lesson never came. He and Arturo had paved the way for their younger siblings to be successful. Their interaction with Brick was an abject failure, but their interaction with the criminal element in Memphis and the surrounding area was a complete success.

They were twenty miles north of Cape Girardeau, Missouri when Junior decided to stop for gas. He loved the Suburban, it drove good. However, even with a big tank, it wasn't a great gas efficient vehicle.

He gassed up first, paying with a credit card under a pseudonym at the pump. Senior was still sleep and he saw no reason to wake his father. If he needed to use the restroom later, he would stop again. He then went into the convenience store to use the restroom and get something to drink. Upon his return, he put the keys into the ignition and looked at his father. He stopped in his tracks when he saw the blood seeping from the slit throat of his father.

Before he could react, he saw a fellow Mexican standing in front of the car. Through his peripheral vision, in the rearview mirror, he saw another man standing at the back of his vehicle. Then both men opened fire simultaneously.

Kendra Harvey answered her phone on the first ring. The caller on the other end of the phone only said two words, "It's done." She didn't say anything in turn. She hit the end button on her phone and looked at her mother, who was laying down in the back of Santana Garsay's Learjet.

She looked outside and was surprised. The weather had been drearily cold for the past couple of weeks, but today was a nice day. How fitting, she thought to herself. Her head was full of thoughts of memories of her brothers, primarily Arturo and Junior. She was already missing Arturo, now she would miss Junior as well.

She then thought about the phone call she had received from Santana. He told her the plan and her role in its execution. She begged for her father and brother's lives, but Santana would only commit to sparing the lives of she and her mother. And to add insult to injury, he told her that his men would call her when the job was done. Why? She didn't know. After all, in the big scheme of things, she was one of Santana's soldiers as well, just like those who'd killed her brother and father.

"It will be alright." The voice of her mother, Mariana, surprised her. Her mother was standing in the back of the Learjet before walking towards her daughter. She was dressed warmly in a thick overcoat and short fur-lined boots. "Santana promised me that you would be his lead attorney going forward and his United States operations will all report to you. Don't worry about your protection, Santana will provide you some of his best men."

"This is your doing, mother?" asked Kendra, with raised eyebrows. Not that her mother noticed, but Kendra's eyes were blazed with anger.

"Yes, dear," stated Mariana Harvey resignedly. "My sons wouldn't listen to me. Therefore, I couldn't help them. Santana has always sought my counsel. Giving you a spare set of keys to the castle is better than being dead, young lady. Wouldn't you say?"

Kendra sat stonily in her seat. And returned to thinking about the good times she'd shared with her brothers.

CHAPTER 60

THE EDGE OF WHAT THE HELL.

I was still on the floor when I woke up. I didn't have plans on sleeping so late. It was past ten in the morning, so I got my butt up and started my day. My body was sore, but a hot shower made me feel better. After throwing on some clothes, I trekked to the kitchen, where I found Max and Sondra eating breakfast.

When I sat down at the small kitchen table between the two ladies, Sondra got up and came back a few seconds later with two slices of toast and a glass of orange juice. The toast was covered with strawberry jam, my favorite. Then she went to the refrigerator and came back with both white and red globe grapes. Hell, the grapes were green, I never understood why anyone called them white.

"Thank you, young lady," I said, as I took a bite of toast.

Both Sondra and Max had what I considered to be a pretty big breakfast. Bacon, sausage, eggs with cheese, biscuits and grits.

I said, "Damn, I guess both of you are pretty hungry."

"Tough day, yesterday," Max replied. "Long ass drive with food we threw in a cooler. Quick restroom breaks, then we had to save your sorry ass."

I looked to my left where Sondra was sitting and she had a big, toothy grin pasted across her face. Max wasn't laughing, but she was good with one-liners. I had to laugh at her sense of humor as well.

Sondra hit a key on her laptop that sat in front of us on the table.

I recognized the room. It was the police director's office. The cameraman did a screenshot of the room and I noticed it was a small audience of six reporters. I'm sure what we didn't see were accompanying cameramen from the local television networks.

At that moment, Director Sam Wanamaker walked in and sat down at his desk. His computer monitor was removed from the desk, along with his phone. Wanamaker sat tall in his chair. I was intrigued by what he had to say.

Wanamaker began, *"I know you all have plenty of questions. So, I decided to call this informal, yet, very intimate press conference to provide the city some answers. I say we just jump into this. But before we dive into the events of yesterday, I have some breaking news for all of you. This morning, at a gas station outside of Cape Girardeau, Missouri, Hector Harvey Senior and Hector Harvey Junior were both victims of foul play and I'm sorry to report, both were reportedly killed this morning."*

"Say what?" said Sondra incredulously. She leaned forward, picked up several grapes and paid closer attention to the press conference on her laptop.

On the laptop, the reporters were excited with questions. Wanamaker pointed at one reporter and he stated, *"Director Wanamaker, thank you for breaking my story."* He laughed at his joke, as the director flashed a smile. *"My sources told me Hector Senior was found with his throat slit from ear to ear, and Hector Junior was shot mafia style, with both the front and back windshields shattered from multiple gunfire. Care to verify that information?"*

Wanamaker didn't hesitate. *"From the information I received from the Missouri State Police, your information is correct."*

Max walked over to the island in the center of the kitchen and grabbed another laptop computer off the counter. She then returned to her seat at the table and began pecking on her keyboard.

"If you were sleep, then who killed the Harvey father and son?" asked Sondra.

"Santana Garsay," was my two-word answer.

"The cartel guy?"

"Yeah, the cartel guy," Max answered, as she positioned her laptop on the table so we all could see.

It was a few photographs from the Harvey father/son killings in Missouri. The photographs were graphic. Hector Senior was probably lying comfortably before meeting his demise. Their SUV's front and rear windshields were riddled with huge holes from multiple gunshots. A shooter in front of the car, another in the rear. The news report stated Junior was shot over twenty times, front and back. Expert shooters. Not worried about stray bullets.

"Holy shit!" Sondra suddenly exclaimed.

I gave her a look. "She's nineteen," added Max coyly.

I didn't say anything. I returned my focus to the laptop and the press conference. The next reporter wanted to know about Ronaldo and Damian Harvey. The director told the reporter the MPD nor the federal agencies knew the current location of the Harvey boys. However, he added that there was a warrant for their arrest.

Now I had a smirk on my face. The warrant was real, but it too was a joke. The smart money was on whoever found the Harvey boys first would put a bullet in each of the brothers' head.

"What about Mayor Archibald?" I heard a reporter asked. *"One, Director, did you notify the mayor that his chief of staff, Ryan Robison was under investigation, prior to subsequent arrest. And secondly, is the mayor under investigation."*

Wanamaker looked exasperated. My thinking was he had to expect that question at some point. How could he not expect a question of that sort?

"I serve at the pleasure of the mayor and the great citizens of this city. In other words, Mayor Archibald is my boss and if I thought the mayor was skirting the edges of a crime or near troubling waters, it would be my responsibility to inform the mayor of those facts."

I was watching a master of spinning bullshit while making it sound like chocolate cake. Before the same reporter could re-ask his question about the mayor knowing about the investigation into Robison, another reporter asked the director a different question. I was sure that's exactly what Sam Wanamaker wanted to happen.

We continued listening to Wanamaker and the reporters. The man was always a natural when it came to cameras and microphones in his face. He re-hatched yesterday's events and gave credit to his staff, especially his deputy director and five deputy chiefs. He was working the reporters, while also smoothing things over with his staff, the mayor and other city officials.

I laughed to myself. I was imagining the conversation with his deputy director and his deputy chiefs. I knew they all were clueless to this side of Sam Wanamaker and the parasites in his police department. I also realized Wanamaker on television was setting up his eventual departure, as he gave credit to those who definitely didn't deserve it.

Then I heard the question and my hand gesturing to Max and Sondra was in the form of keep the chatter down. The reporter asked Wanamaker, *"There are rumblings that former Detective Zachary Brick was involved in exposing the corruption in your department. Care to comment?"*

Wanamaker didn't hesitate in responding, *"Many of you know the former detective. He worked for me when I was the chief*

324 | John A. Wooden

of detectives, and he and his partner, Detective Alaina Rivers, were the absolute best at solving crimes in our city. That's my way of saying I wish he was still a member of the MPD. As some of you may have heard, someone offered some decent money for information on the whereabouts or even a sighting of former Detective Brick. That I know of, nothing came of that. I think the Harvey family was making up a boogeyman. I think the former detective was thrown into the equation to give you media types something to chew on and put a scare into the local community.

"With all of the negative press regarding law enforcement, it wasn't hard to convince the public that the former detective was a rogue officer. However, Zachary Brick left the city five years ago. He was an honorable person and detective then, and I'm sure he is just as honorable now...wherever he may be."

Sam Wanamaker was full of shit. I, for one, was glad he could spin the truth into the biggest fairytale or lie ever told.

Another reporter followed up with a different question, *"Director, if that's the case, then who is responsible for all of the recent criminal activity in the city?"*

Wanamaker paused before replying. I knew the man. It was for effect, like a wrestler teasing the crowd before punching an opponent. He had a captive audience and he knew how to manipulate them. *"From our investigation of the Harvey brothers, Ronaldo and Damian, and information shared by several federal agencies, who are also investigating the brothers, we are convinced Ronaldo and Damian Harvey are responsible for the recent activity in the city."*

Another reporter quickly jumped on that answer, *"Are you saying Ronaldo and Damian Harvey killed their father and two brothers, as well as killed their own men."*

This time, Wanamaker leaned forward as if he wanted the camera to do exactly what it was doing, zooming in on his face and answered immediately, *"Yes, that's exactly what our investigation have uncovered. The primary purpose of this press conference was to share what led to the arrests yesterday of my law enforcement officials who have brought shame to this department...my department. I own this. This occurred under my watch and I am responsible to the citizens of this fine city. I sincerely apologize to my family, the citizens of Memphis and my fellow officers who do things the right way and represent the city the right way. Yesterday...was about cleaning up the city and cleaning up this police department, and regaining the confidence and trust of the public we serve.*

"And lastly, this message is for Ronaldo and Damian Harvey. We are coming for you. My people and the fine agents of the ATF, FBI and Homeland Security. We are all coming for you. The smart thing for both of you to do is turn yourselves in. If not, we will hunt you down."

Wanamaker didn't take any more questions. Instead, he said his last word, stood up and marched out the room. His *drop the mic* moment.

I was surprised. I wasn't the only one. Sondra and Max were just as surprised, and I assumed everyone in the city who had just saw Wanamaker challenge the Harvey brothers was as well.

"Sondra, where are the Harvey brothers?" I asked with a sense of urgency in my voice.

She tapped the keys on her laptop. She was fast. Within thirty seconds, she had the information. "Still in West Memphis."

"Max, is the gang still in place?" I asked. The gang was a party of six that had trailed me from Shelbytown. They had performed menial tasks for me during their stay. Now was no different, but this assignment would be their biggest.

Max replied, "Yeah, four are directly across the street, and the other two are next door."

"What?" Sondra expressed excitedly. "Y'all have six other people in the city? What the hell? I thought it was just you two?"

"It is," Max meekly responded. "But we have friends who believe in having our back."

"Really?"

"Really," I intervened before Sondra could get started again. "Time is of the essence. Have the other two guys next door come over to the house and keep Sondra company. Let the folks across the street know what's going on and that their sole responsibility is keeping Sondra safe. Have one of them go to the house next door and keep an eye on the backdoor. Then gear up, we have things to do."

Max grabbed her phone, got up from the table and began accomplishing what I asked.

"No, I'm going with you and Max!"

"No, Sondra, you're not," I stated. I gave her the thumb drive I had received from Lucy Bankwell. "This is from your mom. She left one for me as well. I haven't looked at this one. But if it's anything like the one I received, you will need some time."

She didn't say anything. Just looked at the thumb drive, then at me. I didn't want to just drop the thumb drive in her lap this way, but this way served my purpose at the moment.

"If you get done and still want to help, we really need you on the computer helping us out."

With that, I leaned down and kissed Sondra on the forehead.

She was mad at me at the moment. I knew this would pass. Regardless of a lack of parental blood between us, I was the father and had to make fatherly decisions.

CHAPTER 61

THE TIC...THE TOC...THE BOMB...THE CLOCK.

"I want to kill that motherfucker today, in broad daylight!" Damian Harvey brusquely stated. He wasn't happy. He, Ronaldo and five of their most loyal bodyguards were held up in a house that belonged to a lady friend of Ronaldo in West Memphis, Arkansas.

"For once, I agree with you. We need to figure out the best way to do this," Ronaldo returned.

The two brothers were sitting on an oversized sofa in the family room, watching their pictures flash over the television. The newscaster said, *"Be on the lookout for these persons of interest wanted for questioning by the Memphis Police Department, Ronaldo and Damian Harvey."*

"We can send the boys when the sonofabitch gets off work or we should just kill his fucking family!" exclaimed Damian. He took a swallow of his beer and sat it on the coffee table. The bottle was one of six bottles on the table. Only one belong to Ronaldo.

"We need to send a message and we can't fuck with the family," replied Ronaldo sullenly. "We have to be subtle in our attack, but we must send the right message. Whatever we do has to be smart and get the attention of these fucks. The attention of Santana Garsay, that motherfucker. I can't believe he killed Senior and Junior."

Ronaldo grabbed the television remote and began flipping through the channels. The cable network consisted of two-hundred fifty-six channels and he was determined to flip through every channel. He was thinking. He didn't care what was on the television. He cared about what wasn't on the television—photographs of he or Damian, or any mention of his father and brother's deaths.

He was hanging out with one of his lady friends when he got the phone call from one of his three bodyguards outside the townhouse. "We have to roll, Ro," stated the voice with a sense of urgency. "The Feds and 5-0 have gone mad and is arresting everyone. Plus, there are rumors that the warehouses and all the other facilities are under attack."

Ronaldo got dressed, grabbed his phone and rushed out of the townhouse. He got Damian on the phone, wanting to find out if he knew what was up. His brother told him what he knew and said that he was headed to their parents' house. Ronaldo diverted him to the house in West Memphis instead.

Just like that, the game had changed. Within minutes, Ronaldo gleaned that Lieutenant Fontaine was killed by his brother, and all of their properties had been sieged by the local cops, ATF, DEA and the FBI. Additionally, Detective Franklin was in jail, and neither the mayor nor any other local government official was answering their phone. That included police director, Sam Wanamaker.

He was equally upset and disappointed in his sister. He knew Kendra served Santana Garsay, but he never thought she would choose the cartel leader over her own family. He was convinced Kendra set-up her father and brother. He wondered how could she live with herself. He would ask her when he found her. His mother needed him and Damian, and he knew Kendra probably made their mother follow her.

Kendra and their mother's cell phones were disconnected. All of their houses had been raided in the wee hours of the morning. He was happy that he and Damian had taken all of the money they had stashed in their homes. They knew it was stupid to try and hide anywhere in the Memphis metropolitan area. Although West Memphis was smaller, the house which they were hiding out was off the beaten path.

Ronaldo knew the history of his family and he didn't like it. The same man had caused all of the consternation for his family. Santana. Garsay. They had to leave Mexico for California, and when it seemed things were great in California, it went from bad to worse. Once again, Garsay made them depart the sunny skies of the golden state for the redneck hicks and depressing ghettoes of Memphis.

It was time to stop. To fight back. The time had come for someone in the Paz/Harvey family to take a stand and stand up to Santana and his family. It would start with he and Damian. He could visualize he and his family running the cartel in Mexico. If he could visualize it, he could live it—he could make it happen.

Damian was talking, but Ronaldo was still in his thoughts. He was convinced they needed to make the Memphis Police Department and every federal agency invading the city take notice. What would they do if they were in Tijuana or any other city or town in Mexico? They would kill the police chief or sheriff and let the citizens know who was responsible.

"You are right, D," commented Ronaldo. "We are going to kill the police chief and his protection team in front of his home. Let the boys do it. Our pictures are all over the place, and there is a bounty on our head

"Two teams. One team of three waiting outside of his home. The other team of two following him and his team from a distance. Let's be like the FBI and CIA and give it a name—

Operation Bloodbath. Also, let's make up a sign with red paint on a cardboard with those words on it. Tomorrow morning, we make our way to Mexico. It's about time we take back what is rightfully ours. We should be leading the cartel. We have proven we can make money, we can deal with local and federal officials, and we are ruthless. We are the future, D. Now we need to show the world who we are and what we are capable of doing."

CHAPTER 62

A MOTHER'S LOVE.

Sondra wasn't mad at Zach. She was disappointed and upset at him. He was stern, firm and unwavering. She got it. He was responsible for her now. She really got it. He was really her father. It was crazy, but that's how she felt. She had never had strong feelings for her real father. She had spent a little time with him, but she always felt like she was his dirty little secret.

With Zach, she wasn't a secret. She was his *lil' girl, his baby girl, his lil' knucklehead*. She loved every nickname—and she loved the man.

Max introduced her to her two new bodyguards as she was leaving the house. Then she grabbed her laptop and went immediately to the bedroom she had slept in last night. She situated herself on the king-sized bed with her legs crossed and connected the thumb drive. After hitting several keys on the keyboard, she took a deep breath and hoped she was mentally ready for what she was about to experience.

The screen showed her mother in her bedroom, dressed in blue shorts and an oversized tee-shirt. She had no make-up on, but Sondra was used to her mother abandoning make-up. At best, she put on make-up sparingly. She saw something she wasn't used to seeing in her mother. She was nervous. That made Sondra equally nervous.

"I don't know how many of these I have done," Alaina began. "I think I have done three or four of these per year since you were born. And yes, I have them all. I'm sure you will find them. That's one of the things I love about you sweetheart. You are very resourceful and resilient. You so remind me of me when I was younger and you also remind me of your grandmother. I hate that. You are so like your grandmother. She was a remarkable woman. As many times as I have tried my best to tell you about her, I always get emotional. Your grandmother and I had such a crazy relationship. Like you and I, it was just she and I. Unlike us, your grandmother and I fought constantly. Verbally fought. She wanted so badly for me not to have to live the life she had lived. Though she could be a nutcase at times, I truly loved the woman. Regardless of her faults, at the end of the day, her life was about me. Unfortunately, you were only a baby when your grandmother died."

Alaina paused. She was gathering herself. She was trying not to be emotional, but she knew this recording might actually be the last one she made for her daughter.

"I'm rambling, baby. Every time I do one of these, I think back to your birth and the life you have lived. It has been great seeing you grow into a young woman. I remember every moment of your life and every day has brought a smile to my face. I have regrets in my life, but Sondra, you have never been one of those regrets. I had a child out of wedlock and I didn't blame your dad for not being there or for getting me pregnant. There was no blame to go around. You were my blessing and I thanked God every day for your life and for blessing me with you.

"As bad as it sounds, sweetheart, I won't be around. What relationship you decide to have with your dad is on you, baby. The one thing I did do right was bring a man in your life who loves you as his own and will never forsake you. I know you have lived with me being this woman on her own, but Zach did change me. He gave me two things I never thought I would truly have in my life—happiness and love.

"If you are viewing this, it means I fail in my mission to bring the Harvey family to justice. It means I probably died with one more regret—not listening to Zach and letting this whole thing go. It means I also failed you as a mother...again.

"I love you. There is so much I want to say. Please, baby, watch the other videos...together, they will say and explain everything I ever wanted you to know about me and how I feel about my little girl. You have grown into a woman and I know you will make a difference in this world. Be your own woman. Be the woman you want to be.

"Lastly, baby, every woman has this idea of their perfect man and the perfect father for their children. Unfortunately, your father was not that person." Alaina laughed at that moment, which also caused Sondra to laugh as well.

"However, Zachary Brick came into my life...our lives, and I saw how you and he bonded. It was crazy for me to see you two interact. It really was as if you two were father and daughter. It was you who let me know that that man loved me. And you probably knew before I did how much I loved him. Or how much I needed him."

Alaina hesitated. She was looking directly into the camera and Sondra could feel her eyes burning through her soul. Tears had begun flowing down her face several minutes ago. She knew where her mom was going with this. And she got it.

Then Alaina continued, "I hope both of you are there for each other. Be there for him, Sondra. He will always be there for you.

"I love you, baby. As much as I don't want to push the STOP button on this recording, I have to. Duty calls. Unfortunately, I know it will be the death of me. I love you, Sondra. More than you will ever know."

Sondra had a consistent flow of tears running down her face. She quietly said, "I love you more, mom."

Then she closed her laptop and wished the day would end faster. But she couldn't do that.

Her mother wanted her to be there for Zach.

She wanted to be there for Zach.

CHAPTER 63

I SERVE AT THE PLEASURE OF ...

The phone call didn't surprise him. The voice did. When the mayor needed to see his director of police services, he would have his secretary call. Today was clearly—a different day. When his boss told him to be in his office in ten minutes, Sam Wanamaker told him he would be there.

When he walked in the mayor's office, he wasn't surprised to see the man sitting on his sofa in the oversized room. What should have surprised him was the mayor replaying Wanamaker's words in his impromptu conversation with local reporters, specifically, the question one reporter asked about whether the mayor was under investigation.

Wanamaker and Kenneth Archibald had known each other for three decades. The two had been partners as uniformed police officers and as detectives. They both knew of each other's secrets. They knew each other's families. The one thing both men did not know was the connection each man had to the Harvey family.

"I love your strategy Sam," said Archibald dryly. "I like how you play the innocent cop, who is uncomfortable with the press, but is also able to deliver your message so subtly that everyone buys your shit."

The police director didn't respond. He was still standing, looking down on his boss. He knew the man and he could tell his nervousness and fear was getting the best of him. During their time together, Archibald had been the corrupt cop, who had his eye on bigger things. He had achieved those things—from chief of detectives to deputy chief of special operations to deputy director to mayor. But it hadn't come without a price—paranoia.

"Nothing to say Sam?" the mayor baited. "I have been here thinking about all of the stuff we used to get into as well as how many meals we have shared over the years and how, when I moved up, your promotion was on my heels."

If looks could kill, Sam Wanamaker knew he would be dead. Everything the mayor had just said was true. But Wanamaker knew why he moved up. Someone had to protect Archibald's ass, and that someone was him. He knew how reckless and careless the man could be. He was one of the smartest people Sam knew, but his weaknesses were a huge detriment to the man.

"Ken, I told you I would always be there for you," said Wanamaker warily. "But I have told you a million times since we were uniform cops that you were a danger to yourself. That philosophy of doing this or that and worry about the fallout after has finally caught up with you and it may be very costly. Only time will tell."

Archibald responded, "So, they are coming for me?"

"Hell, I don't know Ken." The director pulled up a chair and sat it down in front of his former partner. "Special Agent Painter hasn't told me a thing about what he plans on doing. He didn't discuss his plans to raid the Harvey enterprise or arrest my officers or come after Ryan or Turner. But I was able to make sugar out of shit by taking responsibility and getting in front of this whole thing. I put our names on this, and that includes you. But even that comes with a price, Ken."

Both men exchanged glances. Kenneth Archibald wasn't sure what the price would be. Regardless of what it was, he wasn't ready for whatever it may be.

"I'm stepping down next year around this time, Ken. That's my price. Your price is similar, maybe a little steeper." He paused. He knew Archibald had to mentally prepare himself. "Step aside in six months. Let your deputy take over the position. Then take the money you have and you and the wife and kids move to an island or some other exotic place."

"Can you guarantee me no one will come looking for me or my family?"

"Ken, I can't guarantee you anything. But I promise you, I will talk to Special Agent Painter and present my plan to him for both you and I to resign in a reasonable time. He seemed like someone who preferred problems went away versus persisting. I think my plan is viable. I think the governor would go for it as well."

"Are we going to talk about the eight-hundred-pound gorilla in the room?"

Wanamaker stood up and return the chair to its original spot. Then he said, "Ken, I don't know if the gorilla is the Harvey family or former Detective Brick, and you know what? I don't give a damn. I don't want to know."

He walked to the door and turned around. He had no idea what was on the mind of Mayor Kenneth Archibald.

Truthfully, he didn't want to know, as he opened the door and made his way to his office.

CHAPTER 64

MERCY, MERCY, MERCY . . .

"Why are you sitting at my desk?" asked an irritated Director Wanamaker when he walked in his office. I was indeed sitting at his desk, with my feet resting on top of the desk, and surfing through my phone.

"Because your seat is the most comfortable damn chair in this damn office," I stated.

"Get your ass up, Brick, and why in the fuck are you in my office." I loved Wanamaker's gruff exterior. He really was a man of multiple personalities and every one served him well.

"Nice press conference," I replied, as I stood up and walked around the desk. We did what two black men who respect each other do, we shook hands and gave each other a hug.

"Nice seeing you, asshole," Wanamaker softly murmured in my ear. "I really want to kick your ass, but to my understanding, you kicked the shit out of Franklin and he is younger, bigger and more fit than me."

"Well, I don't abuse the elderly," I joked, as we disengaged from our embrace.

"Let me guess, you are here to protect me from the Harvey boys?"

I sat on the edge of the desk, while Wanamaker took a seat in a chair in front of his desk. I was surprised, the man looked relaxed and at peace with the world. That was a good thing.

"We need to take a ride," I said. "Your press conference, as you probably wanted to happen, has stirred up some feelings in Ronaldo and Damian."

"How do you know?"

"There are three of their men at your place and another two waiting outside on you to depart work for home."

"I'm not worried," countered Wanamaker, with a smirk on his face. I didn't know if that was good or bad. "I have a team at my place, plus I had the family relocate out of town as soon as your buddy, Special Agent Painter, surprised us with his blitz attack on my city."

I smiled. "Cal took care of you, sir. He actually made sure your guys were a big part of the arrests and raids, and he made your press conference possible today."

"That's all true, Brick, but a little heads up would have been nice."

"I get it, sir, and I agree. But that's water under the bridge. I'm more concerned about making sure you see tomorrow."

"So, what are you recommending?"

"I recommend you allow me and my partner to drive you to your place. Your team will discreetly follow behind the two thugs working for the Harveys. When we hit your street, we will take out both teams that work for the Harveys—the three-man team at your house and the two-man team in the vehicle."

Wanamaker thought about my proposal. I could tell he had other things on his mind. What? I had no idea. Before I could say another word, he said, "There is something cynical going on in my city, Brick. I want to know, who is this Painter guy and why did you leave when you did?"

I wasn't expecting a question and answer session, but I got it. I would probably have the same questions if my city was invaded. However, the city was invaded years before the Feds made their way to Memphis.

"Painter. He is above both of our pay grades. He is probably who he says he is. The man is not much of a liar. If he told you he worked for Homeland Security and he has the ear of the president and every other high-ranking dick in D.C., then he told you the truth."

Wanamaker didn't speak. I could tell he was impressed though. "I left to protect Alaina and her daughter. It's that simple. End of story.

"Now, let's go."

It was past work hours and besides his security team, there were no others in the director's office area. I knew his security team. Knew them well. We had something in common—we both respected and cared for Detective Alaina Rivers.

The most important element of a great operation is coordination. I had been on the phone most of the day making sure this would end well. I had touched base with Painter and let him know what was going on. I also told him I needed him to make some phone calls. That was earlier. Everything I needed for a successful operation was in place. I didn't worry about Painter. He was a man of action, the quintessential mover and shaker.

Now it was on me to bring home the wrath of vengeance.

Many times, it's the things you don't say. I didn't tell the director that his saviors tonight would be members of the Garsay cartel. That wasn't the kind of information he needed or could process.

I introduced Max as Maxwell. No first name or surname, just Maxwell. That was all he needed to know. Max was driving, I was in the front passenger seat and the director was in the backseat.

"What's the play, Brick?" asked Wanamaker. I looked back at the director. I saw the fierceness and confidence in his eyes. He was ready for action. On the seat next to him was a Glock 17.

"The play will be transparent to you, Director," I stated. "As soon as we pull into the driveway, all five Harvey men will be put down before any of us open our door."

"So, basically, the team I have stationed at my house, along with your men...or should I say Special Agent Painter's men, will take down the perps."

"Not your men, Director. And you can say Painter's men, if you'd like." I caught Max looking at me through her peripheral vision.

"So, Miss Maxwell, what's your story?" Wanamaker asked.

Max replied, "Just Maxwell, Director Wanamaker. No story, sir. I needed employment and Mr. Brick gave me a job. Whenever he needs me, I usually accept the task."

We rode in silence for the next few miles. When we were turning into the director's street, I saw the director bring his gun to his torso.

Then I could see in the sideview mirror, the car that was following us sped up. Just as rapidly, I heard six shots from two assault rifles and the car sped up as we turned into the driveway. I knew what was going on. The driver was dead and his foot was dead-weighing on the gas pedal, causing it to increase speed before it jumped the curb and slammed into a tree in a yard several houses across the street from the director.

I didn't hear the other shots. Being on the cautious side, I told Sam we were staying in the car for several minutes.

"Who took out the guys in the car, and shouldn't we make sure they are dead?" asked Wanamaker, as he was looking back and down the street at the wrecked vehicle.

"No, Director, we are good," I reassured him. "We will be good in here for now." At that moment, his protection team pulled him behind us. This was his driver and extra protector. They were driving my vehicle.

Then I got the phone call. I put it on speaker. The voice was in Spanish, "All clear. Three down, head shots and we have taken care of the bodies. Since the car hit the tree, it would be best for the cops to take care of the bodies."

I replied in Spanish, "Estoy de acuerdo. Gracias." *I agree. Thank you.*

"You do know I speak Spanish as well, Brick?" It was more a statement than a question from Wanamaker. "My men will process the scene across the street. However, I think it's best I don't ask about the voice on the phone."

We all got out the car. Sam shook Max's hand and she walked away. When I came around the car, Sam Wanamaker shook my hand and gave me a hug. The same routine we went through when he saw me in his office earlier.

"I didn't say it earlier, but I'm sorry for your loss, Brick," said Sam, with sadness in his voice. "She was a helluva woman and one helluva detective. I think many of us suspected you two had a real thing for each other, but I know you loved that woman. If not, we wouldn't be here. I apologize for not protecting my detective. Please forgive me. And thank you for this. You saved my life."

I took a step back, and Sam and I exchanged glances. I didn't speak. I didn't know what to say. Then I just walked away.

No other words were exchanged. Nothing was left to say.

CHAPTER 65

DEATH TO THE SPIDER THAT HAS NO TEETH.

Ronaldo Harvey laid in bed, looking at the ceiling. He often wondered what would have come of his life if he had chosen another profession. If he would have stayed clear of the family business. He knew that was his sister's plan. How did that work out for her?

He recalled going to a recruitment seminar for Ivy League schools and he realized his dream could be real. The purpose of the team was to find the most qualified candidates to attend Harvard, Yale, Brown, et cetera. He wasn't stupid. He knew it was a recruitment effort for black, brown, red or yellow students from the western states. Hell, he had a 4.0 grade point average and he definitely qualified. After a full day of unexpected testing, which was described as voluntary testing, there was one more examination. He was summoned to a room with five seminar officials. There was only one question: how many blades were on the overhead fan that was spinning rapidly, probably on the highest setting. The answer was four. He didn't know if his action caught anyone by surprise, the officials' facial expression or body language never changed. But he did what he needed to do, which was walk over to the power switch and turn the selector to OFF.

He heard one *Thank You* from one of the officials and left the building on the San Diego State University campus feeling good about the day. Two weeks later, a woman showed up at her house and offer him a four-year full scholarship to any Ivy League college of his choice. His father made the decision for him and that decision was an undeniable *no*.

He didn't say anything. His father controlled his destiny then. Not now.

He needed sleep. He had been up almost forty-eight hours, so he had to sleep. Lying down, his goal was a couple hours of shuteye, not the six hours he did get. He was upset at himself. The last thing he wanted to do at this drastic time was leave his fate to Damian.

His instructions to his brother were simple—wake him up when the team killed Director Wanamaker, and to contact the Death Squad via his burner phone and tell them the mission was still on for tomorrow morning. That mission included going after Zachary Brick's best friend, Major Cal Hillsmeier, and his family, and raiding the house of Lucy Bankwell. She was the money woman. She was also Detective Smokey Franklin's ex-wife, and Smokey admitted on several occasions that she controlled Brick's money which, based on Smokey's account, Brick had boatloads of money.

That was what they needed, a boatload of money.

"Damian!" he called out loudly. "Damian!" This was followed by two more loud calls to his youngest brother. The lack of a response made Ronaldo jumpy and concerned. He grabbed his Glock 43 on the nightstand and slid his feet off the bed. He was in the master bedroom on the second floor of the house, and the good news was that the room was directly over the garage. He could also look out the window and see the driveway, the front yard and some of the front of the house.

Everything looked normal. As much as he could see. There were lights on both sides of the driveway, plus there were three outside lights on the house.

Hopefully, everything really was normal.

It was nightfall. Past eight o'clock.

He put his Glock on the dresser and grabbed his two shoulder holsters. Three guns. At least six extra clips, two for each gun. The door was closed.

He took his time slowly opening the door. Then he looked right, that was the only way to look. He debated with himself whether he wanted to look in the other two bedrooms on the floor and in the bathroom. He hadn't looked in the master bedroom, but he was convinced if someone was in the master bathroom, he would already be dead. Brick or whoever would have killed him in his sleep.

He was sure that applied to the whole upper floor, so he chose not to look in the spare bedrooms or the spare bathroom.

"Fuck, I hate this staircase," he quietly said to himself. The staircase was V-shaped and did not allow you to see anything downstairs until you physically were downstairs. There were seven stairs, then a landing, then another seven stairs to the bottom of the staircase. He walked slowly, his Glock in the ready, shooting position—pointed out, his right arm completely stretched out, while his left hand served as his leverage, his balance.

The bottom of the staircase ended in a hallway. To the left led to the living room, the family room, the kitchen and the dining room. The right led to the garage.

He still took his time making his way to the living room. He didn't want to call out. He wasn't nervous. He wasn't afraid. However, the sweat on his forehead and nose told him he was something. What that something was, he wasn't sure.

He looked around the corner in the living room and saw Damian lying down on the sofa. He sighed a sigh of relief.

He walked over to the sofa and decided to have some fun. Damian's back was to him and he didn't know how he missed it. Damian was snoring loudly. In one quick motion, he put his hand over Damian's mouth and shouted, "Give me your money motherfucker!"

A startled Damian struggled to get himself together and get his bearing, while reaching for his gun on the coffee table. Then Ronaldo heartily laughed. He loved that Damian was surprised and scared.

Then he saw it. And it pissed him off.

"Why in fuck is your cell phone on and not the burner?" screamed Ronaldo at Damian, who was now sitting on the sofa, rubbing his eyes.

"What?"

"D, why in the fuck is your phone on? Ronaldo repeated himself.

"Chill, Ro'. The burner wasn't acting right, then the juice ran down. So, I had to use my phone."

Ronaldo sat down in the chair near the sofa. He wasn't happy. He could only hope and pray that the Feds or anyone else, namely Brick, wasn't tracing or pinging his phone.

"Go grab your shit, D," ordered Ronaldo. "We need to be out of here in five minutes." He got up, with his Glock in his right hand. He looked down at Damian and said, "Get your ass up and let's get a move on it." His brother finally did what he asked.

Five minutes later, they were in their car in the garage. Damian was in the driver's seat. He hit the garage opener and pulled his car out the garage before noticing the three vehicles blocking their escape.

Damian reached for the gun in the middle compartment, before Ronaldo's hand landed on his hand. Damian looked at his brother and then he saw the figures outside passenger side window. Then he noticed Ronaldo was looking past him and outside his driver's side window.

Damian looked around and he saw the five men cladded in black garb, to include black hoodies, pointing semiautomatic assault rifles at him. Outside Ronaldo's window was another four men with similar weapons.

"Santana Garsay," were the only words Ronaldo Harvey whispered.

CHAPTER 66

THE MENIAL THINGS IN LIFE PASS US BY...THANK GOD.

"Are you alright?" I asked Sondra, as she sat at the kitchen table looking at her laptop computer. She was comfortable in a blue cotton shirt and pink sweatpants.

She glanced at me. "You know what?" Before I could say anything, she continued, "Your secret weapon is mind control. People respond to you. You can walk in a room and people pay attention to you. It's not like you are looking for attention. It just happens. Women. Men. Gay. Straight. Black. White. It doesn't make a difference, people are just drawn to you."

I didn't know how to take that. Maybe Sondra meant it as a compliment. I wasn't sure. She wasn't smiling. But she wasn't sad. That was a win in my book.

"What brought this on?" I ask. "Or better yet, where is this going?" I had taken a seat at the table as well. I wasn't directly across from her, but we could look at each other, without turning our heads.

"How did you clone the Harvey boys' phones?"

"I didn't."

That two words answer stopped her in her tracks. Then she smiled. I smiled back.

"It was the housekeepers, gardeners and bodyguards, right?"

348

I laughed slightly. "Yes," I said. "Now, they all have departed from Memphis to other parts of the world and have been handsomely taken care of financially."

"With your money or the Harveys' money?"

"The Harveys, of course." Then Sondra let out a hearty laugh and it made me smile and feel good.

"You are too much, Zach," said Sondra in a low tone, as she got up and went to the refrigerator. She grabbed a can of soda, opened it and stood by the kitchen sink.

"She loved you," stated Sondra. "In so many ways, she died happy. Way before her time. Now, I want to give her what she wanted."

"What is that?" I asked.

"She wanted us to be close, to love each other as if we were father and daughter."

We continued to exchanged glances. Occasionally, Sondra would take a sip or swallow from her soda.

"Don't worry Zach, I have always looked at you as the closest thing I have to a father. Our family is different now. It's you, me and Max." I laughed.

I rose up from the table and Sondra quickly walked over to me and hugged me, resting her head on my chest. I held her just as tight as she held me.

"I love you," she said. I said it back and kissed the top of her head. "I want Max to go with me tomorrow to see my dad. We are meeting for breakfast."

"Understand." It was the only word I could muster. I really didn't know how I felt about that, but she did have a father. I did what I needed to do and accepted the moment for what it was.

"I want him to know that I love him," she said. "And I do. His blood, like my mom's blood, courses through my body. However, he was more a sperm donor. You are...my dad. Whether in

Memphis or Texas, you have been the one there for me. You are the father I never had."

She held me tighter. I didn't want her to let go. We were sharing a loss, but also sharing a love. Alaina was the finest woman I have ever known. She loved people and people loved her. She had her enemies and nemeses, but many of those were bad guys.

I realized that Sondra had a huge part of her mom in her, both the good and the bad. I didn't know her future. I didn't know if she'd stay with computers or would decide to try her hand at something else. I did know that she had a good heart and that would be her saving grace. The goodness she brought to the world would be rewarded.

"I hope I find a man like you one day, Zach," she surprised me with that statement.

"No, I hope you meet someone much, much better than me," I replied. "I could say your mom caught me by surprise, but it was the other way around. I was the lucky one, Sondra. She made me the man I am today. The goodness in her is the goodness in you.

"There are at least fifty songs a day I hear that reminds me of Alaina, or me and Alaina. I miss her just as much as you. But life goes on and we will press forward and make the best of life. Understand?"

"Yeah, I get that," she stated weakly. With Alaina's death, her world was derailed and truthfully, she didn't have time to grieve because Ronaldo and Damian Harvey wanted me, so they kept eyes on her. And they made sure to be seen. I would be seeing both brothers sometime before the sun rose again in Memphis. That, I was sure of.

"She thought she was a bad mom," Sondra surprised me again.

"Every parent feels that way," I retorted. "Parents want to get it right. Those who feel the way your mother did, felt that way because they want their kids to come out great and live a great life.

"And you will live a great life. Bank on it."

"Can I get my mom's laptop?"

"Look under the mattress in the master bedroom."

We didn't speak anymore. It was an emotional period for both of us. I was lucky. I had a daughter. She wasn't my pretend child or child by birth or even by adoption. But she was a part of me and I, a part of her.

Ten minutes later, Max came into the room and touched her watch. That was her subtle way of telling me the night was just getting started for her and I.

I realized, I still had someone to come home to—my daughter, Sondra Rivers.

CHAPTER 67

HOW OLD IS TOO OLD?

I left Sondra with her mom's laptop, so she could see the old recordings Alaina had made over the years for her daughter. I had viewed several of them from years ago, when Sondra was a baby before realizing it was not my place to view them. She was a survivor and she would eventually get over this. Unfortunately, we had that in common. My mother was killed when I was only twelve and it made me grow up. I had my sister, but she was three years younger than me. Hopefully, those two things would be the differences for Sondra. The fact that she had Max and me to get her through this and that she was nineteen-years-old, which is much better than finding yourself the guardian of a younger sibling at the age of twelve.

Max and I were riding together. It was around midnight and we were headed to a nightclub in downtown Memphis to offer some southern hospitality to the self-proclaimed Death Squad. It was a group of ten killers from Mexico, who supposed to be killers for hire, but in actuality, only worked for Ronaldo and Damian. They loved Memphis. The city was non-threatening for them. Yes, Memphis had home grown criminals and killers, but the Death Squad knew cutting a person's heart out sent chilling messages to those in Memphis, more so than to those in Mexico.

Additionally, in Mexico, killers eventually had to deal with the cartel as well as other killers worse than they were.

I left two of my six-men team at the house with Sondra. The other four were dispersed to a warehouse outside the suburban area of Cordova, east of the Memphis city limits. It was the only Harvey warehouse the Feds didn't hit. That was my choice.

"About time you guys made it," Seth Painter voiced amusingly. He met us on the next street over from the nightclub. Our plan was simple. Kill ten gang members, then go out the backdoor, which led to the alley we'd be walking through in order to get to the front door of the club.

Seth was a man itching for some action. He was a retired colonel, who turned down a promotion to brigadier general on four occasions. He started out as my savior and somewhere down the line he became my friend. In many ways, I was still his subordinate. In other ways, I was his partner. During my first year in the CIA, he told me one day he may have to kill me, I took it in stride. That day did come, but he didn't try hard enough. Now he, Max and I have formed our own team.

"I think we should make this interesting," said Painter, as we walked through the alley. The man was like a kid in a candy store. He was a bureaucrat and didn't come out to play often. Although he was confined to a desk, carrying weapons on his person was just second nature for him.

"What's on your mind?" I asked.

"How about five thousand dollars if we can do this in five minutes?" he replied.

"Is that high point?" I asked. High point was the maximum amount of time it took to take out the ten criminals.

"It all depends on you and Max's numbers."

"My number is three minutes," responded Max. But before I could say anything, she expounded on that answer. "Hold on, how are we doing this? Are we doing this back-to-back-to-back, making sure we have three hundred sixty degrees coverage...or are we spreading out?" Back-to-back-to-back meant exactly that—the three of us would be standing with our backs to each other, shooting anything that came our way.

"I like the back thingy," stated Painter. "Does the time start as soon as we walk in or as soon as we take the first shot?"

"You already know the answer Seth," chimed in Max. "As soon as we walk in, because as soon as the firefight begins, it will go fast."

I said, "Cool, my time is four minutes. However, before we make a decision on how we are going to do this, let's just play it by ear. It's not your typical club. There is a raised area in the back of the club, which is where the three leaders usually hang out. Plus, to the right, is a staircase to a second floor and the second floor looks down on the first."

"Interesting," said Max. "You have been pretty busy since you have been here."

"Yes, he has," Seth snidely remarked. "Let's do this!"

The line outside was lengthy. We bypassed the line and walked to the front of the line to the objection of many. They were doing wand checks at the door, but I knew the doorman, and he knew I would be coming through tonight. I told him to tell everybody the place was packed and they wouldn't be allowing anyone in until at least another twenty people left the club.

I think I had instantly aged ten or fifteen years. That's how I felt as I walked in Club Ricardo. I was never a nightclub guy but in my profession, you spend your fair share of time in clubs. I had spent time in clubs in over twenty countries. I could dance and I got a thrill dancing with Alaina, but the club scene was not my scene.

The club was indeed packed—and that was an understatement

Club Ricardo was a nice sized club at best. It definitely wasn't small, but equally it wasn't too big. It was designed with the latest trend in mind—a lounge club. That trend included no traditional area for a dance floor. Yes, there was a so-called designated space for dancing, but on that space, patrons were standing around and some were dancing in place. That seemed to be the biggest theme change for most of the newer clubs—lounging, more so than dancing. It still focused on people making connections and socializing. The biggest change, to me, not being a regular club guy, was the dancing in place.

The club belonged to the Harveys. Officially, Ronaldo and Damian's names were on the legal paperwork. I loved the set-up. The bar was in the middle of the club and it had 360 degrees coverage. The numerous bottles of liquor were on full display in a lighted area that was at least twenty to thirty feet high. There was a sliding ladder that covered the complete circular area of the bar. It was impressive.

There was one sitting area to the left as you entered the club, with seven small tables, which also included a wall-attached long sofa sitting area that ran from the entrance to the place to the wall. As you entered the club, you had to walk down three or four stairs to get to the main floor, then another two stairs to get to the sitting area. In the back of the club was another sitting area, with seven bigger tables than the other area. Additionally, there were three sofas in the sitting area. Two were traditional big sofas that could sit at least six normal size patrons, while the other sofa was a wall-attached sofa that had a longer table. That table was reserved for the owners.

On the right side of the club was a circular staircase that led to the second floor. We all had the faces of the Death Squad members committed to memory. I saw two of the criminals go up the staircase.

356 | John A. Wooden

We all had silence suppressors attached to our guns. However, once the shooting started, the place would empty out and empty fast. This wasn't the smartest move. Max, Seth and I all knew this. But this was about making a statement. We all hoped the same thing—that no one else got hurt, no innocent bystanders. In our business, we didn't like rolling dices. Tonight, the dices were in my hands and I was shaking them up, getting ready to toss. Hopefully, they came up sevens, meaning we hurt no one else besides members of the Death Squad.

"We need to split up!" Max shouted into my ear, trying to speak over the loud music. I, in turn, did the same to Seth.

Max headed to the second floor, while Seth went into the direction of the raised area in the back of the club. I headed to the left side. What I didn't like was the bar in the middle of the club. Because of the raised shelves, it was almost impossible to see the other side of the club. Now I was thinking we should have done a back-to-back-to-back technique. At least we would be together and able to see what's going on.

I reached both hands into my jacket. I had on a double harness with attached holsters, and a gun in each holster. Soon, it would be jumping off fast and I wanted to be ready.

I had eyes on Seth as he approached the raised area. There was no security protecting the area. I was sure the patrons of this nightclub knew who the club belonged to and would only enter that area if requested. In the area closest to the door, there were two other members of the Death Squad.

I had my eyes on them and on Seth. The three leaders of the Death Squad were sitting together on the long sofa in the raised area. They were flanked by a total of seven women. As many people that were on the sofa, this would be easy for Painter. His targets were all men. Easy.

I saw Seth reach in his jacket with both hands and I knew it was showdown.

He came out with two Glock 17s with silence suppressors attached and I didn't hear the shots, but I saw the results. Then I saw the reactions of the nightclubbers in that area. As expected, hell was breaking out.

I pulled my guns as well and shot the two criminals near the door area, before they could pull weapons. Then a body came crashing to the first floor from the second floor, and I knew that was all Max.

Then I was looking around for bad guys and I knew Seth was doing the same. The chaos was real. People were running over each other trying to get out of the club. I didn't panic, but my eyes were still searching the club, even the second floor balcony. I didn't see anyone else with a gun.

Then it hit me. The restroom. Before I took a step, I saw Seth shooting at the bar area. Then I saw blood and brain matter fly out the back of one of the bartenders' head. The music was still blaring. I wasn't sure anyone in the restrooms could hear anything. Plus, I was wondering if everything was well on the second floor with Max.

I was cautiously approaching the men's room. I had just passed the door to the women's restroom, which was before and across the hall from the men's room. Then I saw the gun and the guy had the bead on me. Then he didn't. His gun jammed, which gave me time to squeeze the trigger. I didn't take any chances. It was a shot to the head.

By my count, I had counted eight dead. I didn't know if I should try the restroom or not. I decided not to, which was a good decision. As I slowly and cautiously made my way out of the poorly lit hallway, I saw Seth and Max.

"Hurry your ass up, so we can get out of here!" yelled Seth.

I did as I was told and we made our way to another poorly lit hallway before going out the backdoor of the club. We were in the alley that led to the street where we had parked our vehicles. Max volunteered that she had killed the other two criminals I was worried about. I called Cal and told him to send his men in. Unfortunately, there would be no arrests tonight, just police reports. The patrons of the bar had scattered and I wouldn't be surprised if some of them weren't speeding, trying their best to get away from the area.

"You two owe me," said Seth. "Not only did I get the time right, five minutes, but I also killed the most members. Four."

Max and I laughed. This was mission one. We still had two more missions.

Seth followed in his car as we made our way east of Cordova.

CHAPTER 68

I'M NOT MY BROTHER'S KEEPER!

Max was driving while I was getting myself together for our next mission. It wasn't really a mission. It was a get together with Ronaldo and Damian Harvey at one of their warehouses on the outskirts of Memphis. The warehouse was their most secretive location. Only a few minions who worked for the Harveys knew about the location.

I had to get it together though. Alaina had been on my mind... all day. I was missing her. Probably more today than any other time. I couldn't explain it. I didn't want to explain it. Maybe finally robbing the Harveys of their ill-gotten fortunes and eliminating all the Harvey men meant this was the end of the road. *Finality.* Maybe I realized it was time to move on from holding on to Alaina. Soon, I had to let go.

Then, Sondra, Max and I would be a family. Maybe it was a hope...or maybe a dream.

I picked up my phone and called my nemesis—Santana Garsay.

"You can only kill one Harvey brother," Santana declared, with his Mexican accent. "I must restore order. I need to send a message. You owe me this."

We were approximately five minutes from the warehouse. Santana had his own death squad. Except he had a unit of nine, not ten. They had already killed Hector Senior and Junior...and captured Ronaldo and Damian.

The warehouse was in a valley, which made for a good staging area for my four men team. They were each situated on high ground, looking down on the warehouse. Each had a long-range tactical rifle pointed at a target near the warehouse.

"Santana, no, I don't owe you anything," I replied. "You can kill both Harvey brothers, but hear me out. Triple your security, because I will be coming for you. That's a promise."

"Touchy, touchy," answered Santana immediately. "You fucking Americans, always with the exaggerations. I got my money, I got my product, do what you must with our friends. We will meet again, Mister Zachary Brick. Then I will kill you."

"It's a date," I responded. I looked at Max as we were pulling up outside the warehouse. Six of Garsay's nine team members were outside as well. Seth was right behind us. I got out of the SUV and went to the back hatch. I didn't bring an assortment of weapons this time. I just needed a few—a sledgehammer I had just retrieved and the guns I had on my person.

I didn't speak to anyone as I walked in the warehouse. The scene reminded me of the one in Arkansas. Except this time it was Ronaldo and Damian Harvey tied up and sitting down next to each other. Both men had been stripped down to their underwear.

The warehouse had been emptied of the money and drugs that used to occupy the place. There were some empty shelves outlining the walls of the warehouse, but at one point, there were pallets of money and drugs throughout the warehouse. Being in the place now, it looked to be much bigger than I thought it was.

Ronaldo and Damian sat side by side, looking small and sad. They were awaiting death. I couldn't imagine the feeling.

Garsay's men had done what I asked, which was to bring a container of fuel and placed it between the two men. I was sure the red gas can added to their anxiety. Additionally, me walking in with a sledgehammer wasn't the gesture of a potentially good meeting.

"So, we finally meet," I said to the two brothers. Max and Seth stayed at the entrance of the warehouse. Three of Garsay's men were inside the warehouse as well. I wasn't expecting trouble, but we were covered if the unexpected happened.

"I know you," said Ronaldo, with a perplexed look on his face. "I have seen you a couple of times. At the barbeque joint off Park Avenue and at our club."

I smiled. "Yep. By the way, we just left Club Ricardo and killed every member of your death squad. But those guys were just great pretenders anyway. Now these guys . . ." I pointed to the three guys at the doorway of the warehouse. "They are the real thing. A true death squad. They lose a member here or there, and have another five or ten ready to step up. Fuck, I don't know how many of these assholes I have killed over the years and they continue to add more bodies."

"Who gives a damn?" exclaimed an excited and afraid Damian.

I placed the sledgehammer down near the only other chair in the warehouse. I then positioned the chair several feet from Ronaldo. I picked up the gas can and began pouring it on the head of Damian. As he shouted his displeasure, I said, "Say another word and you die sooner than later."

Then I poured the rest of the fuel over Ronaldo, who didn't squirm or object like his younger brother. He was trying to be a man about his death.

"I will make this easy, Mr. Harvey," I stated, as I pull the chair up and sat down within a foot of Ronaldo. The sledgehammer was by my side. "I just want the name of the Fed who was pulling your string and calling the shots."

Ronaldo was angry. I wanted to laugh. His eyes were red and watery from the fumes of the fuel. He wanted so much to accept his imminent death, but it was useless. The man was afraid. I could see it in his eyes. He had a deep fear of dying.

"Fuck you, bitch!" Damian shouted out. As soon as the words came out of his mouth, I picked up the sledgehammer and swung it at his face, connecting with the tip of his nose. I hit him hard enough that the blood gushed from his nose and he cried out.

"Next time, I promise I will beat you to a pulp with this hammer."

"Fuck!" he screamed out again. He said this repeatedly. "Stop the bleeding!"

I stood up with the sledgehammer in hand.

"Damian, shut the fuck up," said a calm Ronaldo. "Stop acting like a little bitch. Be a man."

I sat back down. "Name?" I said to the older Harvey.

"I don't know his name."

"You know, Santana always thought you would be like your sister, like your father, an attorney. But you decided to be the tough guy. Crazy as hell. You were so fucking smart. Probably smarter then Kendra. Now, this is how it ends."

"Santana doesn't know shit about my family," sneered Ronaldo. The man looked brazen. It was still the tough guy act. Ronaldo couldn't look or act contrite. Even on death's door, it was about dying a respectful death.

"Sorry, Ronaldo, he knows all about your family," I corrected. "Santana is your family. That's why your father has repeatedly beaten death. Your father had a trump card and he never knew it. Knowing your dad, I'm sure he never suspected or realized that he had his guardian angel sleeping next to him every night."

The man had an incredulous look on his face. He was wondering what in the hell I was jabbering about.

"Your mother is Santana's half-sister. They have the same father. Your mother has always been an advisor to her younger brother. Your father and brother were killed by this very death squad, and you know what? Your mother gave Santana permission to kill your father and brother."

"That's bullshit!" snapped Ronaldo, as he tried to wiggle out of his binds.

"No, that's the truth. But now, I want a name. I want to know who ordered the death of Detective Rivers."

"Fuck that bitch!" screamed Damian.

In one motion, I picked up the sledgehammer and swung it hard. It connected with his head with such an impact, that his entire body fell over from the hit. I wasn't sure if Damian was dead, but he was definitely brain dead. I didn't care. I swung the hammer down on the left side of his chest, near his heart, if he even had one. It was with enough force that I could hear the cracking of his ribs. I was about to swing again, when Ronaldo yelled out, "Stop! I will tell you!"

I looked at Ronaldo and tears were flowing down his face. The man was broken. I had no sympathy. I was mad. Whatever niceness or fairness I had previously had, had left the warehouse. The only thing left was the man who remembered the deaths of Brittany Zachary and Alaina Rivers. The man who remembered the deaths of his mom and twin sisters.

The man left behind was Hunt Collins. My CIA persona. The person who represented death. The person I needed to be at this moment, until this was over.

"Brice Sloane. His name is Brice Sloane. And he did it to bring you back to Memphis. He didn't know if you were alive or dead, but the only way for him to know was to kill the detective."

"Did the mayor tell you to kill Detective Rivers, or was it Sloane?"

"Initially, it was the mayor. I didn't believe him and told him to set up the meeting with Sloane. It was my first and only time meeting the man, but he told me about you guys history and your history with Garsay."

I didn't say anything. I was still standing. I dropped the hammer. I was probably more focused than I had been since arriving in Memphis.

"Is it true about my mom and Santana?" Ronaldo Harvey was the last of the Harvey men. He had a son as well as Arturo had a son. Hell, they may have multiple sons. I really didn't know, nor did I care. If their mothers were smart, they would change their names and keep their children far from the family business.

"Garsay wants you alive...to make an example of you for his other operations here in the States and in Mexico. What do you want?"

"I want to live."

I pulled my gun out and pulled the trigger two times to Ronaldo's head. Then I shot Damian once in the head. I didn't linger. I left the sledgehammer and walked away.

Neither Max nor Seth Painter said anything. We got in our respective vehicles and headed to our final destination.

On our drive, Max and I did not speak a word.

CHAPTER 69

THE GREAT THING ABOUT DEATH—IT
ONLY COMES ONCE!

Officially, it was day three. For me, it was a long extension of day two. Either way, Brice Sloane was occupying my mind.

Brice was both a planner and a thinker. The man loved being in charge. In his mind, it was his calling. He was third generation CIA and he loved sharing that tidbit of information. Something to be very proud of, and I got that. There are not many who can say their family history dates back to the Office of Strategic Services. The OSS.

Sloane could do that.

What a true disappointment the man was to his family. However, he would be celebrated as an American hero. I didn't give a damn.

He earned his death.

Napoleon Bonaparte. That was the thought I had whenever I saw Brice Sloane dating back to the first time we ever met in the hallways of Langley. The man had been an asshole from day one, and that continued throughout the many assignments we worked together. The unfortunate thing for me was that I was the asset and he was the handler.

He and his two bodyguards disembarked from the black SUV. I laughed internally. Seeing his two over six feet tall protectors and seeing him giving up at least eight inches to each man was funny to me.

I was surprised. The man was dressed down with a beige, lightweight jacket and blue jeans. As always, he looked awkward in regular clothing.

I was in the cockpit of a CIA-owned Gulfstream G550. Seth Painter was sitting next to me. It was ironic that there were two Gulfstream aircraft on the Memphis airport ramp that belonged to the Company. Sloane's family history meant something at the agency. Plus, the man had been with the Company for over thirty years. Half of that time had been dishonorably, but that was another story. Regardless, his status allowed him the honor of borrowing the company Learjet whenever he wanted.

Even more ironic was Seth Painter. His paycheck did say Homeland Security, but the man was the property of the United States government. He was still CIA and would always be CIA. Asking for the CIA jet was just a matter of letting it be known he had to use the aircraft for several days.

I didn't know how long Sloane and his protectors had been in Memphis, but from the amount of luggage they were dragging behind them told me that they had been here at least a month or more.

Some bags were thrown in the baggage compartment of the aircraft, which was on the underbelly of the Learjet, but each bodyguard had two big duffel bags as well. I knew what it was. Money. Stolen money.

When the three men climbed the staircase of the Learjet Sloane led the way. He took a seat as his men were trying to put the oversized duffel bags in the small overhead compartments.

The sound of Max's gun wasn't as suppressed in the confines of the aircraft as one of bodyguards fell over from the shot in the head.

Brice Sloane jumped up, while his other bodyguard dropped his duffel bag and tried to reach in his coat and get his gun out unsuccessfully. It was too late and he was too slow. Max double tapped the man with a bullet to his throat and another to his forehead.

Before Sloane could reach for his weapon, Seth, who was alongside me entering the cabin of the aircraft, ordered him to sit back down.

"Seth, is this really the move you want to make?" asked Sloane. I gave the man his due credit. He was sounding confident, as if he had no worries in the world. "This is not the smartest play... for any of you. And Seth, you know this."

"Why did you kill her?" I asked calmly. "You could have held her hostage. Did an exchange, me for her? So, why did you kill her?"

We exchanged glances. The confidence he had just displayed was gone. His certainty turned to uncertainty before my very eyes. What bravado he had possessed two shakes ago, had abandoned him upon the opening of my mouth.

"I honestly didn't think about taking her hostage," he said. "I just wanted you. If she was killed and you were still alive, I knew you would be back in the city within a couple of days to protect her daughter. Unfortunately, I was wrong. You actually took your time and came in with a plan. Beat me at my own game."

I didn't say anything. I was actually basking in the man's fear.

"Seth, tell Hunt why he won't be killing me today or any other day." He tried his best to speak with confidence, but his heart and soul had already abandoned him.

Seth didn't speak. It was my show, my play. And however it played out, was fine with him.

"Detective Rivers used to have a saying whenever we ran across a dead body," I said. "The great thing about death—it only comes once."

I saw the sweat on the man's forehead and nose. I saw the fear in his eyes. He was tapping his feet and wiping his sweaty hands on his pants' legs. "Seth...Seth." That was his mercy cry. He was hoping Seth Painter would save him. Not today. Nor any other day.

His eyes were on me. My eyes were on him. He opened his mouth to speak. In one quick motion, my shots hit him in the mouth and forehead.

CHAPTER 70

AND LIFE GOES ON ...

I don't know how long I slept, but I did sleep. It was a new day. A new time in my life. Alaina was officially gone in my head now. I still had one thing to do.

The cemetery had fast-tracked Alaina's headstone. It was nice—off-red granite. I laughed internally at the crazy titles of colors today. It was a light red color and actually looked good. The groundskeeper told me that headstone had been up a couple of days.

Loving Mother and Dedicated Police Officer and Detective. You Will Be Missed!

Those were the words that graced the headstone. It was all true. She was missed now. As much as I had on my heart and as much as I wanted to say, I didn't talk. I was on one knee. I had placed the twelve red and white roses that I had bought in front of the headstone. The roses actually complemented well with the headstone.

I let the thoughts and memories run through my mind. The good times. The bad. The car rides. The stakeouts. The late nights.

"I don't know what to say, woman. I definitely love you, miss you. Don't worry about Sondra, she will be good. She is meeting with her dad now, and whether she decides to come back to Memphis and live, or stay with me, I will always make sure she is good.

"I was trying to think what I miss most about you. Your smile, your loving personality, your kindness, your this, your that. I could actually go on forever about everything I miss about you. At the end of the day, it all comes back to one thing...I miss you. I never knew love before, never wanted love before...before you.

"In many ways, I was broken when I met you. Hell, you were broken as well. That should have shattered my dream. You weren't the perfect woman I envisioned. However, you were the perfect woman I needed. You were perfect for me, and I like to think, I was perfect for you. I think we healed each other, made each other whole."

I was stuck for words. Detective. Alaina. Rivers. We were good together. Now she was gone. Now I wanted to be gone. But life goes on. Dammit. Life goes on.

"I know you are up above looking down. I promise you, I will make sure Sondra continues to grow and be the woman you want her to be.

"Know that I love you...I miss you! Bye for now. I hope and pray we meet again."

I was searching for something within, but I didn't know exactly what that was. I think I was both physically and emotionally drained. I realized that death and I had bad history, and worse, I didn't process death well. I cried when my mother died, but I was twelve. Brittany's death hurt me to the core. Alaina's death devastated me.

Now I was emotionally drained to the point of being speechless.

I left the cemetery without saying another word. I was disappointed in myself. Alaina was on my mind and would stay on my mind. We would talk. Or I should say, I would talk to her. Hopefully, I would have more to say than I did today.

Several hours later, I was at the house. Seth was headed back to the nation's capital. Garsay's death squad was back in Mexico.

The warehouse east of Cordova was set afire and two burnt corpses were found inside. I suspected it would take a while to figure out the identities of the two bodies that were no doubt burnt to death.

Mayor Archibald had already stepped down and Memphis now had a new mayor. I was convinced Director Wanamaker would do the same in a couple of years.

I was in the kitchen when Sondra sat down. She only sat for several seconds, before getting up and hugging me. I stood up and we hugged for several minutes.

"My dad's wife was at the café too," she said to me, while we were still hugging. "Max sat at the bar. I told him the truth. Told them the truth. She seemed like a nice woman. He wanted to be a dad now. I told him I have a dad. That you had been there since I was nine years old. I told him about you and my mom. That we were a family. Then I thanked him and told him, my dad was waiting. Then we left."

She hugged me tighter.

"Time to go, you two," stated Max, as she had bags in her hands. "Let's do this."

"Yeah, let's do this," Sondra said.

As I got in the car, I remembered something else Alaina used to say, "Life goes on, Boy Scout."

Yes, it does, woman. Yes, it does.

Life goes on . . .

ACKNOWLEDGMENTS

Special thanks to Tammy LeJack, Yolanda M. Johnson-Bryant, Jessica Tilles and Jene A. Wooden for making this book a reality. You guys rock! More importantly, you guys keep me on my toes, bring realism to my crazy thoughts and storytelling, and make my books worth picking up. I give many thanks and really appreciate all you guys do for me.

Sending love to my family and friends for always being in my corner, having my back and supporting my dreams.

As always, to my fans and audience, I appreciate you all and say thank you for supporting me and reading my books. I love the written word and love manipulating words into something called a story. I will always love the art of storytelling—and I hope this book, like my other books, resonate with most or all of you and you continue to support me.

ABOUT THE AUTHOR

John A. Wooden is a retired Major from the U.S. Air Force, a feature writer/columnist for *The Perspective* magazine in Albuquerque, New Mexico, and a freelance editor and ghostwriter whose clients have appeared on several bestsellers' lists. *Welcome Back Zachary Brick* is his introduction of assassin Zachary Brick. He has written three novels in his Special Agent Kenny "KC" Carson series. He has also collaborated on a novel, *UnAuthorized,* with bestselling author, Shelia Goss. John is the proud father of a son and daughter.

To learn more about John and his novels, visit his website: www. jwooden.com.

CPSIA information can be obtained
at www.ICGtesting.com
Printed in the USA
LVHW050916080419
613326LV00017BA/780